To the real Allison

GEMINI

Penelope Ward

ω |อๅอห

GEMINI

First Edition, May 2013

Copyright © 2013 by Penelope Ward

Cover by RBA Designs. Stock photo © Shutterstock.com
Formatting by Polgarus Studio

CHAPTER 1

ALLISON

Your ruler, Mercury, is set to go forward motion, Gemini. You can sense you are coming out of a fog. Get Ready To Invite Romance Into Your Life!

How nice it would be if my horoscope actually came true today. Because something in the air shifted when *he* walked into the Stardust diner.

The feeling was indescribable.

Barry Manilow's *Mandy* had been playing but the volume of the song seemed to fade with the feel of the brisk wind that blew in the door when the most gorgeous man I had ever laid eyes on walked in and sat down in booth number three.

That table wasn't in my section, so from behind the counter, my eyes and ears focused in on him as he ordered a salt bagel with butter and a side of coffee. Then his crystal blue eyes proceeded to find me and stare back at me…right through me.

Hot flashes permeated my body and I instinctively turned away immediately, but the pull to look back at him was stronger than I could control.

Whoever he was, he was dressed to kill. From the neck down, it was all business. He wore a button down shirt that hugged his protruding muscles and tailored pants. From the neck up, he was ruggedly sexy with wavy hair that looked like it had just been messed with in bed. And he had just the right amount of chin scruff.

I tried my hardest not to stare, but the interest seemed to be mutual. Even when I wasn't glancing in his direction, I could still feel his gaze following me when he thought I wasn't looking and every time he did it, it was like everything turned from black and white in here to color.

So, this was turning out to be a far from typical Monday.

Sure, nice looking guys walked in here all the time: cops, firefighters…but this guy was…well, there are no words to describe the level of utter beauty. He was drop-dead—not someone you typically found visiting a suburban diner, that's for sure.

Why did I have to be wearing this dumb waitress uniform right now? Max, my boss and the owner, tried to give the diner a retro feel, so we waitresses wore dresses reminiscent of those worn by the characters Flo and Alice in Mel's Diner from that seventies TV show. The light blue uniform had my name, *Allison*, stitched over the left breast pocket and everything.

The customers often gave me the same line: *"Someone as pretty as you shouldn't be waiting tables. You must be an actress too, right?"* The truth was, this certainly wasn't what I wanted to do with my life, but for now, waiting tables was the only career I had.

I had dropped out of the special education graduate degree program at Simmons College because I couldn't afford it anymore. I had always wanted to major in something where I could eventually work with special needs kids and make a difference, but the Simmons program was intensive and expensive. Plus, certain life circumstances in the past year made it impossible for me to focus on my studies. So, I decided to give my brain a rest until the time felt right to go back. I made pretty good money at the diner, mainly because I put in so many hours and the patrons were generous with their tips. So, I would be more than able to get by and save up, so that someday I could do something I was passionate about. Max was my neighbor and when he offered me the job, I took it.

And at the moment, with Blue Eyes here…I was *really* happy to be a waitress and wouldn't have traded it for the world.

Even though Delores had taken the gorgeous man's order, which I overheard since my ears and eyes were in tune to him from the moment he walked in, she gave it to me to serve. I didn't know whether to thank her or kill her. She knew what she was doing.

Holy Shit.

My heart was really pounding and my throat seemed to close up. I placed his tray on the counter and hesitated before walking over.

At the moment, he was looking down at the Boston Herald the previous customer left on the table. This meant I could study him for a few seconds before having to face him.

He was truly stunning with a chiseled face and thick, shiny chestnut brown hair, slightly parted in the front and long on the sides curling just above his ears. And I mentioned the piercing blue eyes. He was tall too, at least six feet, I would guess.

Under the table, I saw he wore black argyle socks and shiny black dress shoes. I squinted my eyes to get a better view of the muscles trying to escape through the blue satiny dress shirt he wore and knew the form underneath had to be exquisite. This guy oozed sex, but he was also definitely a professional of some sort, dressed like that. The combination meant he stood out like a sore thumb here.

His expensive-looking navy suit jacket lay across the opposite booth and I was glad I had wiped down that greasy seat before he arrived.

A shiver ran down my spine when he licked his finger to turn the page of the newspaper.

That was one lucky finger.

I inhaled deeply, lifted the tray off the counter and walked over as my heart beat out of my chest. The fluttering of the butterflies in my stomach intensified with each step toward the booth.

After placing the bagel down in front of him, my hand trembled causing the coffee cup to clink against the spoon set on the saucer beneath it. I somehow managed to empty the tray without spilling anything and cleared my throat.

"Can I get you anything else?" I asked.

"No, thank you." He smiled flashing beautiful white teeth. The

3

combination of his smile, scent and smooth voice was so sexy it was painful not to reach out and touch him.

"Well, just let me know if you change your mind," I replied.

"Will do," he said, nodding slowly but continuing to look at me after he stopped speaking. His eyeballs briefly moved side to side a few times as if he was trying to take a picture of my face with his translucent eyes.

There was an awkward silence between us, but I could hear his breathing. His eyes never left mine. I turned around suddenly without saying anything more, taking in his musky scent and feeling the weight of his heated stare on my back as I walked toward the kitchen. Sweat droplets trickled down my armpits and I hoped I remembered to wear deodorant.

In my haze, I bumped right into a customer who was getting ready to leave.

"Excuse me, I am so sorry ma'am," I said nervously without making eye contact with the woman. Of course, Blue Eyes' head was still turned in the direction of my mishap.

Back behind the counter, I snuck peaks at him as he bit heartily into the bagel and swallowed.

That was one lucky bagel.

He wiped his hands from the salt crumbs and took a sip of coffee, revealing what looked to be a Rolex watch wrapped around his sleeve.

When he turned his head in my direction again, I quickly turned away, focusing on a conversation between two elderly women who sat at the counter, as I refilled their coffee cups. One was talking to the other and when the woman on the left got up to go to the bathroom, the other one looked at me with lipstick on her teeth, and confessed, "I couldn't hear one word she was saying to me." I laughed and looked up when I heard chimes signaling the front door opening.

One of the regulars, Mr. Macchio, walked in. He came from Italy forty years ago, and still had the strongest accent. His loud voice snapped me out of my cologne-drunken stupor. He headed straight for his favorite seat in the corner, motioning to me. "Hey, Bella…why-a don-cha get me a green-a tea-ya today, eh? My wife, eh, she say, I should cut down on, eh the coffee, so I gonna try a green tea, o-key?"

I smiled. "Sure, honey."

From the corner of my eye, I could see my mystery man turn around and look in Mr. Macchio's direction as I went to the kitchen to put in the green tea order.

When I came back out, I nearly dropped the tea in a panic when I saw Blue Eyes suddenly get up from his table, plop money down, grab his jacket and quickly walk out. No...he practically *ran* out. The abrupt sound of the door chimes and wind that blasted through upon his exit were like a slap in the face.

So fast?

My heart was pounding harder upon his exit than it had been when he was here. Panic quickly transformed into a feeling of emptiness that washed over me. I actually felt like crying, which was pathetic. I had imagined him maybe striking up a conversation with me before he left or at least maybe getting his name off of a credit card.

As Stevie Wonder's *My Cherie Amour* played over the diner speaker, I had the urge to rip off my apron and follow him out the door. That, of course, would never happen...but I sure did want to.

Without saying more than a few words, this guy had managed to awaken something in me that had been dead: desire. Not only that, but it was a level of want...of need...*of lust*...that I had never experienced in my entire life. He had such an effect on me and now, I could quite possibly never see him again.

It felt like the room was swaying as I walked over to the table that still smelled of his amazing scent and I noticed he left behind more than just his smell: fifty bucks on a bill that was under five-dollars. I almost wanted to chase after him (...again) in case this was a mistake. Did he forget change? Who leaves that big of a tip to a flustered, mediocre waitress, at that?

Faster than I could think of the answer, I remembered Mr. Macchio's tea still sitting on the counter where I left it. After delivering it, I went to the register and sniffed the fifty before depositing it and gave Delores half of the sizeable tip Blue Eyes left.

"What the—" Delores said as I handed her twenty-five dollars cash.

"I know. That gorgeous guy! He left us a fifty. There is your half," I said walking solemnly into the bathroom where I tried to grab my bearings.

I locked the door and sat on the toilet with my head in my hands.

Silly girl. You really need to get some.

Every day in life, people we will likely never encounter a second time, pass us by. For some unknown reason, I just couldn't accept that he was one of them.

For the rest of that afternoon, I fantasized about the beautiful, generous stranger and what it would have been like to thank him properly…with my lips.

CHAPTER 2

CEDRIC

Oh fuck.

Fuck.

Sweating profusely, I ran down Main Street as far away from the diner as I could get.

Where the hell did I park my car?

I needed to think. There it was.

I got in and slammed the door. Silence.

She was so fucking beautiful.

My God.

I had an idea of what she would look like, but never could have imagined her to look as amazing as that. I was imagining a girl…but so much time had passed, I should have known that clearly, she would be a beautiful woman.

Those gigantic green eyes…

God, I hope my staring wasn't that obvious. I just couldn't look away.

Will do…WILL DO? That was the best I thing I could think of to say to her?

And why the hell did I leave a fifty-dollar bill? Way to slip under the radar. I was so flustered and it was all I had in my wallet; I just couldn't stay for change and risk saying something stupid or unintelligible while I waited for that. I could tell by how fast my heart was beating in there, that if I had stayed, I would have fucked it all up.

My heart rate had yet to slow down.

I had to get out of there. It was bad enough I had a forty-minute drive back to the agency in the city. Who travels forty minutes for a bagel? Crazy stalker men, that's who.

I must have been doing eighty-five miles per hour down I-93 when I thought about her name: *Allison.* It was pretty just like her. But of course, I knew she would be more than pretty. And she smelled like green apples.

She seemed nervous. Her hand trembled and her cheeks turned rosy when she approached me and that made me want to rub her sweet face with my hand.

I wondered what her story was, why a girl that looked like that was waiting tables in a diner in the suburbs. Surely, she at least could have done better at one of the trendy bars in Boston. She could have anything she wanted with a face and eyes like that.

Not to mention her slamming body…the way that tight uniform hugged her ass.

Fuck!

She was the last woman I should have been thinking like that about. Yet, all I could focus on was whether she tasted as good as she smelled.

Snap out of it, Callahan. She's the one woman you can't have.

Which is why I wanted her.

I needed to control my thoughts, but I didn't expect to be so fucking captivated liked this.

I had to see her again when I calmed the fuck down. I just didn't know how I was going to manage it. The next two weeks were jam packed with client meetings.

***

I got back to the office in record time, passing my assistant Julie who immediately pointed to my office.

"Karyn is waiting for you," she said.

Karyn.

8

I had been in a relationship for six months with Karyn Keller, an attractive blonde television reporter I began representing after she walked into the agency and demanded to be added to my client roster. We were immediately attracted to each other and decided to ignore the agency's non-fraternization policy.

D.N. Westock represented some of the biggest names in broadcast news and I was their highest grossing agent and rising star after nabbing one of the hosts of a national morning show as a client. Not bad for a kid from Dorchester.

To say I had humble beginnings was putting it lightly. I grew up on the third level of a triple-decker apartment house in one of the highest crime sections of Boston, the middle child of an Italian mother and Irish father. My parents, older brother Caleb and I and my sister, Callie, who's ten years younger, shared the two small bedrooms in the apartment. My parents, Paul and Bettina, went with the whole 'C' name thing for the kids, which went even further because our last name is Callahan.

Money was tight, but our parents did the best they could to provide for us. My father worked as a steelworker and my mother was a maid. Even so, no one was surprised when I, the boy who survived an accidental drive-by shooting on my fifteenth birthday right outside our front door, left home as soon as I graduated from high school. Marked with a bullet hole on my left arm, I managed to get into Northwestern on a merit-based scholarship because studying and school came easy to me, plain and simple.

Northwestern was known for its Communications program and I knew that I wanted to major in something where I would be able to use my innate ability to write and speak publicly. Mostly, I was good at mouthing off and could have taught an AP class in Bullshitting 101.

It was there in Chicago, nearly twelve years ago, during my senior year that my life fell apart. Even with what happened, though, somehow I managed to finish up and graduate.

Three years after the nightmare senior year, while working in Chicago, I began an affair with an older woman named Lana Ford, who happened to be a broadcasting agent. I had taken a position as her intern and even though Lana was fifteen years older, she taught me everything she knew—in the boardroom and the bedroom. I would follow Lana around during the day while she met with clients and then we'd head back to her loft at night. I was closed out emotionally after what happened to me back at Northwestern anyway, so the fact that she was using me for sex and I was using her to get ahead suited me just fine. I didn't want to feel my heart break ever again. I didn't want to feel anything at all, for that matter.

One day, Lana found out I took one of the other young female interns back to her loft, so she cut me loose. She had to know it wasn't going anywhere romantically, but she was…understandably, very bitter. I thought she might try to sabotage me, but I immediately got another better internship, safely working under a male this time.

I eventually used the (non-sexual) experience I gained from watching Lana, to snag an actual junior agent job in the Chicago office of D.N. Westock. I worked my way up the ladder and began representing some major names in the Chicago area before being transferred to the Boston office. I requested the transfer to Boston four years ago after my father died suddenly of a heart attack.

I wished I could say the day my father died was the worst day of my life, but I had already experienced that day eight years earlier.

After I moved back to Boston, I was more determined than ever to forget everything that happened in Chicago. That is, until now. Four years after arriving back home, I now have to face my past again. I just couldn't believe out of everywhere in the country, *she* was so geographically close to me. I have to see her again, if nothing else, just to stare at her beautiful face.

For now, I'd have to see Karyn.

"Hi, hon. What took you so long?" Karyn asked, sitting with her high heels crossed over my desk and clutching her usual "venti non-fat two-pump vanilla latte." She handed me a now cold cup of coffee.

I lied. "I had a meeting with a potential client outside of the city."

"Anyone good?" She batted her eyelashes and twisted her straight blonde hair into a bun.

God, yes, someone good, I thought.

"Yes, this one might have a lot of potential." I immediately pictured Allison and lost all attention to what Karyn said in response. Allison was simply gorgeous and my girlfriend's looks paled in comparison.

I thought about Allison's features: small nose, full lips and straight long, beautiful dark hair that landed in the middle of her back. She could have easily passed for a model, except for her shorter height. And I mentioned her eyes...*her eyes*. They were unusually huge...a light green with speckles of gold. There was something about those same eyes though that made me sad. I sensed something in them that told me her life hadn't been easy as of late. I couldn't take my eyes off them but did just long enough to glance down at that tight uniform that had her name stitched on the front of her perky breasts.

Karyn interrupted me from my stupor. "Where do you want to go eat tonight...Sonsie?" She winked sarcastically. She knew I hated going to those fancy places on Newbury Street. I was much more a takeout and Netflix kind of guy. Plus, I spent most afternoons wining and dining clients at frou-frou restaurants.

"Actually, I'm thinking we should stay in tonight, I had a long day," I said.

I was emotionally exhausted from the experience at the diner and wished I could just be alone tonight.

"Ok, whatever," Karyn hissed, walking over to me to sit on my lap. Running her fingers through my hair, she asked, "Any word from WANY in New York? Didn't you send my demo reel there last week?"

"Karyn, do you know how many agents are trying to get their clients that anchor gig? Believe me, if they are interested, we'll hear from them. Personally, I think it's a long shot for you. You have no desk experience, just street reporting. I think they are looking for more of a bubbly type; it's a morning show gig and babe...bubbly you are not."

Karyn frowned, "Well, I want you to push for me anyway."

Karyn was the I-team reporter for one of the Boston stations. While she was pretty, her tone on-air was serious and it pained her to smile. Not my usual type, she could be brass and cold, but deep down, I liked to believe she was a good person. She came from a wealthy family in Darien, Connecticut and got her start based on the fact that her mother was a big broadcasting exec in New York. Her father was a brain surgeon and Karyn wanted for nothing growing up, having gone to private schools and private resorts her whole life…nothing like *my* childhood.

Dating Karyn was convenient, though. She understood the industry and the demands of my job and she was available and attractive. She never seemed jealous when I worked closely with young, attractive wannabe TV stars, coaching them. Best of all, she didn't push me to open up emotionally, something I haven't done in years with a woman. Karyn didn't seem to expect much except keeping up appearances and sex. I was happy to oblige on the latter, but after a while with Karyn, the sex had become ordinary without the chemistry that existed in the first months of dating. It was still good, just vanilla (like her predictable latte).

***

That night, Karyn and I got Thai food from the place on the corner of my street and later, she left to sleep at her apartment on the other side of Boston. She had to wake up early to work the morning show and introduce her exclusive investigative report on the rise in Chinatown massage parlors being used as fronts for prostitution. Just as well. I wanted to be alone with my thoughts tonight.

It was bad enough that the entire time Karyn was going down on me, Allison was the only thing I could think about. How pathetic that I imagined it was her instead of Karyn and that it was the only way I could finish.

As I lay in bed, the moonlight was exquisite. Beacon Street was quieter than usual and that helped, because I had a lot on my mind tonight, namely deciding whether I would venture back to that diner ever again once I calmed down and whether I would open the can of worms that would emerge from that. I had to come up with a story if I were ever going to show my face again there. I reached for my iPod and immediately searched for my smooth jazz play list, putting on some Diana Krall. I looked up at the ceiling, thinking about the woman who mesmerized me at the diner today, wishing I could have met her under different circumstances and knowing that the truth would turn her world upside down.

CHAPTER 3

ALLISON

The train ride back to my apartment in Malden seemed to go by in a flash tonight. Maybe it was all the fantasizing about Blue Eyes and his fifty-dollar bill. And of course, the number fifty led to thoughts of the book I just read…which leads to thoughts of bondage and billionaires. That guy certainly could pass for a real-life Christian Grey. Heck, he was better looking than the man I imagined when reading that delicious smut.

I blamed my roommate Sonia for introducing me to my favorite pastime and escape: erotic romance novels. She knew I needed a distraction from the year I have had. Even a scandalous book couldn't have kept my interest right now, though.

My mind was all over the place as the train went underground, and the darkness of the tunnel matched my depressive state.

Thinking about him almost made me miss my stop. What was wrong with me? So, a good-looking guy came into the diner, left a big tip and walked out. Why couldn't I stop thinking about him? Maybe Sonia could analyze this for me.

My roommate was nothing like me. She was from England, short with red hair, huge boobs and a fabulous personality. I, on the other hand, was thin, with long nearly black hair, average breasts and tended to be melancholy most of the time…at least lately. Sonia was a good balance for me.

I arrived back to my apartment eager to tell her what happened.

"Hey, Sonia," I said as I walked in the door and threw my keys on the table.

"Sup, bitch," Sonia said.

She had the coolest British accent and "bitch" was her term of endearment for me.

"Ugh...where do I even begin?" I sighed.

"Why...what happened?" Sonia opened a bottle of, ironically, *Bitch* brand wine and took out two stemless glasses from the cupboard. Our kitchen was retro with big black and white checkered laminate flooring and yellow painted cabinets. The apartment was dated, but the vintage style could almost pass for hip. Between the bright sunny kitchen, old-fashioned dark wood moldings and built-in shelving, I loved our apartment.

"You are never going to believe what happened to me today," I said as I sat down and grabbed one of the glasses she poured. "Okay, so I'm in the diner and the most beautiful man I have literally ever seen walks in—"

"Damn...why wasn't I on shift? What did he look like?" Sonia asked as her eyes widened. She also worked at the diner part-time.

"Just...I don't know. The whole nine: beautiful, tall, blue eyes, sexy hair. Let me finish."

Sonia nodded, gulping down half her glass of red.

"This guy was staring at me for some reason. When I pretended to be busy, I could see out of the corner of my eye that he was still following me. When I gave him his order, he barely said anything, just smiled and continued to look at me with these intense eyes."

"Okay," Sonia said as she poured more wine.

"The staring continued for a while and then I went into the kitchen and when I came out, he was abruptly booking it out of there. He didn't even finish his bagel." I took a sip of wine, hoping for a quick buzz to calm my nerves.

"Hmn." She poured me some more wine, even though I had barely had any yet. It's clear that this was becoming a "you had to be there" kind of story, since Sonia clearly wasn't seeing the significance.

"There's more. When I went to clean up his table and collect the money, there was a fifty-dollar bill. His check was only like five-bucks and he left me a fifty!"

"Wow." Sonia's eyes lit up.

"Yeah. I don't know. I guess this kind of thing happens, but never to me. I don't know why I can't stop thinking about him. If he wasn't so damn good-looking, I might have just stopped by now, but he was…so…ugh…" I sighed.

Sonia finished her wine, moved into the living room and lay down on the couch. "Why is it so inconceivable that a handsome guy would walk into the diner, take one look at you and want to leave you a nice tip? You're gorgeous, luv. You know these encounters happen all of the time in the books we read."

Sonia adjusted her bra and took another sip of wine. God, her boobs were huge. The poor thing could barely stand up without tipping over. She was under five feet, which made the whole situation that much worse. Sometimes, I couldn't tell if she was tipsy from the wine or if her chest was defying gravity. I certainly didn't have that problem.

"It's not about the tip, Sonia. That only added to the mystery. What I can't get over is the way I reacted when he was around, like a silly schoolgirl. My body was so aware of him. My uniform practically melted off of me." I said.

Sonia smiled, "Hmn…I think you just need to get some. Well, maybe he'll come into the diner again and you can find out more about him."

"I don't think so. He didn't strike me as someone who would frequent Stardust. Trust me, if he comes in again, I will just about die."

Sonia paused and looked down at the floor then abruptly changed the subject. "I wasn't sure whether to tell you this, but I saw Nate today."

"What? Where?" I asked, freaking out.

"He was coming off the Red Line when I was getting on at Alewife." She stared at me looking for a reaction.

Nate and I dated for almost a year and broke up three months ago. I met him on the train back when I was commuting to Simmons College. At first, I thought he was the most handsome, sensitive, artistic guy I had ever met. You could tell Nate anything and he genuinely listened. Being with Nate was so easy...during the early days. I hadn't been used to guys that had feelings and who seemed genuinely interested in what I had to offer on the inside. We had a great first few months and in many ways, he really introduced me to Boston, even though I had grown up here, showing me all of the museums and taking me to concerts. Nate taught guitar at Berklee College of Music. We had bonded over the fact that we were both adopted. Eventually, we moved in together into an apartment near Fenway Park. It was during that time, I discovered Nate was an alcoholic. The sensitive guy I met slowly shown himself as someone I felt I didn't know anymore. He was very good at hiding it from me in the beginning, but eventually wasn't able to.

"What did he say to you?" I asked.

Sonia never knew Nate when we were dating, since I met her after we broke up, but she encountered him the couple of times he came to the apartment looking for me when I wasn't home. He had somehow gotten my new address here.

"He just said to tell you to call him." Sonia handed me a card Nate had given her. It was a new cell number on a Berklee College of Music business card.

I stared at the card. "Hmn. Did he seem ok?"

"Yeah, I mean, he looked fine, just a little sad, maybe. He also said to tell you he was sorry about how everything turned out." Sonia frowned.

"Well, I think it's best to leave well enough alone don't you?" I asked.

"Yes, I do. I never want you to have to go through that again." Sonia didn't say it, but we both knew what she meant.

One night when Nate was particularly hammered, he came home, saw two empty wine glasses and accused me of having an affair with my friend Danny. Danny is gay, but Nate always insisted that he looked at me like he was interested, or that he could be bi. He said that Danny was pretending to be gay just to be close to me. Danny and I did spend a lot of time together, enough for me to know he was *definitely* gay. When I continued to deny Nate's accusations that night, he hit me so hard across the cheek that I had a bruise that lasted over a month. That was finally the straw that broke the camel's back and I moved out a week later, staying with various friends, including Danny, until I found a place and met Sonia. She helped me get the job at Max's since she worked there part-time while going to nursing school.

Working at a diner was certainly not how I pictured my life at almost thirty. But I was lucky to have a good group of friends there and a place to bide my time while I figured out the next step. I had no real family guidance anymore and so my friends, like Sonia and Danny, were very important to me.

My mother, Margo Abraham, adopted me as a baby, but died of cancer a little over a year ago. Mom never married, but didn't want to miss out on having a child, so she visited an adoption agency when she was forty-two years old and after a three-year wait, was finally blessed with a newborn baby girl. She was my whole life and aside from her sister, my Aunt Reeni who lives in New York, I was virtually alone.

Thankfully, Mom had saved a lot of money over the years. She did well working for the city in the Mayor's office so I have a little nest egg that I'm reluctant to dive into and was even more reluctant to waste away on an expensive college so soon. I had a liberal arts degree from a small community college and spent many years after high school and college working odd jobs until I decided on special education as a career. But after Mom's death, I decided until I could save enough money of my own and focus on my studies, finishing grad school was not going to be happening in the near future.

"Are we going out tonight?" Sonia asked. She was antsy and went out practically every night, even if just for coffee in the North End. I was a homebody and happy to stay home and watch movies most evenings.

"What did you have in mind?" I asked, knowing full well, I would probably stay home anyway.

"I was thinking of calling Tom and seeing if he wanted to meet up with us somewhere, maybe get some cannolis at Mike's Pastry. They are divine."

Sonia loved sweets and Tom was a guy she was crushing on lately. He lived in the neighborhood and they met while he was walking his dog and she was taking out the garbage. They exchanged numbers and met for coffee once so far.

"You should go, but I think I'll just stay in." I said, pulling off my beige Ugg boots.

"Suit yourself, babe. You are not gonna call Nate while I am gone, are you?" Sonia lifted her brow at me.

"Of course not." The truth was, I wasn't so sure about that. I had no intention of getting back with him, but I was curious as to how he was doing. He was pretty devastated when I moved out and called me every day for two weeks. I know what he did was unforgivable, but I also know that had he not been drunk, it wouldn't have happened. Nate had never laid a hand on me sober. I just didn't like the way I ended things, essentially abandoning him and I do struggle with that guilt.

"Alright, I am going to shower," Sonia said as she walked out.

I crashed on the oversized green sofa, closing my eyes, thinking about Blue Eyes and the smell of his cologne. I wondered who he was, what his name was and what he was doing right now, as I drifted to sleep.

CHAPTER 4

CEDRIC

The rest of the week after Monday's diner incident went by in a flash.

After just returning from a quick business trip to the New York office, I met Karyn for dinner on Friday night. The Italian restaurant she chose was dark and noisy and I just wanted to get the hell out and go home.

"You seem distant tonight. Everything okay?" Karyn asked me, straightening her napkin as she perused the drink menu.

"It's just been a busy week, babe. Everything is fine." The truth was the need to see Allison again was consuming me and only got worse as the days passed.

"What do you want to do this weekend?" Karyn said before being interrupted by the waitress who came to take our drink order.

"I'll have a margarita. Cedric?"

"Um…Sam Adams on draft. Thanks." I was hoping the beer would take the edge of this anxious feeling I have had all week, but I probably could have benefited from something a hell of a lot stronger.

"So, what do you want to do this weekend?" Karyn repeated.

"I was hoping you had that mapped out. I'm not feeling very decisive tonight." I said, throwing the menu down.

"Actually, I was hoping we could drive out to Brimfield for the antique fair. I hear great things. It's only about an hour and a half away." She beamed.

"Hmn. Ok, sounds good." Really, I had no use for antiquing, but it would do some good to get out of the city, clear my head and decide what my next move was going to be as far as Allison was concerned.

***

Saturday's scenic drive out to Brimfield was pleasant enough. Brimfield is a rural town in the Western part of Massachusetts and it took about two hours to get there. It was a crisp, fall day and perfect weather if you had to endure trolling around for other people's mostly useless shit.

"Look at this pashmina!" Karyn squealed as she lifted up a hideous pink piece of fabric.

She took out her wad of cash and paid for the scarf that she "just had to have" along with about twenty other items I lugged around in an uncomfortably feminine Vera Bradley tote while she ran ahead of me to the various vendors.

Oh, yeah, I felt real fucking manly today.

At one point I lost her and found myself in a tent run by a woman who looked to be in her eighties. She was selling silver and gold rings and necklaces.

The woman approached me. "Can I help you find something for that special lady?" she asked.

"Oh, no thank you. My girlfriend has a mind of her own," I said rolling my eyes.

The lady ignored me, reaching for something in her stash. "How about this? She lifted out of the clear glass case a silver butterfly on a rope chain that was actually pretty cool looking. The center of the butterfly was encrusted with what looked like diamonds.

"How much?" I decided to humor her even if I had no intention of buying anything.

"You tell me," she said.

The old lady had such a sweet look in her eyes and frankly no one else seemed to be coming by.

"Is it silver?" I asked.

"Actually, this one is white gold. You can see the 14K stamp here." She turned the charm around with trembling hands and looked up at me with bright blue eyes, smiling with a toothless grin. This woman was probably beautiful sixty years ago and spoke with an Irish brogue.

"This belonged to my mother. All of this jewelry was hers. She was a collector. I held onto all of it for so long, but I have been having some health issues and really need to sell it off to pay my bills," she said.

I lightly tapped her arm. "I'm sorry to hear about that," I said.

As the lady put the butterfly back in the case, my eyes caught sight of a ring with a unique colored green stone. The shade of green reminded me of a certain waitress's eyes. It was a lighter green than an emerald, almost a forest green, with just a hint of gold.

"What about that one?" I pointed to the ring. "Is this a real stone?"

She handed it to me and I examined it closer to my eyes.

"I can't be sure. This ring was given to my mother by my father when he was courting her. They were married for sixty years before my father passed away. It's not an emerald, but it looks to be a real gemstone, maybe of the citrine family. This one is also white gold. See the marking inside?"

I squinted to look inside the ring. "It's beautiful. But I would have no idea what to offer you for it."

The woman thought about it for second. "The filigree style of the setting is just not something you see anymore. You can't buy stuff this well made these days. How about one hundred? I'm sure it's worth more, but you seem like a good boy. Are you Irish?" she asked.

"Actually, I'm half Irish on my father's side. My mom is Italian." I grinned.

"That explains the dark hair from your mother and blue eyes from your father, I take it. I'd venture to say that wicked grin is the Irish side as well. For a good Irish boy, I'll give it to you for eighty. Just promise you won't give it away to a lass unless you truly love her. That ring has special meaning and I believe it should be passed to a woman who is truly cherished like my father felt about my mother."

"Ok, it's a deal." Smiling at the woman, I took my wallet out of my pocket hoping I had enough cash to cover the ring. I had two hundred and emptied my wallet, handing it all over to her.

She closed her eyes and shook her head back and forth. "No, dear. I can't accept this. Eighty will do," she said

I shoved the money into her hand. "Please, take it. You can use it and you are giving me a special part of your past. Let a lad help out a lass, ok?"

The woman gave me the biggest toothless grin I have ever had the odd pleasure of experiencing and stood up to hug me.

"Bless you. What is your name, lad?"

"Cedric…Cedric Callahan."

She clapped her hands together. "Callahan! My mother was a Callahan! Mary was her name. Who knows, we could be linked. Thank you so much, Mr. Callahan. I'm Maeve."

"Anything is possible, Maeve," I said, taking the ring which I placed in my shirt pocket.

Just then, I spotted Karyn walking toward me with more junk and nodded my head to the woman who stood smiling as I walked away.

Karyn handed me another small bag, which I placed in the larger one I was carrying. "Did you buy something?" Karyn smiled.

Looking back at Maeve, I lied. "No, no just chatting to that nice lady."

The old woman must have overheard me because when I looked over at her again, she winked. I think she probably sensed as I did, that Karyn wouldn't be the person getting her mother's ring. She was wise, that Maeve.

***

The ride back to Boston was not as relaxing as the ride to Brimfield, since Karyn and I got stuck in bumper-to-bumper traffic on the Massachusetts Turnpike.

After going on and on about the great finds that took up most of the back seat of my Audi RS5, she decided to listen to an audio book on her iPod while I took free reign of the radio.

As I flipped through the channels, I stopped at—of all songs—*Mandy* by Barry Manilow. Definitely not one of my favorites, but it freaked me out because I remembered that it was playing when I walked into the diner that day. It reminded me of the moment I first laid eyes on Allison. It was weird how I hadn't heard that song in years and now I have heard it two times in a week. Maybe it was a sign that I should go back.

Mondays were the only days in my schedule where I had that kind of time in the middle of the day to make the forty-minute drive to the suburbs. Tomorrow was Monday and I was nowhere near ready to step foot back in there and face her yet. I would have to come up with an excuse to talk to her, but somehow explain the tip I left, if she remembered me and asked. Maybe she wouldn't bring it up, but I had to be prepared. No, I wasn't ready to face her. It wouldn't be tomorrow.

***

Several weeks passed before I finally decided to drive up to the Stardust diner again.

I figured if I dressed casually, maybe she wouldn't remember me as the *tip guy*. So, I wore my favorite pair of Levis and a gray cotton shirt under a leather jacket, letting my chin hair grow out a little more for the past few days as well.

I needed to start fresh, grow some balls and somehow start a conversation without coming across as too forward. I didn't want to scare her off. Guys must try to pick her up all of the time and I didn't want her to think that was what I was trying to do, because it wasn't. I really just wanted to get to know her. She had no idea how much. Aside from stalking her at her job, I just didn't know exactly how else to make that happen.

Lucky enough to find a space right in front of the diner, I put the car in park and took the deepest breath I could, remembering the breathing technique I learned in the Bikram Yoga class Karyn dragged me to in Brookline last week.

Breathe.

Ok, F-this. What I really needed was a cigarette. I had been trying to quit, but if there were any moment to make an exception, this was it. I reached into the glove compartment, grabbed my stash of Marlboro Lights, took one out, lit it and inhaled.

Breeaathe. That's better, I thought, as I exhaled. I am so going to Hell. After a few puffs, I tossed it and popped an Altoid before getting out of the car.

You dumb fuck. Now you're gonna smell like smoke.

Bells chimed when I opened the door to the diner. It was much noisier and more packed than the last time and there didn't appear to be any available booths. *The Long and Winding Road* by the Beatles played on the stereo system and the only seats available were right up on the counter. Damn it. I conceded that I had no choice and walked over to the counter seats.

An older woman with very bleached blonde hair and bright red lipstick handed me a menu and told me she would be right back. This was the same waitress who worked with Allison last time...*Delores*...according to her name tag.

But there was no sign of *her* as I looked around. The diner wasn't a big place, so there wasn't a lot of area to cover. The doors to the kitchen swung open and I could see one other waitress in there, shorter, red hair with...gigantic breasts. No Allison.

Delores came out of the kitchen and the other waitress followed. I could have sworn they were looking over at me in unison and whispering by the coffee station. The other waitress then came towards me with a bit of a maniacal smile.

"Hi, my name is Sonia, I'll be your waitress today. Can I get you started with some coffee?" she asked in a strong British accent.

"Ugh, sure. That'll be good. I'll take a coffee and a salt bagel with butter, please." I realized after the fact that I ordered the same thing I got last time, having not really looked at the menu. I had no appetite anyhow once I determined that this had been a wasted trip.

"Sure, thing. I'll be right back with your order." She winked.

The waitress walked back over to the coffee station to pour my cup and I noticed her whispering to Delores again, but this time, Delores turned around and stared more blatantly in my direction. The other waitress…*Sonia*…she said her name was, jumped up a few times, laughed giddily, and then went into the kitchen.

Delores came over with my coffee and smirked.

What was up with that? Perhaps, she was expecting a big tip again.

When Sonia came out three minutes or so later, she set my bagel on the counter in front of me.

"Can I get you anything else?" she asked with a grin.

What a fucking miserable experience.

"No, thanks…just the check."

I smiled but inside I felt like absolute shit. For all I knew, Allison didn't even work here anymore.

I gulped the coffee down and ate half of the salt bagel by the time the waitress came back with the bill. I set my credit card down, and she took it away.

When she came back, she was staring and hesitated for a minute before handing it back to me. I opened the leather binder, added a tip and signed my name as fast as I could.

"Thanks a lot," I said as I got up from the stool.

The waitress smiled. "Thank *you*, Mr. Callahan. Have a brilliant day."

I grabbed my jacket off the back of the chair and headed for the door. The bell chimed again on my way out and I left the diner feeling empty.

As I ran to the car, I realized I should have had the balls to ask if Allison still worked there. But that would have been too random and didn't feel right. What if I lost the only means I had to see her? I decided I would go back a few more times on different days before I jumped to any conclusions.

***

The ride back to Boston was slow and painful. It was cold out, but I opened the car windows anyway and let the frigid air hit my face in an attempt to snap out of my depression.

I had to stop at the condo to change back into my work suit, seeing as though I wanted to dress down for the diner so as not to *tip* Allison off.

I pulled my jeans off, replacing them with my black Armani pants. Just as I was taking off my shirt, the phone rang. I usually let my answering machine pick up calls to my landline phone, since all of my important contacts have my cell phone number. It was normally just telemarketers calling me at home.

As I slipped my purple pinstriped dress shirt on and fastened the "trendy" suspenders Karyn bought me, I heard a female voice on the machine.

Hi, Mr. Callahan. I got your number from the Boston white pages. I am hoping it's the right Cedric Callahan, but there was only one. I'm calling from the Stardust diner. You were in here about an hour ago. I am so sorry, but you must have been in a rush and you left your credit card in the bill folder. Your waitress tried to catch you, but you had already left the area. Anyway, if this is your number, we are open until eleven tonight, so feel free to come by anytime; we'll hold it here for you. My name is Allison; I'll be working tonight, so you can ask for me.

CHAPTER 5

ALLISON

It was rare to be home during the afternoon. Sonia and I had switched shifts today, so that she could go out with Tom tonight. I offered to take her evening shift instead. Sonia was part-time at the diner and only worked a few nights a week. When the phone rang, I had just stepped out of a relaxing bath, wrapped in a towel and decided to let the answering machine pick up.

A loud British voice startled me. "Al...Al...pick up...you're never gonna believe—"

I picked up the phone once I realized Sonia sounded frantic.

"Sonia? What's up...aren't you at work?"

"Oh my God—yes. Your guy...he was here. Al....Blue Eyes...Blue Eyes was here...except he has a name. It's Cedric. Cedric Callahan!"

"Wha...what? How do you know it was HIM?" I shouted into the phone.

"Delores recognized him immediately. She pulled me aside and Oh my God, he was actually how you described him: piercing blue eyes...hair you want to run your fingers through...sexy as all hell. He was dressed down, too, Al. He looked so friggin' hot. And get this: he ordered the salt bagel and coffee again so there was absolutely no doubt that it was him."

"Wait...how did you get his name?" I was shaking. Words could not describe how devastated I was that I was not working today. *So. Utterly.*

Pissed.

"Ok, here's the best part. Are you ready for this? He paid with a credit card. That's how I got his name. But when he went to sign it, he rushed off so fast...he friggin' left it here! I am standing here holding Cedric Callahan's credit card!" Sonia screamed into the phone. She better be out of Max's earshot.

Cedric Callahan. Oh my. The name certainly suited him.

"Are you going to try and look his number up, call him...so we can let him know we have his card?" I asked.

"Well, I figured since you'd be in here in an hour, I'd wait to give you time to get here, unless of course, he figures it out first. Allison, you'd better get your ass up here in case he comes back."

I didn't know how I felt about this. I had been waiting hopelessly for this guy to come back to the diner for weeks. I was fairly certain that he was a one-time thing and that I would never see him again...ever. Now, he would definitely be coming back.

"Ok, I'll be there as soon as I can." I hung up the phone without waiting to hear her response. I needed to get out of my house as fast as possible AND make myself look decent. I grabbed the blow dryer and shook it through my hair faster than ever before. I stopped to put on under eye concealer, eyeliner and mascara, which I never bothered to do when I was just working at the diner, but I had to look my best in case he came in tonight. I hated having to put on this ugly uniform but threw on a short fitted navy cardigan to cover the top. I dabbed on a few spots of mauve colored lipstick, threw on my corduroy beige pea coat and slammed the door behind me.

It was a cold fall day outside and the chill of the air hit my still damp head hard. I grabbed my knit hat out of my tote. Waiting for the commuter rail train seemed to take forever as my heart pounded out of my chest in anticipation.

***

Seven stops later, I exited the train and walked (well, jogged) the two blocks to the Stardust. My heart was pounding as I entered the chaos of the diner lunch crowd.

"Al!" Sonia rushed over to me. "He hasn't come back yet. I just searched the white pages on my phone and found this listing in Boston. It's the only Cedric Callahan in Massachusetts. It's got to be him."

"Did you call?" I asked.

Sonia grinned. "No, you silly bitch...I'm going to let you do the honors."

"Me? I don't want to call him! You do it...please?" I begged. I was so nervous. I couldn't imagine what I would do or say if he picked up.

"Nope...no way. Come on...this is your chance to talk to him and then when he comes in, it'll make it easier to strike up a conversation because you will have already spoken."

"Sonia, we don't know anything about this guy. You are assuming he is not married and that he is heterosexual. I am not getting my hopes up and I really don't want to call him, nor do I expect that he would be thinking about anything more than getting his credit card back." That was a lie. *My hopes were totally up.* I didn't see a wedding ring that first time, so I was pretty sure married was out. Gay, though, that was certainly a possibility.

"He is not bloody gay." Sonia laughed. "You said he was staring at you. Any normal hetero single guy would be checking you out. Come on, make the call...now! Just do it and get it over with."

She handed me the cordless diner phone and I reluctantly grabbed the slip of paper from her hand that had his name and number written in pen. Without thinking it over, I grabbed the phone and dialed the number...6-1-7...5-8-9...9-6-5-8.

Riiing...Riiing...(My heart is thumping hard.) Riiing...Riiing...Riiing... Hello you have reached the voicemail of Cedric Callahan. Please leave your name, number and the time you called and I will get back to you as soon as I can. BEEP. (Heart Thumping)

I don't remember exactly what I said, because I was so nervous. But I don't think I sounded like an idiot. The gist was that he left his card, that he could come get it until closing and that he should ask for me. Done. That was over with. *Phew.* Ok. Now, the wait begins. How was I going to get through this shift?

Sonia was smiling at me. "See…that wasn't so bad! Good luck, bitch…I am heading out. Sonia kissed me on the cheek, grabbed her purse and headed toward the door. I knew she was eager go shopping for a new outfit for her date with Tom tonight, before heading to the apartment to get ready.

"I can't believe you are leaving me. Have fun," I said smiling.

"You too…call me if you snog him later…cheerio!" Sonia winked and left.

***

The slower late afternoon turned into an unusually busy evening at the diner. All of the booths and tables were full and the orders were non-stop during the dinner hours. I was so busy; I shouldn't have had time to notice who *wasn't here*. But of course, it was all I could think about. Every time I would hear the bells chime at the door, my heart would stop for a second.

Maybe it wasn't the right phone number.

Maybe he had no idea he left his card here and would not be coming in tonight after all.

At about 7:30, I took my dinner break. That was the good thing about working at a diner: I could have my choice of anything I wanted to eat. (That might be a bad thing depending on how you look at it.) I usually tried for a salad with grilled chicken, but tonight…tonight I was going to eat my nerves away. I opted for a Reuben sandwich smothered in Thousand Island dressing, banana milkshake and chocolate cream pie for dessert. I was going to *throw down*.

I sat down next to one of the regulars, Mr. Short, who was ironically, ridiculously tall, at about six foot seven. The other patrons called him Big Bird behind his back. Mr. Short was such a nice guy though and would probably find that funny.

"Hi, Mr. Short…mind if I join you?" I sighed and sat down before he could respond, because we always sat together when he'd come in for lunch during my normal shift.

Mr. Short was a Vietnam veteran and widower. Since his kids all lived in different states, the diner was like home to him and he had breakfast, lunch and dinner there. I enjoyed keeping him company whenever I was on duty.

"How ya doing tonight, Allison? It's nice to see you here during the dinner hour." Mr. Short looked at my tray full of food and lifted his brow.

"I know…a different variety for me, right?" I laughed.

"Yes…I should say!" he laughed.

"I'm a little preoccupied with something tonight, so I am thinking food might help me calm my nerves." I took a huge bite out of the sandwich and again, glanced at the door. This would not have been the right time for Blue Eyes to walk in.

"Anything I can help you with?" he asked.

"No, no…I'm fine, really," I said, taking a big gulp of my shake.

He opened the newspaper. "Ready for your horoscope?"

Mr. Short and I often checked our horoscopes during lunches together and he would always read mine to me.

"Yup…shoot," I said.

Mr. Short read for me and I listened intently as I took another huge bite out of my sandwich.

"*You may receive word from a friend today with a career tip or inspiration for a new hobby. Whatever the case, Gemini, a friend will play a significant role in your life bringing forth business opportunities.*"

"Interesting. I'll keep it in mind," I said.

He gestured silently that I had dressing on the side of my mouth and I wiped myself with a napkin.

"Are you sure you are okay, Allison?"

"Yup," I said with my mouth full of food, as I wiped it again.

I could never admit to what I was really obsessing over tonight. It would sound so stupid to him, really, admitting that I was nervously waiting for a man who would probably never show.

I changed the subject and started asking him questions about Vietnam, his favorite topic, which inevitably led to as long of a story I was willing to sit for.

***

The crowd in the diner died down after about ten. At that time of night, it was more about cleaning up and restocking for the next morning. There were a few stragglers sipping on coffee and eating pie, but for the most part, the real work was done for the night.

I finished wiping down the last of the empty tables and grabbed the broom from a side closet to sweep the floor behind the counter as Patsy Cline's *"Crazy"* played. I was *crazy* all right. I thought about how stupid I felt looking at the door every thirty seconds tonight, when, even if he had come in, he would have taken his card and gone away just as fast back to his cosmopolitan life. It might not have mattered even if he came in. Why was I obsessing over this guy anyway? Was there something truly missing in my life that I had to create this imaginary drama? Was the significance of him all in my head?

I thought about the past year as I swept the floor: how much I missed my mother and how badly the relationship with Nate ended. I hadn't focused on anything other than my problems until the distraction of Blue Eyes...*Cedric*. If I could take away anything from this situation, at least I knew I had the capacity to be interested in something again.

***

It was 10:55 and time to start shutting down for the night. Max and whichever waitress worked the late shift would always walk out together before he locked up.

I turned off the neon "Open" sign in the window and grabbed my coat. I waited by the door for Max to come out of the kitchen and looked out at the streetlights. He wasn't quite ready to leave yet and I could hear some last minute washing and clanking of pots and pans. Besides that, the music was off, and overall, the diner was eerily silent.

I couldn't wait to get out of there, back to my apartment and into a hot bath. Pathetic. What a waste of energy today was, I thought, as the draft from standing near the door made me shiver.

The last train would be leaving at 11:20, so I was hoping Max would hurry up. I closed my eyes imagining how good that hot water bath would feel.

I opened my eyes just as a silver Audi pulled up out front.

CHAPTER 6

CEDRIC

I had been sitting at this business dinner for over two hours and I couldn't tell you one thing that was said. I was aimlessly nodding and nursing a scotch because I didn't want to get hammered tonight if I had any chance in hell of making it to the diner before they closed. I would have much rather been on the highway headed north but couldn't get out of here to save my life.

Earlier this afternoon, after I got the voicemail from Allison that I had left my credit card at the Stardust (*idiot move by the way*), I rushed back to the office elated and nervous but determined to make it back to the diner after work.

In the midst of this development, I realized I had forgotten about a major client meeting followed by dinner scheduled at night. Westock was trying to woo Boston's top sports anchor from a rival agency and he and his wife had scheduled a meeting with my colleagues and me. It wasn't until I walked in and saw a panicking Julie waiting in my office that I remembered.

Sports anchor Scott Ellis was already waiting in conference room B and he didn't look too happy. Thankfully, I was skilled in the art of schmoozing and ass kissing and by the end of the meeting, I had him wrapped around my finger. I offered to take a lower percentage commission than he was paying his current agent and guaranteed that I could get him a higher salary. I had already had a meeting setup with TV station management who owed me a favor anyway, after I stopped another client of mine from suing them for breach of contract. I knew the higher salary was a given and I knew Ellis would be my client before the week was over.

***

No longer needing to kiss-ass, I joined Ellis, his wife Maureen and a few of the other agents to celebrate the new business relationship at Ruth's Chris Steakhouse in the city.

It was 9:30 and I knew I needed to wrap this up soon if I wanted to get to the diner and allow time to go home and change out of my work clothes first.

Just when I was about to make up an excuse and leave…Karyn showed up. Apparently, she had called my assistant's cell phone to find out where we were and decided to join us. Karyn worked with Scott at the same station and must have thought her presence would help; little did she know how much worse she made this night for me by showing up when she did.

"Hey, babe. Hi, Scott…Maureen…" Karyn said as she walked in like she owned the place, asking the waiter for an extra chair and squeezing in beside me.

"Karyn…what a pleasant surprise." I lied, flashing a fake smile.

"I didn't realize you two were an item," Maureen said, looking over at her husband who was grinning.

Karyn wasn't exactly the most liked person at her TV station. She was known for being overbearing in staff meetings and throwing out story ideas that management didn't always agree with ethically. Ellis seemed amused by her, though. I ignored Maureen's question about our dating and turned to Karyn to whisper in her ear.

I flat out lied. "Babe, I wish you had gotten here sooner. I have an early commuter flight to New York City in the morning and was just about to respectfully excuse myself, since I have some preparation to do for the meeting at WANY."

I didn't know what else to do. I didn't feel good about lying, but the thought of missing out on seeing Allison…*who was expecting me*…was killing me. If I hadn't intervened, knowing Karyn, this would have turned a long night into a never-ending one. I would have to make up a story tomorrow about the meeting being cancelled suddenly, but I can deal with that later.

Karyn's eyes popped. "WANY! You are going to talk to them about the anchor position…the one I want?"

The truth was, I did have a meeting to discuss Karyn and a few of my other clients at WANY *next week*. So, the lie was not 100-percent ruthless. In fact, my idea was becoming more brilliant by the second since next week's actual meeting would look like I rescheduled the fictitious one.

"Actually, yes, that's on the agenda, Karyn." I looked up at Scott realizing that Karyn shouldn't have been discussing jumping ship in front of her current co-worker. This was my fault. I didn't want to jeopardize Karyn's job, and I knew she really didn't stand a chance at the New York anchor position. In fact, I had two other clients I would be pushing harder for to get that job, because they were better for it, plain and simple.

Karyn rubbed my shoulder. "Honey, I completely understand if you need to go. I can't believe I didn't know you were going tomorrow, but I am happy you are." Karyn then did a little happy dance and giddily stomped her feet.

"Thanks, babe. You stay…have fun," I said.

On that note, I got up from the table, shook hands with Ellis and gave Maureen a friendly kiss on the cheek after she leaned in.

"Thanks for a great meeting, Scott. I'm sure this is the beginning of a great working relationship. I'll call you later this week once I have had a chance to talk the guys in suits." I leaned in and kissed Karyn on the cheek, slapped down eight hundred dollars cash that should more than cover the bill and walked out.

***

Halle-friggin-llujah. When I exited the restaurant onto the busy street, I felt relief as the cold air hit my face. I waited for the valet to bring out my Audi and gave him a higher than normal tip, patting him on the back, simply because I was so friggin' happy to have made it out of there in time.

I didn't have time to go back to the condo and change, so I would have to see Allison dressed up the same way I was that first visit. She was definitely going to remember me now. I was not sure how I felt about that, given what an ass I acted like that day.

I revved the engine and sped onto I-93.

It was 10:20. I would be just getting there in time if I were lucky.

I passed a broken down Toyota Corolla and thought about the fact that if this were any other night, I would have helped the poor bastard. Not tonight, though…not tonight.

10:45…I was almost there. I started to feel my heart pounding, knowing how my body would react when I saw her again. I continued to drive focusing on that beautiful, haunting face.

10:50…I exited the off ramp and made my way down the side streets, noticing the black and orange lights adorning the houses and stores on Main Street in preparation for Halloween.

I could see the Stardust in the distance, but noticed that the Open sign was not illuminated.

Fuck.

I slid fast into the space right in front and without thinking, rushed out of my seatbelt and slammed the car door closed.

When I looked up, my heartbeat accelerated when I saw Allison standing with her coat on facing me through the front window of the diner.

She looked like a doll, standing there in a fitted brown coat and a pink knit cap, with flushed cheeks. She was gorgeous.

The chimes sounded as I opened the door, bringing us face to face and into a few seconds of silence where I stood in awe of her before speaking.

"Hi…I, um, am so sorry I'm so late…I'm Cedric. You called about the credit card I left here earlier today?" I couldn't stop looking into her eyes. They were so unique, yet familiar.

"Hi…yes, that was me who left the message. It's no problem. We aren't technically closed. I'm waiting for Max, the owner to finish up before we lock up. Let me get your card," she said.

She definitely seemed nervous.

"No rush," I said.

No rush...stupid thing to say. Why wouldn't she want to get the hell out of here? It was the end of her shift.

I watched as she walked behind the counter toward the register. She was the perfect height, about five feet six inches, not too tall, not too short and was wearing light beige Uggs. She must have changed out of her work shoes. She was really ready to leave. I was inconveniencing her. She looked frazzled as she rummaged through papers and folders near the register. I heard her whispering to herself. I thought I heard a faint 'fuck.'

I hadn't moved yet from my spot near the door, so I walked over to her.

"Is everything ok?" I asked.

"No...um...it's not. My co-worker told me she left your card in this folder and it's not in here. I'm afraid I have to call her and find out where she put it because it's just not here."

I smiled, wanting her to relax. "No worries. It's gotta be in this place somewhere, right?" I'm in no rush. Please take your time, Allison."

The credit card was the least of my concerns right now. It could have been on its fucking way to Nigeria for all I cared.

Just then, an older black-haired man with a moustache who looked like Super Mario came out from the kitchen, dressed in a coat and hat with a newspaper stuffed under his arm.

"Ready to go, Al?" he asked. This must have been Max.

"Max, if it's okay, I need to use my key to lock up. This customer left his credit card here earlier today and I don't know where Sonia put it. I just tried her cell and there is no answer, so I am gonna look around for it."

"No problem. You know how to lock it, right?" Max asked. He didn't seem worried. You could tell he trusted her.

"Yup...done it before plenty of times. Thanks."

The bells chimed as Max left the diner, leaving me alone with Allison.

Alone with Allison.

This was my one and only chance to get to know her. It was now or never. I hoped she never found that goddamn card.

"Cedric, I'm really sorry about this." She looked over at me quickly while still rummaging through cabinets and drawers, her big eyes frantically searching. "I know Sonia wanted to put it someplace for safe keeping, but apparently, that backfired."

Her cheeks looked red. She was actually really upset about this. I wished I could tell her how happy the situation was actually making *me*, but then if she knew that, I'd probably end up in the back of a cop car heading back to the city.

"Allison, it's really ok. Please, don't worry about it. Do you mind if I sit down while you look?" I asked.

"Please...yes...can I get you a slice of pie or something?" she asked.

"That's really sweet of you. Yes, I would love some." Pie actually sounded really good.

"Apple or coconut cream?" Allison held the door open to the kitchen as she waited for my reply with the sweetest look on her beautiful face.

My heart was fucking toast.

"Aw, man...that's easy...coconut cream...thanks."

Could this night have gotten any better? Now there was pie in the mix?

Allison walked out of the kitchen with a small plate that had a huge slice of pie on it, a generous dollop of whipped cream and a maraschino cherry on top.

"Here you go." She smiled and placed the pie in front of me.

"Thanks." I stared up at her again for a few seconds. This time, she was staring back at me, her hand slowly backing away from the pie plate. It reminded me of the awkward pause we experienced the first time I came into the diner. God, I just wanted to grab her and sniff her hair. Thank God she couldn't read my mind because if she could, this pie would be in my face and the cherry up my ass.

Allison abruptly walked away and said, "I'm going to try Sonia again."

She picked up her iPhone and scrolled down to a number and this time she got an answer. I watched and listened to her as I stuffed my face with pie.

"Sonia!" she shouted. "Where the hell did you put the credit card? I looked there. It's not there! You said the green folder. What do you mean top shelf? Oh...the shelf in the pantry. Crap. Alright...yes, he is...later...later...I can't now. Alright...thanks."

She hung up and ran into the kitchen.

When she came out, she flashed me a big smile showcasing her perfect teeth.

"Cedric, I'm so, so sorry. Apparently, she left it in a green folder, but it was a different green folder in a different spot. Anyway, I am really sorry for the mix-up."

Allison handed me the card and our fingers brushed together, the feel of her skin sending a shiver down my spine and an awareness somewhere else. That was the first time I actually touched her.

"Please, don't apologize, Allison. Sitting here enjoying this pie has seriously been the highlight of my day. And I should be apologizing to you for putting you through the trouble of having to look for it when it was my asinine mistake, leaving it here."

"Well, it all worked out, I guess."

"It did," I said.

Then, there was more tense silence as I got lost in those gigantic green eyes.

"Allison, I hope you have a safe way of getting home tonight. It's pretty late."

"I actually usually walk to the train station with Max, but...wait, what time is it?" She looked at her watch. "Crap," she said.

"What? What's wrong?" I asked.

"The last commuter train left at 11:20. It's 11:25. I missed it." She sighed.

"Well, it's obviously my fault. Please let me drive you home. Where do you live?"

This was too good to be true.

"I live in Malden. It's about a half-hour drive from here. Are you sure? I could call a cab."

"No way. You are here because of me and it's actually right on my way home. I live in the city."

"I figured that."

"You figured I lived in the city? Why is that?" I asked with a curious gaze, not able to take my eyes off her swollen lips.

"Well, you're always so well-dressed, like a businessman from Boston, I guess. I mean…uh…I remember the first time you came in," Allison said shyly.

Shit. Ok, so she remembered me as tip guy.

I had to think quickly and then lied. "Yeah, I have a client up this way which is why I've stopped in before."

Allison searched her bag for the key. "Ready to go?" she asked.

"Absolutely."

Absofuckinglutely.

I walked out first, watching her shut the light, lock the diner door and check it a few times. I disarmed the car and stopped at the passenger side to let her in.

Her smile was mesmerizing as she stepped into the passenger seat and I gently closed the door, wondering again how I got so damn lucky.

CHAPTER 7

ALLISON

Holy shit. Was this really happening?

Cedric opened the driver's side door, turned on the heated seats and started the car. He smelled so incredibly good. I swear, I could have died happy right there in that seat, intoxicated by his scent. It was a mix of musk, sandalwood and leather.

He was so damn hot, dare I say the most handsome man I had ever laid eyes on. Just like I remembered, but with even more of a five o'clock shadow on his chin, which made him even sexier. There was a roughness about him that directly contradicted the business attire.

As he grabbed his stick shift *(pun intended),* a slight piece of his shiny hair fell over his forehead and I nearly died.

He wasn't wearing a jacket, just a purple, fitted dress shirt that showed off his muscular chest. He was even rocking suspenders that wouldn't have been sexy on any other man. He could pull those off really well, though. I had the urge to pull them and snap them back against his chest.

I turned around and saw that his suit jacket was thrown in the backseat, along with a bottle of wine on the floor. I wondered who would be drinking that with him.

Nervous chills ran through me as his big, slightly scuffed hand grabbed the stick shift and moved it in a jerking motion. My body was fluctuating from cold to hot, reacting to these feelings of lust. I could feel my armpits welling with sweat again and a tingle in my nether regions. I realized at that moment, how little control I actually had over my own body.

Cedric broke the silence. "So, you remembered me, huh?" he said, suggestively in a low, smooth voice as he turned to look at me with a sexy side glance, before returning his eyes to the road.

"Well, you were kind of hard to forget. I mean…you left quite a big tip." I was sure to add that last part. I didn't want to give away too easily the real reasons I thought he was unforgettable, which had nothing to do with the money.

Cedric seemed to hesitate, shaking his head and said, "Yeah…I guess I did, didn't I? I was in a bit of a rush, so I left you what I had in my wallet."

"Well, thank you. It truly brightened my day and was very generous. I had wanted to thank you, but you left so fast. I thought maybe it was a mistake. I have never received such a big tip in my life. I actually split it with Delores since it was technically her table to begin with. Delores is really cool. She's a hoot. She makes working at the diner fun." I shut up immediately. *Oh God, I was rambling like a bumbling idiot and making no sense.*

"Well, I am really glad I could brighten your day," Cedric said as he glanced at me and smiled.

"Thanks again." I turned to look out the window when a sudden bout of bashfulness took over.

In my periphery, I could see his head turn in my direction and I looked back at him.

"So, Allison, tell me, how long have you worked at the diner?" Cedric asked as he sped onto I-93, returning his eyes quickly to me once he entered the highway. I loved watching him drive.

"Just a few months. I'm just biding my time there. I was in a special education program at Simmons, but I am putting that on hold for a while. But working with kids with disabilities is really my passion."

"Simmons is a great school. Special education? That's an honorable field. What made you decide to go in that direction?"

He switched gears and continued to alternate between looking at me and the road.

"Well, I really love kids and one summer when I was a camp counselor for the YMCA, I bonded with a little girl with Down syndrome. Her parents had actually given her up for adoption at birth, so she lived temporarily with foster parents. I am also adopted, so that made me even more attached to her. I was crushed when she was transferred to another family out of town. We still write to each other to this day. Ever since that summer, I wanted to work in some capacity with special needs kids. Even though I can't afford Simmons right now, I'm hoping to find a way to get into the field while I wait to get back to grad school."

Cedric nodded slowly as if he was thinking of what to say next. "I think that's amazing. I give you a lot credit for that."

"Thanks," I said.

He paused and licked his lips, his expression turning serious. "Actually, I don't tell too many people this off the bat, but my younger sister, Callie…well, she has autism. She is twenty-four now, but she is a lot like a little girl in many ways. Back when she was diagnosed as a child, there were not a lot of autistic people. Nowadays, it's something like one in every fifty kids is on the spectrum. Incredible. So, there really is a need for people who can work with them." The emotions that talking about his sister conjured up were written all over Cedric's face. After a pause, he said, "My sister…she's…she's special."

I was caught off guard at how impassioned he became when talking about his sister.

"Wow. Is your sister verbal?" I asked as I thought to myself and smiled when I realized her name would be *Callie Callahan*.

"Yes, somewhat. She can ask for simple things. She can read, but she doesn't have the ability to converse like you and I. She is totally dependent on my mother and has someone coming to the house a few hours everyday to work with her on daily living and to help Mom out in caring for her. They actually go with her to a job where she helps sort books at the local library, which is pretty cool."

You could tell he was very proud of his sister, but also a little sad about it. The tender look on his face made me want to grab his hand.

"She sounds amazing. I am sure having her in your life gives you a different perspective on things."

"Yeah. It sure does. We neurotypical people take so many things for granted." He smiled.

"I would love to work with autistic kids, myself," I said.

Cedric scratched his chin. "Hmm. There's an agency that provides the services Callie receives. I know they work with children, as well as adults. Maybe I can ask my mother for a human resources contact there and email it to you. My mother complains a lot that the turnover rate of people working with Callie is high, so maybe they are looking to hire. We can exchange emails."

Yes.

"That would be fantastic, Cedric. Really, that would mean a lot." I was truly amazed that he cared enough to offer to look into this for me. We've known each other less than an hour.

"My pleasure. I wish I could say I had a meaningful career like that. My profession…well, it's about as shallow as they come." He shook his head and glanced at me.

"What do you do?" I was dying to know.

He held his breath with a mischievous smile and then glanced at me again, seeming hesitant to tell me. He rolled his eyes and said, "I'm a talent agent. I represent mostly TV journalists…news anchors and reporters and we handle things like contract negotiations for them and we also do some consulting for the news stations."

"That sounds exciting, actually. So, you represent people like Katie Couric?" I asked.

Cedric laughed. "Kind of like her…but not her, yeah. It can be exciting at times. But it's really quite a cutthroat business."

"How so?" I was curious.

"Well, sometimes you have clients who are both competing for the same job and you have to make both believe that you're in their corner, otherwise, you could stand to lose them, but you also want one of them to get the gig, because the agent gets a commission on their salary. And then there's the consulting end of things, where you basically walk into these TV stations and tell management everything they're doing wrong...which reporter needs to lose weight...which anchorman is getting too old to relate to the target audience...that sort of stuff," Cedric said as he looked over at me for a response.

"You're right. It does sound kind of nasty," I smiled.

He nodded his head in agreement and we both laughed. "Yeah."

I continued to ask him questions about his job over the next several minutes. That turned into my telling stories about some of the characters that come into the diner. We laughed *a lot* and it was so easy to talk to him.

Then, at one point, neither of us said anything for about a minute. He licked his lips again and I turned away embarrassed suddenly when he seemed to catch me staring at his mouth.

Breaking the silence, I spoke up. "You're going to want to take exit 32, by the way, to get to my house."

I glanced down at my watch willing the time to stop going so fast. I wished I lived farther away. I wanted to stay in this car forever with him.

"Great. So, do you live alone?" Cedric asked.

"No, actually, I live with Sonia...the waitress who took your order today? She and I met through Craigslist. She was looking for a roommate and thankfully, it worked out. She and I get along really well."

"You're lucky she wasn't a murderer if you were looking for roommates on the internet."

We both laughed. "No kidding."

After a bit more silence, Cedric turned the heat down and looked at me. "I hope I am not prying, but you mentioned you were adopted? Did you grow up here in Boston?"

"Yes. I have always lived here. My mother adopted me when she was in her mid-forties. She had always wanted a child, but never married and so, she took things into her own hands. She was really lucky, since in those days, single parent adoptions were rare. But Mom was a professional and made a good living for the city with good benefits and they had no reason to deny her."

"What does your mother do?" he asked.

"Well, she worked for the mayor's office before she retired. She passed away about a year ago."

The look on Cedric's face turned suddenly sullen and he was briefly silent before letting out a deep breath that made me shudder.

"Oh, I am so sorry, Allison. I lost my father. I know how hard it is," he said, frowning.

It made my heart hurt that he had endured losing a parent too. "Thanks. I was an only child. So, it's been tough," I said, fighting back watery eyes.

Cedric looked at me and then turned away staring ahead in silence at the road. The expression on his face showed that he seemed genuinely affected by my revelation that I was essentially alone.

He turned to me again. "Allison...you don't have any other extended family?"

Well, my aunt Irene...I call her Reeni...lives in upstate New York. She has a son, but he is a bit of an ass clown...Cousin Arthur," I said rolling my eyes.

Cedric's head rolled back as he shook with laughter at my use of that term. "Good old cousin Arthur the ass clown...I love it."

He was cracking up and had such a deep, smooth laugh. It was the first time I heard it.

I was laughing as well now. "Yes...cousin Arthur. He's thirty-five, has incurable acne and spends most of his days playing video games and chatting online with other Trekkies. This is my next of kin. He works in a comic book shop part-time and mooches off my aunt the other times. So, essentially, I am indeed alone. Although, I have some wonderful friends, so I never feel it, really."

"Well, that's good. I'm glad to hear it." Cedric smiled.

"Um...the exit is coming up next." I pointed to the green highway sign that showed we were a quarter of a mile from my neighborhood. I was bummed that this was coming to an end. It was not like I could invite him inside.

Could I? God, I wanted to.

Cedric pulled off the highway and I directed him down the side streets of Malden.

I pointed. "Turn left here, this is my street."

"Nice little neighborhood you have here," he said, looking out the window.

"Yes, it's very family-oriented, so it's pretty safe. You can park right here," I said, pointing to the space in front of the green two-family house that I lived in on the second floor.

Cedric pulled into the space, put the car in park and then surprised me when he turned the car off completely. There were no moving cars on the street and it was quiet except for the sound of a train horn in the distance.

We both just sat in silence for several seconds and then he turned to me. The streetlights were shining on his blue eyes, which were now glowing. He seemed like he wanted to say something and we stared at each other before Cedric spoke. "I hope this isn't too personal, but do you know anything about where you came from?"

That caught me off guard. "You mean my biological parents?" I asked.

Cedric nodded tenderly looking into my eyes and whispered, "Yeah."

His question surprised me, being that we had just met, but I felt comfortable enough with him to be open.

I shook my head. "I don't know anything, actually. Mom always said it was a closed adoption, so it would be very difficult to find her or…them. I never really tried to find anything out. I never wanted to hurt Mom's feelings and truthfully, in my eyes, she was my real mother in every way. I never knew anything else."

That was the truth. I had no desire to meet the person or people that gave me away. My mother was everything to me and I never felt slighted until the day she died.

Cedric looked down at his shoes pondering my response and looked back up at me, his eyes seemingly staring into my soul. "Do you feel differently about it now that she's gone?"

I broke from his intense gaze, looked at the ceiling of the car and thought about that for a moment. "I haven't really given it much thought to be honest. Mom's only been gone a little over a year. But no…I think my birth mother or birth parents probably would have found me by now if they were interested…and if they never wanted to find me, then I certainly don't want to look for them. So, I think I'll continue to leave well enough alone. Hopefully, someday I'll start my own family, you know?"

Cedric nodded slowly, soaking in my answer then said in a low voice, "I am sure you'll make a wonderful mother someday."

Chills ran down my spine at the sound of his soothing voice saying words that evoked so much emotion in me. I secretly wished he were right and that by some miracle of my imagination, he could be the one to give that to me someday. My feelings for him were growing by the nanosecond. It was strange to feel so close to someone I had just met.

"Thank you for that." I smiled and was hopeful that we could drop the subject of my history. I had never been fully comfortable discussing it. Bringing up the subject of my birth parents was something I had always avoided. Talking about it seemed to demean in some way the only true mother I had ever known. I could never fathom how a mother could give up her baby as easily as my birth mother must have given me up as a newborn.

I decided to change the subject. "I can't believe all these years we lived in the same city and never crossed paths," I said.

Cedric laughed, his eyes now turning mischievous. He looked down and shook his head. "I think that might be a relief on my end. I was a bit of a punk growing up. You wouldn't have liked me then."

"Oh really?" I said.

I just couldn't get enough of looking at those eyes. He had a darkly impish grin on his face now.

God, he was drop dead gorgeous.

Then, he continued. "Seriously, looking back, I realize I was a bit of a dickhead when I was a kid, used to start fights and break windows. My friends used to joke that's why my initials spelled cock. Cedric looked at me for a moment and then broke out in laughter as he waited for my reaction.

I shook my head and laughed. "What, now?"

"My middle initial is O, so Cedric and Callahan wrapped around that…you have C-O-C…cock." He laughed.

"Ah…makes sense." I continued laughing then realized something. "Wait…your middle initial is O? My middle initial is O too!"

Cedric's mouth dropped. "Really?"

I nodded and grinned. "Yes…my middle name is Ophelia."

His eyes widened and glistened in amazement. "Allison…you're friggin' kidding me," he said.

"No, I'm not. What's wrong with Ophelia?"

"Nothing at all. It's absolutely beautiful…but when I tell you my middle name, well—"

"What? Cedric tell me…what is it? Oscar? Omar? O'Shaughnessy? Obi Wan Kenobi? Tell me!" I laughed, waiting in suspense.

Cedric put his hand on my headrest and moved in closer which startled me. I could feel his breath near my face when he said, "Allison…your middle name is Ophelia…"

"Yes…don't tell me your middle name is Ophelia, too?" I joked.

Cedric shook his head. "No…not Ophelia…but—"

"But what?"

"You'd never guess it."

"Give me a hint."

He rubbed his chin and smiled. "Okay…it's from Shakespeare too."

My jaw dropped and I did guess it. "Oh my God…*Othello?* You're telling me your middle name is…Othello?"

He nodded. "That's *exactly* what I am telling you."

This was really bizarre and hilarious.

"You mean to tell me we are both named after Shakespeare characters?" I stared at him in awe before thinking about it again for a few seconds. "Wait…are you shitting me?"

Cedric burst out laughing. "It would seem that way wouldn't it, but unfortunately, I'm not. I swear on my father's grave," he said.

Now, I knew he was being serious. You just don't joke on someone's grave. "Wow," I said.

Cedric seemed really amused by this coincidence too. "Wow is right...you're telling me. My father was a huge Shakespeare fan and insisted on my middle name being Othello. The Othello board game was pretty big back then too. For some reason, he thought it was the coolest name. It started as a joke, really. My mom was dead set against it and one night, they were with some friends and she lost a bet and well...there you have it...Cedric Othello Callahan."

"I guess maybe this is a sign we were meant to meet," I said, immediately regretting the suggestive comment.

Cedric smiled, his white teeth glistening. "I think so, Allison Ophelia."

He was so surprisingly easy to talk to and I didn't want this night to end, but I was apprehensive about asking him to come upstairs.

No, there was no way I could do that.

Cedric turned the interior light on and reached across me to open the glove compartment when I got my closest interaction with his body yet, breathing him in. The heat beneath my ass from the seat was nothing compared to the warmth throughout my body as his hair sat inches from my nose. His arm brushed against me and I fantasized about pulling it towards me, putting his hands on me.

He looked frantically for something, eventually grabbing a pen. I spotted a pack of cigarettes in there as well. Strange...he didn't seem like a smoker and I didn't smell it in here.

Mmm...I think the cologne might be Cool Water.

"Aha. Here it is," he said after grabbing a pen. "Do you happen to have a piece of paper in your bag?"

"Let me look." I opened my purse and dug through all of the crap: hairspray, gum, mace, wallet, change...not one darn piece of paper?

"Ok, don't worry about it. My phone is dead; otherwise I would enter your information that way. Here, give me your hand."

Cedric reached out his palm and I placed my hand in his. He clicked the pen and began to write his cell phone number and email address carefully on top of my hand, while holding it steady with his. His hand was big, rough and warm. A wave of heat rushed through my body as he breathed out slowly and I felt his hot breath on my hand.

I never wanted him to stop writing, never wanted him to let me go. He did though, but not before squeezing my hand, a silent farewell gesture before he let it loose.

Then he just stared at me for a few seconds with his icy blue eyes and my nipples got hard.

I cleared my throat. "Um…let me give you my information as well," I said, grabbing his hand *(ballsy, yes?)* as he handed me the pen. My hand might have trembled a little as I wrote all of my information on his. I could have sworn his thumb brushed across my hand intentionally before I reluctantly pulled away.

Cedric turned the interior light off and we stood in silence for a few more seconds before he spoke. "Well, then…Allison, it was really great talking with you. Again, I am sorry about your having to look for the card and your missing the train…but I can't say I didn't enjoy your company on the ride home."

"Me too…I mean…I enjoyed your company too. *You have no idea.* And thanks for, you know, looking into that contact at the special needs agency."

I lingered a bit, hoping Cedric would ask me out. When he just continued to stare at me, I opened the car door, leaving him sitting there.

He flashed his beautiful teeth one last time as I shut the door.

As I walked up the stairs, Cedric started the car. Fiddling with my keys, I looked back, noticing he was still idling waiting for me to safely enter. When I cracked the door open, I turned around and waved and saw him wave back. Then, he took off.

I ran upstairs and when I entered the apartment, I realized Sonia hadn't come home yet.

I started tearing off my clothes and ran to the bathroom to see what I looked like. Not bad. The mascara was a little runny, but for having worked all day, I guess I looked somewhat presentable.

I turned on the faucet to the bathtub and I pulled off my socks. If I thought he was amazing before, I was speechless now. In that short time, Cedric managed to make me laugh, almost cry and possibly gave me a job lead. Not to mention, my underwear was soaked from just the touch of his hand on mine. The only thing that could have made tonight better was if he had actually asked me out.

I poured lavender bath salts in the water and waited for it to fill up. As I entered the white ceramic tub, I smelled my hands, which were coated in Cedric's cologne and made sure not to dip them in the water, so it wouldn't wash away. I smelled him as I soaked the rest of my body and fantasized, imagining a different ending to our night: one where I had asked him if he wanted to come upstairs. I knew I couldn't have done that, but I couldn't help wishing I were that kind of girl. Because if I were, he might be here with me right now and I wouldn't feel this tremendous loneliness.

I then burst out laughing at the crazy thought of Sonia coming home seeing me mounting Blue Eyes on the couch. As it was, she was going to have a heart attack when I told her about my more platonic ride.

CHAPTER 8

CEDRIC

I pulled into the parking space in back of my brownstone, but couldn't get out the car. I was paralyzed by thoughts of her, running our entire conversation from the ride over and over in my head. Shutting my eyes, I turned off the engine and listened only to the sounds of the city night. Church bells in the distance rang to signify the start of a new hour. It was one in the morning

When I opened my eyes, I reached over to pull out the cigarettes from the glove compartment, lit one and took a long drag. I couldn't give a fuck about the repercussions of smoking right now.

Even though the October weather in Boston was cold, I was sweating from the intense anxiety that had overcome me. I needed that cigarette.

She had no family. She was alone.

Even though she was a waitress, you'd think she'd come across as unattainable and materialistic, based on her stunning looks. That couldn't be further from the truth. She was a person with a passion for helping people and a humble upbringing much like my own. She was so easy to talk to and made my normally frigid soul feel warm inside.

I wanted more.

I didn't even know what that meant.

I only knew that every emotion I was capable of feeling, belonged to her when I looked into those mammoth eyes. Nothing else mattered in those forty minutes, no one else existed.

No other woman, not even the one I had considered my first love, had ever made me feel like that. It was an instant connection I had never experienced before with anyone at all. But realistically, I knew I couldn't ever have more with Allison. Because I could never be with someone like her and deceive her. I've *already* deceived her, though, haven't I, making her believe our meeting in the first place was coincidental?

She had already lost everything. And if she knew the whole story, she wouldn't want to be with me. But at the same time, I couldn't just walk away and never see her again. Even if that made the most sense, I felt that it would be physically impossible for me to stay away now that I've met her.

I needed more time, even if it meant just being her friend. *Friend.* There was nothing friendly about the raging hard-on I was trying to fight when I touched her skin.

I wanted her so badly it physically hurt.

I nearly lost it when I could feel her soft breath on my neck as I leaned over her to look for a pen. I wanted to feel her breath all over me.

And that was wrong on so many levels.

I did have a girlfriend after all. Oh, yeah…that minor detail. I remembered that I had lied to Karyn. Karyn didn't deserve a boyfriend that deceived her either. As superficial as Karyn could be at times, underneath it all, she was a decent person who told me she was in love with me even though I never returned the sentiment. I've lied to her so many times in the past month since I became obsessed with Allison.

Before this, I had vowed to at least try and be a better person, try to think about settling down, if not for myself, for Mom and Callie. I'm thirty-four for fuck's sake. I had spent most of the past decade drowning my sorrows in the wrong women. It had always been just sex with each and every one of them, many of them just one-night stands, with no emotional connection. I didn't want anything more than that. I just needed sex to wash away the pain and devastation I had endured so many years ago. Karyn was the first long-term relationship I have had in a very long time, but even with her, the emotional connection was never there.

I didn't think I even had the capacity to feel anything for a woman again beyond sexual attraction. But I knew what I felt for Allison in the car tonight was more than just sexual. Even though I had never wanted a woman as much sexually, the emotional connection was even stronger; I couldn't even find a word to describe it. It just felt right being with her. I instantly felt like I could trust her and mostly, I never wanted to leave her. I could have stayed there all night asking her question after question. It pained me to have to say goodbye so quickly. I was just getting to know her and had no idea how I would manage to get that kind of alone time again.

This I knew for sure: I needed to see her again and I wanted to help make her life better, even if mine had gone to shit. I wanted to make up for my past mistakes. God, this was all too much to handle. My life was so simple before I found Allison: shallow job, shallow girlfriend…shallow life…no risk of getting hurt again whatsoever.

But as of tonight, I had entered into a lose-lose situation and it's turned my world upside down.

If I vowed to never contact Allison again, my heart would break. I also knew that getting to know her and having to tell her the truth would absolutely shatter it. So, I am inevitably going to get hurt. I vowed I would never let myself hurt again.

Fuck.

I took one last drag of the cigarette before rolling down the window and tossing it out, deciding to get out of the car at last.

Once inside my condo, I collapsed onto the leather couch, holding my head in my hands. I looked at the clock and saw that it was now 1:30 am. Glancing down at the phone number and email written on my hand in beautiful feminine script, I got up immediately to transfer the information into my newly charged phone before the ink faded away.

I had an intense urge to email her right then and there but decided that would come across as strange. I also had no job information to give her, which was supposed to be the reason for emailing in the first place. *Dummy.* So, I nixed that idea and instead decided to text Karyn the lie that I received an email about the New York trip being postponed a week, suggesting that we have dinner tomorrow night, since I'd be in town.

I entered the bedroom, taking off my clothes that now reeked of smoke and walked into the master bathroom to turn on the faucet in my large walk-in shower.

I got in and willed the hot water to wash away these feelings of agony.

The one girl you can't have Cedric, is the only one you want.

Thanks to all the tension built up tonight, though, my thoughts quickly turned impure as I closed my eyes and imagined Allison naked here in front of me, wearing nothing but my handwriting on her breasts.

I grabbed the shampoo and roughly stroked myself to release the tension that had built up all day and concluded that I was screwed.

CHAPTER 9

ALLISON

Do you feel like a new person today, Gemini? Something has grown back, and unless you're a reptile with a new tail...that probably means that some part of your soul has woken up from a deep sleep.

When the alarm clock sounded at 5-am, I felt like even though I had barely slept, I was more alive than I had been in months.

It took me a while to get to sleep last night because I couldn't stop smelling my hands and thinking about him. I sniffed them until every last drop of Cedric evaporated.

The sight of the sun rising through my bedroom window was bittersweet.

It was Tuesday and I had to be at the diner for the breakfast crowd at 6:30. I hurried out of bed, ran to the bathroom to pee and as I sat on the toilet, I looked at the now fading writing on my hand, the only proof left that Cedric wasn't a dream.

I snuck a peek into Sonia's bedroom on the way to the kitchen and saw her mop of red curls hanging over her pillow, her shallow breathing evidence that she was sleeping soundly. She must have come in really late, sometime after I fell asleep.

The coffee machine I set to brew last night made its last bubbling sounds, telling me the java was almost ready. I grabbed my favorite mug (It said "Dy-no-mite" and had a picture of J.J. from the show Good Times on it.), plopped two teaspoons of sugar into it and poured in some cream and coffee. Taking my first sip, I jumped, startled by the sound of footsteps behind me and turned around.

"Oh no ya don't! You didn't think you were going to sneak out of here, without filling me in on last night did ya…you little hussie?" Sonia hoarsely yelled, groggily wiping her eyes and pouring herself a cup of coffee.

"Well, I didn't want to wake you!" I laughed

"So…what happened with Cedric?" Sonia was chomping at the bit, pulling out a chair to sit and taking a first sip of coffee. She cringed at how hot it was.

"Ohhhhh…Sonia." I sighed. I didn't even know where to begin shaking my head and closing my eyes.

"Oh my God. Shut up! You have that look. I know that look. Did you sleep with him?"

"Sonia!" I shouted. "Of course not!" I suspected my face was beet red.

"Ok. So…what happened?" Sonia laughed, leaning toward me in suspense.

I sat down at the table across from her and relayed the entire story from how he arrived at the diner just in the nick of time to the conversations on the ride home. I was running late, so I had to give her an abbreviated version without missing any of the important details like the subtle hand squeeze.

Sonia sighed. "I am gob smacked, Al. This guy sounds too good to be true. Did you ask him if he has a girlfriend?"

I shook my head. "No, the conversation never got personal in that way." *Of course, I wanted to know.* "He never went there, so I never asked him either."

I was so curious as to whether he was available. I felt such a connection with him. It was scary how quickly I developed feelings for a total stranger. It was so much more than his perfect looks. It was the look in his eyes when he talked about his sister. It was the way he seemed affected when I told him my mother had died. It was the way he looked at me when he let go of my hand, like he didn't want to. It was the way he looked at me like he could see through me into my soul. It would break my heart if there were never a chance of experiencing anything more than last night. I didn't know if I could survive without a taste of him.

"Allison. You have to let him know you're interested. Guys are stupid sometimes. And a guy who looks like that probably has a million women hitting on him. He's not going to bother with someone who seems complacent or who plays hard to get. It's 2013. It's ok for the woman to make the first move, like I did with Tom."

"I am sorry, Son…but I'm not making the first move here. He said he would email me that contact information. If I email him first, it's going to seem way too desperate," I said.

"Well, why don't you just email him just to thank him for the ride home?" Sonia suggested as she got up and put her coffee in the microwave.

I dumped mine in the sink because I was running late. "Sonia, I'll catch up with you tonight and we'll talk more. I've got to run. I'm going to be late." I rushed out of the kitchen and threw my uniform on foregoing a shower since I had taken a bath last night.

***

By the time I got to the diner, I realized I was ten minutes late. As I walked in, the breakfast regulars were already there and I was relieved to see that Delores had a good handle on things. She grinned when she saw me and called me over to ask how last night went. Apparently, Sonia had sent her a text that I was alone with Cedric after I called looking for the credit card.

I gave her an even shorter version of the story as she listened to me, her eyes popping out of their sockets with interest while I filled small containers with sugar packets.

Wedding Bell Blues by the Fifth Dimension was playing on the overhead and I couldn't help this giddy feeling I was experiencing. I felt alive. I took orders with enthusiasm, chatting up customers more than usual. I was giddy for a man who I wasn't even sure was single.

I couldn't shake this amazing feeling that came over me today. I felt that he wanted me last night. I could see it in the way his eyes seared into mine.

***

Right around 1:30, I checked my phone and saw that I had three new emails on my Yahoo account. My heart nearly jumped out of my chest when I saw the third one was from Cedric. I clicked on the email and it seemed to take forever to load (of course).

Allison Ophelia,

It was nice getting to talk to you last night. I spoke to my mother this morning and she gave me three contacts you could try at the agency that provides Callie's services. It's called Bright Horizons. The main office is ironically based in Malden, where you live, but they provide services to most of the Greater Boston area and nearby suburbs. Here are three names: Beth Stephens (Human Resources) 617-856-9899, Michelle Aguiar (Clinical Supervisor) 617-856-9881 and Shannon Bryant (Social Worker) 617-856-9890.

She said to try them in the order listed above. So, you'll have to let me know how it goes.

Good luck with everything. Maybe I'll see you around the diner again.

Best, Cedric

P.S. Sorry you had to work late because of the ass clown who left his credit card ;-)

Allison Ophelia. I laughed out loud at the last line too, covering my mouth in amazement. Wow. He operates fast. I read the email a few more times…okay…maybe ten and exited out of the screen, putting my phone back in my purse. I was even giddier than before. Even though I wanted to respond right away, I decided to wait until I got home because I couldn't stand to type on the touch screen of my iPhone.

***

That afternoon, I ran into the apartment, dropped my keys and purse and went straight to my laptop. I opened a blank email screen and began to type and erase over and over again. My lack of focus was made worse by the distraction of looking out the window and noticing that the leaves on the large tree outside had transformed into beautiful fall foliage.

Or was it just that everything in the world seemed brighter today?

I decided to get up and make a cup of jasmine green tea before returning to the laptop. After that first sip of steamy goodness, I finally just bit the dust and typed.

Cedric Othello,

You are so **not** an ass clown! Thank you so much for providing me with these contacts and please thank your mother too. I look forward to calling them in a few days. I can't believe Bright Horizons is based right here in Malden. I looked on their website and it's just a stone's throw from my apartment. I will definitely keep you posted. Please do stop into the diner again if you are up in that neck of woods. I'll save you a slice of coconut cream pie now that I know you like it. Even though I was working nights yesterday, my usual shifts are Monday through Friday 6:30am to 3:00pm. Also, thanks again for the ride home. I really enjoyed talking with you too. Take care. — Allison

I stared at what I wrote for about five minutes before hitting send. Once I sent the message, I sighed and abruptly closed the laptop and put it away. I was happy that I decided to let him know what shift I worked. I was worried that he would come back when I wasn't there thinking that my normal shift was at night because of yesterday. Not that he was necessarily planning to come back to see me, but I could hope, right?

***

One week later, I received a call from Bright Horizons after leaving one voicemail for each of the contacts Cedric gave me. It was almost 4:00 in the afternoon and I had just returned home from the diner and was resting on the couch watching *The Ellen DeGeneres Show* when the phone rang.

"Hello?" I answered.

"Yes, I am looking for Allison Abraham?"

"This is she," I said in my most professional voice, suspecting it might be job-related.

"This is Beth Stephens from Bright Horizons. How are you?" she said in a friendly voice.

"Great. I have been expecting your call." I hoped that didn't sound cocky.

"I got your voicemail and was wondering if you had some time to come into the office this afternoon. I remembered that you said you lived in town and I had a meeting just cancel, so I would have some time to meet with you," she said.

"That would be great. I could be there in twenty minutes." I was beaming.

"Excellent. Just give them your name at the front desk and I'll come out. Please bring a current resume and valid license. I'll see you then."

"Thank you, Beth. See you shortly."

I hung up the phone and immediately went to my bedroom to pick out something professional to wear. I wouldn't have time to shower. I picked out a pink satin sleeveless blouse with a bow on the front and a gray wool pencil skirt. I ripped off my diner uniform and threw on some nude colored pantyhose. I changed into the skirt and put on the blouse, sniffing my armpits. I added a short gray cashmere cardigan over the top. As I looked in the mirror above my bureau, I decided that my long hair made me look messy, so I twisted it into a bun and secured the sides with two bobbi pins. I dabbed on some concealer, very light eyeliner and some lip gloss. I was ready to roll. I grabbed my coat, left the apartment and walked the three blocks to the Bright Horizon's office.

***

The small brick building housed three offices, one of which was Bright Horizons. A middle-aged Hispanic woman sat at the front desk and I told her my name.

Beth Stephens, a tall middle-aged blond woman, came out shortly after and we shook hands then made our way to her office down the hall.

"So, tell me about your experience at Simmons, Allison."

"Well, I had completed almost a year in the special education graduate degree program there. I took classes like child development and psychology. My mother passed away a little over a year ago and I decided to take a leave of absence until I could save enough money to continue. I have been waitressing full-time but am looking for a way to get some experience working with kids with special needs."

"Ok, very good. I have to tell you though, while Bright Horizon's does offer services to kids and adults, the only openings we have right now are in our adult services program, which places employees with adults in their homes and also in group homes. You would be trained initially and after a background check, you would be assigned to an adult, mostly likely with autism, helping with things like job assistance and daily living. Would you be interested in working with an adult?"

I hadn't really expected that. Without thinking, I said, "Absolutely. I believe it would still be good experience and training for me. I think I would be up for the challenge."

Three weeks later, those words would bite me in the ass, quite literally.

***

I completed the intensive training, which included CPR and restraint classes over three weekends, shadowed two employees after work at the diner, passed the background check and was now a part-time therapist for a twenty-year-old non-verbal autistic man named Lucas. Well, technically, Lucas was a man, but he acted more like a boy.

I was assigned to go to his house in Cambridge three afternoons a week, leaving straight from the diner. He was chubby with shaggy blonde hair and was almost six feet tall, but had a baby face with rosy red cheeks.

The job requirements were to spend time reading books to him, helping him do chores like taking out the recycling and helping with his dinner and bath. I would then leave right before his bedtime.

Lucas was basically in his own world and loved comic books.

On the first day, Lucas ran from me and hid in his room. His mother, Pat, finally got him to come out by telling him I was Wonder Woman. He was obsessed with the character. So much so, that his mom suggested that I dress in costume, because this worked with a previous therapist in getting Lucas to respond. Apparently, he only bought the act when the worker had dark hair, so she told me I was lucky. I guess I was the closest match physically so far. Evidently, there had been many wonder women who came and went in his life. She happened to have a costume lying around.

So, here I was on my first day on the job, wearing the red and blue Wonder Woman costume, crown and all, bathing a grown man. At one point, I bent over to get a towel when he reached out of the tub and bit me playfully in the ass. (I told you it literally happened!) When I turned around, he was laughing and splashing me with water. I couldn't help but break out in hysterical laughter myself, splashing him back. When the ruckus died down, his mother reported that this particular evening was the calmest and most content she had ever seen him with a new worker.

Later, she told me that he slept through the night for the first time in weeks that day. Maybe I had finally found my calling: Lucas' hot piece of ass superhero.

CHAPTER 10

CEDRIC

It had been a few weeks since that night in the car with Allison. Business trips and deadlines at work had kept me busy and unable to visit her during the weekdays at the diner.

Not one hour of any day went by when I didn't think of her. The feel of her soft skin in my hand replayed in my head over and over as I held onto the memory of the only actual physical connection we had.

I considered emailing or calling her, but never got up the nerve to deal with the repercussions, at least until things calmed down.

Then, came the weekend when I realized that I couldn't hold out any longer.

***

We had spent Thanksgiving weekend with Karyn's parents in New York City. They had rented three rooms at the Ritz Carlton. Karyn and I stayed in one room, her parents in another and her sister in the third.

Friday afternoon started off innocently enough with breakfast at the hotel and then a long day of walking through Central Park and shopping on Fifth Avenue.

We somehow ended up right in front of Tiffany's. Karyn and her sister, Krystina, stopped in the window, which displayed a handful of diamond engagement rings. Right in front of me, Krystina started blatantly asking what kind of ring Karyn liked. I immediately stepped away from them and faced toward the street, but my ears were still in tune to them.

"Princess cut, two carats," I heard Karyn say, loud enough for me to hear.

I got the impression the conversation was some kind of set up by Karyn to let me know what type of ring she wanted when that time came.

Princess cut, two carats.

This was my first realization that Karyn and I were on two totally separate tracks, because I knew that time would never be coming…with Karyn.

Then it all really came to a head later that night. During dinner in the hotel dining room, the pianist played a rendition of Billy Joel's *Always A Woman*. It was beautiful but haunting and melancholy at the same time.

As I sat listening to this song in the candlelit room, I drowned my sorrows in scotch and realized how lonely I had been the entire weekend, just robotically going through the motions. A volcano of emotions seemed to fly out of me with every chord of the song, pouring out the things I had been harboring for the past month.

I missed the sight of Allison so much.

I didn't deserve her.

I could never have her.

I hated myself.

I didn't love Karyn.

Why was I here?

Princess cut, two carats…Princess cut, two carats…

I was losing my mind. Karyn was oblivious, chatting with her sister about our plans to visit the Guggenheim the next day.

I stayed in my own little world until Karyn abruptly suggested we go back to our room for an early nightcap. I was half-drunk and numbly followed her out of the restaurant, neglecting to say goodbye to her family.

In the elevator, I remembered her nibbling on my ear, undoing my tie and grabbing my crotch as I stared numbly at the numbers at the top of the elevator door.

When we got to the room, she immediately went to the bathroom and put on a green and black lace and satin lingerie set she had bought with her sister at Barneys earlier that day.

When she came out, she pushed me down on the bed and started to unzip my pants. She grabbed a condom from the nightstand and started to pull down my boxer briefs when I began having what felt like a panic attack.

My vision blurred, my heart pounded and my breathing became rapid. We hadn't had sex in weeks, so you would think I would have wanted it badly. Instead, I felt nothing except guilt, as if I was being unfaithful because my heart was somewhere else entirely.

My heart was with a woman who didn't even know she had it.

I started panting, pushed Karyn off of me and got up off the bed, zipping up my pants.

Sitting on the bed with my head in my hands, I became ashamed of what I was about to do.

"Cedric? What the fuck is going on?" Karyn stared at me with daggers in her eyes, which were starting to well up with tears.

"Karyn...I...I...don't know." I really didn't even know how to explain what I was feeling: why all of a sudden, being with her no longer made sense.

I certainly couldn't tell her the truth: that I thought I might love someone else, someone I had only spent barely an hour with and by the way, she has no clue that I have been stalking her for weeks while I lied through my teeth to both of you.

Karyn's mascara ran down her cheeks as she cried out. "Well, you better fucking figure it out! You have been so distant this past month, Cedric. I have tried everything to get you to come out of this funk, but apparently you don't want to be brought out of it. I seriously hate you right now."

Not more than I fucking hate myself.

"Karyn, I don't blame you. I am so sorry. I think I need to go back to Boston tonight. I need some time. I didn't mean to hurt you. I just...can't do this anymore. I'm so...so sorry."

I truly meant it. I never wanted to hurt her, never meant for things to turn out this way with her.

"Fuck you," Karyn spewed as she went toward the bathroom and slammed the door. I could hear her crying and gasping for air. Then, she turned on the water, possibly to hide the sound.

I felt horrible but grabbed my suitcase anyway, packed it as fast as I could and left.

***

I was determined to see Allison come hell or high water the Monday after I abandoned Karyn, along with our relationship, in New York City.

The weekend seemed to drag on. I sat unshaven in my condo, my ass glued to the leather couch as I smoked and listened to old discs. At one point, I freakishly came across the song *Allison* by Elvis Costello, which nearly put me over the edge.

With that, I had an intense urge to see her and almost drove to her apartment in Malden without a plan. I thought I could make up a story about why I was there, but nixed the idea because I didn't think I was of sound mind to see her and couldn't come up with any excuse that made a lick of sense.

I was still exhausted since I had driven late Friday night back to Boston from the Ritz after I sobered up and rented a car. Karyn and I had originally planned to fly back together on Sunday.

By now, I hadn't gotten any sleep, looked like ass and I reeked.

***

On Sunday, I decided I couldn't keep my thoughts to myself any longer; I needed to talk to someone. The only person I could trust with this was my older brother Caleb.

Caleb and I were two years apart, and he was the only one in my family that actually knew what happened in Chicago.

I could never bear to tell my parents anything. They were going through so much with my sister Callie at the time, and then as the years went by, I continued to keep the past in the past and away from my family…except Caleb.

To this day, my mother knows very little about my time in Chicago, including the sordid intern years after graduation. But Caleb had come to visit me shortly after everything went down senior year and was a huge help in getting me back on track to finish school. He kept in touch by phone every single day after he left. I couldn't have graduated from Northwestern without my brother.

Caleb lived about ninety minutes away in New Hampshire with his wife Denise. They owned a large new colonial style home that sat on three acres of rural land. I liked to go to Caleb's whenever I needed to clear my head. They had no kids, so it was a peaceful place away from the noise of the city.

Denise had been trying to get pregnant for a few years with no success. They had planned on kids, which is why the house they built was so big. The echo in their home was like the elephant in the room. I hoped it would happen for them one way or another because they were both such good people and would make great parents.

After the hour and a half drive to my brother's door, I pulled up to the circular driveway of their house, which was located on a quiet cul de sac.

Denise greeted me at the door with a warm hug and I could smell the pumpkin and turkey—aromas of Thanksgiving leftovers heating in the oven. It was nice to have a home-cooked meal after the cold Thanksgiving I suffered through in Manhattan.

"Hey, little brother! You look…tired. Come on in, sweetie." Denise hugged me. I liked that she thought of me as a brother. She was a great girl and had been Caleb's college sweetheart at UNH. Denise was petite with medium length dirty blonde hair and the kindest eyes you have ever seen.

"Saying I look tired…is that another way of saying I look like shit? It smells wicked good in here," I said, tending to resort to Boston-speak when in the presence of my family.

Caleb ran down the stairs and we gave each other the usual quick manly hug. It was good to see him. It had been a couple of months.

Caleb was two years older than me, about fifteen pounds heavier, three inches taller and worked as a contractor. We shared the same brown hair and blue eyes, but while I typically wore dress shirts and designer shoes, Caleb was often seen in a brown Carhartt Jacket and boots. Today, I was unshaven and dressed more like Caleb, wearing jeans and a hooded black sweatshirt.

"Hey, man, let's go into the garage and talk while Denise finishes up dinner," Caleb said as he opened the fridge and grabbed two bottles of LandShark beer, leading the way to the heated three-car garage off the kitchen.

"First of all, you look like absolute shit," Caleb said once we got into the man cave.

Giving him the finger, I said, "Yes. Denise already made that clear. Thanks, shithead."

Caleb took a swig of his beer and after letting out a huge belch, turned serious. "Ok, you sounded upset on the phone when you said you needed to talk. I know it's important, because you never say you need to talk."

Caleb took another sip and sat down on one of the swivel chairs next to his tool bench.

The room was quiet as I looked at my brother, leaning against Caleb's pickup truck and sighed. "Yeah, man. Something major's happened. I think you know what I'm gonna say."

He nodded slowly. "You found her. You talked to her?" Caleb whispered.

Denise didn't know anything about what happened in Chicago either because I swore Caleb to secrecy. If my mother ever found out I kept something like that from her she might never forgive me.

"Yeah," I said, not knowing where to begin.

"What's she like?" he asked.

I paused, not knowing how to sum up all the feelings Allison conjured up.

"She's amazing, man. But the problem is…my brain sort of misfired when I actually laid eyes on her that first time. I forgot all the reasons I was looking for her in the first place and now…I can't stop thinking about how much I want her…for myself. It's all kinds of wrong. I have been fucked up ever since that first day."

I then filled him in on all of the details from the first diner meeting to the car ride to my freak out with Karyn.

Caleb burped and pointed his beer in my direction to make a statement. "First of all, Cedric…I'm glad you finally broke it off with that cold bitch. That's all I am gonna say about that. No one in this family liked her and if it took this situation to do it, then so be it. Second, I will say that given what happened twelve years ago, I think the feelings you have for this Allison are completely normal. You can't help how you feel. I don't know why you are beating yourself up about it. Any man in your shoes would feel the same way."

"You know why I can't go after her. It's one thing to have urges and another to act on them, knowing that it could never work out," I said, staring into my brother's eyes, which were identical to my own.

Caleb's tone softened. "You know I have never looked at what happened in Chicago exactly the way you do. We've gone through this before. You're being too hard on yourself. What you need to do is go down to this diner again, grow a nut sack and ask her out, plain and simple for the sheer fact that you are not going to be able to function until you get this out of your system. Find out if she's even available, for Christ's sake! Then, you need to really get to know her and if you continue to feel this way and things develop, you need to tell her the goddamn truth. Let her decide what she wants instead of assuming you know how she is going to react. If she sees the guy that I see, knows the guy I know…she'd be nuts to leave."

Leave it to Caleb to turn crazy into something that kind of made sense.

I took a deep breath and nodded trying to ingrain my brother's comforting expression into my memory. I would need it tomorrow.

Denise came down the stairs and interrupted our conversation to let us know dinner was ready.

We moved upstairs into the kitchen and enjoyed the feast that my sister-in-law had spread out for us, sitting casually on stools that surrounded a granite island. I watched the way Caleb caressed Denise's back and stared at her throughout dinner, like she was the most beautiful woman he had ever seen.

For the first time in my life, I think I was starting to want what they had.

I wanted to share my life with someone.

After dinner, I hugged my brother and sister-in-law goodbye, leaving the warm candle-lit house for the cold November air and drove back to Boston feeling more confident about tomorrow.

***

When I walked into the diner, I saw her immediately.

She didn't notice me right away. I stood at the door and my heart nearly skipped a beat because I had forgotten how pretty she was.

Allison was sitting in the corner with a freakishly tall older man, laughing at his jokes. She seemed to be on her break.

I stayed by the door until she looked in my direction and waved over at her with a half-smile when she noticed me.

Upon seeing me, the happy look on her face abruptly turned surprised and then serious…almost pained.

Fuck. That wasn't what I was hoping for.

"Allison," I said, walking slowly over to the table from which she was just getting up.

"Cedric…what a surprise."

Allison looked nervous, not at all the comforting presence I remembered from our car ride.

"I wanted to stop in and say hello. It's been a while…find out how the Bright Horizons thing went."

She still looked serious, nothing like the sweet, happy, Allison I left in the car that night.

"Oh, it's going great. They paired me with a twenty-year-old in Cambridge. He's a good kid. Thanks again for helping me with that."

Allison stood awkwardly, leaning her arm on the counter, almost as if it were helping her balance, then she looked up at the ceiling, down at her nails…anywhere but at me. Her hand started to tremble.

What happened to her?

"Great to hear it," I said.

I stood frozen, perplexed at the standoffish vibe I was getting. For the first time, I realized that maybe my advances were unwelcome. Maybe I had misread her all along.

"Can I get you anything?" she asked as if I were just any other customer.

The fact that she looked more beautiful than ever was like a dagger in my heart right now. Her long, dark hair was half up, half down and there was a tiny white flower in the corner of her ear. She smelled like green apples again and I wished I could taste her and see if she also tasted like green apples.

Get a grip.

"Yes. I would love a piece of that coconut cream pie," I said, wondering how I was going to stomach the pie feeling like I was about to throw up.

"Sure. I'll be right back. Sit wherever you like."

Allison suddenly went into the kitchen and came out with a piece of pie, placing it on the table of the booth that I sat myself in. The goddamn pie didn't even have whipped cream or a cherry on top. I took this as a cryptic "fuck off."

"Thanks, Allison," I said as I desperately searched her eyes for any sign of hope or recognition of our past connection. Instead, they looked pained but distant, and I realized there was so much I didn't know about her. So much I still wanted to know even in this troubling state.

"You're welcome, Cedric." It blew me away that she said nothing else, turned around and walked into the kitchen.

We've Only Just Begun by the Carpenters was playing over the speaker and depressing the crap out of me, making an already shitty situation so much worse.

I took a couple of bites of pie and stared at the kitchen door. Fifteen minutes passed before Allison came back out, proceeding to clean off tables at the other end of the diner.

I was shattered. Speechless. She was either ignoring me intentionally or genuinely had no interest at all. Feeling like a complete asshole, I took a ten-dollar-bill out of my wallet and placed it on the table.

I walked over to where she was standing. She was calculating something on a pad of paper.

I swallowed my pride and offered one last attempt to talk to her. "Allison, I better get going. Thanks for the pie. I left money on the table. I hope things continue to go well with the new job. I'd still like to hear more about it sometime?"

And then it came…

"Bye, Cedric." She might as well have taken her pen out her pocket and stabbed me in the fucking heart.

CHAPTER 11

ALLISON

Ouch, Gemini, this is not one of your better days. It's best to steer clear of negative energy. The Moon is not happy with Mercury, your ruler. So, just for today, avoid confrontation.

When I heard the chimes sound, signaling his exit, I turned around to look at the door that had slammed behind Cedric. I couldn't take my eyes off of it for about five minutes.

The pounding of my heart and the swaying of the room finally seemed to slow down with each passing minute.

When I knew he was gone, I let the tear being held captive in my left eye fall freely and finally walked over to the table where his piece of pie still sat in the dish, only one bite taken out of it. I realized I was so flustered, I forgot to add the whipped cream and cherry before serving it. The pie looked as pathetic as I felt and I picked it up along with the ten-dollar bill.

As I put the money in the register, I felt another teardrop stream down my cheek. *Get it together, Allison.*

I didn't expect seeing him to be so hard. If this had been a week ago, his coming to the diner would have been the highlight of my life. He had clearly come in to see me today. The fact that he barely touched the pie proved that...but why? Why did he come here? Did he feel sorry for me?

After I found out that all of my romantic delusions about him were false, I had to conclude that he must have just seen me as a charity case. Didn't the tip the first time around confirm that? Even though I had resigned myself to this fact, it still hurt more than I thought it would to see him again, knowing that I couldn't have him.

If it was possible, he looked better than ever. His hair looked a bit longer on the sides, curling around his ears and it was parted slightly differently framing his beautiful face.

And I had never seen him dressed down before. He wore dark blue jeans and a hooded maroon sweatshirt that hugged his muscular frame. He looked younger and so goddamn sexy when he stood before me with his hands in his pockets, seeming almost… nervous.

But why?

When he first came in and started to approach me, I froze, feeling faint and had to hold on to the side of the counter just to grab my bearings. I could barely get the words out when he asked me a question, staring into me again with those penetrating crystal blue eyes. The heat of him standing so close to me, that damn intoxicating scent of his again and knowing now that he was off limits, was too painful to take.

And to think if I hadn't opened the paper that day, I would still be wasting my time thinking that he could want someone like me.

***

It was the Tuesday before Thanksgiving. My friend Danny and I planned to meet at Starbucks in Copley Square for coffee after my diner shift, since I didn't work with Lucas on that day. It was so nice to catch up with Danny who wanted to fill me in on his new boyfriend, Paolo.

"Danny!" I shouted and I saw him waiting in line, rushing to join him amongst the crowd of people waiting for their drinks to be called out.

He knew me so well. "I already ordered you your caramel macchiato," he shouted through the sounds of foaming milk as he stood in the barista receiving area.

We took our drinks over to the velvet purple couch in the corner. We were lucky to get that coveted seat. Everyone knows the Starbucks couch is always inevitably taken by one person unnecessarily taking up all of the space with multiple newspapers, when two people are forced to take the small table with the hard uncomfortable seats.

"So, tell me about Paolo!" I crossed my legs and took a sip of the foamy drink as I anticipated his story. It tasted so good.

"He is awesome. Did I tell you he is a performer?" Danny was beaming.

"No…what kind of performer?" I laughed and slapped Danny playfully on the shoulder.

Danny gave me an impish grin. "Well, let's just say, by day he goes by Paolo…by night he is Paula."

"He is a cross-dresser?"

"No, no, no…a drag queen. Big difference. He chooses to dress as a man in real-life, but performs as a woman…for other men. Believe me, he is all man," Danny said winking.

I laughed. "Oh boy, I bet. That is too cool, though. Can we go see him…um…*her* on stage?

"Sure. We can take your billionaire blue-eyed boyfriend. You can finally test his sexuality once and for all," he said jokingly.

"Very funny." I pushed Danny's shoulder in jest again.

I had filled him in on my Cedric crush last week over the phone, getting his thoughts on whether I should send Cedric another email under the vise of updating him on the new job.

After fifteen minutes of gushing on the couch about our respective men, Danny had to run to get back his hairdressing job.

I decided to go back to the counter for one of those gigantic rice krispy treats.

When I turned around, of course, someone had taken the couch, so I made myself comfortable on one of the hard seats by the door. At least someone left me a free newspaper here.

I immediately admired a striking cover photo of a turkey taken by my friend Angela, who was a photographer for the paper. The story was about a family that purchased a live Thanksgiving turkey originally intending to kill it and cook it on Thursday. Instead, their five-year-old daughter convinced her parents to save its life and keep it as a pet. The photo showed the turkey sitting at the dinner table with the family as the father stood under the table sticking his head through a hole, creating the illusion that his head was on a plate. I couldn't help but laugh out loud at the caption: *"Eat Me."*

As I munched on my rice krispy treat, I immediately skipped to my favorite section of the paper, which was the local celebrity gossip column. Well...it *was* my favorite section. Not anymore. I wasn't prepared for the shock of my life that I would encounter on its pages that day.

My heart pounded faster than I had ever experienced as I saw Cedric's electric eyes staring back at me from the page.

A piece of my rice krispy treat fell out of my mouth and onto his face and I wiped it away.

He was dressed in a tux. On his arm, was an exquisite blonde with an up do, who seemed to be smirking. Cedric's smile of course was beautiful and genuine. He looked happy. I immediately started to regurgitate the rice krispies I had eaten. And I am embarrassed to say...I peed a little...just a drop. I lost control down there.

The caption under the picture read:

"Boston television reporter Karyn Keller attended the Boston Symphony Orchestra's ALS Fundraiser at the Boston Omni Parker Hotel Monday night on the arm of her long-time boyfriend and former most-eligible Boston bachelor candidate, hot shot J.D. Westock agent, Cedric Callahan."

I must have read that caption fifty times in the hopes that maybe I read it wrong.

Long-time boyfriend
Boston bachelor
Karyn Keller
Karyn Keller
Karyn Keller

I HATED Karyn Keller. I hated Karyn Keller so much in that moment.

But not more than I hated Cedric. I hated him for making me feel that he wanted me with just the stare of his eyes that night in the car. All along, he had a girlfriend…a gorgeous, famous one, at that. How could I have been so stupid to think that someone like him would want to date…me…a lowly waitress charity case?

I stayed frozen in my seat. I took the paper, folded it and placed it in my tote. I closed my eyes and took a deep breath.

The door at Starbucks continued to open and close before me as I sat in a haze for an undetermined amount of time. I felt the cold wind blow in every thirty seconds and wished that I were any one of the people walking in. I wanted to be anyone but myself right now.

I felt so much heartache for a man who never once considered me romantically. Even if he had, for even a moment, the reality was that he was in a serious and public relationship. No wonder he never actually asked me out that day in the car.

Stupid Allison…don't you think he would have asked you out then and there if he were really interested?

It all made sense now. The email…that's all it was…a damn message with a job lead. I had blown everything out of proportion. Cedric as I knew him was all in my head. The real Cedric Callahan wouldn't give me the time of day. He took me for a ride all right. Fuck my life.

***

You need to be part of something larger than yourself, Gemini — so if you need to find a spiritual community or a service organization, now is the time. You should expect to get some inspiration soon.

The days that followed after Cedric's diner visit were a blur. I threw myself into my work and asked Bright Horizons if they could give me some more hours on the two afternoons I didn't work with Lucas. I was on Wonder Woman duty Monday, Wednesday and Friday. I didn't need to go home after the diner in the afternoon and sulk on the other days of the week. I needed to get my mind off the breakup of my imaginary boyfriend.

I was eventually told there was an opening working with an autistic woman named Calista two days a week on Tuesdays and Thursdays. This would fill my entire workweek and still leave the weekends free.

On the first Tuesday of December, snowflakes were flying and it was blistery as I headed out to my new assignment.

I knocked on the door of a small ranch style brick house in Boston's Savin Hill neighborhood and the warmth of the heat inside immediately sucked me in. I was greeted by a friendly woman with graying, black hair that was tied back into a bun. She looked to be in her mid to late sixties and was quite beautiful. This must have been her mother.

"Hello…you must be Allison?" She smiled.

"Yes, hi…it's great to meet you," I said nervously, not knowing what to expect from my new client. Wonder Woman boy, I had down pat, but I had no idea what was in store for me here.

"My daughter is in her room playing on her iPad. I'm afraid that's all she likes to do with her free time. But it keeps her occupied and out of trouble. Let's have you meet her and then we'll talk about the routine here." She smiled. She seemed like a sweet lady.

I followed the woman down a hallway and smelled the delicious aroma of cinnamon, reminding me that I never had lunch. The house was warmer and more comforting than any I had ever been in.

The woman opened the door to her daughter's bedroom.

Through the door I saw a beautiful young woman in her twenties with long brown hair tied into a side braid. She wore blue jeans, pink sneakers and a pink Hello Kitty hoodie. She sat on the bed looking down, transfixed by a musical video she was watching on You Tube. She hummed and rocked a bit, curling her fingers in excitement and did not seem to notice that we entered the room. I then got close enough to hear the song: *The Wheels on the Bus.*

I could see that there was an animation to go along with the song, various cartoon characters and a big yellow bus. She waved a long green Starbucks straw over the screen and looked like she was conducting an orchestra. She laughed when the video ended and pressed play again immediately. It was amazing to think that this was a woman in her twenties, because she seemed so childlike.

In an attempt to get the girl's attention, her mother reached out and grabbed the iPad from her daughter, who was still laughing to herself. When she finally looked up, the most beautiful blue eyes stared back at me...through me.

I knew those eyes.

"Callie, this is Allison...can you say hi?"

I froze. Calista...Callie: Cedric's sister.

***

Bettina Callahan closed the door to Callie's room, allowing her daughter to remain in her own world for a bit while she led me to the kitchen.

Oh my God!

I sat down and could feel my heart pounding rapidly, still reeling from the realization that I was in Cedric's family home. It pained me so much to think about him and now I wouldn't be able to escape it.

I felt almost as if I were an imposter, even though I had every right to be here. This was my job now and I wasn't going to let Cedric or Karyn Keller or anyone screw it up. It wasn't Callie's fault I had a delusional crush on her brother.

"Allison...can I make you some tea while we go over Callie's routine? I already have some water boiled."

Again, this place was like heaven.

I did not get the impression that Bettina had any clue that I was the same person her son inquired about for the job information and figured Cedric never used my name.

"Yes, I'd love some," I smiled. Tea sounded good and maybe it would calm my nerves. For some reason, I was not as freaked out as I might have figured I'd be in this situation. Cedric's mother actually seemed like a really nice lady with a very reassuring tone.

As she prepared the tea, I looked around curiously. The kitchen, as did the rest of the house, seemed to have a cozy, country feel, lots of reds and greens with floral curtains and plaid seat pillows. It was homey but small, so I assumed it was just Callie and her mother who lived here.

"May I use your bathroom?" I decided I really had to go and figured since she was preparing the tea, this would be my window.

"Sure, dear, it's back down the hall, last door on the left. Before you go, would you like black or green tea?"

"Green will be perfect. Thanks so much," I said as I got up and walked down the hallway.

Before I opened the bathroom door, I noticed some family pictures on the living room wall diagonally across from the bathroom. I scurried over to the framed picture collage hoping she wouldn't notice since I heard her clanking things back in the kitchen.

There he was.

If this wasn't confirmation that I was in Cedric's mother's house, I didn't know what was.

The picture I focused in on appeared to be a photo of a younger Cedric on what looked like his high school graduation day. The same beautiful eyes were framed by even longer, shaggier hair. Cedric was flanked by his mother, father and whom I assumed was his brother. He had the biggest most beautiful smile and looked so happy. I immediately felt sad, remembering that during our car ride he mentioned that his father had passed away a few years earlier. Cedric was tall like his father and had his blue eyes. But his facial features and smile resembled his mother overall.

I didn't want to take too much time staring at the picture, in case Bettina wondered what the hell I was so interested in her family for, so I entered the bathroom.

I splashed a small amount of water on my face to help calm me down from the surprise of this situation and quickly peed. I washed my hands and walked back out and down the hall.

Bettina had placed my tea in front of my seat in a beautiful ornate yellow ceramic mug and had her legs crossed sitting in the chair relaxed across from me and began to speak.

"Ok, Allison, so basically you met my daughter. You can see that she likes to be in her own world most of the time. What I hope when someone comes to work with Callie, is that they help to structure her time to make the most of it. I don't want her just sitting there rocking back and forth, looking at online videos, like she does when she is alone. It's really hard to break her out of her shell. I want you to try and play with her... try to get her to speak...I know it's not easy getting her attention...the autism assures that. But you can read to her or try to get her to sound out the words, things like that. A group of her favorite books are in a large basket in her room. She can read many sight words but she just can't always comprehend complex themes. So, she may not answer you if you ask what generally happened in the book, but might answer a simple question like 'what are the characters doing in the picture?'

I nodded silently, as she continued.

"I'll also have you sit with her and make sure she eats appropriately and puts away and washes her dishes. She also does some light chores likes recycling and swiffering the floors. She works at the library sorting books, accompanied by her other staffer on Mondays and Wednesdays, but you don't need to worry about that since you are here Tuesdays and Thursdays. What questions do you have at this point?" Bettina looked at my quizzically.

I had so many questions.

"How much detail can she relay about what she wants?" I asked.

"A bit. Simple requests are her strength in terms of communication. She can say 'I want' and then list the item or even describe it somewhat. For example, 'I want red sweater cat' might mean I want the red sweater that has the black cat on it. Eye contact is a problem though. She doesn't like to look at people."

Bettina sipped her tea and then reached out for my hand, which startled me and continued. "You'll get used to her, get a feel for what she likes. I can tell you will be great with her."

Smiling, I said, "Thanks for the vote of confidence. What should I do with her for starters today?"

"Why don't you just sit in her room with her for a while. Let her get used to your being there. Then, in about an hour, I can show you what her dinner routine is like."

"Sounds good."

I followed Bettina into Callie's room and she quickly backed out and shut the door. I think she was intentionally separating herself so that I didn't feel pressure from her watching me. I appreciated it because I was extremely intimidated by this situation, which left me feeling clueless.

I sat on the bed next to Callie, on a pretty Pottery Barn floral quilt. She continued to look at You Tube, but this time she was focused on a video that played television station identification music backwards. It looked to be vintage music from the cable station Nickelodeon. She would keep rewinding it to the same point in the middle playing the same three-second chime over and over again. I was fascinated that she actually found this entertaining and that she never once acknowledged that I was sitting next to her. She could have cared less that I was there, if she even realized it.

I decided to just sit next to her for a while and not say anything. Maybe she would eventually look at me or ask me for something. I looked around her room at the various pictures hanging on the wall, some butterflies, some drawings of stick people in crayon, some marker scribbled right on the wall.

There was one cluster of photos that particularly stunned me.

There on a bulletin board above her headboard was a collage of the CNN anchor Anderson Cooper. Yes, the Silver Fox. Apparently, Callie had the hots for him or something. It was such a strange contrast to the Dora the Explorer dolls and grade school board books that lay strewn on the floor. There were pictures of Anderson Cooper posing with other celebrities, headshots of him and an autographed picture.

I then decided to try something. I suddenly grabbed the iPad from Callie. She finally looked at me…like I was pointing a gun at her.

I quickly typed into the You Tube search bar: *Anderson Cooper.* Hundreds of search results displayed on the screen and I selected one that said *Anderson Cooper Cracks Up During Newscast.*

I pressed play.

Callie spotted Anderson right away and yanked the iPad from my hands.

Upon the first sight of Anderson losing control and laughing hysterically in the clip, Callie started jumping up and down on the bed frantically, with a look of utter excitement. She began to smile and then…a volcanic eruption of laughter came out of her.

I stopped the video, barely containing my own laughter at her response. And she *looked at me.*

"Callie, what do you want?" I asked holding the device.

"Anderson," she said looking at the iPad.

"Ask better," I said.

"I want Anderson," she replied, her eyes still glued to the screen.

"Good!" I said and played the video again.

Each time the video played, Callie's reaction was bigger than the last. And each time, I asked more of her before playing it again.

"Callie, what do you want?" I asked.

"I want Anderson," she said.

I pointed to the still of the video. "Callie, this is Anderson Cooper. What do you want?" I asked.

"I want Anderson Cooper," she said.

I played the video again and paused it mid-way. Callie, frantically curled her fingers and rocked back and forth, obviously wanting the video to continue. I had paused the image on Anderson's smiling face.

"Callie, what is Anderson doing?" I asked.

"Smiling," she said.

"Who is smiling?" I asked.

"Anderson Cooper is smiling," she said with a grin.

"Good girl." I resumed the video.

When the video stopped, Callie looked at the screen and said, "I want Anderson Cooper smiling."

I held the iPad and wouldn't budge.

"I want Anderson Cooper smiling!" Callie laughed staring away from me.

I held back and did nothing.

Then, what I had hoped for happened. *She looked at me.*

I immediately played the video to reward her for the eye contact to send her a message that looking at me would be a requirement for getting what she wanted. When the video stopped, she *looked at me again* immediately and said: "I want Anderson Cooper smiling."

I played the video and stopped it mid-way, turning to her.

"Callie, my name is Allison. Ask me for the video."

"Allison, I want Anderson Cooper smiling," she said looking at the iPad.

I waited.

Waited some more.

She looked at me.

"Allison, I want Anderson Cooper smiling," she said *with eye contact.*

I played the video. When the video ended this time, she looked at me without my having to say anything.

"Hi Callie," I said.

"Hi Allison." She smiled.

"It's nice to finally meet you, Callie."

***

Almost three weeks into my new position working with Callie, she had become more and more aware of my presence. When I would enter the house, she would look at me unprompted and say, "Hi Allison."

We developed a good routine each shift. At the start of each afternoon, we would play some of her favorite videos, but she would need to request everything with eye contact and answer any questions I asked her before I let her continue watching. Then, we'd move into the rest of the house and I would assist her with various chores, like sweeping the floor, folding laundry and taking out the recyclables.

After the chores, we would go back to her room and work on some reading and trying to get her to read aloud. Last, we would head to the dinner table and I would sit with Callie while she ate and made sure she fed herself properly and cleaned up.

Bettina insisted that I join them for dinner on the nights I worked, so I, too, would get fed, which worked out great, since by the time I got back to my apartment it was quite late. Bettina was a great cook and every night was a different Italian dish: things like lasagna, gnocchi or eggplant Parmesan. Thank goodness it was only two nights a week or I would need a new wardrobe.

Some nights if dinner were early enough, I would help Callie bathe and dry her hair before bed. I would marvel at the fact that someone with the mind of a child had the body of grown woman, voluptuous in all the right places. It saddened me, because I also realized that this would be a curse for a girl who could so easily be taken advantage of. No wonder Bettina only allowed women to work with Callie and never considered putting her in a group home, since many were male dominated.

Bettina told me that when I wasn't there, Callie would ask for me. That made me so happy to hear. I could tell she liked being with me, too, because I was getting more and more eye contact, smiles and sometimes she would hold my hand when we sat together. It warmed my heart.

***

Get your dancing shoes ready, dearest Gemini, because celebration is in the stars. You will be jubilant in the very near future and you are going to party. A good time will be had by all.

One Thursday evening, just a few days before Christmas, Bettina asked if I would be willing to stay a bit later since she was having some friends over for a pre-holiday dinner party. She wanted Callie to be occupied and someone to keep an eye on her. She offered to pay me extra, but I insisted that she pay me in the form of the delicious holiday treats she had spent most of the day baking and that I would surely nosh on at the dinner party.

I helped Callie get into her plaid party dress and then we set the table together. Having advanced warning about the dinner party, I decided to wear a red sweater dress today.

Together, we placed a red and green table cloth over the oval table in the small dining room and followed that with my showing Callie the order of the place settings.

I felt nervous about not knowing exactly who was coming over. The guests were expected to arrive at 7:30. Of course, it dawned on me that it could be Cedric walking in that door, but he hadn't shown yet and I really didn't feel comfortable asking Bettina who she was expecting, although she did mention that it would be "some friends." Or maybe I didn't really want to know if he was coming. I would find out soon enough.

I realized that Cedric probably didn't know I was working here, since his mother never mentioned anything to me about her son acknowledging that he knew me. She never asked me if I was the same person her son had inquired about the job information for, so I knew she had no clue I had ever met Cedric.

I was doing a good job letting go of the whole Cedric fiasco, aside from the fact that being in his mother's house twice a week assured that I couldn't exactly forget about him altogether.

Not to mention the fact that Callie looked so much like her brother.

I decided that I needed to be strong and prepared for whatever walked through that door, even if it were Cedric and his girlfriend. Oh God, I really hoped that didn't happen.

But Bettina needed me here for Callie and that was all that should matter.

At 7:25, the doorbell rang as Callie and I sat in the living room reading.

My eyes nervously followed Bettina as she opened the door and let in a couple who appeared to be in their sixties, hugging and kissing them.

"Allison, this is my dear friend, Maria and her husband Kurt," Bettina said.

I got up from the couch and shook their hands.

"Allison is Callie's new therapist. She is going to join us for dinner tonight." Bettina smiled.

"It's great to meet you," I said, holding out my hand to greet them and then quickly returned to my seat next to Callie on the couch.

White Christmas played softly from a cd player.

Bettina brought her friends into the dining room, as I continued to wonder who would be arriving next. There were two additional place settings. My heart started to pound as I thought about the fact that it could very well be Cedric and Karyn. That would be so incredibly awkward.

The doorbell rang. My heart pounded faster.

Bettina clicked her heels as she rushed from the dining room to the front door, which was off of the living room.

"So glad you could make it!" Bettina shouted.

I couldn't see who was coming in because they were lingering and it sounded like they were wiping snow off their boots.

Relief consumed me as I saw an older man who also looked to be in his late sixties or early seventies walk in the door.

"Allison, this is my friend Bruno. Bruno, meet Allison, Callie's newest therapist."

Bruno walked toward me and startled me when he grabbed my face. "Hello, sweet Allison. My goodness if I were fifty years younger." He winked.

"That is very sweet. Great to meet you," I said and sat back down.

Bettina grabbed the bottle of wine that Bruno carried in and they both disappeared into the dining room.

"Allison, why don't you join us with Callie in here?" Bettina shouted from the other room.

This Christmas now played on the stereo as Callie and I entered the dining room.

Callie went straight for the chips. When I spotted her licking the salt off them and sticking them back in the bowl, I immediately stopped her.

"Allison, can I get you some wine?" Bettina asked as she opened a bottle of red.

"Oh, no, thanks. I'm on the job." I'll help myself to some soda later, Bettina."

The guests picked at the appetizers that sat on a buffet table at the corner of the room. I counted the place settings again and thought to myself: *Bettina, Callie, Me, Bruno, Maria, Kurt…and one more.*

I would likely not be able to relax until the last person arrived, so that I could be sure it wasn't Cedric.

A half hour passed, as I sat with Callie while she ate a plate of appetizers that I gathered for her to deter her from attacking the chips.

Bettina began setting some food that had come out of the kitchen on the table: a roast surrounded by potatoes and carrots, French style green beans, salad, a rice casserole and a chicken fettuccini Alfredo dish.

Then, I jumped as the doorbell rang.

My heart started pounding furiously again.

"Allison, would you mind answering the door for me? I think that's my son," Bettina shouted from the kitchen.

Oh God.

Oh God.

Oh God.

Without having time to think or prepare, I got up from the chair, took a deep breath and slowly walked to the door and opened it.

CHAPTER 12

CEDRIC

Peggy-Rose Kim was an aspiring news reporter, a few years out of Columbia University's journalism school. Her father was the general manager at one of the stations I consulted for in Chicago. Peggy-Rose lived in Boston now and as a favor, I agreed to a coaching session after hours at the agency, where I would meet her, look at her resume reel and critique it.

When she walked into the office, I was immediately drawn to her exotic look. Her mother was Korean and her father was Caucasian. But she used her mother's maiden name—Kim—on her resume.

Her vanilla perfume was really strong.

"Hi Cedric. It's a pleasure to finally meet you. You have quite the reputation," she said flirtatiously holding out her tiny hand.

"Peggy, the pleasure is mine," I said as I shook her hand, not exactly sure which *reputation* she was referring to.

She batted her eyelashes. "I brought my demo disc; it's mostly stuff I did in school and footage I was able to put together while interning at one of the Boston news stations. I have no real experience on-air. That's why I am hoping for your advice, so I can land my first real job."

I nodded, staring her up and down. "Ok, Peggy. Let's get to it."

I closed the door then slid the disc into the machine and we both stared at the screen.

The video started with a shot of Peggy in front of a building talking in an uncomfortably high pitched voice: *"This is Peggy-Rose Kim reporting live from the scene of a fire on Broad Street."* It then cut to a clip of her reading the news from what looked like an amateur college TV station news desk: *"Police are investigating a homicide in Boston's Roxbury neighborhood..."*

If I could have chucked the video into the garbage then and there, I would have. In the second clip, Peggy was actually smiling on camera when talking about the murder.

She sucked ass.

I stopped the DVD abruptly and turned to her.

"Peggy, I'm friends with your father which is why I am here now looking at your reel. If I were a news director, that is as far as you would have gotten. Do you realize you were smiling in that footage while you were talking about a murder?"

Peggy looked at me dumbfounded. She said nothing, looked down, and then looked up at me with tears in her eyes. "I am sorry. I should have never come here. I know I'm not ready to be showing a big agent my tape. I needed your advice, but obviously I am way out of my league," she sobbed.

Aw, shit. I grabbed a tissue from my desk and handed it to her.

"Whoa, Whoa, Whoa...come on. It wasn't that bad. I was just trying to make a point, that there is a lot of competition out there, but you do have a great look; you just need to work on your voice and presentation. You get ten seconds to wow a news director before he shuts off your demo. But you have potential." I put my hand on her shoulder as I lied through my teeth because I felt like shit for making her cry.

"You think I am pretty?" she asked.

"Yes, I think you're gorgeous, Peggy." I immediately regretted my use of that word. She was gorgeous, but that was inappropriate under the circumstances.

Before I could clarify what I said, Peggy stopped crying, looked me in the eyes, grabbed my tie, pulling me toward her and kissed me suddenly and fiercely.

I froze but didn't stop her. We continued to kiss for about thirty seconds, when I pulled back.

"What's wrong?" she asked, huffing and puffing.

I wiped my lips. "Nothing, Peggy...I meant what I said, but this isn't right. Your father would kill me." It was the truth. But I hadn't been this close to a woman since Karyn and felt conflicted.

She grabbed my tie again, and we continued kissing. Just as I was about to push her off me, she kneeled down and started to unzip my pants. I had to stop this, but my brain and my body were on a break and not speaking to each other.

Should I let her do it?

She pulled my boxers down and my decision got easier as I noticed the desperate look on her face, which made her less and less attractive and my dick less and less hard by the second.

I abruptly pulled my pants up. "Peggy, this is not right."

"What my father doesn't know won't hurt him," she said, grabbing at my pants again.

This time, I was saved by the bell when my cell phone rang. I stood up with my pants still hanging down and moved away from Peggy.

"This is Cedric," I answered hoarsely, my breathing erratic as Peggy continued to try and kiss my neck.

I covered the receiver. "Please, stop," I whispered to Peggy.

"Cedric, it's Caleb. I need to talk to you. I'm at Mom's."

Why was he at Mom's and why was *he* whispering?

"Is everything ok?" I panicked.

"Yes, it's not an emergency, but—"

"Hold on, Caleb."

I turned to Peggy, zipping up my pants. "Peggy, this was a mistake. If you want to mail me your future demos, I'll be happy to look at them and give you my feedback but this...here...can't happen again. I need to leave. Something's come up, so you'll have to go, so I can lock up the office. I am very sorry."

With that, Peggy took her DVD and stormed out without saying a word. I waited until she was out of sight.

"Caleb, are you still there?" I said as I left my office and locked the door, walking toward the elevators. I noticed the elevator door that Peggy just entered closing shut. I pushed the down button for myself.

"Cedric. Did you know that Allison has been working with Callie?"

My heart nearly stopped. *What did he just say?*

"What...what do you mean?" I asked.

"When was the last time you spoke to Mom?" he asked.

I ran my hands through my hair. "About a week ago, but she never mentioned anything to me about an Allison working there. She's working there?"

"Cedric, she's here now."

What?

Caleb continued. "Mom knew Denise was away on business, so she invited me to this holiday dinner she's putting on for Bruno, Maria and Kurt. I drove down. Allison opened the door and let me in. I knew immediately it was *your* Allison."

My Allison.

I was silent and in shock.

Allison has been at my mother's house...with Callie? She's there now? This was unbelievable.

Caleb kept talking as his voice competed with the numerous thoughts floating through my head. "I played dumb, Cedric. She told me she was assigned here after Callie's Tuesday-Thursday person suddenly quit. She has been working here for a few weeks now."

I stayed silent in shock as I exited the elevators and walked aimlessly out the revolving door onto the noisy hustle and bustle of State Street. I ran my fingers through my hair again as I absorbed what I was hearing, looking up at the evening sky.

"Cedric...are you still there?" Caleb asked.

After a long pause, I responded in an exhausted and dazed whisper. "Yeah."

"Cedric, she's amazing with Callie. I have never seen Callie so content. Callie is looking at her in the eyes and they are feeding each other dessert. It's really cute, actually. And you were right about how you described her…holy Jesus. You have to get down here."

"Whoa, Whoa, Whoa, Caleb, I don't know. I told you what happened when I went to the diner. She acted like she never fucking wanted to see me again. I still can't figure why. I've been a mess these past few weeks. I almost made a huge mistake tonight in my office with some girl because I have been so fucking down in the dumps over this. I can't even process anything having to do with Allison right now, let alone show my face there."

I closed my eyes for a few seconds and opened them.

"Well, I think she is only going to be here for about another hour, so if you decide to come down, you need to do it fast," Caleb said.

"Ok, thanks." I hung up the phone abruptly and walked in a daze down State Street to the garage where my car was parked. I disarmed the car and got in, sitting there in silence for a minute before starting the engine.

As I drove out of the garage, I hadn't made my mind up about whether or not to go to my mother's. I just started driving.

It made sense that Allison could have been assigned to work with Callie, but the possibility that it would happen had never occurred to me.

I decided to stop at home and change out of my work clothes, which reeked of Peggy-Rose's vanilla scent.

I threw on a plain, fitted white long-sleeve shirt, my favorite Levis, some brown shoes and a brown leather jacket.

I went into the master bath and threw some water over my face and wet down my hair.

I sat back on my bed bouncing my knees nervously. Should I stay or should I go? (Go ahead, sing the song.)

Without thinking further, I shot up, grabbed my keys and ran out the door.

Speeding down the side roads to my mother's house, I had no idea what I was going say to her if she was still there, what I was going to do when I saw her or how she would react when she saw me. I wondered if she had even figured out that this was my family. Would she be shocked to see me show up out of the blue? So many thoughts raced through my head. But more than anything…I was excited to have a reason to see her again. Maybe she would be cold, maybe she didn't want me in the way I wanted her, or would treat me like she did last time at the diner. But to be able to see her face again was something I simply couldn't pass up.

I pulled into the spot across the street from my mother's house. I could see the Christmas tree was lit up and the house was covered in lights. The bright lamplight from the living room shined through the window and silhouettes of people moved back and forth. As I approached the front door, I could see right into the house. No one noticed me looking in like a creeper.

Through the glass, I saw my mother and our family friend, Bruno, sitting on the couch talking.

I saw Caleb walk from the living room into the dining room holding a beer.

I waited, continuing to stay by the window. No Allison. I was too late. She was gone. My heart sank.

I rang the doorbell and was greeted by my mother.

"Cedric! What a surprise. Come in, son. Did Caleb call you?" She beamed.

"Hi, Ma." I hugged her tightly never wanting to let go.

"I didn't even think to call you over, because you said you had been working so late this week. I am glad you decided to join us, honey."

"Me too," I sighed into my mother's neck.

I greeted Bruno, Maria and Kurt who were now all sitting in the living room. Caleb must have been in the bathroom because I didn't see him in the dining room or kitchen.

I decided to peek in on Callie who was surely in her room playing on her iPad in bed away from the commotion of the guests.

As my fingers touched the doorknob to her room, the door swung open suddenly.

There was my beautiful sister.

She was riding piggyback on the shoulders of another beautiful woman.

My heart raced when I realized I was face to face with Allison.

CHAPTER 13

ALLISON

Once I realized, Cedric was not going to show up, I started to relax. I had told Bettina I would stay until 9:30, so I had a little over an hour more to go.

Callie and I had finished dessert and retreated back to her room to play Connect Four while listening to her favorite *Laurie Berkner Band* c.d. I had discovered the Connect Four game was a good way to teach turn-taking and patience. I was red, Callie was black and each time before she threw in a piece she would have to say "my turn." Then, she would have to look at me and say "your turn" before I would put my piece in.

When we finished the game and I was cleaning up the pieces, I felt the weight of a hundred and something pounds on my shoulders behind me.

Callie had jumped on me piggyback style and was giggling infectiously. I couldn't help but laugh hysterically along with her. I decided to humor her and stand up, allowing her on my shoulders. She got a kick out of being up so high and watching us in the mirror this way. We made faces like this at each other in the mirror.

Callie looked down at me from atop my shoulders and said, "Show Mommy."

"You want Mommy to see piggyback, Callie?" I asked.

"Yes!" She laughed.

I opened the door thankful for the high ceilings in the old house.

I could never have been prepared for what stood before me when the door opened.

I stood there frozen looking into Cedric's blue eyes, which were the iciest crystal blue I had ever seen them.

His face was flushed and his eyes wide; he looked just as surprised to see me, as I was to see him.

"Allison," he whispered and smiled warmly looking into my eyes, blinking rapidly as if to process this.

I barely got the words out. "Cedric."

The weight of this shock and the weight of Callie nearly dropped me to the floor.

"Show Mommy!" Callie yelled breaking our awkward silence. Cedric and I both laughed nervously, eyes still on each other.

Cedric's hand reached past me and up to caress his sister's cheek. "Callie, are you having fun with Allison?" he asked as he stepped aside, letting us pass down the hall into the living room.

"Bettina, Callie wanted you to see this," I said.

Cedric's mother, who was heavy into conversation, Caleb and the company all clapped unanimously at the sight of Callie on top my shoulders.

I then sat down on the couch so that she could climb off of me. It felt as though the weight that lifted off my shoulders transferred to my chest with the way my heart was pounding.

Callie and I walked back over to her room and Cedric was sitting on her bed, waiting for us.

Callie grabbed her iPad and sat next to her brother as he put his arm around her and kissed her on the cheek. My heart hurt with a bittersweet joy at seeing how tender this masculine man could be with his sister.

Bettina had said just to let Callie have some down time with the iPad for the rest of the night until bed.

I sat down on the other side of Cedric and as always, I was intoxicated by the smell of him. Aside from a brief moment during our car ride, we had never been this physically close to one another.

After a bit of silence and both of us pretending to be transfixed on the video Callie was watching, Cedric turned to me. "Allison, I don't know how I had no clue you were working here," he said looking straight into my eyes.

I cleared my throat. "I haven't mentioned to your mother that we had met each other. I wanted to prove myself with your sister without any expectations. I wasn't sure if I was going to be good at this and didn't want it to reflect poorly on you if it didn't work out. I was told I would be working with someone named Calista before I came here. I know you referred to Callie in the car that night, so I didn't realize until later on that first day when your mother used the nickname, that she was actually your sister."

Cedric nodded, looking over at Callie for a few seconds and then turned back toward me. "It seems to me you're doing an awesome job. I don't think I have ever seen my sister this content."

I smiled. "Thank you. That means a lot." *It did.*

Cedric didn't move his eyes from me for even a moment. "Are you still working at the diner?"

I cleared my throat, becoming nervous at the intensity of his stare. "Yes, this is my second job. I'm still working with another young man as well after the diner on the days I don't see Callie."

Cedric nodded slowly as if to think about what to say next, then looked up at the headboard collage and flashed a smile at back at me. "So, you must have wondered what the Anderson Cooper fixation is all about," he said laughing.

"Yes! What *is* that all about?"

Cedric shook his head in laughter. "No one can figure it out exactly. We think he might remind her of our dad, because of his white hair, maybe she misses him. But since she can't tell us what she's thinking, for the most part, no one knows for sure. A friend of a friend is his agent and I got her that autographed picture."

"That's very sweet. I wondered how she got that." We laughed together until that dissipated into more staring.

Just as I was getting lost in his eyes, the light in Callie's room started to flicker. It was almost as though the Awkward Gods were trying to intervene and save me from imminent death.

Then, the lights went out completely.

Here I was, sitting on Callie's bed, next to Cedric, listening to the *Wheels on the Bus* song in the dark. I certainly could not have imagined this night ending up like this, not in a million years. But I knew I never wanted it to end.

"Ohhhhh…kay," I said and we both laughed at the sudden darkness.

Callie remained unphased, the light of her iPad the only illumination in the room.

"Hang on. I'll be right back," Cedric said as he got up.

Cold air replaced Cedric's warmth as he exited the room.

I didn't want him to leave my side even for a second. After being near him again for only minutes, I wondered how I would survive staying away from him ever again after tonight.

I shouldn't have been having these thoughts, knowing he had a girlfriend, but I couldn't help being so attracted to this man. The resilience I had to stay away from him last time was nowhere to be found tonight.

I wanted him…badly.

And this beautiful man was also so sweet to his sister. I would have given anything to be with someone like him that way…to go with him wherever he was going tonight.

Get a grip, Allison.

Cedric returned with a new light bulb and began twisting Callie's light fixture off. As he replaced the bulb, the light returned. It was brighter than before. He seemed to be having issues with securing the fixture back over the light.

As he struggled with it, his white, cotton shirt rode up high as he lifted his toned arms and…*holy hell*…I could see almost half of his bare right side torso. I was stunned to see a large tattoo there. As I suspected, it seemed Blue Eyes did have a wild side.

I hadn't thought it was possible to be more turned on by Cedric but seeing that took it to a new level. It was hard to make out the image, but it seemed to be a cross with roses on a vine with thorns wrapped around it and the word ART in the middle. *Not that I was looking closely or anything. Was he an artist? Art. Interesting.*

"Ok, got it." Cedric smiled as he finally twisted the fixture successfully and stepped down.

The curtain to his sexy side tattoo peepshow had officially closed.

"Let there be light," I said. *What a dork I could be sometimes.*

Cedric sat back down in between Callie and me. This time, the side of his leg was pressed up firmly against mine and I immediately felt my underwear getting moist from the heat of his touch. His leg was not brushing against mine; it was *pressing* against me. He was deliberately sitting as close to me as possible and it made me crazy.

"Allison, can I tell you something?" he turned to me, his icy eyes were piercing into mine again, and I started to sweat.

I barely got the words out. "Sure," I said.

Just when Cedric was about to speak, Bettina entered the room and we both turned towards her in unison.

She smiled at us curiously. "I see you've met my son, Cedric. He surprised us tonight."

"Yes." I smiled nervously offering nothing more.

"Allison, I was just going to say you could leave anytime you want, but if you two are chatting, feel free to stay as long as you like. Bruno just left. Maria and Kurt are staying for more pie and coffee," she said.

"Mom, I'd love some coffee…Allison?" Cedric turned to me, his eyes seemingly urging me on me to stay.

"Sure. Coffee would be great," I said.

"Cedric, you come into the kitchen in about five minutes. It'll be ready then," Bettina said as she walked away back to her guests.

Just then, Caleb appeared at the door. "Sorry I didn't get to spend much time with you, little bro. I have to head back to Cow Hampshire."

"Bye, buddy," Cedric said as he stood up and they clasped hands. I saw Caleb give Cedric a knowing look. He was definitely thinking something was going on between us. I just couldn't figure out if he was encouraging it or not, given his brother had a girlfriend.

Caleb reached for my hand. "It was a pleasure meeting you, Allison."

"You too, Caleb," I said as I shook his hand goodbye. His hands were strong and firm like Cedric's.

Caleb shut the door behind him, which hadn't been closed entirely all night...until now.

Cedric returned to his seat next to me on the bed and the sexual tension was almost unbearable. This felt all sorts of wrong, especially with Callie sitting there next to us. Then again, the only naughty things actually happening were in my head; we weren't actually doing anything wrong.

He turned his beautiful blue eyes toward mine again, "Allison, what I wanted to say before was—"

The door opened suddenly and in walked Bettina with two coffees. She knew how I liked mine since she often made coffee for me when I worked in the afternoons. She handed me a cup and handed Cedric his and left without saying a word, just smiling as we thanked her.

"This is just what I needed," I said as I took a sip of the hot coffee, thinking that what I really needed was a cold shower.

"Mmm." Cedric purred into his mug as he sipped. Hearing him moan like that was so erotic and my nipples felt it.

"Allison...um—"

Just as Cedric was about to get the words out again, Callie started humming and jumping up and down on the bed. I could see she was watching a clip from Anderson Cooper 360 on the iPad when it happened. Some of Cedric's coffee spilled on the lap of my dress.

Cedric freaked. "Oh, God...shit...Allison, I am so sorry. Are you okay?"

I lied. "It's fine. This is...a thick sweater material, it didn't seep through to the skin."

Truthfully, I probably lost some leg hair and may have lost feeling in my right thigh...but it's all good.

Cedric rushed out of the room and returned with a wet dishrag. He began rubbing the area with it and I swear I thought I was going to die. He was rubbing the top of my thighs. He was so close to me at this point that I thought I was going to melt into him. I felt like a pile of mush with him touching me like this and my being able to smell, not only the cologne, but the smell of *him* being so close. I think I briefly closed my eyes and bit my bottom lip.

He finally stopped and threw the rag on the floor, shaking his head.

"I'm really sorry," he said again, sighing, but never taking his eyes off mine.

I felt like I must have turned fifty shades of red. "Cedric, it's fine, really."

I looked over at Callie to distract myself from him. A wave of sadness suddenly overcame me and something inside me told me I should go home. I was sitting here on a bed with my poor autistic client who was oblivious to the fact that I was getting off on her brother who happened to be someone else's boyfriend. I got up suddenly.

"Cedric, I really have to go. I have an early morning at the diner tomorrow. It was nice catching up again."

Before he could respond, I rushed out of the room and put my mug on the kitchen counter. I kissed Bettina who was still heavy in conversation talking in Italian now to Maria, grabbed my coat and ran out the door—literally—before Cedric could offer me a ride home.

The next train left at 9:45 and I would be able to make it if I jogged the five blocks to the station. That's what I did.

***

I got there just in nick of time and hopped the train.

As I sat with my head leaning back on the wall behind my train seat, I started to cry. I was filled with so many emotions tonight, between my growing love for Callie, my lust for Cedric and the overall longing I felt to be part of a family like theirs.

My running wasn't about how much I wanted to leave tonight. What was bothering me was how much I desperately wanted to stay.

As the train swayed, I thought about my mother and how much she loved me and hoped she was watching over me. We had so many good times, just the two of us. Memories of Mom flashed through my head as the train swayed and the tears fell: trips to Castle Island, mother and daughter Lifetime movie marathons, praying at St. John's Church together, being able to confide in her about anything. I couldn't have loved her more if she had given birth to me. As the thoughts of Mom continued, I thought about how I just wanted to do something in life that would have made her proud. I think she would be happy that I found Callie and Lucas and that I was making a difference in their lives.

Just then, my phone chimed and I looked down at a text that gave me the chills.

> Allison, you are so beautiful inside and out. Your mother would be proud. That's all I wanted to say. You left before I could. – Cedric.

***

Still reeling from the irony and timing of that text, after much internal debate, by the time I got back to my apartment, I had decided I would respond to him. I needed to find a way to acknowledge such a sweet sentiment without encouraging something that could never be. I plopped down on the sofa, noticing the eerie silence of my apartment since Sonia had just left for the UK for the holidays. I wished she were here so that I could tell her what happened. It was too late to call the UK.

I wanted to cry, looking at the text over and over. Cedric's words could not have been more perfectly timed since I had been deep in thought on the train about my mother when the text came in. The fact that he told me that my mother would be proud of me cut deep. The fact that he told me I was beautiful was the icing on the cake.

Tonight left me feeling very emotional.

I didn't want to be alone this Christmas, which was Sunday, so I planned to have dinner at Danny's house in Boston near Fenway Park and finally meet his new partner Paolo.

As I lay down, I tried to think about how to respond. Looking out the window at the Christmas lights adorning the house across the street, a tear fell down my cheek. Why did everything have to be so complicated? Why couldn't Cedric be single? Why did he send me that text if he has a girlfriend? Why did it touch me so deeply?

As I pondered these things, I stared at my phone and turned it to camera mode. I could see my reflection in the screen and noticed mascara running down my cheeks. As I looked down at my red sweater dress, I noticed the stain from where Cedric spilled his coffee and decided I would definitely endure more burns if it meant being able to be close to him again.

I was struggling with my feelings over him tonight and the fact that even though he had a girlfriend, I couldn't shake this connection. He apparently felt it too. Those very feelings and my being able to sense his, were what drove me out of there so fast.

Karyn Keller. I had to remember he had a girlfriend. I needed to snap out of this.

I unlocked my phone and clicked on his message and typed a response.

> Cedric, thanks so much for those kind words. I can't tell you how much I enjoy working with your sister.
> Send.

A tear rolled down my cheek and I let out a deep breath. I immediately regretted the casual tone of that message, but it was too late. I had already sent it. A part of me felt I should have taken that opportunity to let him know how I truly felt even if he had a girlfriend. He wasn't married, after all. My thoughts began to race and my heart pounded furiously because I knew what I was about to do.

I typed again.

> And I think you are beautiful too.
> Send.

I waited and waited for a response, but it never came. Technically, he didn't have to say anything, since I was responding to him. But I had hoped he would continue the dialog. The ball was in his court. I had no regrets. The first text was the message I thought was appropriate to send, followed by the second text that came from my heart. He could take either one and do what he pleased.

After an hour of lying on the couch staring at the Christmas lights across the street with my phone in my hand, I knew I wasn't going to get a response, so I retreated into my bedroom and tried to get some sleep.

CHAPTER 14

CEDRIC

I stared at the blazing fireplace in Caleb and Denise's living room. It was Christmas and my entire family had gathered in New Hampshire to be together and celebrate.

Callie sat on the couch next to me playing on her iPad while Mom helped Denise in the kitchen. I could smell the ham cooking and couldn't wait to sit down to a home-cooked meal, especially when my mother was doing the cooking.

Caleb was stocking the bar down in the basement with drinks since that was where we usually hung out and watched movies after dinner.

Denise had the house all decked out with garland and white lights. Their Christmas tree was huge...tall and fat with a strong, pine scent. It was loaded underneath with presents we had opened after brunch this morning.

As *Have Yourself A Merry Little Christmas* played on the iPod speaker, I looked at the fire and couldn't help but think about what Allison was doing tonight. She didn't have any family, so who was she with tonight? It took every ounce of my strength not to text her that very question right now.

I looked down at my phone and stared at the text she sent me in response to my message a few nights ago. *And I think you're beautiful too.* My heart sank. It sank each of the dozens of times a day I stared at those words on my phone.

And I think you're beautiful too.

I remembered the exact moment I received it. I had just returned home from Mom's dinner party Thursday night. My body had been aching with pent up desire from sitting so close to her and then feeling her soft skin as I cleaned off the spilled coffee.

I had sent her my text twenty minutes before arriving back home that night. I had decided to text her just as I was walking out my mother's door some time after Allison bolted, leaving me dumbfounded. I could sense that she was running from me that night, but why...I couldn't understand. If she knew the truth about everything, then running would have made sense, but under the circumstances, I couldn't figure it out.

I had felt like I needed to tell her how I felt anyway, because she mesmerized me. I couldn't stay away and needed to get it off my chest. That night, I had texted her that I thought she was beautiful and I got no response, so I had pretty much given up and decided to drive home and call it a night.

So, later that evening, when my text alert sounded as I was taking off my clothes getting ready for bed, my heart had skipped a beat. It could have been anyone, but it was her.

The first text was a generic thank you, which made me feel like shit. Just as I was about to toss the phone across the bed in despair, the phone sounded again. I looked down and my heart started beating rapidly when I saw what she wrote.

And I think you're beautiful too.

My heart kept pounding and my fingers were ready to start frantically typing to pour my heart out to her. I wanted to text her back, but I hadn't been able to put into words what I was feeling.

I remember starting to sweat and breathe heavily when the realization hit me that I actually might be able to have her if I wanted her. Those words she texted were the first confirmation I had received that she returned my feelings at all. Was I really ready to take the next step, knowing where it would lead—that I would inevitably break her heart?

I knew either I was going to tell her I was crazy about her right then and there or that I needed to stay away. There was no in between. This situation was black and white. In my heart, I wanted to let it all out and run to her wherever she was. But I didn't. I never wrote anything back that night.

Every moment since that night became consumed with thoughts of her. And now, three days later, it was Christmas and all I could do was sit there by the fire and wonder about her yet again.

What I realized since the night of that text was that I really didn't have a choice. I thought that by not responding, I could somehow make this situation easier or less complicated, but that wasn't possible. Just the opposite happened, really. My draw to Allison was a completely uncontrollable pull that wouldn't go away despite my knowing the consequences of acting on it. I would never stop wanting her. And I would inevitably hurt her either way once she learned the truth, whether I was involved with her or not at the time. She was going to find out with or without me. Maybe just maybe, if I could show her who I was and get her to trust me, she would find it in her heart to see past everything. It was a long shot but a dream I needed to cling to right now. Because I knew what I was about to do: I was about to lose control.

My ruminations were interrupted by the sound of my mother's voice telling me that dinner was ready in the dining room. I pulled myself away from the fire and seated myself next to where Callie was already sitting at the table.

I helped serve my sister food and watched as she began devouring mashed potatoes before anyone else even sat down. I just laughed at how nice it must be to be Callie Callahan sometimes…to not give a shit about the consequences of anything.

As the rest of the family sat down, I led the table in prayer. "Bless Us Oh Lord for These Thine Gifts For Which We Are About To Receive…"

As I continued the prayer and held hands with my sister and mother, I felt truly blessed to be here with these wonderful people and wondered again where Allison was without a family on Christmas.

We all sat down and began devouring the meal which consisted of ham, mashed potatoes, sweet potato pie, green bean casserole, cornbread and barbecued beans. Denise and my mother were amazing cooks and even better when cooking together.

The family dinner discussion ranged from what movie we would be watching later to the latest gossip from my mother's church. I continued to stuff my face not contributing much to the conversations.

Then, my gluttonous consumption was interrupted by a shocking and abrupt question from my mother. "Cedric, what was going on between you and Allison the other night?" she asked.

Caleb's eyes immediately darted toward mine, eager to see my response.

"Why do you ask?" I nervously asked and reached for another piece of bread and started to butter it.

"Well, I am not blind, son. I can see how gorgeous she is and happened to notice the fact that once you got a look at her, you didn't leave her side all night in Callie's room except to change that light bulb. For the record, I think she is amazing and you would be stupid not to go after her." She winked.

"Who's Allison?" Denise interrupted.

My brother had clearly been good at keeping my secrets.

"Allison is Callie's new therapist and your brother-in-law here is smitten."

I broke in. "Mom, you wanna know something?"

"Yes, honey. What?" She smiled.

Like I said, my control over this situation was dwindling and I responded, "You are absolutely friggin' right. I was smitten. She is amazing." I felt a rush of heat in my face at the balls it took to admit that small part of the truth in front of my mother.

Caleb laughed heartily then downed his beer.

"Well, what are you going to do about it?" she asked.

I shook my head not knowing what to say or why I even told my mother how I felt about Allison.

Then, she gave me a brilliant idea.

"Cedric, Allison doesn't come back to work until the Thursday after next because Callie and I are visiting your aunt in Maine. I had meant to give her a Christmas gift at my party, but she left suddenly. I have the gift wrapped in my car. I was going to drop it off at her house this week because I am going to Malden to meet with some people on the board of Bright Horizons. Why don't you find out if she is home and tell her you are dropping it off as a favor to me tonight?"

It seemed a little nuts. I mean, why couldn't my mother wait to give her the gift the next time Allison worked with Callie? But if this gave me even a shitty excuse to go to her house and see her, I might need to take what I could get.

I didn't respond, just sat in deep thought.

Of course, my mother had no idea what I'd really be getting myself into. I hated that my mother thought all of this was so innocent, but I had kept the secret too long to ever tell her the whole truth now. I sometimes wished I could get her take on the true dilemma I faced.

"Well, you think about it, Cedric. I'm not going to put any pressure on you. She may not even be home," Mom said before resuming her dinner.

My mother was right. Allison was probably with friends tonight.

As Denise, Mom and Callie cleared the table, I followed Caleb downstairs to the basement to help pick a movie for after dessert and to get his opinion on things.

"So, Mom's on to you, huh?" Caleb smirked taking a swig of beer and plopping down on the leather sectional.

"If she only fucking knew. I realized tonight that I am also deceiving Mom with this whole charade." I sighed.

"Cedric, please. Stop doing this to yourself. You have every right to feel the way you do. You need to let go of the past and move forward. Just think about you and Allison and nothing else. You deserve to be happy, dude."

"I can't stop this thing if I tried, man. It's a runaway train," I said as I joined him on the couch, leaning my head back.

We were then interrupted by Mom, Denise and Callie, all of whom were walking down the basement stairs carrying a different dessert and some paper plates and napkins.

We turned on the DVD player and opted for *It's a Wonderful Life*, mainly because it was Dad's favorite and he was always here with us in spirit. This movie always depressed me though, even before Dad died. Now, it was even more bittersweet.

My family sat together cuddled on the couch eating apple pie and chocolate cake, transfixed by the movie. Callie was the exception and opted to watch Anderson Cooper clips on You Tube with her headphones on.

I escaped upstairs to sit by the fire again, taking a bottle of Shiraz with me from the basement bar.

I stopped by the kitchen first to open the wine and pour a glass then returned to my spot on the recliner right in front of the fire in my brother's living room. The Christmas music still played low from the iPod speaker. I took a sip of the wine and looked down at my watch. It was only 8:30.

I leaned my head back, closed my eyes and imagined Allison straddling me on this chair in front of the fire. Just the thought was enough to make me hard. I shook my head to get the image out so I could think straight. I couldn't. Remember that runaway train? It was about to derail.

I took my phone out of my pocket, hit her name and typed.

Merry Christmas, Allison.
Send.

I closed my eyes and held my phone, having no clue whether I would hear from her. My hand shook when I immediately heard it chime back.

Allison: Merry Christmas, Cedric. Where are you?

Cedric: At my brother's in New Hampshire. How about you?

Allison: I just got home from dinner with my friend Danny.

Danny? Is she dating him? Fuck. And then as if she could read my mind...

Allison: Danny and his boyfriend live over by Fenway Park.

Phew.

Cedric: Ah, I see. Was it a good time?

Allison: Yes, it was. What is everyone doing over there?

Cedric: Watching It's a Wonderful Life down in the basement. That movie kind of depresses me.

Allison: Oh my God…me too. My mother loved it though.

Cedric: I'm sorry.

Allison: Sorry for what? It is depressing.

Cedric: I know, I mean, I am sorry that your mom is not with you tonight.

Allison: Thanks. Me too.

I knew what I had to do next.

Cedric: Allison, how late will you be up?

Allison: Pretty late. Why?

Cedric: My mom asked me to drop off a gift for you that she forgot to give you last Thursday…on my way home tonight if you were around.

Allison: I'll be around. Sure. That is so nice of her.

Cedric: Great. I'll probably leave here in about twenty minutes, so I'll be there sometime after ten.

Allison: Sounds good. I'll see you soon.

Cedric: Ok. See you soon.

My heart was pounding out of my chest. I was going to see her *tonight*. What a Christmas this was turning out to be.

I immediately went to the bathroom, grabbing the first toothbrush I saw not knowing whose it was and brushed my teeth. I wet my hair back and stared at myself in the mirror. I had looked better, but if I had known I would be seeing Allison, I might have dressed differently. I was wearing a maroon button down shirt, rolled up at the sleeves and dark jeans. I hadn't shaved for a couple of days, but it would have to do.

I ran down the stairs and pulled my mother aside letting her know my plans. She gave me her keys and I ran out to the driveway, took the wrapped present out of her glove compartment and transferred it to the passenger seat in my car.

I went back in the house, returning the keys, putting on my black North Face parka and hugged and kissed each of my family members goodnight.

Caleb patted me strongly on the shoulder, since he was the only one who knew how difficult the situation with Allison really was for me.

I felt bad leaving early, but my mother was practically shoving me out the door when she found out I was going to take her up on that idea.

I got in my car and blasted the heat because it was freezing out. I put on some smooth jazz and tried to relax as I pulled out of my brother's driveway.

As I sped south down I-93, I thought about what I would say to her when I saw her. I needed to tell her how I felt about her without scaring her off. I hoped that she would invite me to stay beyond just handing her the gift, so that I had the chance to talk to her for once.

I finally got to her exit and drove slowly down the side streets leading to her house. I parked across the street from the two-family house where she lived. Once I looked up into her second floor window, I really started to freak out.

CHAPTER 15

ALLISON

Be certain to take your vitamins, as this is your low point of the month, my Gemini friend. It is a good day to curl up with your favorite book or video, sip herbal tea and avoid the world. Tomorrow brings new energy.

I couldn't believe this was happening. Cedric was coming over...on Christmas night. We would be alone. This was so dangerous, but I was not about to stop it.

I didn't care about his girlfriend right now. And why wasn't he with her tonight anyway? The consequences of this couldn't compete with the uncontrollable desire I had to see him. I just wanted to look into those beautiful blue eyes tonight. I wanted nothing more than to get lost in them and forget about the despair of being alone on Christmas without my mother.

Dinner with Danny and Paolo had been good. They actually invited a few other nice people and put together a Mexican buffet-style menu. Danny knew that Mexican is my favorite type of food.

But seeing Danny and Paolo all over each other and so in love only reminded me what I was lacking. I ended up making up a story about not feeling well and leaving early, because I wanted to go home.

Soon after I got in, I kicked off my shoes, went straight to bed and lay down staring at the ceiling.

A few minutes later, my phone startled me when the text came in.

Merry Christmas, Allison.

It was a Merry Christmas…now.

I needed to look better than ever before. After our texting exchange ended, and I knew Cedric was coming over, I sprung up and ran to the bathroom. I tied my hair up while I showered, careful not to get it wet, because there would be no time to wash and style it before he arrived.

As I stepped out of the shower, I sprayed myself with a Victoria's Secret fruity scent and walked over to the closet. I could not decide what to wear. I put on a cream- colored lacy bra and matching thong…just to feel sexy. I wouldn't be going *there* of course, tonight…would I? Clearly, I didn't trust myself, or else I would have chosen the more comfortable granny panties.

I then picked out an emerald-green, cotton, fitted v-neck shirt and tight dark blue skinny jeans. I threw black leather high-heeled boots over the jeans and finished the look off by brushing my hair, leaving it down. I gave myself a smoky eye and put some light gloss on my lips, puckering in the mirror. I had to admit; I looked pretty good for someone who was about to turn in for the night twenty minutes ago.

I went to the kitchen and took a bottle of cold Chardonnay out of the fridge. I hadn't had too much to drink at Danny's because I was taking the train home and didn't want to be drunk and vulnerable on public transportation. So, I decided to pour a glass now to help loosen me up.

I suddenly started to get really nervous. I didn't wonder if something was going to happen tonight. I knew deep down, it would.

The only thing keeping us from each other last time was the fact that Callie was in the room. I could tell by the way he was looking at me that night and by the way he made me feel, that had we been alone, something more would have happened. And that scared me. Knowing what he later texted me that night…that I was beautiful…confirmed what I already knew in my heart. He wanted me. I wanted him. It was the reason I ran.

I figured I should have some kind of food to offer him when he got here, so I quickly put together a fruit plate since I had just stocked up at the market yesterday. I also cut some Cracker Barrel cheese onto Ritz crackers and arranged them on a plate. I nearly dropped the plate that I was carrying to the table when I heard a knock at the door.

My heart felt like it was thumping out of my chest and I started to sweat instantly.

Cedric was early.

"Just a minute!" I yelled as I gathered my bearings, taking in a deep breath.

He may not have heard me because the constant knocking continued and got louder as I walked toward the door.

I opened it and a wave of nausea and the smell of vodka hit me like a ton of bricks.

"Nate."

***

I hadn't seen Nate since I ended our relationship. The man I was met with at the door was nothing like the man I knew before I discovered his addiction. His eyes were bloodshot red and his hair was dirty and inches longer than I had remembered. I usually like longer hair on guys, but Nate's was just messy and unwashed. It was clear that alcoholism had been taking its toll during the months since our breakup.

"What are you doing here, Nate?" I asked nervously.

"Allison...we need to talk," Nate slurred as he leaned against the doorway.

"I can't, Nate. I am sorry, not when you are drunk like this."

I started to close the door and he stopped it with his hand.

"Allison, please...it's Christmas. I'm so lonely. I miss you so fucking much."

"Nate, please leave. I don't want to see you like this. You're drunk and you're scaring me."

I tried to push the door closed again, but this time, Nate slammed the door all the way open and pushed past me into the living room.

"Allison, you can't shut me out like this. I fucking love you. I need you."

He stumbled into the kitchen, grabbing the Chardonnay I had left on the table and started to drink it down fast like water. The glass shattered into pieces as he threw it on the floor. More alcohol was clearly the last thing he needed.

"Nate, you can't stay. Please go home." I was shaking.

I immediately remembered the last time that we were together when he hit me across the face after accusing me of cheating on him with Danny. He wasn't even half as drunk then as he was now.

"Allison, we never got to talk...abou...about what ha...happened between us," he said as he started walking slowly toward me.

I walked in reverse into the living room, my back facing the window.

I grabbed my cell phone from my purse and held it in my hand in case I needed to dial 911. The smell of vodka got closer and closer and made me nauseous.

"Who are you calling?" Nate backed me up against the window.

"No one," I said as my hands that held the phone shook profusely.

"You're lying."

Nate grabbed the phone and threw it to the ground. His putrid breath hit my face as he pressed his body into mine.

"Nate, you're scaring me. Please back away," I whispered, barely having the energy to talk audibly because I was truly terrified that I didn't know this person anymore. I didn't really know anything about Nate on alcohol, except for the fact that he had it in him to use force against me when he was intoxicated like this.

"Allison, I missed you so much. The way you smell, the way you taste, please just let me touch you," he said leaning in toward me.

I stood frozen with my back still against the window as he started kissing my neck. I wanted to vomit. Not only did he reek of vodka, but he smelled of body odor. He wrapped his hands around me, and I began to feel his hard-on and became truly worried that he might take this further than kissing my neck.

I tried to remain calm. He then started putting his hands up my shirt, and I instinctively pushed him away.

"Allison, we've done this a million times. Please just relax," Nate slurred, his eyes half closed.

"Nate, stop!" I screamed as his kiss on my neck turned harder and he started undoing my jeans.

"Allison, don't you know how many times I've made you come? What's one more time?" he asked.

I kept trying to push him off of me, but he felt like dead weight. The tops of my pants were undone and I was shaking. I couldn't let this happen.

"Nate, get off of me!" I yelled and pushed him with all of my might.

He fell back and when he regained his balance, he rushed toward me and slapped me so hard across the same right cheek as the last time he hit me.

I started to see stars as he struggled to get my tight skinny jeans off. I was again frozen and could feel tears starting to form quickly.

I decided I would rather die right here and now, than let him force me to have sex with him. I needed to try harder to get him off of me and then, I needed to run like hell.

I came up with a plan that I was going to pretend like I was giving in for a moment and then when his senses were wrapped up in the act, I would knee him in the balls and run for the hills.

I stopped resisting and let him continue to kiss my neck with his hands nudging on my pants, still trying to push them down.

Now, one of his hands was down my underwear and he was touching me.

I suddenly made my move with a swift kick to Nate's groin and managed to break free, running to the door, but Nate caught me by the hair and tackled me to the floor.

I started to scream bloody murder.

"Help! Help me!"

Nate covered my mouth and continued to push me down to the ground with all of his body weight.

I closed my eyes, not wanting to see what was about to happen to me. As I whimpered in the darkness, a tear fell down my cheek as I felt him press against me.

Then, my eyes shot open as I heard the sound of my door busting open and a voice.

"Get off of her, you MOTHER FUCKER!"

CHAPTER 16

CEDRIC

I almost turned around and went home. As I looked up into Allison's second floor window, I saw her beautiful long, dark hair plastered against it and male hands caressing her back.

Was this some kind of sick fucking joke? Did she forget I was coming by and in the meantime, get a Christmas booty call?

I felt like I was about to vomit as I sat in my car and watched this guy kiss her neck. I could seriously taste the apple pie I had eaten come up on me.

My heart was breaking and beating rapidly in anger and shock, but I couldn't look away. I punched the steering wheel and threw my head down onto it.

Fuck. Me.

I looked up again. Her back was still to the window. But the scene this time looked different to me. Allison's hands were flailing and I immediately jumped out of the car, so that I could possibly hear what was going on even though the window was closed.

I couldn't hear anything but then saw what looked like Allison pushing forward, and then she disappeared from sight.

Shit. Something wasn't right. I had to know what was going on and got out of the car, slamming the door behind me.

The front door leading to the hallway stairs up to Allison's second floor apartment was open.

I walked up the stairs and began to sprint when I heard a cry for help…Allison's cry for help.

Adrenaline pumped through my veins, and when I reached the top, I busted through the door to find the man lying on top of Allison, who was crying. Before I could process what was happening, I charged toward him and pounced.

"Get off of her, you MOTHER FUCKER!" I yelled.

I managed to push him off of her and tackled him to the ground, pinning him under me.

He swung at my face and missed. He smelled badly of alcohol.

"Cedric! Oh my God, Cedric!" I heard Allison cry.

The man spit in my face as I held him to the floor. "Who the fuck are you?" he yelled.

"Call 911," I shouted over at Allison who ran to the kitchen dialing the phone.

"What were you about to do before I walked in…huh? HUH!?" I spat back at the man and yelled louder. "WHAT THE FUCK…WERE YOU…ABOUT TO DO TO HER?"

"I was about to take back what was mine," he said as I pinned him down to the ground as he continued to struggle to release from my grip.

Who the fuck was this person?

Just then, Allison appeared after having called the police. "They're on their way," she cried, tears pouring from her eyes.

Just then, the drunk man pushed up from under me and managed to get up on his feet. He swung at me and I swung back, hitting him. I ducked again, missing his punches and pushed him down to the ground, causing him to hit his head on the coffee table.

He sprung back up and charged toward me, smacking me down to the ground and hitting me as hard as he could in the chest.

I punched him in the face in return and immediately felt warm blood trickling down my hand.

Allison was screaming, "Stop! Please just leave, Nate…please."

Nate? She knew this guy? Who the fuck was Nate?

The last punch I threw at *Nate* seemed to stop his resilience.

He was lying down on the floor for a few minutes and I wasn't sure if he was injured from the punch or whether he just passed out from all the booze he drank.

I stood staring at him on the ground and then moved my stare toward Allison.

She had mascara running down her cheeks and was trembling. I wanted to go to her, but I had to keep my eyes on him in case he got up again.

A few more minutes passed with Nate lying on the ground.

Allison and I just stared down at him in shock.

The sound of distant police sirens got louder by the second, and then came the sounds of running footsteps from the hallway.

Three officers with guns drawn burst through the door.

"He's there, officer. That's the man who attacked me. His name is Nate Hutchinson. He is my ex-boyfriend. He is an alcoholic," Allison said.

Wow. So, Allison actually dated this asshole. Up until now, I had no idea who this guy was.

While two officers lifted Nate off the floor, a third large man approached me for questioning.

"I'm Officer Derin with the Boston Police. I am going to have to ask you some questions," he said.

"Sure, ask me anything." I sat down on Allison's sofa, only realizing now just how much my hand was bleeding.

"You may want to wrap that. Feel free to take care of it and come back here," Officer Derin said, pointing to my obvious wound.

I quickly got up and grabbed a wad of paper towel from the kitchen and temporarily wrapped my right hand tightly, noticing that one of the officers was now taking a groggy Nate away in handcuffs.

Allison was on the other side of the living room answering questions for the third cop and I could hear her sobbing.

I returned to Officer Derin and told him the story exactly as I saw it happen. He assured me that no charges would be filed against me for the injuries Nate sustained, since I was acting in self-defense.

When my questioning wrapped up, I looked over and saw Allison still tearfully relaying her side of the story to the officer. She nodded her head slowly and thanked the policeman for his help.

"We may need to call you in for additional questioning, depending on Mr. Hutchinson's recall. I am hoping that won't be necessary, though," Officer Derin said.

"Thank you so much, officers, for your help," Allison said as she shook hands with the two men.

I sat on the couch staring down at my bloody hand. Everything happened so fast and I felt like I was just starting to process it.

She closed the door after the policemen left and rushed over to where I was sitting on the couch.

"Cedric," she said as fresh tears fell again.

"Allison…what the fuck did I walk in on tonight?" I said, my voice hoarse. I was still in shock.

Before answering me, she rushed up and went to the bathroom, bringing back a first aid kit.

Tears fell from her eyes. "Cedric, you are hurt because of me. I'm so, so sorry. I don't know how to thank you enough for getting here tonight when you did."

She took my injured hand and began pouring peroxide on it. I looked down silently at it and back up at her tearful face. She was crying harder now and it killed me to see her in so much pain.

"Allison, please stop crying. Please, it really hurts me to see you cry," I said. It did. *It really did.*

Allison started to wrap my hand in gauze while she spoke.

"Cedric…that man…Nate…he was my ex-boyfriend. We broke up months ago as soon as I realized he had a serious drinking problem. He was a good person for a long time, taught music at Berklee and everything. I had no idea he was an alcoholic until the very end of our relationship. He hid it well for most of the time we were together. One night, he came home drunk and hit me and that was the last straw. I never wanted to see him again and I never did after that. Tonight was the first time I saw him since that night almost six months ago. I opened the door without checking, because I thought you were early."

Allison shook her head, crying and repeated, "I thought it was you. I thought it was you."

My heart was breaking as more tears fell from her eyes. I wanted to touch her, comfort her, but resisted. To think that I had something to do with him gaining access to her tonight made me physically ill.

"Did he…do anything to you?" I asked. *I needed to know.*

She sniffled. "He forced himself on me but only kissed me and groped me, but he wasn't able to do anything more. You came in right when he was…about to, though. I don't know what I would have done if you weren't here, Cedric."

It made me sick that he even got that far. And to think, I sat there and witnessed some of it through the window first hand before I realized she was actually being assaulted.

Allison finished wrapping my hand and kept her hands on mine when she finished.

The will I had to resist her moments ago disappeared as I took my hand from her grip and wrapped it around her shoulder pulling her into me with my forearm.

Her head leaned against mine and I just held her there and closed my eyes, listening to her heart beating rapidly against my chest. She must have been able to feel mine too, because it was absolutely racing.

We stayed like this for about five minutes before I pulled away to look at her.

She looked up at me with those beautiful green eyes and I noticed a small bruise on the right side of her face and pushed back suddenly.

"That fucker hit you too?" I seethed.

"Yes. Right before you walked in," she said, never looking away from me.

"Mother fucker," I said, taking my good hand and gently caressing the area.

My feelings were so strong for this woman. It hurt me so much to see her physically harmed.

She closed her eyes as I held her face with my hand and rubbed my thumb gently across the bruise.

"I am so sorry this happened, Allison," I whispered.

"Thank God you were here. I can never thank your mother enough for sending you tonight. And I'll never be able to repay you," she said.

My emotions were running wild and I pulled her head back toward my chest, holding her there.

I didn't know if I could ever let her go tonight. She had been through hell, but she still looked so incredibly stunning even with mascara running down her cheeks and a bruise on her face.

Looking down, for the first time, I realized she was wearing such a hot little outfit and wondered if she had dressed that way for me. But instead, she got Nate showing up. That thought made me sick all over again.

After many minutes passed while I held her head to my chest, listening to her heartbeat, she looked up at me with those beautiful, green eyes again and we continued to stare into each other. But this time, instead of pulling her face back into my chest, I placed my hand on her chin, pulled her mouth straight into mine and buried my tongue down her throat.

CHAPTER 17

ALLISON

Lying in Cedric's arms felt like home. He was cradling me as we both tried to process what had happened with Nate. I had expected to get close to him in some way tonight, but the circumstances that got us here were far from what I could have ever predicted. His saving me from Nate's advances forced a quicker and more intense connection.

As he held me in his arms, I thought about how much this man's mere existence had consumed my mind over the last two months.

I had imagined being touched by him for so long but never could have predicted exactly how amazing it felt actually being this close to him. I couldn't quite understand my unusual obsession with him that began from that very first time I laid eyes on him at the diner. We hadn't even been around each other for any significant amount of time, but I feel so attached to him, like he was always mine in some way. But that was the problem...he wasn't.

I wanted so badly to kiss him but couldn't muster the courage to make the first move. I closed my eyes and prayed that he wasn't turned off by what happened tonight and that he understood that Nate was a distant part of my past and not a reflection of me.

His heart was beating against mine, and I looked up at him. I didn't say anything, but the voice in my head silently willed him to kiss me.

Please kiss me.

We stared at each other for what seemed like minutes and then he gently put his warm hand on my cheek. I thought he might pull me close to him again, but this time he pulled my face into his and our lips smashed together.

I immediately opened my mouth and let his warm tongue slide into it, feeling a blast of heat from his intense breathing.

At first, he kissed me slowly, alternating between tasting my tongue and kissing me softly on the lips. At one point, his teeth gently brushed against my chin.

I wanted more.

I opened my mouth wider and kissed him harder and faster. He immediately reacted and grabbed my face, plunging his tongue as far into my mouth as it would reach. Our tongues danced roughly and when he moaned, the vibration sent shivers throughout my body.

He stopped kissing my mouth and moved his lips down to my neck, kissing it gently, but stopping just short of my cleavage. This felt so good, but I licked my lips missing the feel of his mouth on them. I wanted his mouth everywhere and closed my eyes, relishing every warm breath on my body.

I wanted him to go lower onto my breasts, but he immediately worked his way up my neck again, but this time his lips were rougher. Our mouths met again and I returned his kiss feverishly, grabbing his shiny, thick hair and running my fingers through it as I pressed my mouth firmly into his.

As our tongues circled one another, his hot mouth tasted like sugar and wine. The taste mixed with his musky scent was driving me mad. The heat of his chest pressed against mine was too much to bear. I sighed into his mouth as we continued to kiss hard and he responded with a louder moan that I felt at the back of my throat.

I had never wanted anyone more in my entire life and felt like I was about to lose it.

I pulled back, never turning away from his electric blue eyes, which were now darker with want. Breathing heavily, he continued to hold my face and stare at me.

My feelings were too strong. I had to do this. I had to know. It was killing me.

"Cedric," I said, my voice raspy. I could feel my armpits sweating.

"Yes?" he whispered, smiling softly at me.

"Your girlfriend…where is she?" I asked, clearing my throat.

Cedric's face turned beet red, but his eyes never moved from mine. He shook his head back and forth as if to snap himself out of a trance. "What? What do you mean?"

"Your girlfriend. Karyn. Karyn Keller."

Cedric moved back suddenly as if taken aback by my knowledge of her name. The sudden absence of his touch and the seriousness of his expression scared me.

Was he mad at me for asking?

"What? How…how…what about Karyn?" he asked, looking confused and a little furious at the mention of her name.

"I saw a picture of you with her in the newspaper," I said.

"The paper? What?" His eyes squinted in confusion.

I nodded. "Yes…in the gossip section. It was taken a few days before Thanksgiving at some fundraiser."

He turned away from me as if to process something and then closed his eyes for a moment, opening them and looking back up at me.

I turned away in discomfort, moving my gaze down to the floor and felt his hand on my chin slowly directing me to look at him.

"Allison. What you saw was me and my EX-girlfriend, Karyn, attending a fundraiser a few days before I ended the relationship for good. I haven't been with Karyn since the day after Thanksgiving."

My heart pounded at his revelation.

"So, you…don't have a girlfriend?" I felt so stupid having confronted him about something that I was apparently misinformed about.

"No. I don't," he said firmly.

Relief washed over me when his intense look turned into a crooked grin.

I shook my head fast, placing my hands over my face. "Oh my gosh. I feel so stupid. I just assumed…I mean, what are the chances it was taken just before you broke up? I'm sorry for prying."

"Please…you had every right to ask. I just mauled your face. If I had a girlfriend, that would obviously make me a real jackass." He laughed.

I laughed nervously, too, noticing that his ears had turned red as a result of my sudden confrontation.

Our signature awkward silence returned for about a minute and Cedric took my hand in his, rubbing it gently with his thumb, looking down deep in thought until he was ready to speak.

"After that night that I drove you home, I couldn't stop thinking about you. I *did* have a girlfriend then. Karyn and I were still dating at that time."

A lump formed in my throat remembering my strong feelings that night, touching his hand as he wrote on mine. Hearing that he did have a girlfriend then upset me immensely. I couldn't help being jealous of anyone that had him in more ways than me.

He continued, "The more days that passed, the more I couldn't get you out of my head, Allison. Karyn and I…we weren't meant to be together regardless of my feelings for you. Some stuff happened over Thanksgiving and I knew I needed to end it, sooner rather than later. So, I did."

I stared in silence at his beautiful face as he continued to speak.

"I went to the diner that following Monday hoping to ask you out. But you didn't seem to want to talk to me. So, I decided not to."

Oh. God. Shit. I was so rude to him that day. The whole thing was making total sense now. I sure had fucked that up.

"Allison, I was floored to see you at my sister's. I was so happy, though, to have another chance to get to know you." He beamed.

After he said that, I really wanted to open up to him. "Cedric…I felt it too in the car that night. When you came into the diner that Monday after Thanksgiving, I had just seen the photo in the newspaper and well…that's why I was cold. I thought you had a girlfriend. I still thought you had a girlfriend up until you told me tonight, but for some reason—" I paused, not knowing how to explain my sudden change of heart in that matter.

"So, wait, you kissed me thinking I had a girlfriend?" Cedric's eyes turned dark again as he gave me a mischievous smile.

I felt flush and was sure my face was red. "I guess I did. But technically, you kissed me first."

"You bad girl."

"Cedric—"

"I'm just kidding, sweetheart," Cedric said, squeezing my knee.

I shivered at his use of that term of endearment. We both laughed and he pulled me toward him and that turned into another round of passionate kissing.

I was on cloud nine after realizing that this man was available and had just confessed that he had been thinking about me like I was thinking about him all of these weeks. I didn't want to ruin this and if I continued to kiss him, it would certainly turn into more because I had very little willpower when it came to him.

So, I reluctantly pulled myself away from him.

"Cedric, I think we should take this slow," my brain said, while my body swore at me, continuing to betray me, still rubbing against him.

He immediately stopped kissing me and placed his forehead on mine, closing his eyes. He said nothing, but I knew this meant he agreed if we kept kissing, there was no turning back. Our attraction was just too strong.

"I think I should go," he said, still leaning against my forehead. "I don't want to, but I need to."

I looked down and noticed the bulge in his pants illustrating that point.

I wanted him to stay so badly. I couldn't stand to be alone tonight. I especially couldn't stand to be away from him.

"Ok," I said, pulling away as he stood up, knowing it was the right thing for tonight.

"Promise me you'll lock your door and you have my number if you need me," he said.

"I do." I smiled.

We walked to the door and stood facing each other as he put his hand on my cheek.

"Listen, I have to fly to L.A. tomorrow night to meet with a consulting client this week. I won't be back until late Thursday. Can I take you out

Friday night?"

"I'd love that," I said.

"Great." Cedric said as his eyes shined.

"Good night, Cedric."

"Good night, Allison."

Cedric gave me a peck on the mouth, and he hugged me tightly for a few seconds.

Then, without another word, he turned around and walked swiftly down the stairs.

I heard the front door shut behind him.

I closed the door to my apartment and leaned against it, my eyes closed and my heart still beating from the elation I was feeling. Elation then turned to emptiness. God, how I wished I just asked him to stay. I couldn't bear being alone tonight and wanted to feel his warm body against mine just one more time. I must have stayed leaning against the door like this for a few minutes until I heard footsteps coming back up the stairs.

CHAPTER 18

CEDRIC

As the cold night air hit me, I was over the moon. Snowflakes were starting to fly and it was well past midnight.

God help me, I was crazy for her.

I managed to put all of my anxiety about my past away for a while. I couldn't think about anything beyond tonight and how she made me feel in the moment. And she returned my feelings.

All this time she had thought I had a girlfriend, which was why she shied away, and I finally had an explanation for her earlier distant behavior.

I scurried to my car across the street and got in. I immediately noticed that I had left the wrapped gift from my mother—my supposed reason for coming here in the first place—on the passenger seat.

Shit.

Should I go back in? I wasn't sure I trusted myself seeing her for another second again tonight. But Mom would be pissed if I had forgotten to give it to her and how would I explain that?

It took all of my willpower to leave her there in the first place. The chemistry between us was unstoppable and would have led to things she probably wasn't ready for. I didn't want to fuck this up, especially because of her working relationship with Callie. I had decided I was going to drop it off in front of her door and text her that it was there after I left.

I grabbed the gift and made my way back up the stairs, but before I could place the gift on the ground in front of her apartment, Allison opened the door, startling me.

"Hey...I heard footsteps. Back so soon?" she said softly, blinking her beautiful long eyelashes.

"Forgot to give you this." I smiled, handing her the present. "Mom would have killed me."

"Thanks." She grinned, taking the small, wrapped box from me but not taking her eyes off mine.

I stood with my left hand in my pocket and since my right hand was still covered in gauze, I placed it firmly behind my back. My hands needed to be in a good, safe place ...away from her where they would inevitably cause me trouble.

Coming back was a bad idea.

Already, I was finding it hard to walk away and stood there frozen.

"Cedric...um," she said before hesitating.

"Allison...I...really...should go," I said, staring at her lips and not moving an inch. That was it. My last attempt to leave, but my body stayed in place. So help me God, if she said anything about staying now, I would be a goner. I couldn't seem to leave this girl tonight and couldn't even think about how I'm going to spend the entire week in L.A. not getting to see her until Friday.

Then, Allison reached for my arm.

"Cedric, I don't want you to leave. I don't want to be alone tonight. The second you left, I regretted it...and then you came back and I just—"

I cut her off, pulling her mouth toward mine and backed her into the apartment, slamming her door shut behind us with my foot. I. had. no. control.

She walked backwards as I kissed her fiercely on the neck falling back onto the couch, and I lay on top of her. Her body felt so good. Her breasts were pressed against my chest and I could feel that they were soft, definitely not fake, like Karyn's.

Allison smelled like citrus and her erratic breathing was driving me nuts. I have never felt so out of control with a woman before, never wanted anyone this badly.

She pulled back and looked at me. We were both panting and I caressed her face, but I knew what she was thinking, why she pulled back, so I broke from her.

"Allison, you know we don't have to go *there* tonight, right? I could just stay and we can do…you know…*this*…without…*that*. I don't want you to think I expect anything more than just being with you tonight. I know we haven't known each other for very long…but I just…love…being with you."

"I love being with you too, Cedric. Yes, I think it's best if we don't go there tonight. It's too soon…but I am really glad you came back."

Allison hugged me and I buried my nose in her neck, breathing in the scent of her skin deeply.

I lifted her off the couch and pulled her into the bedroom. We both collapsed onto the bed, exhausted from earlier. I lay down behind her and breathed in her fruity scent mixed with shampoo. *She smelled amazing.* I kissed the back of her neck softly until she fell asleep in my arms, the sound of her breathing my lullaby.

This girl is going to be the end of me, I thought before drifting to sleep.

***

I woke to the smell of eggs, bacon and coffee coming from Allison's kitchen.

I got up from her bed and snuck into the bathroom off the hallway to catch a glimpse of myself in the mirror and take a leak before meeting her for breakfast.

I looked like ass, so I wet my hair down and rubbed some toothpaste over my teeth with my finger. I lifted the toilet seat and peed, careful to return the seat to its original position. I sure didn't need to be making that mistake so soon.

I had slept in my clothes, which were now wrinkled but would have plenty of time to go home, change and pack before my flight to L.A. tonight.

I snuck down the hallway to the kitchen, catching sight of Allison. She hadn't noticed me yet. She had talk radio on low and was cooking at the stove, her long hair cascading down her back. This beautiful woman was making me breakfast and I was tempted to sneak up behind her and kiss her neck, but I just stood there staring, amazed at my willpower last night and amazed at how lucky I was to be here. There was no doubt in my mind that she was too fucking good for me, in every way.

I walked over to her and gave her a peck on the cheek. She jumped at the surprise of seeing me.

"Good morning." She smiled.

"Good morning. Thanks for doing all this." I wrapped my arm around her waist and kissed the top of her head. I couldn't help myself.

"It's the least I could do after what you did last night for me," she said sweetly.

Allison separated the eggs onto two different plates and placed three slices of bacon onto each one. I grabbed two mugs from the cabinet to start pouring the coffee.

"Oh, do you mind grabbing that one for me?" She gestured to a different mug that had a picture of J.J. from the show *Good Times* on it. I shook my head and laughed out loud.

"This is your favorite mug?" I asked surprised.

"It is. I don't know why. It puts me in a good mood." She laughed.

That smile—Allison's not J.J.'s—made me wish I wasn't going to L.A. tonight.

I poured the coffee into the mugs, placed them on the table then sat down.

Allison grabbed cream and sugar and two pieces of toast and joined me.

"These are the best scrambled eggs I have ever tasted," I said, devouring them. It was the truth.

Allison grinned. "The key is to not mess with them too much when you're cooking them, and I add a dash of milk. I'm glad you like them."

I inhaled the breakfast and helped her clean up the table. We walked over to the couch and sat down, our bodies turned toward each other.

"Do you have to work at all today or just get ready for your trip?" Allison asked.

"No work. The office is closed until tomorrow. I wish I didn't have to go to California."

"Me too." Allison grabbed my hand and I entwined my fingers with hers.

She gestured for my other hand, the one wrapped in gauze.

"We should take a look at that," she said.

"I guess you're right." I removed my good hand from hers and started to undo it until Allison stopped me.

She took over, unwrapping it carefully. It looked a lot better than I expected but was still a little red and bloody.

She got up and returned with peroxide and cotton and began cleaning my hand.

She then did something that blew me away. Before wrapping the hand back in fresh gauze, she took my nasty looking hand up to her mouth and kissed it gently right on the wound, closing her eyes.

I closed my eyes, too, overwhelmed by the raw emotion I felt from that gesture but didn't do or say anything, just watched her as she wrapped my hand in gauze again.

"Thank you, Allison." I whispered.

She couldn't possibly imagine how much I needed to have her right now.

"You're welcome." She moved in toward me and placed her head on my shoulder. I pulled her close to me and we sat like that for a minute.

"Do you have to work at the diner today?" I asked.

"No, I would have been there by now. I took today off and go back tomorrow."

We sat in silence for about a minute then I turned to her and kissed her on the forehead when she looked up at me.

There was so much I wanted to say to her. I didn't know where to begin.

"Allison…if you don't mind my asking, was Nate your last boyfriend? Is there anyone else?"

She straightened herself up as if to prepare to answer my question.

"No, there isn't. I haven't dated anyone since Nate. The whole thing was just such a huge disappointment. Everything was so normal in the beginning with him. Alcoholism is a real beast."

"Yeah, but not all alcoholics are violent. Had he tried anything like that before?" My body cringed at the thought.

"He never tried to rape me, but he did hit me, like I said, the one and only time before last night. That was it. I broke up with him the second he put his hand on me."

"I am so sorry, but I'm glad you were smart enough to leave," I said, suddenly wanting to find Nate again and finish the job.

"Yes. I had never experienced violence in my life. It was just Mom and me since forever. It was a peaceful existence until she died. Everything seemed to fall apart after that." Allison looked down.

I hated seeing her sad. "Things fell apart in ways other than Nate?" I asked.

"Well, Nate happened and that's also when I dropped out of school. My whole life just changed. I felt like I didn't have a purpose and overall I just missed my Mom. It's strange to not have her around to talk to anymore, to be alone. But I have been doing my best."

I put my hand on her knee. "You're not alone, and I know she is watching over you. Hell, I wouldn't be surprised if she had a hand in my showing up last night."

She smiled. "I would love to believe that, Cedric. Lately, things have really turned around, especially since I met Callie and Lucas."

I loved hearing that. "I wish I didn't have to leave tonight," I said.

Allison abruptly changed the subject. "Cedric, what about you? Were you and Karyn serious?"

"No. I mean, we dated for a while exclusively, but the chemistry wasn't there. To be honest, we couldn't have been more different. I really want to settle down with someone who shares my family values, but mostly, those feelings you need to have to want to be with someone forever were not there for me with Karyn."

"I see," Allison said trying to process my answer.

I suddenly felt the urge to be honest with her. She deserved at least *some* honesty, seeing as though I didn't have the balls to tell her the real reason I even met her in the first place.

"I have dated a lot of women, Allison, I am not gonna lie. Most of the women I have dated have been about sex and nothing more. I want more than that out of life now. Karyn was the closest I had come to a serious relationship, but that didn't hit the mark, not by a long shot."

"How many women are we talking?" Allison laughed nervously.

I hesitated, but I wanted to be up front.

"A lot...well into the double digits. But I was protected each and every time with them. Don't worry. I always used, you know, condoms and get myself checked regularly. I wouldn't put myself at risk like that or put anyone else at risk. I don't want that life at all anymore though. I had gotten hurt after a relationship when I was younger and I vowed never to let that happen again. So, I let myself think that sex was all I wanted. But I am realizing more and more lately that it's not all I want anymore."

I stared at her attempting to give her a subliminal message that *she* was what I wanted. I couldn't tell her that yet in so many words.

"What *do* you want, Cedric?" Her blunt question startled me.

I closed my eyes for a moment, trying to process my answer.

"I want it all. I want to wake up in the morning next to someone who rocks my world in every way. Someone who I am so physically attracted to that I can't keep my hands off her but who at the same time fulfills me in other ways, emotionally, on a deeper level. I want to be with someone who makes me never want to be with another single soul and someone who makes me want to be a better person."

I want to be with you, but I don't deserve you.

***

Allison and I spent a couple of hours on her couch getting to know all that we missed in each other's lives up until now.

She told me about growing up in the Roslindale section of Boston, how she used to dance and sing in the Boston Latin School show choir and how she almost married her high school boyfriend before realizing he wasn't the one.

She opened up to me that her mother came out to her as gay when she was a teenager and that her mother's longtime partner had died when Allison was only five. Her mother never met anyone else or fell in love after that. She floored me with her openness and she seemed to trust me enough to tell me anything. That warmed my heart and hurt at the same time.

I told her about growing up in Dorchester with my family, showed her my bullet mark from the accidental drive by, and we found out that we both used to go to Castle Island a lot as kids.

I told her as much as I could…up until Chicago. That was the point I had to stop or rather, skipped right over. She opened up to me about everything, and I gave her only half of myself. But it was too soon to tell her everything, and I wasn't ready to lose her just yet.

As a matter of fact, I couldn't wait to see her again after my trip, and I hadn't even left her yet.

"It's 1:00. You better get going if you need to pack," Allison said.

"Shit. I do."

I got up and she walked me to the door. I embraced her as hard as I could, pulling her mouth toward mine one last time. I could have stayed here all day, so I had to physically rip myself back with force and step away.

Allison stood in the doorway. "Bye, Cedric."

I stood staring at her just shaking my head in awe of her beauty. "I can't wait to take you out Friday night," I said.

"Me too. Text me when you get there, okay?" she said.

I was touched that she would be worrying about me. I knew I would be thinking about her every second of this trip.

CHAPTER 19

ALLISON

Smelling him on my shirt for the hundredth time, I tried to imagine that he was still here. I still couldn't believe everything that had happened in less than twenty-four hours, on Christmas, no less.

I had spent the day cleaning my apartment and doing laundry downstairs in a daze, replaying every moment since he burst through the door and saved me from Nate.

Sitting on the couch, I looked down at the two Alex and Ani charm bracelets that Cedric's mother had given me for Christmas, admiring them for being the reason that Cedric came to me. Each silver bracelet had a single charm, one saying "Thank You" and the other had the Virgin Mary, an ode to both of our Catholic upbringings.

I looked down at my watch. Cedric's flight was at 6:00, so he would be in L.A. sometime before midnight. I wanted to stay up to see if he would text me when he landed. I knew that was lame, but I couldn't help myself. It was only 11:00, so I decided to watch the Sex and the City marathon to occupy my mind.

As I watched the character Samantha put sushi on all over her body to surprise her boyfriend Smith, my phone chimed, and I grabbed it.

Cedric: Just landed. Can't stop thinking about you.

My heart fluttered, and I typed.

Allison: Me too. I miss you already. Get some rest. I know you must be tired.

Cedric: I am. Will you be around tomorrow night?

Allison: Yes. What do you have in mind?

Cedric: I'd like to Skype with you. Do you have Skype?

Allison: I do. Send me an invite. My Skype name is: AllisonAbraham1984

Cedric: Awesome. "See" you tomorrow night. Look for me about 10:00 your time. I should be done with my meetings by then. Good night.

Allison: Good night, Cedric.

I put the phone down and sighed. Oh, God. I had it bad for this man.

A few minutes passed and my phone chimed again. My heart melted at the single and last text from Cedric.

Cedric: ♥

***

It was a miracle that I was able to stop thinking about him long enough to sleep last night. When my alarm sounded, I jolted out of bed with a newfound zest for life. I hoped I wasn't setting myself up for heartbreak.

Cedric had told me he had been with a lot of women sexually. That sort of intimidated me.

I told him last night the truth, that I had only been with three men my entire life: my high school boyfriend, Trent, my mid-twenties boyfriend, Sean…and Nate. But at the same time, I couldn't wait to experience what every one of Cedric's women had.

***

"Allison, you look like you have something up your sleeve." Delores turned to me as she wiped the diner counter.

"It's that obvious, huh?" I smiled, not being able to contain the fact that I was on cloud nine.

"Is it a man?" Delores asked.

"Yes…It's Cedric, actually," I whispered as I poured a cup of coffee for a man at the counter.

"Cedric? *The Cedric*? Blue Eyes? I thought he had a girlfriend?"

"No, apparently, they had broken off after that picture I showed you was taken. It's a long story."

I tried to condense it as best I could and relayed what happened Christmas night to Delores.

"Honey, I don't know how you resisted doing the deed with him. That guy is the hottest thing on two feet and he rescued you, at that. I have to give you credit. I would have been all over him like Ben Gay on an old person." She laughed.

"Yeah, tell me about it. Believe me, it wasn't easy. I'm not sure how much longer I'll be able to behave." I winked.

***

Nervous anticipation consumed me at home that night. I brought home takeout sushi and forced it down, my excitement taking away my appetite. A glass of wine was definitely needed, so I opened a bottle of cold Pinot Grigio and poured myself a large one.

After I had loosened up, I wanted to feel sexy for my Skype session with Cedric, so I perused my closet for something cute to wear. I decided on a pale pink tank top that had a thin border of pink sequins on the top. My house was warm, so the tank top in the middle of winter wasn't totally inappropriate. I put on a tighter, sexy pair of jeans and left my feet bare.

In the bathroom, I ran a blow dryer through my already dry hair to touch it up, did up my eyes and put some lip-gloss on.

It was only 8:53. I decided to go onto Skype to see if Cedric had sent me an invitation to be added as a contact. He did. His user name was CedricCallahan99. I accepted the invitation, of course and could see that he was not online yet.

I finished my glass of wine and sat on my bed, breathing in and out slowly to try and relax and put on some soft music, closing my eyes.

As it got close to 10:00, my nerves started to act up again.

It was 9:55 now. I began to wonder if I was supposed to call him or him call me. I decided it was best if I waited for him to call me. The minutes dragged on.

When 10:00 rolled around, my heart really started pounding.

Jesus, what was wrong with me? I wasn't even going to be with him. We were thousands of miles apart. I couldn't stand the anticipation.

At 10:05, I jumped at the sound of Skype telling me that CedricCallahan99 was online. Ahhhh!

My excitement was short-lived because it was 10:08, and he still hadn't called, so I convinced myself that maybe he was waiting for me to call, since he appeared to be online. I impulsively hit the "call with video" button.

After three times, the ringing stopped, and I could see the video start to load. My pulse raced at the unexpected sight of what I was met with.

CHAPTER 20

CEDRIC

I sat by the Santa Monica Pier, taking in the sights and the ocean as I ate some of the best Mexican food I had ever tasted. It was nice to be in California in December, but I wished she were here with me. I had another couple of hours before my afternoon meeting at KLAG-TV and decided to drive down here to clear my head first.

It hadn't even been two days, and I was falling harder for her than I could have imagined. I missed feeling her next to me, sleeping next to her. Immense sadness came like a wave crashing in the ocean nearby when I realized that I was tricking myself into believing that she might not leave me if she found out the truth.

I wanted to stay in denial forever.

I needed more time with her; I would regret it forever if I left her behind and wasn't ready to leave her, even though it might have been the right thing to do.

I needed a cigarette, but was trying to make a commitment to be a better person for her. She didn't strike me as the type to appreciate me blowing smoke in her face...or for that matter, what I was really doing, I suppose, blowing smoke up her ass.

Amusement ride music and the sound of children laughing faded into the distance as I walked to my rental car and sped onto the freeway back toward Los Angeles.

***

I arrived just in time to meet the news director and general manager at KLAG.

After a station tour, we went over some new theme music tracks for their shows and they showed me footage of their on-air talent.

I met with a few of the top personalities one-on-one to critique each's presentation individually behind closed doors.

The last meeting was with news anchor Brandi Brady, an attractive petite redhead who anchored the 5:00 newscast. After viewing her demo, I had to say, she impressed me with her top-notch look and delivery, and I asked her who represented her.

"I'm a free agent right now, actually. Do you know any takers?" Brandi crossed her legs in front of me and licked her lips flirtatiously. I could tell when a woman was sending me signals.

"Actually, J.D. Westock is always looking for new talent to represent. It would be a conflict of interest for me to entertain representing you myself, since I am a consultant for your employer KLAG, but I'm sure one of our other agents would be happy to set up a meeting with you."

"I was hoping to set up a meeting with *you*, Cedric," Brandi replied firmly, her eyes glancing down, sizing me up slowly.

"Oh?" I said, knowing full well what she was getting at from the way she looked at me and licked her lips.

"I am very impressed by your knowledge and would love to hear more about what it is you do at J.D. Westock. You have quite the reputation. I was hoping you'd let me show you around tonight. I could meet you at your hotel after my shift is over."

Well, fuck, could she be more direct?

"That's nice of you Brandi, really it is, but I'm going to have to pass. I have another meeting tonight."

"Ok, Cedric. Well, I better be going, I need to get ready for the broadcast." Brandi exited the room, looking back at me flirtatiously.

"Bye, Brandi." I watched her walk away. If this were three months ago,

Brandi would have likely ended up naked in my bed tonight. It wasn't that she wasn't appealing, but I was so wrapped up in Allison, I had no desire for anyone else.

***

After a sushi dinner at Koi with the station management, I finally made it back to my hotel room.

All day and night, all I could think about was Allison and lying in bed talking to her on Skype tonight.

One day in Cali was enough; I couldn't get back to Boston fast enough and I had two more days here, with meetings at two other stations.

I logged into Skype to turn my status to online and figured I had a few minutes to jump in the shower before calling Allison.

I took off my suit jacket and was about to unbutton my shirt when I heard a knock at the door. I stupidly opened it without checking the peephole and was surprised to find Brandi Brady standing there in a tight, red dress with ample cleavage.

Shit.

She pushed her way in before I could tell her I was not interested.

"I heard your meeting wrapped up. I thought I would come over and keep you company." She started touching my shoulder suggestively and I instinctively moved back.

"Brandi, um…I appreciate that, really I do…but—"

Brandi cut me off. "Look…I am going to be direct with you, Cedric. When you walked into the station today, I couldn't believe how hot you were, that I could be so attracted to someone. I have never wanted to fuck someone so badly in my life. I want nothing more than to experience that with you tonight. There…I said it. This isn't about business; it's about pleasure. No strings attached. No one has to know."

Tell me how you really feel.

I wasn't really sure what to say to her as she sat on my bed looking up at me. I actually felt sad for her. I hated to think that I would have taken advantage of her a few months ago, but I probably would have, as pathetic as this situation was. But now, tonight…I really only felt sorry for her, and there was no way I would fuck up my situation with Allison for a cheap thrill.

"Brandi, wow. I am so flattered…believe me. If this were a few months ago, things might have been different, but I'm sort of involved with someone right now, so…"

"*You* have a girlfriend?" Brandi interrupted.

Allison wasn't technically my girlfriend—yet—but I felt like my heart belonged to her from that very first day in the diner. I lied to Brandi anyway.

"Yes, I do, Brandi. I'm sorry," I said.

"Okay, Cedric. From what I had heard about you, I didn't think you were the girlfriend type. But if you say so, that's all I need to hear. If you change your mind, you know where to find me. You won't regret it." Brandi kissed me on the cheek, handed me her card and walked out the door.

I had lost track of the time. It was past ten.

I looked at myself in the mirror and realized I had a lipstick mark on my cheek. Even though it was time to call Allison, I ran into the shower and took a quick one, washing my face vigorously and wetting back my hair.

When I got out, I wrapped a towel around me and immediately heard the computer ringing on Skype. I knew it was Allison, probably wondering why I was online but not calling, so I ran to the laptop, out of breath, but excited and picked up. It took a few seconds for the video to load and when it did, she took my breath away.

"Hey, beautiful," I said softly.

"Cedric! Oh my God…you are practically naked!" Allison laughed.

I truthfully was so excited to hear the phone, I had forgotten I was only in a towel and dripping from the shower.

"Yeah…about that. I was just getting out the shower, but I didn't want to not pick up, so, yeah…I am only in a towel." I laughed at myself as Allison chuckled along with me. Her laugh was wonderful.

"Hold on, okay?" I said as I got up and returned to the bathroom, coming out in baggy flannel pajama pants and a white wife beater shirt.

"You didn't have to get dressed on my account," Allison said.

"Well, I figured you already had enough of a show for one night." I laughed.

"I didn't mind. You have a nice body, and I like your tattoo," she said.

"Thanks."

I was hoping she would drop the subject of the tattoo. I didn't want to have to lie to her about its meaning.

"What does the tattoo mean? I actually first noticed it when you were changing that light bulb in Callie's room. It's some sort of cross and the word ART?" Allison asked.

Fuck.

Her inquiry was innocent. She couldn't have known the meaning of the tattoo. I hated lying to her.

"Yeah, it was just a stupid thing I did one night. It's kind of grown on me, but it better because I'm stuck with it, right?"

I attempted to avoid having to explain the meaning of ART.

"What does ART mean?" she asked.

Here we go.

"Ugh…it's kind of a long story. I'll explain it to you some other time."

My heart pounded hoping she would drop the subject of the meaning. It seemed the Gods were on my side tonight when she playfully asked, "Can I get a closer look?"

"I don't know about that. If I show you mine, you might have to show me yours." I hoped she knew I was joking.

"Okay. I mean if that's what you want, we can do that."

Holy shit. She wanted to play.

Allison gave me a look that was an exact cross between innocent and naughty and I could tell she was half serious.

She was wearing a tight tank top with nothing underneath and I could feel my dick getting hard from the mere thought of seeing her bare skin. Lying in bed and being this close to her, even just on Skype, was driving me mad.

"Okay, you want a close up of my tattoo?" I said mischievously.

"Yes, please." Allison smiled.

I lifted my shirt and moved the laptop so that she could see the side of my torso. "What do ya think?"

"I think it's gorgeous," she said.

"Well, I think *you're* gorgeous," I said as I pulled my shirt back down and repositioned the computer.

"Thank you," she said sweetly.

After another moment of us just starting at each other smiling had passed, Allison spoke. "Cedric, tell me something about yourself that would surprise me."

My eye twitched as the irony of that question hit me.

God, she had no idea, but I wasn't going to let my mind go to that dark place tonight. Not tonight.

"You first," I said, giving myself time to recover from that question.

Allison smiled and closed her eyes to think for a second.

"Okay...well, let's see. Something that would surprise you...okay...well, I was once in the Miss Massachusetts pageant!"

"No fucking way. You...a pageant girl?"

"Yeah...my mother convinced me to enter and I actually placed third runner-up."

"Third-runner up? There is no way that pageant is based on beauty then, cuz you would have won if that were the case."

"Aw, thanks...but no...see, there's this little thing called talent? And well, I guess they didn't appreciate my rendition of *Wind Beneath my Wings.*"

I threw my head back. "You did *not* sing that song?"

"I did...and it sucked ass."

I lost it at her use of that term, which I used a lot too.

"Hey...but still third runner-up, it couldn't have been that bad!" I said, wiping my eyes.

"Your turn," she said.

I closed my eyes and thought about it.

"Okay…I know…something that would surprise you is that I have a bit of a musical past myself."

"Oh yeah?"

"My brother Caleb and I used to rap, actually. We had an amateur rap group as teenagers called Triple C."

"Triple C?" she asked.

"Yeah: Triple C for Cedric, Caleb, Callahan. We thought we were the shit. I used to write the lyrics and Caleb did the beats. We had the baggy jeans falling off our asses and everything…Marky Mark and the Funky Bunch wannabees." I chuckled, shaking my head at the thought of how ridiculous we were.

Allison covered her mouth and shook in laughter then shouted, "Rap me something!"

"Seriously?" I asked.

"Yes! Come on…show me what you can put together in three minutes," she said.

My head fell back in disbelief and laughter. She was actually gonna make me do this?

"Okay. Three minutes. Hold on," I said.

I walked over to the hotel room desk and grabbed the pad of paper and pen.

Returning to the bed, I began to write down some lines, laughing to myself at how stupid this was, but I wanted to make her laugh and show her I was up for anything.

Allison stared at the screen for those few minutes smiling and giggling, watching me write.

I looked at the alarm clock. My three minutes were up so I returned to the screen. "Okay…ready? This is for you, sweetheart."

I quickly grabbed my sunglasses and put my baseball cap on sideways and began to sing, gesturing with my hands.

I met her in a diner.
Never seen a girl finer.

She gave me such a thrill.
I left a fifty-dollar-bill.

Left my credit card behind.
But you know I didn't mind.
Took a Ride Unplanned.
Wrote her digits on my hand.

Found out she works with my SIS-ter…
Before I even kissed her.
She tasted so divine.
Now, I want to make her mine.

Allison's face was in her hands, and she was laughing so hard that she had to wipe her eyes. I loved being able to make her laugh.

She lifted her blushing face. "Oh my God. I can't believe you put that together in three minutes! Thank you. That was awesome!" she said.

"You're welcome, beautiful."

After a pause, the mood got quieter.

I wish you were here. You know that?" I said.

"What would we do if I were?" Allison asked.

The images that flashed in my imagination were suitable for mature audiences only.

"Hmmm…let's see. There's this lovely mini bar over there. I might have offered you a frozen Snickers bar if you behaved."

Allison laughed. "What else?" she said.

"Well, I could have interested you in a pay per view movie." I joked.

"That sounds like fun. Where would be watching the movie?"

"I'd probably be in the bed and I'd make you sit over there on that nice hotel sofa across the room."

"Oh really?" Allison's raised her eyebrows in jest.

I laughed. "Ok, maybe not. Maybe I would have you right here next to me and with the way I am feeling right now, that would be really dangerous.

"How are you feeling, Cedric?" Allison whispered.

I paused and gave her the honest answer.

"I am feeling like I want to devour you."

CHAPTER 21

ALLISON

I was pathetic. One simple statement from this man and my underwear was drenched.

I gulped and was sure I turned red. "You want to devour me?"

"Yes," he whispered. "Is that okay?"

His eyes were glowing. I wondered exactly what that meant, and my body reacted to the possibilities.

I silently nodded in agreement into the web cam, closed my eyes and sighed, feeling by body temperature rise.

"I can't wait for Friday, Allison. We never have to do anything you are not ready for…but as soon as you tell me you want it—"

I interrupted. "I want it, Cedric. I want you…all of you."

I couldn't believe I just said that out loud. It was the first time my thoughts escaped my head, and it was like I vomited them right out of my mouth.

Cedric closed his eyes and let out a long, slow breath and nodded slowly. "You have no idea how much I want you, Allison. God, from the moment I first laid eyes on you…"

We stared into each other's eyes at a loss for words. Cedric smiled and had me really wishing I could jump through that screen.

"Cedric, I remember the first time I saw you too, feeling connected to you."

He shook his head and let out a deep breath. "I wanted to kiss you so badly that night in my car."

"Why didn't you?" I asked.

"I should say it was because I had a girlfriend, but that wasn't exactly it. I just didn't have the guts that night. It would have seemed too random. We had just met."

"And the night in Callie's room?" I asked.

"I was *definitely* planning to drive you home that night and was dying to kiss you…but you ran, remember?"

"Yes." I laughed. "I thought you had a girlfriend. It was a self-protective mechanism."

Cedric laughed heartily showing off his beautiful white teeth, which seemed even whiter on the web cam.

I didn't mean to, but I yawned.

"Sweetheart, it's late for you. I know you need to work early tomorrow. Can we please do this again tomorrow night?" Cedric asked.

I loved when he called me sweetheart.

"Absolutely." I smiled. "Same time?"

"I am not exactly sure of my schedule tomorrow. So, I'll text you during the afternoon and let you know what time to log on. Sound good?"

"Sounds great," I said.

"Good night, Allison."

"Good night, Cedric."

Cedric touched his hand to his mouth and blew me a kiss before disappearing from the screen.

***

Mercury, your ruler, is receiving kudos from the Moon, Gemini, resulting in a jubilant day. Romance is in the air, as you crave fun and are easily entertained. Hang on and enjoy the ride!

Well, Wednesday certainly didn't start out like my horoscope predicted. The afternoon spent with Lucas turned out to be quite eventful but not in a good way.

As usual, I was dressed in my Wonder Woman uniform and superhero boots. Today, Lucas' mother, Pat, asked me to take him out on a few errands. I drove with Lucas to a nearby small one-level shopping mall. There was a Walmart inside and a food court where I could have Lucas eat an early dinner and practice using money to pay for his meal. (Yes, I was still wearing the uniform to the mall.)

Lucas liked to go in the mock hurricane machine, so I added the quarters in and let the wind blow in his face repeatedly until he tired of it.

We made our way over to the Chinese takeout restaurant in the food court, and just as we sat down, an indoor train that parents paid to have their kids ride in, started making its way around the mall.

Lucas had always been sensitive to certain sounds, but for some reason, this particular train horn really upset him. As the train approached, he got up from the table so fast and began running down the mall covering his ears.

I abandoned our food and chased after him as fast as I could, but he was such a fast runner. I could only imagine what people were thinking: a grown woman dressed as Wonder Woman chasing after a grown man covering his ears.

Lucas tripped and fell flat on his face before I was able to catch up with him. He had a pretty bad gash on his forehead. By this time, we were far away from the train sound, so he had calmed down. I felt so badly for him but couldn't lift him off of the ground.

A mall security guard helped me hoist him up off the floor and a nice woman got me some paper towel to add pressure to Lucas's cut.

I immediately called his mother to let her know I was going to take him to the walk-in clinic on the way home to make sure he didn't need stitches. It was a pretty bad gash.

***

Pat met us at the clinic, and we had to wait an hour to be seen. By the time the doctor came out, it was almost 7:00 at night. My shift normally ended at 7:00 but I didn't want to leave until I knew he was okay.

As I sat in the office as the doctor examined Lucas, my phone chimed. It was a text from Cedric.

> Cedric: Hi, beautiful. I can't wait to Skype with you tonight. Would 11:00 your time be too late?

I would stay up until any hour to Skype with him.

> Allison: Not too late at all. Looking forward to "seeing" you.

> Cedric: I would tell you to wear something sexy, but a paper bag would be sexy on you. ;-)

> Allison: If you could only see what I am wearing now.

> Cedric: ????

> Allison: Remember I told you about the 20-year-old man I work with? He has an obsession with Wonder Woman and I have to dress like her or else he won't acknowledge me.

> Cedric: LOL. Are you serious?! That is fucking awesome.

> Allison: You should have seen me today at the mall chasing after him in it.

> Cedric: Shit. I would have paid serious money to see that!

> Allison: I have to run. Still with Lucas.

> Cedric: Ok…talk to you at 11.

***

I finally got back to my apartment about 9:00.

Pat had insisted on buying me dinner at McDonald's (Lucas's favorite) before I headed home and thankfully, Lucas did not need stitches because it would have been really fun trying to hold him down for that.

The first thing I did was take a nice hot shower. As I lathered my body with the foamy soap, I closed my eyes and imagined it was Cedric massaging me. I intentionally held off on touching myself because I wanted to do it after I got off of Skype, like last night when I gave myself the most intense orgasm I had ever experienced alone. Cedric had gotten me so worked up. I closed my eyes and thought about his sexy stomach and that tattoo that drove me wild. I really needed to see him again. Friday could not come soon enough.

I got out of the shower and towel dried my hair. I decided to let it air-dry wavy tonight. I put on a fitted, periwinkle blue long-sleeved casual jersey dress and made up my face.

All I needed to do now was sit down, relax with some tea and wait for my call with Cedric.

***

I was surprised when I received a text from Cedric at 10:30.

> Cedric: Hey. Are you home? I got done a little early and so I wondered if you wanted to Skype in like five minutes.

> Allison: Hi. Yes, sure. I'll turn it on.

> Cedric: Can I ask you a favor?

> Allison: Sure. What is it?

> Cedric: Can you show me what you look like as Wonder Woman? Can you wear the costume when we Skype? I've been thinking about it all day since you told me.

> Allison: Are you serious?! I just showered and changed out of it.

Cedric: Ok. :-(Never mind.

Allison: You really want to see it?

Cedric: Yes!

Allison: Okay, I'll change.

Cedric: Really? Yes! Just for that, I'll wear my Clark Kent glasses. My contacts are acting up anyway and I want to be able to see this clearly.

Allison: I'll bet you look sexy in glasses. See you in a few.

Cedric: xo

I laughed hysterically as I ripped off my dress and grabbed my Wonder Woman outfit, which consisted of a strapless, red tank with gold accents and a royal blue mini skirt with stars. I topped it off with the gold crown and put on my red thigh-high boots. In public, I wore a blue cardigan over the top, but I would leave it off for Cedric. I couldn't believe he was making me do this…but I would have done anything for him at this point.

I sat on my bed in character now, feeling like a goof, wondering what Cedric would look like in his Superman glasses.

I jumped at the sound of my phone. It was another text from Cedric.

Cedric: Are you in your costume?

Allison: Yes. I turned on Skype. I am waiting for you to go online.

Cedric: I am not going to be able to Skype tonight after all, sweetheart.

What?

Allison: Okay. What happened?

Cedric: Well, for one there is no wireless in your hallway.

I read over the text again. There was no...wireless...in...MY HALLWAY?

I shrieked, ran to the door and opened it up the sexiest man in glasses I had ever seen.

CHAPTER 22

CEDRIC

As I ran on the treadmill at the hotel gym on Wednesday morning, I got the call that would change my week entirely.

The general manager at KABV-TV cancelled my meeting scheduled for that day, so I immediately called my Thursday morning client and cancelled them too. Figuring I would now have to come back to L.A. another time to meet with KABV, I would reschedule both meetings for another time. Dripping with sweat, my heart raced as I thought about feeling her next to me again. This meant I could go home and be with Allison again almost two days early, so I wasted no time getting myself on the 11:00 am plane back to Boston.

***

On the flight home, I closed my eyes and thought about how I should surprise her. I decided I would text her on my layover in Newark and pretend I was still in California, arranging the time to Skype tonight. I should have enough time to drop by my condo, shower and change, assuming no delays.

The flight attendant startled me out of my fantasies when she offered me a drink. I opted for a glass of Merlot to help me relax. As I slowly sipped the wine, nerves overcame me as I pondered whether I was making the right decision diving headfirst into a romantic relationship with the one woman on Earth that should be forbidden.

Unfortunately, she was all I could think about and all I wanted.

So many people could get hurt if things didn't work in my favor, not only Allison and me, but Mom and Callie. Mom would find out the truth about everything if...*when*...I had to tell Allison. When *would* I tell her the truth? I wasn't ready to go there and needed to make sure she trusted me first. More than anything, selfishly, I needed to have her...at least once...before I ever possibly lost the chance. If that meant I was going to Hell, then so be it.

A cornucopia of emotions flooded through me on that flight home: guilt, longing, grief for something I hadn't even lost yet. Allison wasn't just special for what she meant to me before I laid eyes on her in that diner that first day. Every moment spent with her since, had made me realize feelings in myself that I thought were long dead and some feelings I had never experienced before. Maybe, by some miracle, there would be a way to make her understand why I needed to wait to tell her the truth.

The fasten seatbelt signal snapped me out of my ruminations as the plane prepared to land.

When we arrived in Newark, I had only a half-hour layover. The first thing I did was text Allison. When she responded to me about the Wonder Woman costume she had to wear for work, I nearly lost it. That sounded so sexy, even though I knew she wasn't intending to be. We planned to Skype later tonight, which really meant I would be showing up at her apartment to surprise her. The confused emotions I felt on the plane from L.A. disappeared as my excitement grew.

The trip to Boston, which was a quick commuter flight, seemed to take forever. The jet was smaller and I was sandwiched between two older women, one of whom smelled like gasoline while the other ate tuna. When we touched down at Logan Airport, I grabbed a cab to my condo and was so happy to be off that plane.

***

It felt amazing to be home. I had about a half-hour to shower and change before heading over to Allison's house and I really needed to look good for her tonight.

Unfortunately, the dry air on the plane did a number on my eyes; with my contacts acting up, I would be wearing my glasses. My hair was gelled to perfection and I wore dark blue Levis and a navy blue henley, spraying on ample cologne and grabbing a few condoms…just in case.

I was pretty confident Allison wanted to have sex tonight, but I wasn't going to assume anything; After all, I would be springing this visit on her, but I needed to be prepared.

I was ready to go, but running earlier than our scheduled Skype call. I decided to head over there anyway, impatient as hell to see her.

On the drive to her house, I couldn't get the image of that that friggin' sexy Wonder Woman costume out of my head. By the time I pulled into a parking spot around the corner from her apartment, I decided to text her to let her know I was ready to Skype early and to ask her to wear the costume for our "call." Can't blame a man for trying, right? I was amazed when she actually agreed and I got hard just imagining what she would look like opening that door.

I sat in the car for a few minutes before we were set to Skype and then got out, walking around the corner to her house. Luckily, the front door was open and I only needed to make my way up the stairs before texting her one last time to let her know that I couldn't Skype because I was actually texting from her hallway.

After I typed the words, "no wireless in your hallway," there was a pause as I stood outside her door, my heart pounding violently.

I heard her shriek.

"What?!" Allison squealed from behind the door and this made me laugh out loud.

When she opened the door, my heart nearly stopped at the sight of her.

I rushed into her and buried my nose in her neck, breathing her fruity scent in. She squeezed me so tightly; I could feel her soft breasts against my chest bursting through the red tube top.

I stepped back taking her in and grabbed her face, pulling her lips into mine, kissing her passionately.

She pulled back, suddenly, panting from my kiss. "Cedric...oh my God. Wha...what are you doing back tonight?" she asked, her face flushed and her hands shaking as she cupped my chin.

I gave no response, just stared at her, grabbing her trembling hands and kissing them softly.

Allison looked like there should be a halo of light surrounding her. I felt like a horny preteen whose favorite superhero just came to life out of a comic book. Her dark hair was shiny and flowing underneath a golden crown. Her beautiful breasts spilled out of the sparkly, red strapless top and I could see her hard nipples through the fabric...and the boots...*the boots*...red thigh-high boots.

"God, you are so fucking beautiful," I whispered, pulling her toward me again, kissing the bottom of her neck hard and working my way up to her lips, which she parted as I thrust my tongue into her mouth hungrily.

She moaned as I continued to plunge my tongue deeper into her mouth, never quite getting enough. With each moan, I got harder imagining what she would sound like when I was inside of her.

I pulled back after a few minutes, still holding her face in my hands. "I couldn't wait another night Allison. My meeting was cancelled today, so I got on the first flight I could. I hope this is a good surprise?"

Allison's green eyes beamed with golden speckles. "Cedric...this is the best surprise." She smiled as she ran her fingers through my hair, looking at me affectionately.

"Thank you for letting me see you in this," I said, rubbing my hands up and down her arm, glancing down at her breasts, to her flat stomach then down to her legs.

Laughing, she reached up, cupping my face with her hand. "Oh my God...you were not kidding about the glasses, too. I love you in them. You look so studious and sexy...totally Clark Kent."

I gave her a mischievous smile and kissed her again. "Glad you like them, sweetheart."

"You must be starved. Can I get you something to eat?" Allison asked.

I stared deeply into her eyes and shook my head. I needed her to know how much I wanted her, how little self-control I had left. "The only thing I am hungry for is you."

With that, Allison pulled me toward her face, taking my mouth into hers and walking backwards as we moved in synch and I pushed her into the bedroom.

I broke away from the kiss for a few seconds to just stare at her and take in the moment.

Looking down at her soft neck, I realized that I had given her a small hickey. I pulled her toward me again, sucking on her neck even harder wanting to mark her over and over again, making her mine.

Pushing her down onto the bed, I continued sucking at her neck and felt her soft hands run through my hair, pushing me down onto her breasts, which I started to kiss gently, licking them in circles through the fabric.

Her panting showed me that she wanted me to keep going.

Dying to suck on her breasts bare, I pushed the fabric of her strapless top down, exposing them. Goddammit, she wasn't even wearing a bra. I wasn't expecting to see them right then and there. Like the rest of her, her breasts were perfect...medium sized, firm, with soft, pink buds. Squeezing them together, I buried my face in them, kissing and licking a line up and down her cleavage as she held onto my hair. Taking turns sucking hard on each of her nipples, it was clearly a weakness for Allison. Her legs rustled while I sucked harder and harder.

Pulling her tube top all the way down her waist, I kissed down the length of her soft, flat stomach, flicking my tongue over her beautiful belly button and kissing my way back up to her breasts, stopping to suck on them some more and then moving upwards back to her mouth.

She gripped my ass in both of her hands as I kissed her. My dick was fully hard, bursting through my jeans and I knew she could feel it pressing against her.

I stopped kissing her to look into her eyes.

She looked up at me with the sweetest smile and just nodded, a silent affirmation for me to keep going.

With that, I kissed her harder, stopping suddenly as my hands developed a mind of their own, reaching down, pulling off her boots one by one, followed by her skirt and then sliding the tube top down her legs.

I looked down at her naked body, covered only by the front of a nude colored lace thong, taking the beautiful view in again as her long hair lay messily across the pillow.

So fucking hot.

She looked at me with an intense longing and pulled my face into hers.

I struggled to unzip my jeans fast enough, pulling them down, leaving on my boxer briefs, which could barely contain my hard-on.

I never remembered feeling that intense kind of longing for a woman ever before. All fearful thoughts about the repercussions were buried deep in the back of my mind. All that mattered in that moment was that Allison seemed to want me just as badly as I wanted her.

As she pulled my shirt over my head, I couldn't wait to feel her skin to skin. I pressed down onto her to feel her breasts against my chest as we grinded fast against each other. I thought I might fucking lose it then and there, feeling totally out of control and knew there was no turning back…so I took off my glasses.

CHAPTER 23

ALLISON

I had fantasized about this moment from the first time I laid eyes on him.

Feeling Cedric's rock hard body rubbing against me in the flesh felt surreal.

Just a couple of months ago, this man was a mere dream, a pure fantasy for me.

Now, we were about to have sex.

His utterly perfect physique definitely made me self-conscious. I had truly never been with a man as gorgeous as Cedric, so chiseled and naturally tan, not a blemish on his skin. My body seemed to react uncontrollably to him and I wondered whether he could feel how wet I was becoming through my barely there underwear.

My heart pounded against his chest as he pressed against me. His heart was pounding too and it excited me to know that he was as turned on as I was.

Sliding my hands down his back, I gripped his firm ass through his boxer briefs and he reacted with a moan, kissing me harder.

Suddenly, I felt the slick tip of his bare, hard penis rubbing against my stomach. It seemed to have burst out of his underwear. Jeez…there was definitely nothing lacking in that department.

Instinctively, I spread my legs apart. His moan vibrated down my throat and he began kissing down my torso stopping at the top line of my underwear.

Then, he went lower and started to kiss my inner thighs softly and I could swear that alone was going to make me lose it. He continued this for some time, starting down at my knees and trailing his tongue up to my underwear line, stopping there at the top of my thighs and returning his kisses back down my leg again. One of the times, he pulled my underwear with his teeth, teasing me as he licked me…everywhere *but there*. My legs quivered and shook with the anticipation of what he was going to do next.

Just when I thought I was going to lose my mind, he ripped my thong apart pushing it down my legs, which I then wrapped around his back.

Cedric looked at me with a wicked grin, shaking his head no and pushed my legs back down off of him. He spread me apart, lowering his mouth downward. I felt his hot tongue invade my sex suddenly and fiercely, as I gripped his thick hair.

I rocked my pelvis in synch with the thrusts of his tongue and screamed out for a pleasure that I had literally never felt before. Every time I would shriek, I could feel the vibration of Cedric's moaning in response.

He continued to devour me for minutes until I couldn't take it anymore. I wanted him inside of me, so I pulled his head up to mine and kissed him hard, pushing his boxer briefs down and opening my legs around him.

Feeling his hot erection against my stomach, I panted in frustration as he took turns sucking hard on each of my breasts. This continued for minutes and I closed my eyes, gripping his hair, lost in the ecstasy of it.

Suddenly, the abrupt coldness of his absence hit me as he lifted off of me, reaching for his pants that were strewn on the floor. I heard the crinkle of a wrapper and lifted my neck to see him sheathing himself with a condom. Cedric looked down at me with glowing eyes and smiled, his chestnut hair now a tousled mess. I couldn't help but smile back at his beautiful face.

"Are you sure you are ready for this?" he whispered, looking down at me longingly and rubbing my stomach with his big hands in slow circles.

I breathed out in a combination of frustration and ecstasy. "Yes, Cedric.

I trust you."

I meant it. I trusted him and had no doubts about what I was about to do.

He closed his eyes and inhaled slowly for a moment at my words, as if he was processing what I said. Was *he* having doubts? I couldn't tell what he was thinking at that moment, but he seemed to be deep in thought and breathing erratically.

When he opened his eyes and stared into mine, I smiled back at him. After a few seconds, he exhaled, reached for my face and cupped my cheek, caressing it with his thumb. He stayed like this for a minute staring at me and then, never taking his eyes off mine, very suddenly lowered himself and plunged into me deeply, claiming me, in one movement. The initial burn quickly turned into a euphoric feeling.

"Fuck...Allison," Cedric whispered into my ear as we moved together slowly.

"Oh...God," I said. Feeling this beautiful man inside me was truly the most amazing thing I had ever experienced. I didn't know if it was because of the sheer size of him or because it had been a while for me, but he seemed to fill me completely, like it was my first time without the pain. It was just the most unbelievable feeling in the world.

I closed my eyes, never wanting the feeling to end and opened them to find Cedric staring into me intently. His eyes never left mine for even a moment. I held onto his back, pushing him deeper and deeper into me.

Cedric was whispering incoherently, but then I clearly heard what he said next.

"I love...this...being inside you. You're the most beautiful woman in the world," he said huskily as he continued to rock into me, his eyes still firmly planted on mine, as we developed a rhythm.

"Aaaaaagh." I moaned, unable to respond with anything more coherent.

"God, I wish I could stay inside you forever." Cedric panted and suddenly began thrusting harder and deeper than before.

With those last words and his change in pace, I could feel myself losing control, climaxing suddenly and unexpectedly. "Cedric, I'm coming."

He seemed relieved to be able to let go. "Oh, God. Come, baby. I'm coming too…holy shit." Cedric's thrusts quickened and I felt his orgasm pulsating inside me while I climaxed.

As we both recovered from that Earth-shattering experience, his movements slowed. He stayed inside of me and slowly kissed my neck.

I closed my eyes trying to relish every moment of being here with him like this. We stayed together silent for quite some time before Cedric spoke.

"That was amazing, Allison," he whispered in my ear as he slowly pulled out of me. He turned over quickly and I heard him remove the condom and discard it.

I turned toward him with my head resting on my elbow. "Cedric, I'm so glad you came home."

"Me too," he said as he pulled me closer into him and rested his forehead against mine. "You have no idea."

CHAPTER 24

CEDRIC

I couldn't believe I almost backed out of the most intense sex of my life. It was the moment I asked her if she was sure, when she told me she trusted me.

I trust you.

Hearing Allison say that really struck a cord, and it was the only moment where I momentarily snapped out of the trance she put me in. I had closed my eyes beginning to doubt whether taking this step with her was a good idea, and everything flashed before me: past, present and future.

By the time I opened my eyes again, the sheer power of her sweet face looking up at me crushed everything else and I buried it all again...by burying myself in her.

Maybe I wouldn't be able to live with myself if the guilt caught up again later, but it was a risk I was willing to take. It was worth it to experience making love to her. Sex with her was different from all of the rest. I hadn't ever experienced the feeling of wanting to completely possess someone and of wanting her to completely own me, to be so completely connected to the person, not just the act.

I had meant it when I said I wished I could stay inside her forever. All of my doubts seemed to disappear there. As long as we were connected, I knew I couldn't lose her. This was the opposite of what I normally felt after sex, which was a feeling of wanting to run, where the connection ended with the orgasm.

It was now the middle of the night and Allison lay sleeping beside me rhythmically breathing so peacefully.

A moment ago, a terrifying dream had awakened me and relief replaced panic when I realized she was still lying next to me.

In the dream, Allison and I were walking in the park, when I suddenly started taunting her like a child in a sing-songy voice, repeating, *"I know something you don't know. I know something you don't know..."* over and over again. She had a terrified look on her face and then I woke up. The dream was brief but just enough to make me sweat profusely and remind me how fucked up this was.

But, thankfully, for now, in reality, she was right here sleeping next to me like a baby. God, I loved hearing the sound of her breathing. I wished she could always be peaceful and that there were no secrets threatening to destroy that. I would inevitably take away that peace, but she had a right to know everything.

Yeah...sleep was not happening for me tonight.

Tempted to kiss her awake, I rolled over away from her to squelch the urge and tried to get some sleep to no avail.

After a half-hour, I turned back around to watch her peaceful face again. There was no way I would ever want to hurt her. Unable to resist, I moved in slowly to softly kiss her on the forehead. She moved a little, still asleep and her breathing changed from the interruption.

At some point after 4:00, I dozed off.

When Allison's alarm went off at 5:30, I jolted awake and noticed her yawning next to me. She would have to leave soon for the diner, but I wasn't about to let her go that easily.

"Good morning, sleepyhead," I said as I leaned over, kissing her on the lips gently.

"Hi," she whispered groggily and pulled me in tighter, kissing me again.

"I wish you didn't have to go to work so darn early," I said, rubbing her back as she got up and sat at the edge of her side of the bed. She was still completely naked and crossing her arms over her breasts, her sudden modesty surprising me.

She continued to look around the room probably for some clothes.

"Do you mind turning around, so I can get up and get dressed?" she asked.

She was blushing and adorable.

I turned around immediately pained at not being able to look at her beautiful ass. "Let me know when it's safe," I said.

After a minute, I heard her say, "Safe."

I slowly turned around to see Allison kneeling on the bed over me, wearing my navy blue shirt, her hard nipples poking through the cotton fabric. There was something so hot about a girl wearing your shirt, particularly when she was as sexy as this one. She had also thrown on a pair of sexy, red satin underwear.

"That looks way better on you than on me, sweetheart," I said, tugging on the bottom to pull her down to me.

She kissed me and as I squeezed her ass, she giggled. "I figured if I wore your shirt, you'd have no choice than to let me ogle your chest over coffee."

I squeezed her and rolled her over pinning her down under me in one fast motion. "Oh, is that what you had in mind? Well, I am happy to oblige on one condition."

Allison pushed my face towards hers. "What's that?" she asked.

"You let me make you coffee and breakfast," I said.

Allison nuzzled my neck. "That sounds awesome. Do you have to work today?"

"I'll probably go into the office at some point, but nothing major going on since I was supposed to be in Cali, so my schedule here is free and clear. How about I come down to the diner for lunch?"

She smiled at my suggestion. "I'd love that."

"Good...because I love being with you," I said as I pulled her toward me into another kiss.

Allison broke away from me and walked away toward the bedroom door not saying anything. She lifted my shirt off and threw it by the threshold.

As I shook my head in disbelief at how lucky I was to be here and to have seen that, I heard the sound of water running in the distance and wondered if she was taking a shower. That thought immediately made me hard and I decided I needed to personally investigate.

When I opened the door to the bathroom just off the hallway, I saw Allison's beautiful, naked silhouette through the frosted glass shower door.

"Hey, uh...I just wanted to make sure you were ok in here," I said through the door.

"Yup...okay...doing just fine, thanks," Allison said teasingly as she rubbed her body with soap slowly.

I struggled to see through the shower door. "Well, you, uh, let me know if you need me for anything in there...okay?"

"Nothing now, thanks."

Okay, that plan backfired. Just as I made my way out of the bathroom, Allison stopped me.

"Actually, can you reach under the sink and grab me a new shampoo? This one is kind of empty."

I moved my way back in and searched under the sink, grabbing a fluorescent green bottle.

She slid open the shower door a few inches, reaching out for the bottle, her face dripping with water and smiled. "Thanks." Then, she slid the shower door closed again.

I walked back out of the room, standing just outside of it, peeking in, not certain whether she knew I was still at the doorway.

I stood frozen in awe watching her lather her beautiful, long hair through the frosted glass. God, how I wanted inside (in more ways than one). Unsure of whether it was okay to just barge in naked, I stood there dazed, staring...*dying*.

As a few minutes passed, and the lathering continued, Allison chuckled.

"You're going to give up...just like that?" She laughed.

I opened the door immediately. "Have you been fucking teasing me this entire time?"

"Well, I was hoping you would give in, actually." She opened the shower door completely exposing her wet, naked body. This time, she covered nothing.

I pushed down on my boxers and couldn't jump in there fast enough. Pulling her slick waist into me, the hot water poured down over us and I slid the door shut.

We kissed slowly as the water gushed between our lips.

Kissing down the length of her body, I kneeled down and just held her stomach to my face, kissing it softly and licking the water that trickled down it.

I paused for a moment and closed my eyes, knowing I would remember this moment forever, no matter what happened with us.

Standing up, I grabbed the sponge, adding some of the green apple body wash she had *(that's where the green apple smell came from!)* and began washing her, starting with her arms and rolling over her breasts, down her stomach and between her legs. Allison panted as I continued to move the sponge back and forth there before it fell to the ground.

She completely floored me when she dropped to her knees and took me deeply into her mouth. Closing my eyes, I relished every moment of her unexpected surprise.

After a few minutes of pure ecstasy, I was about to lose it and pushed her away pulling her up, grabbing her face into my mouth, unable to kiss her hard enough.

We continued to kiss as I lifted her up and wrapped her legs around my waist. Just as I was ready to carelessly plunge into her, someone burst through the bathroom door.

CHAPTER 25

ALLISON

A familiar British accent broke Cedric's and my passion in the shower.

"Holy shitballs!" I heard Sonia yell.

Cedric dropped me to the shower floor, shouting "What the fuck?"

"Sonia? Oh my God! What are you doing back?" I asked, mortified at what she saw.

My roommate wasn't due back from London for another couple of days. I saw her flaming, red hair and giant-breasted silhouette through the frosted glass.

"Ok, so apparently...I missed a lot while I was away. Sorry!" Sonia's voice shook in mortification as she walked out of the bathroom and said, "Um...heading...to the kitchen...yeah." The door slammed shut.

"Your roommate?" Cedric held me close, the water still pouring down on us.

My heart was pounding against his chest. "Yeah." I sighed.

Cedric started to laugh and I quickly followed. All of a sudden, we both started cracking up hysterically under the water. It was awkward, but you had to admit, it was funny.

Cedric shut the water off and squeezed the excess moisture out of my hair, pulling me in for one last kiss before we exited the shower.

I looked up at Cedric embarrassed. "We'll have to join her for coffee, I guess."

"Does coffee cure blue balls?" He winked as he wrapped me in a towel, drying me off.

He grabbed a towel for himself and I enjoyed the view as he wiped down his tight abs and sexy tattoo. He placed the towel around his waist and we exited the bathroom, hurrying to the bedroom to get dressed.

Cedric pulled me in for one last kiss before he held his hand out leading me into the kitchen where I could smell that Sonia had started to make coffee.

Cedric came up from behind Sonia and I laughed when she jumped in surprise.

He held out his hand. "Sonia…I'm sorry about that. I'm Cedric. Nice to finally formally meet you."

I kept waiting for Sonia to let go of his hand, but she continued shaking it in awe. "I figured it was you, Blue Eyes. I couldn't make you out through the steam in there. Nice to meet you, too."

"Blue…what? Blue…balls?" Cedric joked, as he looked over at me, and the three of us all started cracking up.

"Blue Eyes, actually. It's a long story," I said as I smiled over at Sonia, pouring a coffee and taking a seat at the table.

I was definitely going to be late to work, so I decided to call the diner and let them know something unexpected had come up and I would be in around 8:00.

Cedric insisted on cooking us a delicious breakfast of cinnamon French toast that was absolutely divine. The three of us inhaled it and Cedric and I filled Sonia in on everything that happened with Nate and how we bonded that night.

"Holy shit, Allison. I can't believe Nate came after you like that." Sonia sat with her arms crossed in shock. "Where is he now?"

I sighed. "His father is a lawyer. Officer Derin told me that his parents came from out of town and cut some deal where he would enter a special six-month rehab program instead of jail time. I don't know much more than that."

Cedric interrupted. "Well, we have to keep tabs on his whereabouts when he gets out. I don't want him ever touching you or anywhere near you, for that matter, again."

I shivered at his possessive tone and relished the fact that this beautiful man wanted to protect me. Cedric glared at me fiercely with his beautiful eyes, a cross between fear and desire, prompting me to reach for his hand from across the table. He entwined his fingers into mine.

Sonia looked down at our connected hands and glanced up at me with a knowing smile. I knew she was flabbergasted at the bond Cedric and I seemed to have in such a short time and the real conversation with her about this situation would come later, one where she would demand to know every juicy detail.

Sonia stood up from the table to give us some privacy. "Cedric, it was an absolute pleasure. Thank you so much for breakfast. I'm gonna hit the hay for a bit; jet lag is a bitch. We should all go out soon."

Cedric smiled and got up from his seat to give her a hug. "Absolutely."

I loved this man.

I ended up calling in sick altogether and Cedric and I spent the day together, followed by another night at my apartment where the sex was even more intense than the first night.

When we weren't physically connected, we were up most of the night talking about anything and everything. I came to the realization that if this didn't work out, it would be the biggest heartbreak of my life.

***

It took all of my strength to separate from him and head to work the following morning.

Thoughts of him invaded my head all day at the diner as I served customers in a haze.

He had driven me all the way here and we decided that rather than come in for lunch, he would pick me up at the end of my shift. He would spend the morning and early afternoon catching up on some work in the office instead.

As I poured coffee for the hundredth time, I kept replaying our amazing nights together, still feeling the soreness between my legs from the times he had been inside me. There, of course, would have been one additional time, if Sonia hadn't shown up Thursday morning. It was just as well, since we were so caught up in that shower moment, there had been no condom in sight. The idea of having unprotected sex with Cedric thrilled me, though, and I wondered if I should tell him I was already on the pill to regulate my periods. I'd need to make sure he was 100-percent clean first, since he admitted to a man-whore past even though he claimed he always used protection. We'll see. There was plenty of time to discuss that.

My lunch break rolled around and I sat down as I normally did at Mr. Short's table.

"Fancy meeting you here," I said jokingly, since we did this almost every day. Mr. Short lived around the corner and came into the diner for breakfast, lunch and dinner most days. He was a true round the clock regular.

Mr. Short smiled and said, "Allison. You look lovely today."

I took a bite of my grilled chicken salad. "Thanks, Mr. Short," I said, munching on the mixed greens.

"You always look great, Allison, but I have to say, I've been watching you today and you seem to have a certain glow about you."

A hot flash suddenly overcame me at his perceptiveness. "You think?" I definitely had to have been blushing.

Mr. Short smiled. "Does it have anything to do with that handsome, young man I saw drop you off this morning? I saw the way you looked at him. It reminded me of the way Marie used to look at me, God rest her soul."

Okay, I was definitely blushing now. "You saw him walk me to the door?" I asked.

"Yes. In fact, he was parked right outside the window by my booth here. Let me ask you, is your boyfriend religious?"

"He is not technically my boyfriend. Why do you ask?"

"Well, like I said…what's his name?"

"Cedric."

"Well…Cedric…after he dropped you off…I watched him for a bit before he started the car. He took a phone call and when he hung up, he put his head on the steering wheel for a bit and then he made the sign of the cross before driving away."

My heart nearly stopped as Mr. Short described this observation. Why would Cedric make the sign of the cross after taking a phone call? That was bizarre.

"Hmm…well, I can't tell you what it means, Mr. Short, but thank you for telling me."

Mr. Short reached across the table and placed his hand over mine. "Anytime, Allison. You know I am always looking out for you. You're like the daughter I never had."

That wasn't the first time he referred to me like that. It was sweet.and I knew he was just as lonely as I had been for a long time.

Mr. Short then made a fist-like gesture with his hands. "And you can tell Frederic that if he ever breaks your heart, I'll kick his ass military-style."

I belted out laughing at his facetious threat and the fact that he called Cedric, *Frederic*. Well, Mr. Short was a former solider, after all. "Thanks, Mr. Short."

I excused myself from the table, and my smile turned to confusion as my thoughts drifted back to the phone call he said that Cedric received, after which, according to Mr. Short, he made the sign of the cross. I impulsively decided to text Cedric, asking how he was doing, just in case, something bad had happened.

Allison: How is everything?

Cedric: Great. I miss you.

Allison: Ok, just checking in.

Cedric: Later, sweetheart

Allison: Later xo

Okay, well that didn't give me any clue. My curiosity was killing me, so I typed again.

Allison: Can I ask you a silly question?

Cedric: No such thing as a silly question...Shoot.

Allison: Are you religious?

Cedric: I am spiritual. Why?

Allison: Someone said they saw you make the sign of the cross in your car after you got off the phone outside the diner after dropping me off.

About a minute passed and no response. My heart started to pound and then he finally responded.

Cedric: It was a work call. Sometimes I do make the sign of the cross when I am asking for, you know, assistance from above on things. Nothing bad. Don't worry. I guess Bettina taught me some things that stuck with me, even though I don't go to church anymore.

Allison: Okay...see I told you it was silly. Sorry for bugging you. Glad everything is okay.

It still didn't feel right, but I was probably just being paranoid. Trying to get my mind off of my insecurities, I focused on being a waitress for the rest of the afternoon, anxiously awaiting the end of my shift.

CHAPTER 26

CEDRIC

I had just left Allison at the door of the Stardust diner and already, I couldn't wait until it was time to pick her up.

Fantasizing about finishing later where we left off this morning, I strolled to my car, feeling on top of the world as the morning sun beamed.

As I settled in, my cell phone rang and my heart dropped as I noticed the Chicago exchange. I picked up.

"This is Cedric."

"Cedric…hi. It's Elaine."

My heart dropped further. "Elaine." I could hardly breathe. "Hi."

"Cedric…Ed and I were just wondering if you have made any progress. We haven't heard from you. Have you found her?"

Closing my eyes, I inhaled and let out a deep breath.

"Um…Elaine…" I hesitated.

"Yes?"

"I…I know where she is, okay? She is doing well. But I haven't found a way to approach the subject yet. I'm hoping you and Ed understand that I need some more time. I have to handle this carefully."

Elaine paused. "Cedric, I have some news. I am not sure how much longer you can put this off."

As Elaine explained the new development that had happened in the weeks since I found Allison, I felt like the wind had been knocked out of me. This news changed everything. It would only be a matter of weeks now and if I didn't tell her the truth, someone else would.

After I hung up with Elaine, I collapsed my head onto the steering wheel. Feeling desperate for some kind of help, I did the only thing that came natural: I made the sign of the cross. *"In the Name of the Father, the Son and the Holy Spirit…help me, God. Please help me."*

Then, I sped away from the diner.

The highway ride was a blur as my mind raced for a solution and before I knew it, I was only a mile from my condo.

Ideas that floated through my mind ranged from taking Allison away on a vacation to never contacting her again and moving to another city. The need to somehow get rid of the situation I had gotten myself into was enormous. Why couldn't I have left her alone and just done what I was supposed to do? For the first time since this entire ordeal began, I felt tears forming in my eyes. A lone teardrop streamed down my left cheek and my jaw began to tremble.

It was at that moment that I truly realized all that I stood to lose. It was at that moment that I realized how desperately I was falling in love with her.

***

Two days had gone by since that afternoon.

I ended up telling Allison that I had fallen ill and couldn't pick her up from the diner that day. It was one of the hardest things I ever had to do, but I just couldn't face her that night and needed time to think.

The walls of deceit I had built were closing in on me. I couldn't bear the thought of her thinking that I was not interested in spending time with her because I had already had my sexual fill.

The timing of that phone call was horrible.

I wanted nothing more than to be able to spend every second of every day with her, making love to her, building on this relationship and having nothing to hide. Again, I wished that things were that simple and that we had met under different circumstances.

I hoped she truly believed I was sick; I hated lying to her…yet again. That's the funny thing about lies; you have to keep covering them up with more lies.

I made sure to text her repeatedly during those days, so she would at least know I was thinking of her. She offered to come by and check on me, but I begged her not to, based on the story that I was afraid she would catch what I had and that Callie was looking forward to seeing her next week. It was the best excuse I could come up with.

The most painful night was last night, New Years Eve. Still in my fictitious sickness bubble, I stayed home alone, too afraid to get caught in my lie. I couldn't exactly go to my mother's house and tell her to lie to Allison next week about having seen me and also couldn't risk being seen or photographed out.

Allison had told me she was going to Boston's First Night celebration with her roommate, Sonia and begged me to let her come by and see me before she went. It pained me beyond belief to tell her not to when I missed her so much but I couldn't let her see that I was obviously fine. So, I urged her to stay away, choosing my words carefully and hoping that she would listen. She hadn't been to my condo yet, so I was fairly certain she didn't even know exactly where I lived and wouldn't just drop in.

As the clock struck midnight, from my couch, I watched television coverage of fireworks exploding over the Esplanade imagining how amazing it would have been to share that moment with her. Looking out the window toward the dark Boston night, it seemed Beacon Street was eerily quiet. As the Boston Symphony Orchestra played on the television and the fireworks continued to erupt, the explosion seemed to symbolize the inner turmoil I was experiencing.

As I pondered that symbolism, no closer to a decision on how to move forward, my cell phone rang.

Seeing it was Allison, I felt an immense pain in my heart and immediately picked up. "Happy New Year, beautiful," I said in a hoarse voice.

"Happy New Year, Cedric. I really wish you were here."

Closing my eyes at the sound of her voice, all the resolve I had to sound neutral went out the window.

The alcohol I had consumed had also done its job in preventing me from masking my emotions. I felt my mouth start to tremble and hoped that she couldn't sense it in my voice.

"I fucking miss you so much, Allison. I want nothing more than to be with you right now."

It was the truth. I was so fucked.

"When do you think we'll be able to see each other? Are you feeling any better at all?" she asked.

God, she was so sweet.

I could barely hear her with the noise of horns and yelling and all of the New Year festivities in the background.

"My fever's gone down a bit and I definitely feel better now that I've heard your voice. I am hoping I'll be done with this by mid-week."

Have I mentioned I really hated lying to this woman?

"Well, you let me know the second you can have me. I mean…not *have* me…you know what I mean…not like I'm thinking about that right now…"

I smiled at her nervously correcting herself. She was so damn cute.

"You will be the first person I see as soon as I beat this thing…I promise."

"Ok…well, I'll let you rest. Happy New Year," she said, sounding a bit down.

"Happy New Year, sweetheart," I said as I quickly hung up the phone before I said anything I would regret. I closed my eyes and silently mouthed, *I fucking love you.*

And so went the worst New Years Eve of my life.

***

After four more nights of tormenting myself, I came to a monumental decision; well, two decisions actually.

One: I was going to come clean to my mother about everything that happened in Chicago.

Two: I was going to ask for her advice on how to handle the Allison situation.

Caleb was the only person who knew the truth, but somehow, this was too important not to have a second opinion.

My mother was the only other person on this Earth that I could trust. She would be disappointed that I wasn't honest with her all these years but would find out eventually anyway, and I wanted it to come from me. Also, I knew she wouldn't say anything to Allison and that I could trust her.

So, Friday night after work, I impulsively drove to my mother's house. Traffic was busy and it felt like I'd never get there.

I knew that Allison wouldn't be there with Callie on a Friday, which is why I chose tonight. I still hadn't seen her since my supposed illness.

Earlier in the week, I told her that my sickness had caused me to fall behind in work having to make up lost hours. I then arranged for a client meeting later in the week in New York to get myself out of town and buy myself more time to think before returning last night.

It had been a full week now since I last saw her. Even though I phoned and texted, I began to feel she was suspecting something because her responses were getting shorter and shorter. But I knew if I went to her and saw her, I wouldn't be able to control myself and needed to give her the respect she deserved until I knew what would happen.

Arriving at Mom's, I used my key to let myself in. The house was unusually quiet as I made my way back to the kitchen. There was no sign of my mother, but I saw a light in Callie's room and could hear soft music playing.

I opened the door and my heart skipped a beat when I saw Allison lying on the bed with Callie.

Her face turned red when she saw me, but she immediately put her finger to her mouth signaling me to be quiet. Callie was fast asleep next to her and Allison slipped away quietly to join me in the hallway, closing the door to Callie's room behind her.

"Cedric, what are you doing here?" she whispered in surprise.

I wished I could have made myself disappear into thin air before saying, "I could ask the same of you. Is everything okay? Where's my mother?"

Allison's face seemed to lose all of its coloring.

"She had to bring some stuff to her aunt Evelyn in the nursing home. She called me over because Callie is sick and her other therapist cancelled. I had to cancel working with Lucas, but it's fine. They were able to fill his shift with someone else. I would rather be here for her. She has a slight fever, but she's okay. How are you feeling?"

"My poor sister. I'm much better, actually. I just got in from New York." I fake smiled, hoping to keep talk of my lies to a minimum.

Allison didn't return my smile and looked down. "I am glad to hear that you're better."

I stared at her in awe for a few seconds, still a bit shocked to have found her here instead of my mother, then immediately lost all control and embraced her, breathing her in.

God, I had missed her.

I leaned in to kiss her but my heart sank when she abruptly pushed me back.

"Were you just coming to visit your mother?"

I realized how crappy it looked that I supposedly didn't have time to see her this week with my workload, yet the first person I came to visit when I got back was my mother whom she knew rarely saw me anyway. I felt like an asshole.

I was an asshole.

"Yeah, I just hadn't heard from her in a while and wanted to check in," I said.

There was a bit of an awkward silence and Allison searched my eyes. The look on her face proved she knew something was off with me.

"I see," she said coldly.

Feeling like my world was crumbling around me, I grabbed her hand.

"Allison...what's wrong? Talk to me," I whispered, my voice breaking up.

"Nothing, Cedric. I'm just surprised to see you, is all. You said you still felt a little under the weather when we spoke this morning when you were in New York and you texted me that you'd be working late into the night after you got back. Then, you show up here, certainly not working, and you seem absolutely fine. I wonder if there is something you are not telling me?"

I seriously wanted to shit my pants.

Sounding like an idiot, I tried to buy more time before responding. "What do you mean?"

Allison's face suddenly turned a shade of red I had never seen before and her breathing was so rapid that her chest rose up and down visibly. I knew she caught me in my lie and I began to imagine that this horrid look she was giving me now would be only a fraction of the pain she would feel when I told her the whole truth.

I needed to go.

I couldn't do this anymore.

I loved her too much to go any deeper into this relationship.

I couldn't lie to her anymore.

Then, she floored me with her next question as her eyes began to water. "Is there someone else, Cedric?"

I stared at her in silence. My heart was exploding out of my chest, and my eyes began to well up. The love I felt for this woman was indescribable and yet, I looked her dead straight in the eyes and lied through my teeth one last time as my breath hitched and my voice shook.

"Yes...yes, there is."

Allison stared at me frozen in shock as tears fell down her cheeks. My hand trembled as I struggled to hold it in place to stop it from rising to wipe her tears away, something I desperately wanted to do but couldn't allow myself to. I had no idea what to do or say and just stayed there watching her cry as my own tears began to fall visibly.

Just then, the front door opened, and my mother walked in. She looked puzzled as she took in the sight of Allison and me staring at each other in her hallway.

"Cedric...what are you doing here? What is going on?" she asked.

I looked over at my mother wishing again that I could disappear into thin air.

"Mom," I said, my voice shaking.

My mother walked over to me, giving me a hug then seemed to notice that my eyes were watery, which prompted her to jolt back.

She then immediately looked over at Allison's sullen face and then looked back at me. Her grim expression showed that she understood something was very wrong between us.

Allison then silently turned around and walked back into Callie's room, closing the door and disappearing from sight.

It took all of my willpower not to go after her, but I knew I had fucked up for the last time. I had no right to touch her ever again.

"Do you mind telling me what is going on?" Mom whispered, looking concerned and a little frightened.

I stood frozen, my eyes staring at the closed door to Callie's room.

"Ma…I really screwed things up. I…I need to leave. I am so sorry."

CHAPTER 27

ALLISON

You and your lover may not be on the same page, Gemini. This is a just passing phase, so don't be too upset or put too much emphasis on the turmoil that arrives. Mercury will be going in direct motion soon, soothing miscommunications.

It has been nearly a month since that moment at Bettina's house, the last time I saw Cedric.

I had told his mother that night, after he left, that I couldn't talk about what happened and asked her to kindly not mention it again. I assured her, though, that I would not be leaving my job with Callie and while still confused, she seemed relieved to hear that.

I heard from him only one time after that night in a text I received a few days later.

The Monday night of the text, I had run a bath after returning from my shift with Lucas. I wanted to soak away the pain of losing him, a pain like none I had ever felt, aside from losing my mother. As I sat in the water, my body ached for Cedric's touch as much as my heart ached. This feeling was what I imagined withdrawal from heroin might be like. My phone chimed, and I lifted out of the water to check it when I saw that the text was from Cedric.

Allison…please forgive me. All of this…it's not what you think. I will explain it to you someday. Please just know that you mean so much to me.

Why?

Fuck you, Cedric.

Fuck you for hurting me so much.

I didn't return the text. Instead, the glass on my iPhone shattered after I threw it across the bathroom and it landed on the tile floor.

A flood of tears poured out of my eyes, and my body shook uncontrollably.

How I wanted to go back a few weeks in time and stay there forever. I had so much hope for the future then, so much love in my heart for that man. *So much love…after such a short time.* I had been sure it was love, not lust, and now I wasn't sure I could ever trust my own judgment ever again.

I felt faint as I sat in the hot bathwater but had no strength to get up. I had eaten barely a morsel since that day and would have to face Cedric's mother tomorrow to work with Callie for the first time since the last encounter. I had considered giving my notice then but decided that I would not let Cedric take away the one good thing I had left, so I was determined to find a way to compartmentalize the two things. Callie shouldn't have to pay for her asshole brother's mistake.

I had no idea what was really going on with him and what his mother now knew, though. *Here's what I knew:* her son abandoned me and there was, as he admitted, "someone else."

The text confused me, though, because he claimed, "it wasn't what I thought." What the hell was it, then? I figured admitting that there was someone else made it pretty damn clear what was going on.

Whatever the exact reason, he had hurt me so deeply that it was beyond repair. I was at least glad he didn't prolong our relationship even further. Only God knew where I'd be then.

***

194

Now, a month later, after weeks of not eating and sleeping, the wrath of Cedric was just starting to really take its toll.

"Al…Al…wake up…you're going to be late for work." I heard Sonia shouting as I lay in bed, having slept through my alarm yet again. I had been awake so much in the middle of the night lately that I would finally fall back asleep about four in the morning, only to have to wake up an hour later for the diner job.

Sonia hugged me as finally sat up. "Al, you know you are going to have to talk to me about it at some point, don't you?

"Sonia, like I told you…talking about it isn't going to change anything. There is nothing to say. Cedric left me for someone else…if we were even ever together at all. My life is back to being shit and I am alone again…end of story," I said hoarsely.

"You're not alone. You have me, Bitch. But that bastard…you were so happy for the first time since I have known you and he seemed to think you were the bees knees. He wrote a fucking rap song for you, for Christ's sake. I just don't get it. I mean…I could see in his eyes how into you he was. I just don't know what to believe in anymore. I'd like to cut his balls off and—" Sonia stopped talking, shook her head and grabbed a brush and started brushing my hair.

"You know I brush my own hair, right?" I said.

Sonia ignored me and kept brushing. "Sure, darling, I do. Just let me."

Tears quietly fell down my cheek as Sonia continued to do my hair as I wondered what my life had come to.

When I got up from the bed, Sonia gasped.

She didn't have to say anything. I knew what she was thinking as she covered her mouth with her hand.

I looked over at my reflection in the mirror on my closet door. I could see my ribs. As the loss of Cedric ate away at me, *I* wasn't eating and had dropped ten pounds. Thinner than I could ever remember being, I was starting to look like Olive Oil. My roommate's frightened face was the wakeup call I needed.

***

By the second month A.C. ("After Cedric"), I had gained about five of the pounds back and was getting back into life a bit.

Bright Horizons had given me another autistic client, a child this time, a ten-year-old boy whom I worked with on Saturday mornings.

Gabriel was a sweetheart and I mostly took him out shopping and accompanied his family on other outings. I didn't have to dress in costume for this one, nor was I dating his brother, so it was a fairly low-key, stress-free assignment. Gabriel liked to snuggle and sniff my hair and would occasionally pull a chunk of it out abruptly and stare at it proudly in his hands. I let him do it because he was a good boy and a great distraction on otherwise lazy Saturday mornings when I had too much time to think about Cedric or rather the fact that Cedric had disappeared off the face of the Earth.

And I was still working with Callie whose beautiful face continued to be a stark reminder of what I lost.

One Tuesday afternoon at Bettina's house, we were sitting down to dinner. I was holding the fork in Callie's hand as she attempted to eat homemade macaroni and cheese. She knew how to use a fork, but liked to eat the pinwheel pasta with her hands. So, my job was to deter her from doing that.

Bettina was watching me intently as I picked Callie's pasta up one by one as the pieces fell off the fork and placed each piece back in the bowl, prompting her to use the fork.

Bettina then startled me with a question.

"Allison...my son won't tell me. Will you?" she asked.

My heart ached at the mere mention of Cedric. It was as if he were dead until his mother mentioned him, reminding me that he was out there somewhere. He was very much alive and not telling her anything either, apparently. I was surprised it took her so long to bring up the subject again but was glad she hadn't...until now.

I looked at her silently, and then cleared my throat.

"Bettina...I don't know what happened and that's the truth. Cedric and I...we dated for a short time, but I was really falling hard for your son. That's all I can say. He ended it that night you walked in on us and I really don't know why, but I'm glad he did it when he did and didn't let it drag on even further." I was proud of my response.

Bettina shook her head and sighed. "Thank you for your answer. I know it's none of my business. I've called him and asked him to tell me what happened a few times and he won't tell me anything. He just shuts down and changes the subject. I am afraid I haven't even seen him since that day either."

The fact that Cedric hadn't seen his mother in two months shocked me.

"He hasn't come at all to see you...or Callie?" I asked.

"No, honey, I am afraid he hasn't. Cedric has always been the closed off one. Caleb is an open book...but my Cedric is different. We keep in contact over the phone, so I know he is okay. But one thing I know for sure...whatever is going on with my son...it hasn't been easy. Allison, aside from his father dying, I haven't seen him that emotional in years, since he was a child, maybe. He had tears in his eyes that night with you. That tells me that whatever happened between you two, it was hard for him, and his feelings for you had to have been real."

Nausea crept up on me at that statement; I hadn't thought of it that way before. Cedric did have tears in his eyes when he told me he was seeing someone else. The thought of him with anyone else, doing the things he did with me, made me sick and I honestly have had to block it out almost immediately. That had been the only way I could function...as long as I don't focus on that. I'd rather just think of him, as gone...dead.

I could feel the tears forming in my eyes now.

"Bettina, I really don't want to talk about this anymore, okay? I said.

She reached across the table and placed her hands on mine. "Okay, honey. I am sorry. We don't have to talk about it."

A teardrop fell down my cheek and I knew Bettina saw it. I immediately gathered Callie's dish, and we walked over to the sink to wash our hands.

"Allison," Bettina called from across the kitchen.

"Yes?" I asked.

"Thank you," she said.

She didn't have to explain why.

I knew she was thanking me for staying.

***

A few weeks had passed and Bettina never mentioned Cedric to me again.

He hadn't sent any more texts either.

With each passing day, I was slowly beginning to accept the fact that whatever we had was over and that I needed to forget him. How that was going to happen exactly was still a mystery since Cedric still occupied most of my thoughts, but at least time had made it clearer what I needed to do: I needed to move on.

Spring was in the air in Boston now and the sun was streaming through the basement windows of Bettina's house. It was a Tuesday afternoon and it surprised me how light it still was outside at 6:00 in the evening. Bettina was usually home at this time but would not be arriving back from a church bazaar committee meeting until the end of my shift at 7:30. She had given me instructions to heat up some pizza she made this afternoon for Callie and me.

Before dinner, Callie and I were hanging out in the basement where Bettina had set up a sensory area for her daughter to let off steam.

There was a small trampoline, an indoor hammock, and one of those vibrating massage chairs from Brookstone that now made me uneasy because Bettina had once mentioned that Cedric bought it for his sister. At the time, that warmed my heart. Now, it just made me sad.

As Callie jumped on the trampoline, I held her hands to help her balance. She was laughing hysterically and saying, "Higher…higher!"

After ten minutes, she finally wore herself out, looked at me and said, "I want chair, please."

"Okay, honey," I said as I walked over to the massage chair, adjusting the settings as Bettina had showed me how, and then she hopped onto it. Callie relaxed in the seat, closing her eyes and letting the vibrations shake her.

As she continued to enjoy the chair, I looked around the basement.

Half of the large space was Callie's sensory area and the other side of the room contained dozens of labeled boxes. I remember Bettina saying something about her kids storing all of their junk in her house, and she joked that one day she was going to have a yard sale, hawk it all and use the money to gamble at the Mohegan Sun casino.

Callie seemed to be happily nodding off in the chair, so I walked over to all of the boxes to take a closer look at the writing in marker on the sides.

Some of them were open and I could see what was inside. Others were taped shut and some were actually large clear covered Rubbermaid containers.

One of the boxes was labeled "Caleb's Wedding Stuff," and that one happened to be open, so I peeked inside. The first thing I noticed was a small white ring bearer's pillow with two fake gold bands attached to the top. There was also a guest book and a few favors: ceramic swans wrapped in white tulle with Jordan almonds. A royal blue ribbon was tied around the swan's neck and on the ribbon it said in gold writing: *Caleb and Denise August 13, 2005.* There was a mini wedding album with the same caption, and curiosity got the best of me, so I opened it. The first picture was a formal portrait of Caleb and Denise. The bride looked beautiful in a satin gown with lace cap sleeves, holding red roses. Her blond hair was down, covered with a rhinestone tiara and puffy veil. Caleb looked a bit more like Cedric back then, since he was a little thinner. Caleb and Cedric had identical eyes, and I could really see the resemblance in this picture. The next photo was of Caleb and his father, a candid where it looked like his Dad was giving him advice. His hand was on his son's shoulder, and Caleb was smiling back at him. This made me sad, knowing that their father passed away just a few years later.

When I turned the page, my heart began thumping hard as I came across the picture of Caleb and his groomsman. Standing in the middle right next to his brother was Cedric, smiling ear to ear, his eyes gleaming. He was dressed in a tux with a royal blue vest and a red rose pinned to his chest. Ignoring everyone else in the shot, my eyes focused only on him. I stared long enough for it to seem like his face was going to pop out of the page. He was clearly younger, his hair was gelled back and parted differently, but it was the same beautiful face and smile that had captivated me. I closed my eyes, took a deep breath and continued through the rest of the album. Denise was a lucky woman, I thought. She nabbed the normal Callahan brother, not the fucked-up one.

I walked back over to Callie who was now fast asleep in the massage chair and brushed a piece of hair off of her eyes. It was rare for Callie to fall asleep during the day, but her mother did say she was up a lot the night before. I decided to let her sleep for ten more minutes until it was time to go upstairs for dinner.

In the meantime, I walked back across the room to the boxes, making sure everything in the Caleb wedding box was arranged as it had been before I looked in it.

I noticed another box that said "Dad's Coin Collection" and another that was labeled "Callie's Childhood Drawings." I was going to peek inside that one, but noticed it was taped up.

There were dozens of containers, but I had to give Bettina credit for labeling everything.

Then, I noticed the first box that had Cedric's name on it, and my heart started to pound. That very large box was labeled "Cedric Miscellaneous," and it was not fully closed at the top. It was also not fully open and I *might have yanked on the tape a bit.*

I considered walking away right then and there, waking Callie and heading upstairs, but morbid curiosity got the best of me. I looked over at Callie to make sure she was still asleep, looked at my watch and opened the flaps of the box. The first thing I pulled out was a Northwestern University banner that was folded. There was also a graduation hat and tassel. Beneath that, were several shot glasses wrapped in bubble wrap. Also in the box: a yearbook, incense, candles, c.d.'s, a couple of notebooks and a huge stack of photos wrapped in an elastic band. If I had to guess, these items looked like they were the contents of his dorm room, like Bettina helped him pack everything up on graduation day and took it all or had it shipped back to her house. I held the photos in my hand, staring at them, suddenly feeling like I was violating Cedric's privacy. *Then, I unwound the elastic band anyway.*

Holy shit…this was overwhelming. The first photo was of a very young looking Cedric with two attractive, blonde girls flanking him on each side. Cedric was giving bunny ears to one of them unbeknownst to her. He had a silly grin on his face and was likely drunk from the look in his eyes and the amount of shot glasses in that box. The next picture was of Cedric and some guys playing beer pong. In another photo, some college kid was pissing on the ground of what looked like the dorm hallway…assumably piss-ass drunk. I rolled my eyes. These photos were totally up on some bulletin board in Cedric's dorm room. Some of them even had tape or sticky stuff on the back. Picture after picture showed more of the same: Cedric with some random girls (in one photo, he was tongue kissing a redhead), college guys goofing around and Cedric giving the middle finger.

I had seen enough, so I rolled the elastic back around the stack and returned them to the box.

There was one last item that caught my eye. It was a small black binder and on it were the letters A.R.T. I immediately remembered Cedric's tattoo which also had those same letters spelled out on top of the cross on his torso. My heart pounded as I slowly unlocked and opened the binder, a decision that would prove fateful.

Three pictures and a dried up pink rose were inside.

As my eyes caught sight of the first image, a sudden wave of nausea and panic overcame me. The room started to spin and my breathing became erratic. I closed my eyes and knelt down, fearing I was about to pass out. With the picture still firmly in my shaking hand, I knelt down on the floor, knowing that if I stood back up, I would surely faint.

On the ground, I dared myself to look at the picture again and squinted my eyes deeply to be sure I was seeing correctly, to make sure I was seeing what I thought I was seeing.

And I was: it was a picture of me.

CHAPTER 28

CEDRIC

"Dude...what the fuck?" Caleb said as he entered my condo.

I ran my fingers through my dirty mop of overgrown hair. "Nice to see you, too."

"What's with the beard...and when did you start smoking again? This place reeks." Caleb reached for my face and suddenly smacked my cheek.

I scratched my head and ignored him, groggily walking into the kitchen, as Caleb followed me.

"Do you mind telling me what the fuck is going on with you? Caleb asked as he poured a cup of cold coffee. "Mom says you have dropped off the face of the Earth and that it has something to do with Allison or some other woman or both, but she couldn't tell me shit."

"Bro, that coffee is from yesterday," I said as I took the cup from him and looked around for some filters to make a new pot.

Where the fuck did I put the filters?

"Cedric...seriously, what is going on?" Caleb crossed his arms leaning up against the kitchen counter.

Filters...Filters...Bingo!

"Cedric...put the fucking filters down."

I looked down at the ground.

"Caleb...I...I'm just fucked up. My life is a fucking mess, so I took my three weeks vacation."

Caleb walked toward me as he spoke. "You call this a vacation…sitting in your apartment, looking like a fucking Chia pet that smells like an ashtray?"

I laughed…for the first time in weeks.

"Fuckhead…it's my house. What do you want me to do?"

"Cedric…seriously…I had no idea. No news is usually good news with you. Why didn't you call me? When was the last time you even spoke to anyone?"

"Mom called me yesterday. She, uh, told me about Denise. I am really sorry, man. I don't want to bother you with my problems."

During that call, my mother told me that Denise had been pregnant but had a miscarriage a few days ago at seven weeks. It was the one thing that made me feel sad for anyone but myself in nearly three months. I felt like an asshole for being so out of touch with my family.

Caleb paused and stared at me. I knew he must be devastated. They had tried to have a baby for so long.

He shook his head. "It's okay, man. We'll try again. We won't give up. She's taking it hard, but we'll be okay."

I sat down. "Caleb…fuck…I've been so wrapped up in this shit. I should have called you. God, I am sorry."

"It's okay…you *clearly* aren't in your right mind." Caleb looked at the ceiling, and then changed the subject. "So, are there any new developments? To what do we owe this shit show?"

Caleb knew about my last encounter with Allison, the night we broke up at Mom's house, because I called him after it happened.

That was nearly three months ago.

I had chickened out about telling my mother anything at all because I wasn't ready, not to mention Allison was still in the house when I left.

I became more and more depressed as the weeks passed. I had disappeared from my own life and chose not to face anything or anyone at all. After a couple of months of attempting to throw myself into work, I was nearing a nervous breakdown and took the time off—all three weeks of my vacation. The agency wasn't happy, but they couldn't stop me because I had the vacation time.

Each day was been spent in my condo, listening to music, smoking, drinking and watching suck-ass television.

I had one picture of Allison and me on my phone that we took at her apartment the day we spent together after the first night we made love and I stared at it a lot.

Lack of sleep had been a constant. Thoughts of her kept me up most nights. I wondered about whether anyone has contacted her, what she knew now, whether she hated me, whether she was with someone else. I had no interest in meeting other women, because my heart still belonged to her.

Each day, I told myself that today would be the day that I'd go to her and tell her my story...her story...the truth. But I could never muster up the courage to face her.

"Nothing has changed, Caleb," I said.

"Why don't you just go to her and tell her the goddamn truth? What is stopping you now? You have nothing to lose anymore," he said.

I put my feet up on the kitchen table and threw my head back.

"I...just...can't bear to tell her I lied to her. She'll hate me for that. She'll think that I was a selfish prick who wanted in her pants. And then, the truth will devastate her. I just don't want to hurt her anymore than I already have. At this point, I'd rather it be someone else that tells her everything."

"You don't think it would be better coming from you, someone she knows? She's got to at least know you cared about her. That's why you lied, to protect her and because you wanted to be with her without judgment. Can't you explain it to her that way?"

"Man, I run through this everyday in my head. I know that would be the right thing to do...but you're not understanding. It will *kill me* to see her...*kill me* to see her cry again. I've hurt her enough."

Caleb put his hand on my shoulder. "Maybe...but you owe it to her."

I threw my head into my hands and whispered, "I know. *I know.*"

***

I knew what I needed to do…but more days passed and I never did any of it.

My "vacation" was almost over and the thought of returning to work and the daily grind was torture. My hair was now three inches longer and my beard was caveman-style. I had become accustomed to a recluse life over these past weeks.

One evening after deciding to take a shower after a few days without, as I was wiping myself down, I heard a frantic knock on the door.

My hair—both on my head and my face—was still dripping, and I grabbed a robe and rushed to see who was knocking.

When I opened the door, Allison was standing there with tears in her eyes, shaking.

My heart raced at the shock of seeing her, and my throat seemed to close preventing me from speaking. All I was able to muster was a faint whisper.

"Allison."

"Cedric?" she whispered through her tears.

I said nothing as I stood in the doorway, then after a few seconds, tried to touch her arm.

My stomach turned as she violently pushed me away and made her way past me into the living room, visibly shaken.

She knew. Fuck me…she knew. But what did she know?

"Allison?" I asked, still unable to form a coherent sentence.

She looked down at the floor and put her hand in her purse. Her hand was shaking, and she pulled out a photo.

Breathing erratically, she said nothing as she stuck her trembling hand out prompting me to take it. Her eyes were bloodshot red as she stared at me with an expression I had never seen from her.

It was fear.

I slowly walked over to her and took the photo out of her hand and looked at it.

Oh God, no.

"Allison…where…where did you get this?" I asked.

She wiped her eyes and looked at me, her voice shaking. "Your mother's basement. I found it."

Fuck. I must have had a box down there from when Caleb took my dorm stuff home after I opted to stay in Chicago after graduation.

"What...what do you think this is?" I asked.

Allison looked at me with daggers in her eyes. "What does it look like, Cedric? It's a fucking picture of me...from years ago. What are you doing with it? Why don't I remember you? Have you been stalking me? Has everything been a big lie?"

"Has anyone contacted you?" I asked.

She looked confused. "What do you mean?"

"When did you find this photo?"

"Earlier tonight."

"No one has contacted you before today?"

"No, Cedric. What is this about? How do you know me? What are you hiding? Tell me...now...please!" she yelled.

No one had contacted her.

She knew nothing beyond the photo.

It was time.

"God...Allison. God, I am so sorry. I need you to sit down, sweetheart, because I have to explain the picture, and I have to explain everything."

She shook her head repeatedly looking down at the floor. "I don't want to sit. Cedric, please."

"Allison, sit down," I repeated in a serious tone.

She finally listened, sitting down reluctantly on the couch.

I stayed standing, knowing she didn't want me anywhere near her. That hurt.

"Allison, first...before I tell you...I need you to know that everything and I mean, *everything* we experienced together was real. Please know that...*please.*"

She said nothing, just stared at me with her red eyes.

A tear fell down my cheek.

"The second thing is...sweetheart...that's not you in the picture."

CHAPTER 29

AMANDA

December 2001

My parents have lied to me for more than half my life.

That's the thought I haven't been able to get out of my head.

A week ago, after dinner, they sat me down in the living room and told me some things that I never in my life expected to hear. I always knew I was adopted but never knew the whole story about where I came from. I was so ashamed that my entire life as I knew it, was a lie.

The story I was told as a child was that I was given to my parents on the day I was born because my real mother didn't want an open adoption and never wanted to even see me. My parents told me they knew nothing about my birth mother nor where I came from. Apparently, they did know something…something important…and they had agreed to tell me everything after I turned eighteen. Why they chose a random night in December, I'll never understand, since I had turned eighteen in June.

Happy Belated Birthday to me.

Since last week, I hadn't told anyone about it, not even my boyfriend, even though I planned to tell him when I was ready. It just all hadn't set in yet.

My parents had given me space over the past week and agreed that I didn't have to talk about it again or do anything about it until I was ready.

Tonight…I just wanted to forget everything and I knew just how I was going to do that: I was going to lose my virginity.

Even though I was a freshman at Northwestern, I still lived at home in a nice, brick house in Naperville, a suburb of Chicago. It was a commutable distance to school and more affordable than living on campus. Mostly, my parents didn't want me living in the dorms, for fear I would go buck wild. I still went to campus parties and slept over friend's dorm rooms, but my parents wanted to maintain some control over me, so they made me live at home.

My boyfriend lived on campus and sometimes I let him into my bedroom window at night after my parents had gone to sleep. Since my room was a converted garage and separate from the rest of the house, they couldn't hear anything when he'd come over. Tonight was one of those nights and I was waiting for him to arrive because I wanted to drown my sorrows in him.

There was one window at the front of my bedroom. Since knocking would wake up my parents, he'd flash a light in the window when arrived. Then, I would open it and quietly sneak him in. That was our routine.

When I finally saw the light tonight, I eagerly ran to the window, opening it.

"You're late, Cedric."

"I know, baby. Sorry. The guys wanted to get beers after class, and then we ended up shooting pool," he said before kissing me hard.

Every time he kissed me, I lost my mind.

My boyfriend was movie star hot with shaggy brown hair, light blue eyes and a sculpted athletic body. He was a popular senior and every girl's dream, and I was only a freshman.

We met at a campus party, and I noticed all these sorority girls throwing themselves at him. Who could blame them? Then, he noticed me from across the room, singled me out, and we started talking as if all those other girls evaporated into thin air. There was no one else in the room but us at that point. He made fun of my Chicago accent and I made fun of the way he didn't pronounce some of his r's because he's from Boston. He'd say things like "Wicked Pisser", except he'd say it like "Wicked Pissa." He was a little rough around the edges, which turned me on. I had never been with a bad boy before. He smoked, drank, swore like a sailor, started fights and seemed to adore me. I, on the other hand, was a shy Daddy's girl, who said "Gosh" instead of "God" and well, who had never had sex. We were opposites…but had been inseparable ever since that first night a few months ago.

Cedric was with a lot of girls before me, but he'd been patient. He was used to girls throwing themselves at him, and I think the fact that I didn't give it up so easily was a bit of a challenge for him. He was experienced but knew I was still a virgin and hadn't pressured me to do anything I wasn't comfortable with. We'd basically done everything—except that—but tonight that was going to change.

He just didn't know it yet.

Cedric took his shoes off and plopped down on my bed. I could smell cigarettes and beer on him, mixed with his cologne, and the combination of all those smells actually turned me on even more.

"What's with the look?" he said smirking.

"Nothing. I was just thinking about how sexy my man is." I crawled on top of him and pulled his face toward mine, straddling him as we kissed.

Cedric pulled away and caressed my long, dark hair, examining me. "You look different tonight, baby."

I had made myself up more than usual. I lifted my shirt and exposed a new black lace bra I had bought today from Victoria's Secret at the mall and said, "I feel different, Cedric."

His pupils dilated as he took in the sight of the lingerie and peeked into my pants to see I had matching lace underwear.

"What does that mean?" he grinned.

"It means…I want you, Cedric."

Cedric caressed my face and his eyes widened. "You want me…to…what?"

"I want…you."

"But you have me." He smiled.

"I know. But…I want…you know…everything."

He started deeply into my eyes and I felt myself get moist with anticipation.

"Whoa…are you saying what I think you are saying?"

I nodded, still sitting on top of him and could feel his hard-on pressing into me through his jeans. "Yes, Cedric, I am."

He moved from under me, sitting up. "Wait. Are you sure, Amanda? I thought you said just last week that you wanted to wait."

"Yeah, well a lot can change in a week." (Life as I knew it.) I pressed my forehead onto his. "I wasn't ready...then. But now, I am."

"What changed?" he asked.

"Nothing changed. I just woke up this morning and realized...I want to fuck my boyfriend. Is that so bad?"

Cedric shook his head and laughed, pulling me into him. "Baby...are you serious? Are you really serious about this?"

I didn't answer him. Instead, I pushed him back down onto the bed and took my shirt off, lowering myself onto him.

Cedric cupped my breasts through the lacy bra and plunged his tongue into my mouth while I grinded against him.

"We don't have to," he said muffled, his lips still kissing me. "We could do other things."

"I'm ready, Cedric. See?" I said as I guided his finger down into my underwear.

Cedric kissed me harder and moaned as he touched me. I moaned back through his kiss at the pleasure of his finger now deeply inside me.

Cedric whispered through our kisses. "Swear on your mother you're ready."

I wanted to swear a lot of things on my mother, both of them. He didn't know the half of it.

"I swear...on my mother," I said.

With that, Cedric kissed me harder as I unzipped his jeans and pulled them down.

I continued to rub against him with my clothes on, kissing him hard and running my fingers through his hair.

"Amanda...you're so fucking beautiful. I've wanted you for so long...waited so long," Cedric said as he unsnapped my bra and threw it on the floor.

"I'm on the pill," I said.

"Okay, baby. That's good. Really good," he said as he continued to kiss me.

Then, he started to slowly pull my underwear down.

I pulled off his shirt and he slid his boxers off. We were both completely naked. He lifted up from under me and flipped me over so that I was under him.

He stared into my eyes as I rubbed his face and stared back at him.

We stayed like that for a while until Cedric spoke. "Okay?"

I nodded and bit my bottom lip when I felt the tip of his penis enter me, followed by a burning friction. I wanted to cry from the pain at first but Cedric moved into me very slowly. I closed my eyes and told myself to relax, no matter how painful. With each slow thrust, I got more accustomed to the feeling until eventually the pain turned to pleasure.

Cedric moaned in ecstasy once he started to realize I was relaxing and enjoying it. His slow movements gradually turned forceful.

Once the pain stopped, I couldn't get enough and asked him to go faster and deeper until I felt myself starting to climax. Cedric knew it, because he covered my mouth with his hand, so that I could scream into it while I came. His translucent eyes rolled back and I knew he was coming too.

When his movements slowed, he stayed inside me and kissed my face over and over again and for the first time whispered, "Amanda Rose Thompson...I love you."

CHAPTER 30

CEDRIC

April 2002

"Cedric...Cedric. Wake up. You really should go home and try to get some sleep at home," Ed said as he shook me.

Shit.

It wasn't a dream.

I was really still here in this hospital room.

A nurse's voice spoke on the intercom in the distance, reminding me exactly where I was. Hospital clerks pushing food carts wheeled by the room. Life went on as usual outside the window; car horns beeping in the distance, part of the hustle and bustle of the Chicago morning commute, as if my life were not falling apart in here.

I wanted to scream out the window at them to shut the fuck up. Someone walked by the open room, laughing at something that was said at the nurse's station in the hallway. Life could not be going on when she was lying here, fighting for her life. It wasn't fair.

"No...no, sir, I can't leave her," I told Amanda's father.

"The doctors said she's not going to be waking up today, Cedric."

I still couldn't believe my eyes every time I glanced over at her. She was so beautiful even with all those tubes and medical contraptions. No, I wouldn't leave...couldn't leave, not for one second.

"Ed, I really don't want to leave her," I said.

He looked over at his daughter and then back at me, his eyes swollen from crying over the past few days. "Okay, son."

Amanda's parents, Ed and Elaine and I had been keeping vigil at her bedside for three days. The whole scene was surreal as this beautiful girl lie fighting for her life in a medically-induced coma.

"Did they say how much longer until they try to wake her?" I asked.

"Could be a couple of more days," Elaine said tearily as she sat by Amanda's side.

What if she didn't wake up? What if she never woke up? How could I ever live with myself?

An Indian doctor walked in and we all stood up in unison.

"Dr. Tripathi, we were wondering if you could tell us when they were planning on ending the coma?" Ed asked.

"The swelling is still too significant. We are going to keep with it for at least another twenty-four hours. Mrs. Thompson, can I talk to you privately?"

"Sure, doctor." Amanda's mother walked out of the room and the doctor followed her out into the hallway.

I walked over to Amanda's bedside and gently touched her silky, dark hair. She was so tranquil and beautiful. She looked so peaceful, nothing like the way she looked the last time I saw her. My heart clenched at that thought. Oh, God, please don't let anything happen to her. Please. I'll do anything. Anything.

I whispered so low that Ed couldn't possibly have heard me. When he had gone out to look for his wife, I spoke louder but still softly.

"Amanda. God, Amanda. I am so sorry, baby. I would take it all back if I could. Baby, if you wake up, I promise I will never leave you again. I was being stupid, baby, so, so stupid. Please just be okay, and I'll never leave you. Please. Please. Please. I love you, baby. I love you."

Tears ran down my cheeks and I began to shake uncontrollably as I recalled the night of the accident.

**

Amanda had taken her father's car to drive to my dorm in the middle of the night after I hadn't returned any of her calls that day. It was the first time I had *ever done something like that. The truth was, I had been having second thoughts lately about being in such a serious relationship at my age. Things were moving really fast and Amanda was starting to talk about a future with me. I loved her. I did. But I was scared and was only twenty-two. She was eighteen. I was her first, and she wanted me to be her last? That was a lot of pressure.*

My mind was spiraling out of control that day, and I was scared that if I talked to her, she would be able to sense it or that I would impulsively break up with her. So, I ignored her all day. I didn't want to hurt her, but I ended up doing worse.

It had all just become too much for me. I had myself convinced that I needed to test the waters...see how I really felt about her...by distancing myself...even if Amanda wasn't aware why.

Sarah was a girl who lived on my floor across the hall on the girl's side. She was tall, blonde and on the girl's basketball team. Sarah had been flirting with me since the beginning of the year, and I had always ignored her because I had a girlfriend.

That night, my door was open and Sarah happened to walk by and stop in my room. At first, it was innocent. We were just talking about music and jobs after graduation. At one point, she put her hand on my leg and gave me a look. I wasn't even as attracted to her as I was to Amanda, but like I said, I wanted to test the waters, test myself. I pulled her into me and started kissing her. That moment was the beginning of the end of my life as I knew it.

My door slammed open, and I threw Sarah off of me. There stood Amanda, in her sweatpants and Beatles t-shirt that she often slept in. Her hair was in two pigtails. She looked angelic but furious, like she had dragged herself out of bed in the middle of the night to come here.

"Cedric? Oh my God. Oh my God," she seethed as she covered her mouth in shock.

I was mute, completely speechless and breathless. This was not what I wanted. I never ever would have chosen to hurt her like this. I finally found the strength to speak.

Panicked, I said, "Amanda, it's not what it looks like. We...just kissed. Nothing more would have happened."

On that note, Sarah jumped off my bed and ran out the door without saying a word. She knew I had a girlfriend, so was just as guilty as I was and certainly not shocked by this scene.

Amanda stood in the doorway, just staring at me. "I'm gonna be sick. I'm going to throw up," she said, before suddenly turning around and bolting down the hall.

By the time I tried to reach her, the elevator doors had closed. I pushed the button frantically, hoping to catch her, but it was too late. When I made it to the parking lot, I could see her father's black Honda Accord speeding off onto the road before it disappeared.

That was the last time I saw her. Her last words to me that night had been "I'm going to throw up."

I raced back up to my room, dialing her number over and over, maybe a hundred times. Pick up. Pick up. She never picked up. After an hour of calling her repeatedly, I had enough.

Running back downstairs, I got in my Volkswagon Golf and sped down the road and onto the highway to head to her parents house in Naperville. I was going to explain everything to her when I got there…let her know that I still wanted her in my life but that we should slow down. I didn't want to lose her. The kiss was a mistake, one big mistake that meant nothing.

On my way to her parent's house, I passed an accident on the highway with multiple police vehicles responding. I didn't bother to look too closely to see what had happened because I was driving so fast to get to her. It looked like the accident was just clearing anyway.

I just needed to get to her.

When I got to Amanda's house, I noticed that her father's car wasn't there. Amanda never came home. Her mother's car was gone too. I knocked on the front door loudly, because I could see from inside Amanda's room in the converted garage that she definitely wasn't inside. She usually slept with a night light, and it was pitch black in there. As no one answered the front door, I felt nauseous and knew something was wrong.

I decided to wait in front of the house, hoping that she or someone would come home. With each passing minute, I worried more and more that something bad had happened.

Then, about an hour later, my phone rang.

"Hello?"

"Cedric, it's Mrs. Thompson. Amanda's been in an accident. You need to come to the hospital. She's at Chicago Memorial."

"Wha…Is she okay?" I asked frantically.

She hung up and the phone went dead.

It wasn't until I got to the hospital that I realized the accident I passed on the highway was Amanda's car. I fell to my knees in the waiting room as her mother's brother, Todd, told me what he had heard.

She was in a coma and fighting for her life.

She had hit a guardrail.

No one else was hurt.

Crying hysterically, I prayed to God to take me, not her.

Please, God, save her. I'll do anything.

I would never forgive myself for causing her to storm off, probably driving erratically and crashing her car. She was so upset. I kept hearing her voice in my head: "I'm going to throw up."

The look on her face would be etched in my memory.

Weeping and shaking my head in disbelief, holding a hand to my trembling mouth, I kept hearing her: "I'm going to throw up…I'm going to throw up."

I cried and begged my mind to stop replaying those words.

***

Looking down at her now, three days later, I made a decision that if she pulled through, I would do everything in my power to be a better person. She needed to know that she mattered to me.

Our Father who art in heaven, hallowed be Thy name…

Ed and Elaine walked into the room as I said the Our Father to myself silently, closing my eyes. Elaine looked white and Ed faced the back wall away from me. My heart dropped as I realized that the doctor had pulled Elaine aside in private. What had he told her? Was Amanda going to die? Oh, Jesus, no.

Ed left the room and I looked at Elaine, still sitting at Amanda's bedside.

"Elaine, please tell me. What's going on? What did the doctor say?"

Elaine shook her head in silence and buried her face in her hands.

"Please…" My voice shook in fear.

"Cedric…nothing has changed with Amanda's condition, but the doctor just gave us some news that I am afraid I wasn't expecting to hear."

"What…what news?"

"Cedric…"

"Elaine…what happened?" I yelled.

She was too shaken up to speak and started to cry, covering her face with her hands again.

Ed reappeared, took one look at his wife and walked over to where I was sitting, pulling up a chair.

"Cedric…the doctor said that…routine tests they performed on Amanda revealed…that she was pregnant at the time of the accident."

I stared at Ed in disbelief, trying to process it, looking over at Amanda sleeping and back at Ed in disbelief.

"Was…was…pregnant?" I asked.

Ed's eyes burned into me and I couldn't tell if he was in shock, upset or wanted to downright kill me.

"That's right…was. The doctors think she lost the baby on impact."

I nodded slowly, got up and walked out of the room.

The hospital hallway seemed to be swaying, and the walls were closing in. A blast of air hit me as I made my way out of the revolving doors in the front of the building. Running down the busy sidewalk, I couldn't catch my breath.

I kneeled down on someone's stoop about two blocks from the hospital, letting my heart rate slowly normalize. My head in my hands, I started to weep like a baby again. The unimaginable situation of the past few days had just gotten so much worse with that news. I had blamed myself for Amanda's accident, kept what happened in my dorm room from her parents and now, the realization that I was also responsible for the death of my unborn child was too much to bear.

As I looked up, I noticed a church across the street. I walked across the busy road in a haze, nearly getting run down. The front door of the gray stone structure was open. "Welcome to St. Mary's" was written on a sign in the entryway. In the distance, down the long aisle, dozens of candles in red votives flickered.

I slowly made my way down toward them at the front of the church near the desolate altar. I reached in my pocket and grabbed a five-dollar bill stuffing it in the donation slot in front of the candles, then lit one of them with a long matchstick.

I made the sign of the cross.

"Dear Jesus, please forgive me for the pain and suffering my actions have caused." Walking over to the front of the altar, I knelt down, closing my eyes tightly. Tears began to fall again, and I rubbed my eyes, grateful that there was no one in the church as my sobs turned to wailing that echoed throughout the vast cathedral.

***

After another night of sleeping poorly in Amanda's hospital room, my body was beginning to ache.

Ed and Elaine had gotten a room at the hotel around the corner and even though you could literally make it here in three minutes, I refused to leave the room. They couldn't make me leave if they tried. I think my being here made it easier for them to sleep at the hotel. There was only space for one cot in the room anyway.

Amanda's parents arrived at the crack of dawn and soon after, Dr. Tripathi walked into the room and told them that Amanda's vitals were looking a little better and that they were going to try and end the medically induced coma later that morning.

My heart raced with a number of emotions: fear, anticipation, relief, anguish. What if she didn't wake up on her own? What if the sight of me upset her when she came to?

A few hours later, we were asked to the leave the room while the doctors worked to bring Amanda out of the coma. Dr. Tripathi said it would be a while before we would be able to see her.

When the doctor emerged, we stood up in synch in the waiting room.

"You can go in now but one at a time, please," he said.

Elaine gasped. "Is she awake?"

"She seems to be trying to wake up. Please go very easy on her. She is still not

stable, but she should be able to hear what you are saying," he said.

Elaine walked in first and Ed and I waited impatiently outside.

Twenty minutes later, Elaine emerged crying and said, "I was talking to her and she was blinking rapidly. I hope she could hear me. Oh, God...Ed...this is just too much. Why our little girl...why?"

Ed comforted his wife and then released her to enter Amanda's room.

The waiting for my turn was killing me.

Amanda's parents were being amazing about letting me stay here. If they only knew that I was responsible. But I couldn't think about how they would feel if they knew. I needed to be here for her and I couldn't risk them keeping me away. That was why I played dumb when they asked me if I knew why Amanda might have been driving poorly the night of the accident. I think they believed that she fell asleep at the wheel. Toxicology reports already showed she wasn't drunk. I knew in my heart that she was upset at me and lost control of her car, although they could never prove it.

Ed emerged from Amanda's room, just as upset as Elaine had been. I don't know if they were expecting her to start talking or something, but the doctor made it clear that wouldn't happen right away.

"You can go in now, Cedric," he said, wiping his eyes.

I swallowed hard and walked into the room. Amanda was lying there just as peacefully as I last saw her.

"Hey, baby...it's me. You look so beautiful. I hope you can hear me," I whispered.

"Amanda, baby? You know what I heard on the radio today in the cafeteria? It was our favorite dumb song by Hootie and the Blowfish. You know the one that goes, "I only wanna be with you?" The one that was playing the night we met? That one. I smiled, baby, thinking of you. It's the first time I smiled since we ended up here."

I bent down and kissed her cheek and could see her eyelids flicker. Grabbing her hand, I placed it in mine. It was cold and clammy and I wished I could warm it up, but I needed to be gentle with her.

"I love you, baby. You're gonna be okay. Can you hear me?"

Amanda continued to lie still, her eyelids flickering again.

Suddenly, I felt pressure on my hand that was holding hers and realized she had squeezed it.

"Baby! You can hear me. You can hear me." My heart jumped for joy that Amanda responded to my voice and a single tear fell down my cheek.

She stayed still, just breathing, for another twenty minutes and hadn't squeezed my hand again, but I kept talking to her gently.

"Amanda…I don't know how much you can understand…but baby, I want you to know that when you get out of here…I want us to take a trip somewhere. Maybe Cancun…somewhere warm. You think your parents will let us go?" I smiled to myself. I knew her parents would probably let her do just about anything if she made it out of here okay.

"And baby—"

I was interrupted by an intense hand squeeze and lots of rapid eyelid movement.

Suddenly, her eyes opened.

Shocked and elated, I said, "Amanda, Amanda…it's me…Cedric. I'm here, baby. I'm here. You're okay. Everything is fine."

Groggily, she looked over at me and said nothing. Did she know what happened? Why she was here?

I ran out of the room and called a nurse. The nurse came in and verified that what was happening was normal, that Amanda would wake up from time to time, but may not be aware of her surroundings. By the time the nurse and I made it back to the room though, Amanda looked fast asleep again.

I let her mother go in again and waited anxiously in the hallway.

After about an hour, I was able to go back in her room. Amanda had not opened her eyes since the last time and I hoped and prayed she would wake up again.

***

The next day, something amazing happened. Amanda opened her eyes and said "Mom."

A couple of more days passed and Amanda was slowly regaining the ability to talk. Her physical condition, though, according to the doctors was still serious. Amanda had a lot of internal bleeding at the time of the accident and may have suffered some irreversible organ damage.

She acknowledged me only one time and it was the most precious couple of minutes of my life.

"Ce—dric."

"Oh my God…Hi, baby. I'm here. I'm here!" I said.

"Love you," she whispered.

"I love you too, baby," I cried through tears.

"Cedric…help me."

"Help you, baby? Help you get better?" I asked, sobbing now.

"Ye—yes. Help me…fi—

"It's ok, baby. Don't force yourself to talk."

Amanda struggled to get the words out then said, "Fi…Fi…Find…my sister."

"Your sister? Baby…your sister? Is that what you said?"

Amanda looked like she was going to cry, nodded and then closed her eyes, dozing off.

Help her find her sister? That made no sense. I wonder if she was delusional from all the meds. My poor Amanda.

When I left her to sleep and joined Ed and Elaine in the cafeteria, I relayed what I thought she said to Ed and Elaine.

The way that Amanda's parents looked at each other showed me there was something to what she said.

Ed coughed nervously and asked, "Cedric…did Amanda say anything to you about some news she received back in December?"

"What do you mean?" I asked.

"Did she tell you what we told her one night?"

I looked down and strained my eyes trying to remember what she told me.

"She said there was something you told her, that she was angry with you, but that she wasn't ready to think about it and talk about it, and I was cool with that. I knew it had something to do with her adoption, but she never said anything again after the first time she mentioned it to me, and I didn't push it."

Elaine closed her eyes and nodded. "Yes. Yes, it did have something to do with her adoption."

"Why was she asking for her sister in there? She has a sister?"

Ed put his hand on Elaine's shoulder, looked at me and said, "Because, Cedric. Amanda was an identical twin. She had a sister born five minutes after she was."

I was floored. There was another half of Amanda out there somewhere?

Holy shit.

Elaine continued, "The adoption agency only told us that the birth mother was having a girl. A woman in Boston had apparently been promised the other girl. Both sets of adoptive parents were told that the mother was having only one girl. Legally, the babies were bound to the respective parents and since both were closed adoptions, there was no information given to us about the other child. The birth mother was a fifteen-year-old drug addict. I knew someone at the adoption agency who leaked this information to me years after Amanda was born, but we chose to keep it a secret until she turned eighteen when we would then tell her, because we felt she had a right to know."

Elaine grabbed a tissue from her purse and wiped her eyes then continued, "We just didn't want to turn her world upside down when the other mother and child had no idea Amanda even existed. We don't have much information on the sister, unfortunately, but promised Amanda that if she wanted, we would look into trying to find her. We don't even have her name."

I sighed in shock at what they just told me. How had Amanda kept this news from me these past few months?

Elaine wiped her eyes again. "She had dropped the subject recently and we thought maybe she was having doubts about finding her. But Cedric, clearly, if she called out to you asking to find her sister, our poor daughter is tormented. My poor baby." Elaine began to cry uncontrollably now as Ed comforted her.

I decided in that moment that I would do whatever it took to grant Amanda her wish to find her sister. I had no clue how I was going to do that, but I knew I owed it to her after all of the damage I had done. I couldn't wait for her to wake up fully, so I could tell her myself and we could work together to find her…maybe take a trip to Boston.

That night, Amanda died.

CHAPTER 31

CEDRIC

Present Day

"What in God's name happened to you?" Allison's roommate Sonia asked as she arrived at the doorstep of my condo, staring me up and down, clearly amazed by my bearded transformation.

"Come in," I said somberly, pointing my head in Allison's direction.

Allison was sitting on my couch with her head in her hands, rubbing her temples, refusing to speak to me. I had grabbed her phone earlier before I started really trying to explain everything, pulled up Sonia's name in the contacts and texted her my address to come pick Allison up immediately at my place without further explanation. Knowing Allison wouldn't have been in any condition to leave here on her own, I wanted to make sure someone could accompany her home.

Sonia arrived faster than I expected, since someone drove her here and she was apparently already close by at a bar in Kenmore Square when she got my text. That had given me under fifteen minutes to try and explain everything before Sonia got here.

Allison had sat in silent shock as I nervously told her bits and pieces of the truth. I wasn't expecting to face this today and was unprepared, to say the least. I wasn't quite sure if she even understood me clearly. She wasn't saying anything and I was really worried about her state of mind.

I got far enough to tell her that the girl in the picture she was holding was named Amanda, that she was her twin sister and they were separated at birth, that Amanda was my college girlfriend and that Amanda died in an accident.

But there were so many holes in my story, and I couldn't seem to articulate it all from the beginning to end.

She wasn't responding coherently to me or asking any questions. She just kept shaking her head in disbelief and wouldn't say anything when I demanded that she talk to me.

Before I could fully explain the role I played in finding her, Sonia knocked on the door. When I opened it, she burst in.

"Al…are you alright?" Sonia asked as she made her way over to Allison.

Allison shook her head no, her eyes red. She was clearly still in shock and my heart was breaking not being able to comfort her. I knew I was the last person she wanted near her, so I kept my distance standing across the room, still dressed in my robe since Allison arrived unexpectedly before I had a chance to get dressed.

Sonia was glaring at me and rubbing Allison's back and after a minute, Allison then managed to look at Sonia and say hoarsely, "Let's go."

Just as Allison stood up to leave, Sonia stopped her.

"Wait…what the hell is going on here? You two weren't even together, so you couldn't have broken up again. What in the bloody hell happened? She looked to me. "Cedric? What's so bad that you thought Allison couldn't manage to take herself home safely?"

Neither Allison nor I said anything.

Sonia looked back and forth at us. "No one is going to tell me what the hell is going on?"

A tear ran down Allison's face and my fists clenched from not being able to wipe it from her cheek.

This moment was one of the worst of my entire life.

I cleared my throat and forced myself to say something.

"Sonia, Allison may not want to say anything right now. She's in shock because I just gave her some devastating news. When she is ready, she'll tell you."

I looked over at Allison, noticing that for the first time gave me a rare bit of eye contact in return.

"And…Allison, when you're ready, I need to explain more to you. I am so sorry I kept this from you all this time, but when you're ready to hear it, I'll try to explain why I did what I did," I said.

I knew she was in no condition to hear anything more from me tonight. I had done enough damage for one day.

"I am not sure I can believe anything you have to say," Allison said as she got up and suddenly opened the front door and walked out in tears.

Sonia followed and looked back at me from the hallway as Allison raced ahead of her. "Good going, asshole."

Her words didn't penetrate. She could have shot me in the chest at that moment and it might not have mattered. About a half hour passed and I needed to do something. I hadn't moved from the same spot I was standing in when she left. I got out my phone and texted her.

> Allison, please don't be scared of me. I have so much more I need to tell you. I know you're not ready to talk to me. It was never my intention to keep this from you for so long. Please, let me know when you are ready and I promise to explain everything, if you'll hear me out.

She never responded and I hadn't expected her to. As sick as I felt seeing her leave like that, an eerie bittersweet calm came over me that night as I realized that everything I feared had finally happened, and it couldn't get any worse from here.

The dread of this day had been eating away at me for months and now, for better or worse, the secret was out. Granted, I hadn't gotten to explain it to her the way I anticipated, but the main facts were out. She would need time to process everything before I would stand a chance of talking to her again and I had to accept that.

***

The next day, trumpets sounded because…I shaved. It was definitely a longtime coming.

Something else that was a longtime coming happened: I finally confessed everything to my mother, and she cried more than I had ever seen in my entire life, telling me that she always felt something was off with me during those months, years ago when Caleb moved out to Chicago to stay with me. She had wrongly suspected it was drugs and that Caleb was keeping it a secret. But of course, at the time, both of us denied that there had been anything wrong.

"Cedric, honey…why did you feel like you couldn't tell me all of this? All of these years you were keeping the fact that your first love died, from me and Dad?"

"I was ashamed. There are so many parts to what happened that I felt would devastate you back then, given how hard things were with Callie on top of things at that time. I am so sorry, Ma."

My mother and I held each other tight as Callie's iPad made noises next to us in the living room.

"Cedric, this is all so hard to believe. How am I supposed to handle seeing Allison now…if she even comes back to work? That poor girl must be so shocked and confused. Tell me again, why you never told her the truth about her sister that very first day?"

I ran my hands through my hair, took in a deep breath and exhaled. "That's the million dollar question, isn't it? I wouldn't be here in this predicament right now if I had done that. That's for sure, Mom. That's something I can't explain to you. She just had me under a spell from the moment I first laid eyes on her and I didn't want it to end. It sounds cliché, but I really think I experienced love at first sight. I wanted to be with her and wanted her to see me for me. I knew it would have ended the second I told her the truth. I was selfish, I know."

My mother pulled me in for a hug. "Selfish, yes, but I know you didn't mean to hurt her."

"No, Mom…no, that's the last thing I wanted, believe me."

"I think you need to write her a letter, son."

"A letter?"

"Yes. She is not going to want to face you for a while, honey. And you won't be able to explain it the way you want to in person. There's too much to the story and from what you told me, you really didn't do a good job of articulating everything to her face to face."

"No, I didn't. I froze," I said.

"Exactly. So, I want you to stay here with us today. Have a nice dinner, spend time with your sister, and clear your head. Then, I want you to go home and sit down and focus on what you need to say to her. Can you do that?"

"I don't think I have a choice."

"No, you don't."

That night, I spent a calm evening with my mother and sister, grateful to have such a wonderful family.

After an early dinner of spaghetti and meatballs and a couple of glasses of red wine, I felt more relaxed and took Callie for a walk around the neighborhood. Holding my sister's hand, I felt for the first time like everything would somehow turn out okay. A lot of that had to do with the weight that was lifted after telling my mother.

At one point, Callie stopped and was pulling me to go across the street.

"No, Callie. This way," I said.

Callie was pulling me harder toward the street.

"Allison," she said.

My heart pounded when I heard her say the name and then saw Callie was pointing to a girl walking across the street with long, dark hair. I soon realized it wasn't Allison, but just the few seconds I thought it might be her were enough to show me how intense it would be when I laid eyes on her again.

Would she even show up here to work with Callie next week? I didn't know how she could. If she did, at least my mother knew everything now.

She knew more than Allison did, in fact.

Not for long. I needed to get home and start working on that letter. I needed to pour my heart out to her even if it would be the first and last time.

CHAPTER 32

ALLISON

Mercury, your Ruler, goes retrograde today, Gemini, so you might be quite reflective. This presents a wonderful opportunity for great spiritual growth and deepening peace.

It had been a few days since Cedric's revelation, and I had asked for the week off from both jobs, citing a family emergency. I guess this could qualify as that.

I sat in my apartment alone listening to the sounds of children playing outside. It was Spring vacation week in Boston, and the streets were filled with kids. The warm air blew through my window screen, and the sounds of birds chirping helped me relax.

Amanda.

I had been sitting on the couch, staring at Amanda's picture, still in disbelief. In the photo, she was alone and leaning up against a tree. The sounds outside seem to add to the scene in the picture and I tried to imagine her coming to life. In the photo, Amanda is smiling lovingly at the photographer. It was obvious who she was looking at and I still couldn't wrap my head around it.

She was dead.

I didn't even know she existed, and she was dead. I would never know her.

But Cedric did.

Cedric knew more about my past than I did, and that unnerved me.

Cedric was my sister's boyfriend…*my sister's boyfriend*. It still didn't fully register. There was so much more I needed to know. Why was he the one looking for me anyway? Did my sister even know about me before she died? I had so many questions. And why did he try to find me now?

There were so many questions left unanswered, but I wasn't able to face him the other day a second longer once he told me the truth.

When I had first found the photo, it hadn't even occurred to me for one second that it wasn't me, even though I hadn't remembered taking that picture. The shock I felt upon hearing that this was actually a photo of my twin was indescribable.

A twin.

This was like a bad Lifetime movie come true. It didn't make sense at first, but the more I thought about it…it was certainly plausible: I never knew anything about my birth mother or the circumstances of my birth.

My mother always said she had no information either. That was the truth because my mother would have never kept something like this from me. How could the people at the adoption agency have allowed the separation of two sisters?

The phone ringing startled me out of my thoughts.

I picked up. "Hello?"

"Al…just checking in," Sonia said.

Sonia would call me everyday from her nursing rotation to make sure I haven't done anything stupid. My mental state the first twenty-four hours after Cedric's condo encounter was not stable. Sonia had considered taking me to a doctor to get anti-anxiety meds, but I refused.

"You don't need to call me every two hours, you know," I said.

"Have you stopped thinking about it for even a minute?"

"Of course not. Would you stop thinking about it if you found out you had a twin? And then found out she was dead a minute later?"

"I can't fucking imagine, Al. I can't. I am so sorry."

We were both silent for a bit and then I said. "I need to get out of the

229

house. Let's go out to dinner tonight."

"Are you serious, Al? That would be fantastic! You really need to get your mind off of things. It's a date."

"Love you," I said.

"Love you, too."

Just as I hung up the phone, it rang again, and I picked up.

"Sonia…come on…this is ridiculous."

There was a pause.

"Allison?"

My stomach turned as I realized who it was. I didn't respond.

"Allison? Are you there?"

"Yes," I whispered as my heart beat rapidly.

"I've been so worried about you."

"Why are you calling, Cedric?"

"I wanted to give you some space, but I couldn't wait any longer. I need to know you're okay."

"I'm okay, but I am not ready to talk to you."

Cedric let out a deep breath into the phone. "Fair enough. I just needed to hear your voice, really. I still care about you…so much, Allison. So much. Please don't hate me. Please—"

I quietly hung up the phone because I was afraid of what I might say next. Tears streamed down my face. He thought I hated him.

That was the problem. I didn't hate him. My feelings for him were still strong, and I hated myself for feeling this way.

***

A couple of more days passed and the funk I was in was slowly lifting.

It was seventy degrees outside and I decided to wear a delicate, pink cotton sundress and take a walk.

Putting on some silver flip flop wedges and grabbing my purse, I headed out the door and breathed in the fresh, mild air as a chorus of birds chirped. Days like these, I swear I could smell the scent of the sun.

I stopped at a corner store and bought something I hadn't consumed in years: a Slush Puppy frozen drink. Sipping it fast through the tiny, thin straw, I got brain freeze as I continued walking down the side streets of my neighborhood.

Two little girls holding hands skipping down the street passed me, and I immediately thought of the sister I never knew. Would we have been close like that? Would she still be alive if we weren't separated? Probably. What kind of mother separates identical twins?

My mood was darkening a bit, and I decided to walk back to my apartment. As I approached my house, I dropped my drink on the sidewalk, startled to see Cedric sitting on the stairs waiting for me.

He noticed me and I froze, stopping about six feet short of him. His beautiful, crystal blue eyes shined in the sunlight and looked like they were glowing. It pained me that he looked so goddamn handsome.

He had shaved that beard away and had just a little hair leftover on his chin. He was wearing a casual, black fitted v-neck shirt and jeans and I could smell his intoxicating scent blowing toward me in the breeze.

We just stood there staring at each other. Even though I was scared, a part of me wanted him to approach me...hold me. I didn't know exactly what this new situation meant for us, but the pull was still strong. It was probably stronger than ever because he just seemed so forbidden to me now.

He was my sister's boyfriend.

Cedric stood up but didn't approach me, as I kept my distance.

"You look good, Allison."

The sound of his voice sent shivers throughout my body.

"Why are you here, Cedric?" I asked.

"Actually, I wanted to give you this."

He reached out a yellow envelope, prompting me to take it. Was he serving me with some legal document? What was this?

"What is it?" I asked nervously.

"It's everything. Everything I wanted to tell you but couldn't...the other day."

Finally approaching him, my hand was shaking as I took the envelope from him, carefully avoiding touching his skin. Cedric stood still, never taking his eyes off mine. He seemed to be searching my eyes for a clue as to what I was feeling and then said, "Promise me, you'll read it, Allison."

I continued staring at him, still wanting desperately for him to touch me, knowing he wouldn't cross that line and that if he did, I would pull back.

"I will," I finally said.

I flinched as Cedric's hand touched my cheek and I briefly closed my eyes, relishing the brief contact before he returned his arm down and said, "Thank you."

I walked past him up my front stairs, taking the envelope with me.

Before walking in the front door, I looked back briefly to find Cedric still standing in place, looking at me with his hands in his pockets. The sun glare made him only partially visible. Then, I closed the door behind me.

***

It was nightfall, and the yellow envelope taunted me from across the room. I wanted so badly to open it but hadn't yet mustered up the courage. I was truly afraid of what I might discover in it.

Prolonging the inevitable, I chose instead to daydream about the Cedric I knew before all of this happened.

I missed the feeling of being on cloud nine and so infatuated with him, being held by him and feeling safe in his arms. It was such a short time in retrospect…but it was truly the best time of my life.

But it wasn't real.

I wondered how much time Amanda had with him…how close they were, whether his feelings were stronger for her than for me. I hated myself for thinking that, but I couldn't help it. I felt sick. I knew that maybe everything I needed to know was in that letter and decided I just needed to just open it already.

So, taking a deep breath, I stood up from the couch and walked over to the letter lying on the table.

Picking it up, I returned to the couch and rubbed my hands over the fairly large yellow envelope.

My heart thumped furiously and I opened a window to let some air in.

I took another deep breath and exhaled, opening the envelope slowly, careful not to rip the contents. Inside was a folded letter with a few pages stapled together and handwritten on heavy high quality stock paper. My chest was heaving in anticipation as I started to read it.

Dear Allison,

First of all, thank you for taking the time to read this. I know it must have been a difficult decision to open this letter. It's difficult for me to even think about you reading everything I am about to write. But I am also relieved to be able to finally tell you everything. I would say that I wished I had told you this story that first day I laid eyes on you, but that wouldn't be the truth. I am fairly certain that if I had bombarded you with the truth about me early on, I would have never experienced what were truly the best days of my life, the weeks spent with you as your friend and as your lover.

*I have to start from the beginning. I was twenty-one when I met Amanda Thompson. She was a freshman, and I was a senior at Northwestern. I spotted her across the room at a campus party and was immediately taken by her. She walked in and immediately fell on her ass after she slipped on the floor that was wet from the keg. I started cracking up, and she walked over to me to kick my ass and the rest was history. She was beautiful in a natural way and easy to talk to. I dated a lot in those days, and it was rare that one girl kept my attention for longer than a week. But Amanda was different. I was a bit of a jackass back then, but she didn't seem to be scared away by that persona. She was smart enough to see that it **was** a persona. I was a kid with a tough exterior from the streets of Boston. She was a sheltered Daddy's girl from the suburbs. But*

Amanda seemed to be able to peel through the fake layers I had built up and had a way of making me want to open up about the real me...my insecurities and fears, my hopes and dreams.

She was young, only seventeen when I met her. I was her first real boyfriend. I got to know her parents, Ed and Elaine, fairly well during that time, and they were pretty cool with everything as long as I didn't spend the night in her room and vice versa. She lived at home, and I lived on campus, so sometimes I would go over to her parent's house for dinner. Ed and Elaine had adopted Amanda as a newborn, and she was their only child. They treated her like a princess because they were so happy to have her since they couldn't have kids of their own. She even looked a little like Elaine.

We dated for almost a year. I was her first. Up until the end, it was the first time in my life that I had never cheated on a girlfriend. She would tell me that she wanted to spend the rest of her life with me. I told her I loved her, but truthfully, I had my doubts about making a lifelong commitment so young. I was getting ready to graduate and possibly move away, and she was just starting college. But Amanda didn't care about all that. She just wanted to be with me. That wasn't enough for me, Allison. What came next is the hard part of my story.

One night Amanda came to my dorm after I had ignored her calls that day. She caught me kissing another girl. It hadn't gotten as far as anything further and probably wouldn't have, but I had lost control of myself in the days leading up to that. I was probably going to end things for her own good but never expected her to see what she walked in on. She was devastated, and the second I saw the look on her face, I was devastated, too. I knew then and there that I cared so much about this person. I felt like I had hurt my best friend, and I had.

Amanda ran out of my room that night and drove

off. She was upset and probably driving erratically. That was the night of the car accident that eventually killed her. I am so sorry to be the one to have to tell you this, Allison. I still to this day feel some of the blame for what happened, most of the blame, actually. Your sister was so strong. She fought for her life for many days in and out of a coma.

What I need you to know is that shortly before Amanda died, Ed and Elaine told her about you. They didn't know your name or where you were living, but Elaine had gotten information from a friend at the adoption agency years before that there had been a twin born to the anonymous birth mother who had you and Amanda. Other than that, Elaine only knew that your Mom was a fifteen-year-old drug addict. Amanda's parents decided to tell her about you after she turned eighteen and vowed to help find you if that was what she wanted.

On her hospital bed on the day she died, her last words to me were to ask me to find you. She said "find my sister."

I had a really hard time after Amanda died. I blamed myself, and Caleb actually came and stayed with me for several weeks. I never even told my mother about anything that happened there or the truth about you until a few days ago.

There is one other upsetting thing that I need to tell you. It's really why I think I have been so afraid to tell you the truth. It's the one part of my past I am most ashamed of, and it's very difficult for me to talk about even to this day. But I want to tell you everything. When Amanda was in the hospital, the doctors discovered she had been pregnant at the time of the accident and lost the baby. It was my baby, Allison. Amanda had not yet told me, and I don't even know if she knew. She told me she was on the pill, and I trusted that I couldn't get her pregnant. I still struggle with whether she knew or

*not when she caught me that night, whether that's
why she had been calling me a lot that day. And more
than that, I struggle with the fact that I helped
cause an accident that also killed my own child. I
know that it is probably very difficult for you to
hear this, and I am sorry to have to tell you that
about me.*

I put down the letter and started sobbing. I couldn't read anymore right now…and there was a lot left unread.

Walking over to the refrigerator, I wiped my eyes with my shirt, poured myself a glass of water and sat down at the kitchen table, taking a long sip. Rubbing my temples, I breathed in and out repeatedly trying to process what Cedric revealed. So many emotions floated through my head.

While I found Cedric's honesty endearing, it was all too much to take at once as shock, sadness and jealousy hit me like a ton of bricks.

I was still in shock to learn about how my sister died. I also felt sad that Cedric blamed himself. Clearly, he never could have predicted what would happen.

Jealousy also consumed me. My sister had been intimate with Cedric, and they had created a child together, something that I would never get to experience with him. Even though the baby tragically died, a child was conceived. That child would have also been related to me.

Shaking my head, I tried to make sense of it all. My breathing slowed, and I wanted to know more. I needed to know more, so I walked back over to the couch and picked up the letter again.

*So, you're probably wondering why all of this is
coming to light now, twelve years later.
After Amanda died, I managed to graduate and
ended up staying in Chicago for about eight years.
That's where I started my career before I moved
back to Boston. I kept in touch with Ed and Elaine
during those years. Sometimes, they would have me
over for dinner, and we would talk about Amanda. I
think I reminded them of her and they liked to see*

me from time to time for that reason. I had even later confided in them about what happened the night of the accident, and they tried to convince me it wasn't my fault. All these years, I still don't fully believe that. Anyway, they're good, forgiving people, and they didn't deserve to lose their only child.

The Thompsons had tried to get information on their own over the years about your whereabouts and kept hitting dead ends. They felt they owed it to Amanda to find you. I think they missed her so much that they wanted to find a part of her alive in you. They used a couple of private investigators and finally hired a different guy a little over a year ago, and this one was able to figure out the name of the person who adopted you (your Mom). With that information, he was able to determine your name and that you lived in Boston. This investigator, named Brandon Samuels, then found out your address and followed you one day to the Stardust diner, which is how I knew where you worked. He gave all of the information to the Thompsons, and they contacted me and asked if I would be the one to meet you first. Ed has been battling cancer, and it wasn't the right time for them to travel to Boston, because it would have interrupted his treatments. We all couldn't believe that you were in the same city as me to begin with. So, it seemed to make sense that I would be the one to approach you.

I had every intention of doing the right thing that first day I walked into the diner. When I saw you, though, I was blown away and lost all sense of reason. It was like looking at a grown up version of Amanda, but you were even more beautiful than I could have ever imagined you'd be. I watched you talk to the customers, and your demeanor was so sweet. I just wanted to watch you like a fly on the wall. I didn't know how I could possibly bring up the subject of why I came to see you, so I just stared at you. I wasn't expecting to have that kind of

237

reaction. I needed more time to just let it sink in. So, I left that day. But I hadn't been able to stop thinking about you. I decided I wanted to get to know you before springing everything on you. So, I planned to go back to the diner another time and maybe strike up a conversation. That was the day you weren't there, that I left my credit card. Obviously, you know that was the same night I drove you home and we talked for the first time. When I found out you had no family, I was floored, but it also made me want to be there for you in some way.

With every second we spent together, I became more and more blinded by my intense attraction to you. I gave into the temptation to continue the façade, because my feelings for you were real, and I wanted desperately to explore them without judgment. I have never felt so drawn to anyone so quickly. You may think that it was because you looked like her, but that's not entirely the case. A lot can change in twelve years, both physically and emotionally. If anything, I was actually surprised at how little you actually reminded me of the eighteen-year-old girl I knew. I was basically a boy when I dated your sister, Allison. I didn't know what I wanted, and it's quite likely Amanda and I wouldn't have ended up together had she lived. I wasn't done sowing my wild oats (and she hadn't even started) and it's possible, I would have fucked things up.

I know my decision to take things as far I did with you was selfish. But I don't regret it, Allison. I just don't. From that first night in the car, I knew there was no going back. I had no control over the pull I felt toward you. I needed to have you, to be with you. I always intended to tell you everything even after we got together—you need to know that. I wasn't going to keep it from you forever; I just didn't feel the time was right. Really, I didn't want to lose you, so I kept putting it off.

Around New Years, things had just gotten sexual between us, and I was falling hard for you. I couldn't get enough of you. That's when my world started crumbling around me. I got a call from Elaine around that time that changed things for me and made me realize I was no longer in control of when you would find out the truth. She told me that in the course of the investigation to find you, Samuels also located your birth mother. Not only that, this woman wanted to know how to find you. I knew that it was only a matter of time before you would find everything out, and that scared the shit out of me. I decided not to make things even more complicated by continuing to get more serious with you until I either I grew the guts to tell you or you found out another way.

The night that I ran into you at my mother's, I had planned to finally tell her everything. I needed to get it off my chest and wanted her advice on how to handle things, because I was obviously not handling them at all. When you asked me if I was seeing someone else, I was caught off guard, panicked and lied. That was a stupid thing to do, but it just came out. I know that didn't help things. I wasn't seeing anyone else and I'm still not. I am so sorry for lying to you.

I am most sorry that finding the photo in my mother's basement upset you. That must have been a shock. I didn't even remember that I had that binder. Those were the only physical items I had to remember her by that were mine. But now, in retrospect, I am glad you found it. It forced me to tell you the truth, which you deserved all along. Just a note, I don't have any other information about your birth mother. Ed and Elaine never heard from her beyond that initial information from the investigator. I don't know if she has contacted you directly, but Samuels can get her info for you if you would like to contact her. I'll send you an email with his contact information, as well as the contact info for Ed and Elaine Thompson. They really want to meet you, and I hope you can make that happen for them. Don't blame them for my mistakes.

I can only hope at this point that you don't hate me, but you'll never hear me say that I regret even one second of being with you. I'll understand if you can't, but if you ever find it in your heart to forgive me—that would mean the world to me. You mean the world to me.

Cedric

P.S. Hopefully you noticed that there is something else in this envelope.

What? I grabbed the yellow envelope that the letter was contained in and reached into the bottom. Inside, was a small Ziploc bag and as I took the note out of it, a ring fell out. *What the—?*

It was a beautiful antique-looking white gold or silver ring with a green stone. The design was really ornate and stunning. What was this about? I unfolded the note that read:

Allison, I bought this ring at an antique fair right after I first laid eyes on you. It reminded me so much of the color of your eyes...the stone even has the same gold speckles. I just had to get it. It was a family heirloom of the old lady that sold it to me. She made me promise to give it to someone special. I knew even then I'd give it to you someday. Even though I know I have lost my chance with you, I still want you to have it because it belongs to you. Please let it remind you always how special you are.

The ring fit perfectly on my right ring finger. A tear fell down my cheek as I wiggled my hand to catch the reflection of the light in the stone. It was the most beautiful thing anyone had ever given me.

CHAPTER 33

CEDRIC

Five Months Later

We were by the ocean in West Palm Beach. Allison was straddling me on the sand, her big beautiful green eyes shining in the sunlight. Callie ran by and poured water out of a bucket all over us, and we laughed hysterically, both getting up and chasing after Callie toward the shoreline. Allison, Callie and I fell to the ground in the water still laughing uncontrollably. We were distracted when all of a sudden a gargantuan wave approached, but Allison was facing me and didn't see it coming. The wave pushed Callie and me to shore, but Allison was gone. "Allison!"

"Allison!"

"Cedric? Cedric. Wake up!" Stephanie yelled, shaking my shoulders.

My eyes blinked repeatedly and my heart pounded. "Wha—Stephanie?"

"You were having a nightmare. Who's Allison?" she asked.

"Huh?" I said, intentionally avoiding the question.

"Who's Allison? You were yelling for Allison," she repeated.

"Oh. Yeah. No one. I don't know. It's okay. Go back to bed."

Good answer, asshole.

Stephanie sighed and rolled over, but I could tell she was still awake. God, I hoped my sleep talk wasn't too dramatic. I dreamt a lot about

241

Allison, but this was the first time I had done it in front of someone.

Stephanie and I had been dating over a month now. She was a lawyer at a firm downtown and we met in the Boston Common during our respective lunch breaks. I had been mulling over life on a bench when she sat down beside me with her Au Bon Pain salad. We shared stories about our jobs and watched together as kids ran around in the frog pond. We ended up meeting for dinner that night and have been casually dating ever since.

I had been forcing myself to move on.

She started sleeping over a couple of nights ago. We hadn't had sex yet, mostly because I wasn't ready to cross that line. I was pretty sure *she* was ready and willing. Actually, I knew that for a fact being that she literally tried to get into my boxers last night. I just hadn't wanted to go there for some reason.

For some reason…who was I kidding? I knew why.

Stephanie was beautiful, Filipino, with nice skin, a pretty smile, a great personality, and she was smarter than probably anyone I knew. It's not that I wasn't attracted to her. Taking it to the next level just didn't feel right.

Stephanie was making waffles in my kitchen when I strolled out of bed.

"Good morning, dreamy."

"Mornin'."

"That dream must have been intense. You were shaking, Cedric."

"Was I?"

Drop the subject. Drop the subject. Drop the subject.

"Yeah. I am glad I woke you up."

"Me too."

Another lie. I would take being with Allison any way I could, even in the form of a bizarre dream.

"What did you want to do today?"

It was Labor Day. I knew my mother was having a cookout, but I wasn't sure if I wanted to go over there. Stephanie and I were supposed to be hanging out and I would probably have to bring her. I wasn't really ready to introduce her to my mother.

"What did you have in mind?"

Just as I spoke those words, my phone rang, and I answered it.

"Hello."

"Sup, shitface," my brother said.

"Wassup, Caleb."

"You better get your ass down to Mom's today, or she's gonna roast more than that pig."

"You and Denise going?"

"Of course. You think we could get away with not going to Ma's cookout? Although I think Denise will throw up when she smells the pig. Her senses have been in overload this pregnancy."

"Who else is gonna be there?"

"Just Callie, Maria, Kurt and maybe Bruno, I think…the usual crew."

"Okay, we'll probably show up for a bit."

"We?" he asked curiously.

I walked into the bedroom so Stephanie couldn't hear everything I was saying.

"I told you about Stephanie," I whispered in a barely audible voice.

"Yeah, you did. But you didn't sound too enthusiastic…so I just assumed—"

"She's cool," I whispered.

"Cool…but not—"

"Yeah. Yeah…I know what you're gonna say."

"You do?"

"I fucking dreamt about her last night…out loud. I fucking wake up to Stephanie asking me who fuck Allison is. How fucked up is that?"

"Pretty fucked up."

"Yeah."

"Well, it's good you're trying to move on. I mean you still haven't heard from her right?"

"Not a thing. I still don't even know where she is."

"Hmmm."

"Gotta go. I'll see you later," I said and hung up the phone.

I waited before going back into the kitchen, sitting on the bed, staring out the window. It was a beautiful, cool sunny day where you couldn't distinguish whether it was late summer or early fall in Boston.

The last time I had seen Allison was the day I gave her the letter five months ago. She looked like an angel that day, wearing a pink dress, her hair blowing in the wind, her cheeks pink from the shock of seeing me sitting on her front steps. Late that same night, I got a text from her.

> Cedric, I really appreciate your taking the time to explain everything to me through this letter. I need time to absorb all of this and ask that you please not contact me until I have had that opportunity. Thank you for the ring. It's beautiful, although I am not sure if I can wear it, but I will cherish it.

It hurt so badly to hear her tell me not to contact her, but I was relieved that she read everything I had to say. I had been completely honest and for the first time since I met her, I had nothing to hide anymore.

That was five months ago, though, and Allison was nowhere to be found now.

Mom told me she had taken a leave of absence from working with Callie three months ago but assured her she would be back. I still didn't know how Allison managed to keep working with Callie for the first two months after the letter, but she did. She was amazing like that.

Walking back into the kitchen, I noticed that Stephanie was already sitting down, drinking coffee and eating her waffle.

"Sorry I took so long."

"No worries, Blue Eyes."

I suddenly felt nauseous when she called me that. It was what Allison said she used to call me before we met.

My mind switched to thinking about whether taking Stephanie to my mother's today was a good idea.

"So, what's the verdict on today?" she asked.

"Do you like pork?"

"Is that what you guys call it these days?" Stephanie winked.

"Ha…no, I mean actual pork, as in pig meat."

"Yeah…it's okay. I prefer chicken."

"My mother has a cookout every Labor Day, and we roast a pig. It's kind of a European tradition she picked up from her grandmother. Would you want to come with me? I sort of can't get out of it."

"Is the pig alive?"

"Oink. Oink." I winked. "Just kidding. No. It's already dead on arrival."

"Oh, thank God." She sighed.

"Don't thank God til you see its face. It's still pretty gross, but the meat tastes great when everything's done," I said, taking a bite of my waffle.

"Sounds like a plan. I'd love to meet your family."

Hearing her say that made me cringe because I knew I wasn't ready for this with Stephanie, but I just didn't have the energy to get out of it.

Not knowing what to say to that, I repeated, "Sounds like a plan."

CHAPTER 34

ALLISON

Three Months Earlier

The harmonious fire Moon brings interesting people crossing your path, Gemini. Their conversations are enlightening and leave you inspired over their encouraging words. You feel refreshed and motivated to continue on the course of those pushed-aside dreams.

The fasten seatbelt sign lit up, and my heart was racing in anticipation of what would greet me once I left this plane. I always hated flying but mostly takeoff and landing.

As the plane slowly descended, I prayed that it wouldn't hit the ground in a ball of flames. My nerves were acting up for a lot of different reasons right now.

When the jet touched down, I mouthed a silent *thank you* to the man upstairs and realized that my breathing was still rapid, even though the plane had safely landed.

Thanking the pilot as I exited, I walked slowly down the long hallway that led to the inside of the terminal.

I didn't know what they looked like, but they said they would find me. I hoped this wasn't a mistake as I looked around and saw that no one made eye contact.

Suddenly, I turned around and saw a smiling woman who looked about sixty wheeling an equally beaming man approaching me slowly. The looks of amazement on their faces confirmed that I had found them.

"Allison!" Elaine said as she hugged me tightly then pulled back to examine my features. After a stare that seemed to last forever, she said, "You are stunning, honey. Oh my God."

I must have been blushing. "Hi, Elaine. It's great to finally meet you," I said nervously.

I bent down to hug Ed who was in a wheelchair. I knew he was being treated for cancer but was surprised to see how weak he actually was. When I pushed back, Ed's tears were flowing as we made eye contact.

"I can't believe this. It's surreal. I'm sorry for being so emotional. I know this must be strange for you," he said.

"Don't worry about that. I understand," I said as I took his hand, still bending down.

I stood up, and the three of us walked silently together to the baggage claim. and I separated from them to get my luggage. The few minutes alone were enough to grab my bearings again.

We resumed walking to the parking garage as I wheeled my suitcase, and Elaine wheeled Ed.

"We thought we could stop for lunch on the way home," Elaine said.

"That would be great," I said even though I was hardly hungry, as nerves had taken away my appetite.

Ed turned around to face me in the elevator. "Do you like pancakes, Allison?"

I smiled down at Ed. "Yes, I do."

"There is this great Pancake House right off the highway on our way home. You can get breakfast or lunch and the best pancakes you've tasted anytime of day, lots of different kinds, too."

"That sounds great, Ed." I could tell he probably wasn't feeling well and hoped he wasn't pushing himself being out like this.

As Elaine helped Ed into the car, I loaded my suitcase into the trunk. The ride to the restaurant was quiet, with Ed occasionally looking back at me and smiling as we made small talk.

"Was the flight okay?" he asked.

"As good as could be. I don't really like to fly."

"I don't blame you." He laughed.

When we got to the restaurant, the smell of the food helped bring some of my appetite back. I ordered blueberry pancakes per Ed's suggestion.

I sat across from Ed and Elaine as we waited for our food, looking around the room to avoid the awkwardness of staring right at them as they examined the similarities between their dead daughter and me.

"So, Allison, is there anything you want to ask us?" Elaine asked.

After a long pause, I started to recall the questions I had gone over in my head prior to the trip.

"I guess I want to know how long you knew about me and why you never tried to find me sooner."

Elaine looked down to gather her thoughts and then raised her head. "We knew for several years...probably from the time Amanda was five that there had been a twin, because a friend of mine who worked at the adoption agency confided in me after she left her job. We had no idea prior to that. She made it clear that there was no other information about your whereabouts. In retrospect, I wished that we had looked for you sooner, so that you could have met your sister. We made a decision when Amanda was young, though, that we would tell her when she was eighteen and let her decide whether she wanted to find you. I am so sorry, Allison," Elaine said.

I looked over at Ed and he was starting to cry again.

"Ed, please. It's okay. You need to save your energy. I am not upset with you. I promise." I reached over across the table and grabbed his hand and we stayed like that until the food arrived. I had just met these people, but my heart broke for Ed, and I wanted to comfort him.

The three of us ate quietly until Ed said, "Mandy used to love this restaurant."

I let that sink in for a minute, and then dropped my fork. "Did you just call her Mandy? Was that her nickname?"

"Only Ed called her Mandy. That was his nickname for her," Elaine said as Ed smiled at her.

Chills ran through me as I recalled the song that played at the diner the very first time I saw Cedric: it was *Mandy* by Barry Manilow.

I picked up my fork and ate again in silence as I thought about that eerie coincidence and seemed to feel her presence in this booth. It might have been my imagination, but I felt like she was here…now. I could sense it. And Ed's use of the name today, and my recollection of the song could be her way of showing me she has been here all along. I kept this realization to myself.

Ed interrupted my thoughts. "Allison, I want you to know, we thought we were doing the right thing all those years. If we had known what would have happened, we would have handled things differently."

I closed my eyes briefly and nodded. "I know."

After a bit more silence, Elaine asked, "Can you tell us a little about your childhood?"

I smiled as I recalled my mother. "Sure. I had a great childhood. I guess you could say Amanda and I were both lucky to be placed in good homes. My mother, Margo, was single and always wanted a child of her own. She made a good living and was on a waiting list and one day out of the blue got a call about a baby girl. I was hers ever since that day. She was my everything and provided a great life for me. I never had a father, but she was enough. She worked, but she never missed a dance class, never missed a soccer game. And when I grew up, there was nothing I couldn't confide in her about. She died from cancer a couple of years ago. So…it's been hard. She was my best friend."

As I started to cry, Ed reached across the table and grabbed my hand again and joined me in tears, saying, "So, you lost your everything, and we lost ours."

I nodded. "Yeah," I said sniffling and over the course of the next hour, I reminisced more about my mother. They shared memories of Amanda, who, it turned out, was a cheerleader and won some competitions. She also studied abroad in Spain during the summer before her senior year in high school and was a grade A student. She had been majoring in journalism at

Northwestern.

The lunch was emotional, but the ride to their house was quiet.

When we pulled up to a beautiful but modest home in a nice suburb of Chicago, I realized my sister must have had the typical suburban upbringing.

Elaine brought Ed inside to his bedroom upstairs and when she returned, I followed her down some stairs off of the kitchen into a converted garage that had been made into a bedroom.

"This was Amanda's room. I thought maybe you would like to sleep here. It's not exactly how she left it, but some of the things, I didn't touch, like the bulletin board of photos over there and the items on the chest of drawers. I donated her clothes some years back, so the closet is empty. Feel free to hang all your things. It's been a guest room for many years now."

I looked around at the pretty pink walls and décor. It was the epitome of a feminine room. There was a pink bedspread with small white flowers—vintage Pottery Barn—and the wallpaper had thick pink and white lines.

There was one window at the front of the room, which let a lot of sun in and a light summer breeze came through it.

"I'll let you get situated. I am going to run upstairs and get you some towels and things," she said.

"Thanks so much, Elaine."

Left alone in Amanda's room, I sat on the bed, looked around and then closed my eyes, relishing the breeze. If I thought I could feel her presence at the restaurant, it was definitely out in full force right here. This room would be the epicenter, actually.

I immediately walked over to the bulletin board that hung on the wall. There were dozens of pictures held up by thumb tacks: Amanda's high school graduation, cheerleading shots, a prom picture with a blonde boy who looked like Zach from the show *Saved By the Bell*. Then, I noticed the same picture that I had found of Amanda in Cedric's binder. I took it off the wall and looked on the back.

To my gorgeous girlfriend, thank you for agreeing to pose for me. Love you, baby. Cedric.

I swallowed hard at seeing Cedric's handwriting and from seeing the words "Love you."

I stuck that photo back onto the board, noticing another one of a young Cedric and Amanda, smiling from ear to ear, wearing St. Patrick's Day hats and green shirts. It was always hard to see his beautiful face, but it was even harder to see him looking so happy with her, especially when she looked identical to me when I was eighteen. It was all so strange.

I turned that photo around and noticed that the date was March 2002. It was taken a month before she died. I felt tears start to form as I tried to block the accident and how she suffered before she died out of my mind.

She was so young. And she wanted to find me...she wanted me there. I had no idea she even existed, and I was probably sitting in a mall food court eating taco bell when she died.

I returned to the bed, clutching the photo in tears. There were so many unknowns. Would she and Cedric have gotten married and had the baby? Would she and I have met and become close? I would never know. As I continued to stare at the photo, my confused emotions continued. The photo made me jealous because he clearly cared for her, but it also made me mad because he was possibly going to break up with her a month later. And was she pregnant in the photo?

Just then, Elaine startled me when she returned with the towels and saw me crying. She sat next to me on the bed and saw the photo in my hand, taking it gently away and looking at it.

"Cedric told me everything, you know," she said.

"What do you mean?"

"Honey, we had put him in a very difficult position, Ed and I, asking him to be the one to find you. We never really considered, his feelings...how he might feel about you, what should now be obvious...that he could fall for you. We just wanted to know you were okay and for you to know about Amanda, because that was her wish. Cedric was already in

251

Boston and with Ed so sick, it made the most sense to ask him to confront you."

"What exactly did Cedric tell you about us?"

"He called sometime after you found the photo at his mother's house. He was in tears, Allison. He confessed that he had found you months before, but had kept it from us and that you two had grown very close all those weeks. He was devastated because he knew he'd lost you."

"That was a real shock, Elaine, finding out about her that way." I sobbed.

Elaine put her arm around me. "I know it must have been. I'm so sorry." After a pause, she continued, "I asked him something that night, though, and I think you should know about it."

I turned to her suddenly. "What?"

"Well, I could hear how tormented he was. I asked him if he was in love with you. He didn't even hesitate, Allison. He told me he was."

I let out a deep sigh. That was hard to hear. Even in his letter, he never used the word love. He had never said those words to me at all.

"Can I ask you something, Elaine?"

"Sure, honey."

"How have you been able to forgive Cedric so easily? I mean, he thinks he's to blame for the accident, but how do you feel?"

"Oh, honey. He wasn't to blame for her losing control of the car. He was a kid who made a bad choice, like so many others. Cedric stayed by her side every second in that hospital. He would have given his own life to save hers and told me so many times. I do believe she was his best friend, but they were kids. Amanda was eighteen and Cedric was only twenty-two. He was older, yes, but still so young and immature. Deep down, I cannot be sure they would have lasted had the accident never happened. Neither one had lived their lives yet. Even if she had survived and had the baby, I still think it would have been too much for them to sustain their relationship at that age.

"How did you feel when you found out she had been pregnant?"

"We were shocked, of course. But we found out after she had lost the baby and while she was fighting for her life, so the issue wasn't dealt with in the same way it might have been had she and the baby been healthy. I knew my daughter was on the pill, because we talked about that so I don't know what happened. I guess nothing is 100-percent."

"Thank you for answering my questions, Elaine. I know it must be hard to relive everything."

"It's okay, honey. You know, when Cedric told me how he felt about you, I have to be honest. I didn't understand how he could fall in love with someone so quickly. But now that I have met you, I think I understand exactly how that could happen."

***

My trip to Illinois was only supposed to be a few days.

We spent most of the time at the house, making meals, playing cards and getting to know each other. Elaine cooked Amanda's favorite Beef Stroganoff for me and showed me how to make it. They also showed me some of Amanda's childhood videos, and we all cried for different reasons: Ed and Elaine for what they lost, myself for what I never knew.

Overall, it felt as though I were visiting a long lost aunt and uncle. We got along well and they made me feel like part of a family, especially, Ed whose calm and welcoming demeanor got me to open up about everything that had been bothering me these past couple of years.

I poured my heart out to him about Nate, dropping out of grad school, losing my mother, finding my purpose and about falling hard for Cedric. He gave me some good advice and urged me to take one day at a time and that everything would work out. He told me to only worry about the day at hand. And today, there was no place I felt more wanted or needed than this brick home in Naperville.

The day before I was supposed to leave, Elaine had to work and someone had come to the house to stay with Ed. Elaine had told me that Ed had to quit his well-paying job as a technology consultant when he began receiving cancer treatments. Elaine, who never had to work during their marriage before, now had to return to the workforce to help pay for medical expenses. So, she worked as a teacher's aide at a local school. Part of that salary also paid for a visiting nurse type person to help take care of Ed while Elaine worked. This person would also help make meals and take Ed to appointments.

Elaine had mentioned that since I had been around, Ed seemed happier than he had been in a long time and he seemed to be stronger.

As I sat drinking my coffee while a woman named Alicia tended to Ed, I had a light bulb moment. Why couldn't I stay a little longer? I wasn't exactly eager to get back to Boston, and if Ed was in good spirits with me here, maybe I could help take care of him for Elaine and save them from having to hire help?

That night at dinner, before I had a chance to propose the idea to Elaine, Ed must have been reading my mind.

"Allison…I really wish you didn't have to go so soon. I feel like we were just getting to know each other."

"Well, it's funny you say that. I was thinking of something and wanted to run it by you both."

"Oh?" Elaine said.

"Well, I was thinking…maybe I could stay for a while. Not just to hang around…but maybe I could be the one taking care of Ed while you go to work? We could play cards and I could keep him company during his chemo. What do you think?"

"My goodness, Allison, that's quite a sweet proposition, but don't you have a life to get back to? What about your two jobs?

"The diner won't miss me, and I can take a leave of absence from my other job. Sure, my clients need me, but I think right now, Ed honestly needs me more. Besides, I owe it to my sister. She would help if she could be here."

Elaine smiled but looked hesitant to accept my offer until Ed spoke up.

He turned to us, clearing his throat. "Elaine, if I might give my two cents on what Allison is proposing?"

We both looked at him and let him speak.

"Aside from losing Amanda, battling this disease has been the darkest time of my life. Allison, whether you know it or not…your being here has taken that darkness away. I don't want to keep you from your life in Boston, but if you are serious about staying here…there is nothing I would want more."

My mouth formed a huge smile and I got up to hug him.

"It's settled then," I said.

***

I needed them as much as they needed me. That's what it came down to.

Two and a half months later, Ed's treatments ended, and he was in remission. I had been there every day with him for every treatment and it was safe to say, I had a new number one fan.

I think my bond with Ed, more so than Elaine, had something to do with the fact that I never experienced having a father. My mother couldn't be replaced, but there was no competition for the role of Dad.

Ed quickly became very protective of me, and the advice he gave me was more to the point and blunt than I remember getting from my Mom. Overall, I was figuring out that even though I never felt I needed one, it was pretty damn cool to have a father figure.

One night after dessert, Elaine was cleaning up in the kitchen and Ed and I were sitting down in the living room when he turned to me. "I want you to know something, kid. If I knew that your birth mother had given birth to two girls, I would have adopted you too that day you were born. You would have been my daughter. It would have been for the sheer fact that you were Amanda's twin. But I never got that opportunity. But let me tell you, now that I know you and the type of person you have become, I know that the right person raised you, because she did a tremendous job. I also know that I would choose you as a daughter today for more reasons that just the fact that you are genetically related to Amanda. You are the best kind of human being, the kind that always puts others before herself and I would have been so proud if your sister turned out to be just like you. I want you to know that from this day forward, you are not a fatherless child. You have a father. I want nothing more in this life than to give you back just a fraction of the love you have shown me these past several weeks."

Tears flowed heavily as I put my head on Ed's shoulder. "Thank you. Thank you, Ed."

He squeezed me tightly and turned to me, "That being said, Allison, as much as I don't want to lose you, I think you need to face your life in Boston. I know that you were running away from all of the hurt, and that hurt let us have you for a while. But I think until you face what you were running from, you won't have the same kind of peace that I have found in facing you."

He continued, "We haven't told Cedric you have been here all this time, because I know that's what you wanted. I know that you don't want to face him…but when Elaine gave me the phone the night you confronted him with the photo, I heard the tears and pain in his voice. I knew then that you must have been pretty damn special for him to be so torn up about losing you. He loves you, Allison. I couldn't have told you whether or not he truly loved Amanda the same way…but he loves you…that I know for sure."

I thought about what Ed said. Cedric was in bad shape that night, barely unrecognizable when I walked in on him with that long beard, and his normally translucent blue eyes were dark and tired. Could he really have been that torn up over me?

Did he really love me?

Did I love him?

I was pretty sure I knew the answer.

***

We decided that I would stay another couple of weeks and head back to Boston the day before Labor Day.

The plan was for me to fly out to Chicago again to visit in a couple of months and then Ed and Elaine would come out to Boston for the holidays.

I notified both the diner and Bright Horizons that I would be returning after Labor Day if they would have me back and requested that I be placed back with my original clients, although I was still waiting to hear on that.

My last day in Naperville, I wanted to go somewhere that I hadn't been yet but needed to visit before I left: Amanda's grave.

I asked Ed and Elaine if it would be okay if I went alone, so Ed let me borrow his car.

As I drove into Pinewoods Cemetery, I followed the directions that they carefully wrote out for me so that I could find the plot.

I had stopped at a florist and picked out pink roses, which Ed told me, were Amanda's favorite. I remembered the dried up pink rose in Cedric's binder, the same binder where I found the photo and wondered if he took it from her burial service.

After driving up a hill and admiring the grassy scenery, I finally found the exact spot where my sister was buried.

Upon seeing the terracotta-colored, granite headstone, I immediately broke into tears, placing the roses down.

Amanda Rose Thompson June 2, 1984-May 1, 2002, Loving Daughter

It crossed my mind that had we known each other, it might have read "loving daughter and sister."

I started to pray silently and willed Amanda to forgive me for all of my conflicting emotions surrounding her. I told her that I loved her, even though we had never met and promised that I would always look after Ed and Elaine.

Staying for about fifteen minutes, it dawned on me that my fresh flowers were not alone, not by any means. There were dozens of flowers, some old and some new, strewn about.

Ed and Elaine had told me that with all of Ed's treatments, they hadn't been there for several months, so I found it peculiar that some of these flowers seemed fresh. They weren't planted; they were just laid down, like mine. Someone had been here…very recently. I wondered who it was, if not Ed and Elaine. I was happy that someone was thinking of my sister, though, and visiting her.

As I turned around to leave, I took one more look back at the stone and blew a soft kiss. It was returned with a gentle breeze, and I liked to think that maybe it was her kissing me back.

When I returned to the car, I felt satisfied that I could now return to Boston having covered all of my bases here in Illinois.

I couldn't wait to get back to Ed and Elaine's and tell them about the flowers. Maybe they would know whom they were from.

As I started the ignition, the car hesitated and wouldn't start. That was strange. I tried it again and the same thing happened. Was the battery dead? I knew nothing about cars.

Shit.

I didn't want to bother Ed and Elaine. Thankfully, I had AAA and immediately took my card out of my wallet and called the number. AAA said the approximate wait time would be twenty to thirty minutes, so I could handle that.

Twenty minutes came and went and as I sat in my car, I noticed another car pull up behind me. It was an older rust-colored Toyota Corolla. It was pretty desolate out here, so I crossed my fingers that it wasn't someone shady.

A teenage boy with shaggy brown hair and tattooed-covered arms got out and walked slowly over to the headstones. He was carrying purple hydrangeas, and my heart dropped when he stopped right at Amanda's stone.

Oh. My. God.

This was the person leaving the flowers. But who was he? He couldn't have been more than sixteen or seventeen.

He stood in front of the stone with his head down and then kneeled to place the flowers down.

I stared at him for a few minutes and my curiosity was about to kill me, so I got out of the car, slowly approaching the boy.

"Hi," I said.

He jumped and turned around. "Oh…hey. You scared me," he said.

"Sorry…um…did you know Amanda?" I asked as I approached him.

The boy was silent for a few seconds then spoke. "Yeah…um…well, not really. I didn't really know her, but—"

258

"What do you mean?" I asked.

"Well, I mean, I never really met her. I don't even know what she looked like…but she was related to me."

"Related? How?"

He looked me up and down. "Who are you?" he asked.

I hesitated, and then decided there was only one answer. "I am her twin sister."

The boy stepped back as if he was scared of me and squinted his eyes as if to examine me.

"What's your name?" he asked.

"Allison…and you are?"

He seemed stunned by my answer and didn't immediately respond.

"Jake. My name is Jake."

"Are you the one who has been leaving all these flowers?"

He nodded. "Yeah…well, not just me. Me and my Mom."

"Who is your Mom?"

Jake didn't say anything. His hands started to shake and he took out a cigarette and nervously lit it, blowing the smoke away from me. He then slowly turned to look at me, and I got the first real look at his eyes. They were amazing…green with gold speckles.

They were my eyes.

"Jake?"

"Yeah?"

"Are you my brother?"

He paused, took a long drag of his cigarette, and then blew it out slowly.

"Yeah."

***

I had a brother…*a brother*…Jake. And he was a badass.

He figured out right away what was wrong with the car and had it fixed well before AAA ever showed up.

We stood outside leaning against the parked cars, just staring at each

259

other and without the distraction of the broken down vehicle, we were forced to discuss the inevitable.

"How did you find out about Amanda, Jake?"

"About six months ago, this investigator guy came to our house. We live on the south side of Chicago. His last name was Samuels. He asked my mother if she had given birth to twin girls in 1984. I was like…what?"

"So, what did your mother say?"

"She just looked at me, like she was afraid to say anything, like she wanted me to leave the room. And then I nearly shit my pants, because she started crying…like really hard and told him, that yeah, she had. I was like…holy shit. She told him she was messed up then, ran away from home and was on drugs and that some dealer had gotten her pregnant."

I nearly fell to the ground at that revelation and felt like I was going to vomit. That answered one of my questions. My birth father was a drug dealer.

Jake continued as I listened stunned. "She wanted to know why he was looking for her and asked if they…you know…you…the girls were okay. The investigator told her that one of the girls had died in an accident a long time ago and that the other one lived in Boston. That's you?"

"Yeah. That's me," I said, shaking my head in disbelief.

"So, Mom was like hysterical because he said Amanda was dead. Then, she asked him how he found us and the investigator explained that Amanda's parents hired him to find the other sister and that in the middle of all that he found my mother, even though they hadn't asked him to."

"Your mom…what's she like?"

"She's cool, Allison, really cool. It's just her and me now. She was real messed up when she was young, like when she was my age, but she ended up getting clean, went to school, became a medical assistant and met my dad, but he died in a motorcycle accident when I was five. So, it's just us."

"I am so sorry about your dad."

"Thanks."

"What's your mother's name?"

"Vanessa…Vanessa Green. Well, Green was my dad's last name. Before that, she was Vanessa Bologna. She's Italian. She looks just like you, actually. It's freaky. That's how I knew you were definitely my sister."

Wow.

I smiled at Jake. He seemed like a really good kid.

"Jake, do you think your mother wants to meet me?"

"I know she does. She told the investigator that when he found you to let her know. But he never got back to her. We don't have a lot of money, so it's not like we could have come to Boston, but I know she wants to meet you. She's just afraid of what you'll think of her, I think. That you'll judge her for giving you up and separating the twins and stuff."

"Do you know if she chose to separate us, the twins?"

"She told me that the adoption people pressured her to do it...something about no family wanting to take on two. She didn't really want to, but they told her the babies were going to two good homes, so she gave in."

I tried to process what he was saying. "I see."

"She begged the investigator let her know where Amanda was buried and he did, so we come out here once a week. We take turns. Sometimes, she comes. Sometimes, I do, and sometimes, we come together. It makes her feel better to come here."

"That's nice, Jake."

Jake put his hands in his pockets and gave me a crooked smile. "You seem really cool," he said.

"You, too. Hey...give me your phone," I said.

I grabbed his flip phone and added my name into his contacts. "I leave to go back to Boston tomorrow. You tell your mom when she's ready, I'd be willing to meet her if she wanted to. No pressure, though, okay? I don't want to make her uncomfortable or anything. I'll be back here in a couple of months for Thanksgiving. If she wants to meet me, then I can come to you. If not, that's okay, too. But...you...you can call me anytime, okay?"

"That's cool. Really cool," Jake said.

"It was really nice to meet you, Jake."

"You too, Allison."

We stood in silence for a bit before we both opened our respective car doors.

Before getting in, I waved goodbye to him again as he faced me looking hesitant to get into his car.

Something came over me as he stood there, and it really hit me that this awkward, tattooed, tobacco-smelling teenager was my kid brother.

I had a living sibling.

I impulsively ran over to him and pulled him into a hug. When we separated, his eyes were watering and I knew at that moment that he was thinking the same thing.

***

On the plane ride back to Boston, I thought about how different my life was now, compared to last time I was on a plane headed to Chicago. I had felt so alone then and so confused.

Those weeks spent with the Thompsons in Naperville had given me a new perspective on my past, on life, on what truly matters and most of all, forgiveness.

I looked down at my phone to the series of texts that I had received last night from Jake.

Jake: Just checking to make sure I wasn't dreaming.

Allison: Hey there!! Nope…it was surreal, though, wasn't it?

Jake: I told Mom. She really wants to meet you when you come back.

Allison: Really?

Jake: Yeah. She was disappointed that you left so soon, but she was happy the two of us got to meet.

Allison: I am happy we got to meet too.

Jake: Talk to you later…Sis. Sounds weird to say it.

Allison: Please keep in touch, Jake. xo

Jake was a sweetheart, but I was glad that I wouldn't be meeting my birth mother for another couple of months. It would give us both time to prepare for that face-to-face encounter and give me time to think about what I wanted to say to her and ask her. She couldn't be that bad of a person because Jake seemed to turn out okay. He was very sweet, actually. I really looked forward to getting to know him more than anything.

Before I faced my Chicago relatives, though, there were more pressing matters back home in Boston that had been waiting long enough to be dealt with.

It was time to face Cedric. It was time to let him know where I had been and to finally let him know how I had been feeling all of these weeks since he poured his heart out to me in that letter.

I had been very careful not to let him know where I was all of this time. For all he knew, I had run away, never to return. I was a little nervous about what I would find out tomorrow. A lot can happen in five months. Had Cedric moved on with someone else? Would he forgive me for leaving town and not saying a word to him about where I was going?

By the time the plane landed in Boston, it was too late to do anything or see anyone. But tomorrow was Labor Day and no one was working, so I had vowed to track down Cedric and get this over with. It couldn't wait any longer.

I would start by going to Bettina's house to check on Callie and to apologize for leaving them high and dry. Then, I would find out where Cedric was and arrange to meet him to let out all of the feelings I had been keeping bottled up.

The anticipation of what I was going to say to him made me nervous, but the memories of both his stunning face and the warmth of his touch comforted me, made me frustrated and giddy.

***

Optimize the fire Moon today, Dear Gemini, as this is a day to be constructive and finish those projects that have been difficult to complete. This is a day to advance in the direction of your goals and tackle unfinished business.

The sun was shining and the air was warm and dry on Monday morning. It was the perfect weather for good hair and I celebrated by giving myself a long blowout.

I also picked out the prettiest aqua tank top and matching skirt I had bought at the mall in Naperville on a rare outing with Elaine during my trip. I finished off the outfit with gray wedges and a thin, gray half cardigan. I made up my face and even tried the smoky eye that the mall cosmetologist showed me how to do.

It might have been the peace I had found in Illinois or it might have been the fact that I was happy to be home in Boston, but even I had to admit, I looked and felt really good when I saw myself in the mirror.

There was no answer when I called Bettina's house from my apartment to see if she and Callie would be home today. I decided I would just head over there anyway in the middle of the afternoon. Hopefully, she and Callie would be home since it was Labor Day. I kind of wanted to surprise Callie anyway. It was possible Bettina would be having something at the house to celebrate the holiday or that she might not be home at all. I would have to take my chances. After I saw Bettina, I planned to text Cedric to find out where we might be able to meet up and talk.

"Damn, you are one hot bitch," Sonia said as she got a look at me.

"Thanks. I want to look decent in case I see Cedric later and don't have time to come back here to change."

Sonia started fluffing my hair. "You're really going to confront him tonight? You just got back. Maybe wait a few days?"

"This can't wait anymore, Sonia. It's been five months since he wrote me that letter. I owe him an explanation of my feelings. It's time."

"And what exactly are you feeling these days?"

I thought about that for a second and it really came down to one thing. "I miss him."

Sonia sighed. "Are you prepared for the possibility that he may have moved on?"

"Honestly? No," I said, putting my head in my hands and rubbing my temples.

"I don't want to see you get hurt," Sonia said.

"I know, but after all that's happened this past year, I owe it to myself to see this through even if I risk getting hurt. I mean, come on. I finally meet the man of my dreams, found a meaningful career path, got attacked by my ex-boyfriend, found out I had a twin, found out she died, found out the man I was falling in love with was said twin's boyfriend and that they conceived a child. Then, I fell in love with my sister's parents and saw her Dad through cancer. And to top it all off, I randomly meet my biological brother in a cemetery! I think it's safe to say, I've built up a little strength to handle what might come my way today."

Sonia hugged me. "Agreed and I am so proud of how you have survived all this. You know, you really should write a book. This would make a hell of a story."

"Seriously," I said as we both broke into laughter.

"Really. You could call it *Gemini*. You know, it's your sign and symbolizes twins.

"That's freaky. I never thought of that," I said.

***

The train ride to Bettina's house went by quickly, and I walked the several blocks from the station to her door, noticing a handful of cars parked in front of the house. Cedric's Audi was not among them, so I breathed a small sigh of relief. I wasn't quite ready to see him yet today. For all I knew, these cars could have also been visitors of the neighbors.

I knocked on the front door and waited for about three minutes before ringing the doorbell, which I wasn't sure worked anyway. I seemed to hear people out back but couldn't tell if it was the neighbor's yard or Bettina's.

Just when I was about to turn away, the door opened. I was surprised to see Cedric's brother Caleb open the door.

"Allison. My God," he said, seemingly taken aback.

"Hi, Caleb."

Caleb's bright blue eyes widened as if he had seen a ghost, and he briefly looked behind his own back and whispered, "What are you doing here?"

"I tried to call earlier, but there was no answer. I…uh…just got back from an extended leave and was hoping to talk to your mother and visit Callie. Is she home?"

"Yeah…um…" he said, looking behind his shoulders again briefly.

Caleb just stayed in front of me speechless.

What was going on?

Before I could think, I heard footsteps and a male voice come up from behind him and say, "Caleb, what the hell is taking so long? I'm fucking thirsty. Who's at the door?"

I knew that voice anywhere.

Caleb closed his eyes in defeat and moved out of the way.

Cedric stood frozen behind him and placed his hand over his heart upon seeing me.

The sight of him nearly knocked me down. Still standing in the doorway, I lifted my hand in a small wave and whispered, "Hi."

Cedric looked at Caleb who continued to say nothing then looked back at me and swallowed.

"Allison," Cedric said so softly it was almost inaudible.

My heart skipped a beat at the sight of his handsome face, piercing eyes and the immediate recognition of his familiar scent. My body tingled in sudden awareness as if it found a connecting part that had been missing for five months.

I cleared my throat. "I am sorry for just showing up here. I…um…thought…I was just dropping in on Bettina. I had wanted to surprise Callie. I didn't mean to startle you I—"

Cedric licked his lips and shook his head and interrupted me. "Don't apologize. Don't ever apologize. God…it's *so* good to see you," he said as he continued to stare at me. His mouth turned slowly upward into a genuine smile that tugged at my heart.

But why were both of them just standing there and not inviting me in?

A few seconds later, I heard a female voice say, "Cedric, hon…where did you go?" and got my answer when an attractive Asian woman walked into the room.

CHAPTER 35

CEDRIC

"Ugh. I'm gonna be sick," Denise said as the smell of the roasting pig wafted in the air. Denise was three months pregnant and the aroma of the meat was making her nauseous.

I was helping my mother rotate it as it sat on the stake over flames. This porker was going to taste damn good though, when the roasting was done, and I couldn't wait to sink my teeth into it.

"I can't believe you guys do this every year," Stephanie laughed.

My mother smiled, salted the pig and said, "Twice a year, actually: Labor Day and Memorial Day weekends. You'll see how good it tastes."

"Well, this is definitely a first for me. Thank you for letting me experience it with you." Stephanie smiled.

"You're very welcome. Don't thank me until you taste it."

I was happy Mom was being cordial to Stephanie. Even though I hadn't wanted to bring a woman I was only seeing casually here, I was finally relaxing, thanks to the passage of time and the passage of beer down my throat. I knew my mother was going to be shocked to see me show up here with someone because she knew how torn up I still was over Allison, but I think even she realized that I needed a distraction.

Allison had all but disappeared from our lives. Even Callie had finally stopped asking about her. I'd be lying if I said I wasn't thinking about her today, though, and wondering how she was spending the holiday, whether she was alone or whether she had found someone else by now. Every time I had even a little alcohol in my system, the longing got worse. My hazy thoughts immediately would shift to her, to her beautiful face and eyes and to memories of the way she tasted. Sometimes, it was downright painful to remember, and I could feel my chest tighten.

My mother interrupted my daydreaming. "Looks about done. What do you think, Cedric?"

"I say about ten more minutes. But it *is* time for another cold one."

Stephanie laughed and shook her head. "Will you get me one too?"

Caleb stood up from the lawn chair he was sitting in. "You guys stay. I'll get them. I have some Octoberfest in Mom's fridge. I wanna break into those. Looking over at a pregnant Denise, he added with a wink, "For you, an O'Doul's."

Caleb sauntered through the sliding glass door into the house. After a few minutes passed and he hadn't returned, I decided to go in and help myself to the beers deciding that he was probably stuck in the john.

I walked through the empty kitchen down the hall toward the bathroom, where I was going to taunt him if he was taking a shit, when I saw him standing instead at the front door.

"Caleb, what the hell is taking so long? I'm fucking thirsty. Who's at the door?"

Caleb moved to the side and I felt like the wind had been knocked out of me.

Allison was standing at the threshold looking more beautiful than I imagined in my dreams. He dark, flowing hair had grown longer, almost to her waist and it was blowing in the breeze. Her green eyes were sparkling, made brighter by the sexy bluish-green tank top she was wearing that hugged her breasts tightly. It took all of my strength to stop myself from rushing toward her.

I could barely get the words out and uttered, "Allison."

She looked nervous but sweet. Her eyes seemed to be welcoming the sight of me. This was not at all the enraged person I saw leave my condo many months ago. This was not the distant person I left at her doorstep

PENELOPE WARD

when I delivered the letter. Something had changed, or rather…returned.

She looked down at her shoes briefly and then straight up into my eyes. "I am sorry for just showing up here. I…um…thought…I was just dropping in on Bettina. I had wanted to surprise Callie. I didn't mean to startle you. I—"

I shook my head. God, she was beautiful. "Don't apologize. Don't ever apologize. God…it's *so* good to see you." I smiled and just stared at the stunning sight before me.

My body ached to touch her, to hug her, but I wasn't sure if that's what she wanted, so I painfully stayed put as we just stared at each other.

I needed to know what she was thinking.

What the fuck was I going to do when she saw Stephanie back there?

Before I could come up with a solution, a few seconds later, Stephanie entered the house and broke the silence.

"Cedric, hon…where did you go?"

Shit.

Shit.

Shit.

I looked back at Stephanie and then over at Allison frantically trying to telepathically tell her with my eyes that Stephanie was not my girlfriend, was not important to me, like she was.

Allison looked sad but then suddenly put on a fake smile and stuck out her hand in Stephanie's direction as she stepped through the threshold. "Hi, I'm Allison, Callie's therapist."

My heart nearly stopped when I saw the ring I had given her gleaming on her right hand.

Holy shit…she was wearing the ring.

Stephanie shook Allison's hand and looked over at me, probably curious about whether there was any relation to the Allison I called out in my dream last night. If she did suspect it, she let it go at that point.

"I'm Stephanie. Nice to meet you."

The four of us continued to awkwardly stand in silence until we heard the words "PIG IS READY!"

My mother was calling from the backyard and when we lingered, she burst through the sliding glass doors. "Didn't you guys hear me? The pig is—Allison!"

My mother ran over to Allison, wiping her hands on an apron and hugged her.

Allison returned the hug. "Hi, Bettina. Sorry to barge in. I wanted to come by and say hello."

My mother gazed at her. "Honey, don't be silly. The door is always open here. I hope you'll stay and join us for the pig roast? I absolutely insist."

Allison looked like she was thinking about it then while looking straight over at me said, "Yes, that'd be nice."

She was staying.

As awkward as this was going to be, I could get through anything as long she didn't run from me again.

The five of us: Mom, Caleb, Stephanie, Allison and myself walked out to the yard.

Allison immediately snuck behind Callie who turned around and squealed louder than ever at the sight of her long lost friend.

"Allison! Allison!" she yelled jumping up and down. I guess she hadn't forgotten Allison after all.

"Callie, I missed you so much," Allison said as she hugged my sister.

I wanted to hug Allison, too…so badly.

Stephanie was looking over at Allison and Callie then over at me, gauging my reaction. "So, she works with your sister?" she asked.

"Yeah…yup…she does." I said flatly, immediately picking up my beer and taking a swig.

Stephanie was looking Allison up and down as she sipped her white wine.

My mother waved everyone over to the table where a dozen side dishes flanked the gigantic roast pig, which had now been carefully sliced into individual pieces of savory pork, garnished with herbs. Thankfully for Denise and Stephanie, the head had been discarded. As good as it looked, I had lost my appetite the second Allison walked through the door.

Stephanie sat next to me while Allison was diagonally across the table from us next to Callie. I watched as Allison carefully tucked a napkin into the front of Callie's shirt and carefully placed slices of pork and sides onto my sister's plate. God, she was so good with her and Callie looked so happy to have Allison back.

Allison glanced over at me, catching me watching her. I didn't even try to pretend like I wasn't and kept my gaze on her. To my surprise, she gave me a slight smile, which I returned. My fists were clenched into balls of frustration under the table.

Everyone was unusually quiet throughout the meal until my mother broke the silence. "Allison, when did you get back into town, honey?"

"Last night. I called Bright Horizons about getting reassigned to Callie but haven't heard back yet. I'll keep on them until they get back to me."

She didn't offer any information on where she had returned from and even though I wondered so badly where she had been and what she was doing these past few months, I couldn't bring it up right then and there.

I nearly spit out my food when Stephanie decided to ask Allison a question. "So, Allison, how long have you worked with Callie?"

Allison seemed startled before answering. "I had worked with her about six months before I took a leave of absence. We get along really well, don't we Callie?" Allison turned to Callie who still had her head face down in her food and then laughed nervously.

Stephanie nodded. "That's so nice."

You could cut the tension in the air with a knife as everyone continued to eat, with only my mother and her friends at the far end of the table making small talk amongst themselves.

After about fifteen minutes, after Callie had cleaned her plate and left the table, Allison excused herself and walked into the house alone.

Stephanie had been trying to engage me in a conversation about her law firm's upcoming yearly banquet that she wanted me to attend, but the corner of my eyes were all too aware of Allison's absence, and my brother Caleb's swift exit to follow her.

CHAPTER 36

ALLISON

I had to get out of there and take a breather, so I locked myself in Bettina's bathroom as a million thoughts ran through my mind.

Who was this Stephanie and how serious were they? She was clearly all over Cedric. Who could blame her? But I couldn't help but feel like he only had eyes for me out there. They seemed to follow my every move while she was going on and on about her job. I wanted to scream as Cedric pretended to listen to her while he clearly wanted to say something to me.

I had also forgotten just how painfully good-looking that man was; he looked hotter than ever. His hair had gotten a little longer and was parted and pieced so perfectly together framing his beautiful face. And his scent had been killing me from across the table. Let's just say, the pork wasn't the reason my mouth was watering.

This was all so awkward and frustrating. I could understand the predicament he was in. He could have never imagined I would show up out of the blue after disappearing for months and never contacting him. Who could blame him for moving on? I might have done the same thing if I were him. Taking a deep breath and grabbing my bearings, I opened the bathroom door to return outside.

As I exited the bathroom, I was startled to see Caleb standing there waiting for me with his arms crossed. "We need to talk, real quick, Allison. Let's go out front."

I took a deep breath and followed Caleb out to the front steps as he gently closed the door behind us.

"Listen, I know this has got to be awkward for you," he said.

I nodded my head in agreement. "Obviously, I wasn't expecting this when I came here."

Caleb blinked rapidly and shook his head. "Where have you been for three months?"

I hesitated for a second, unsure about whether I wanted to tell him where I was before I had a chance to explain it to Cedric, but caved. "I was in Chicago actually…with my sister's parents."

Caleb looked stunned. "No shit…wow. I didn't expect you to say that. Cedric had no clue where you went and you told him not to contact you, so—"

"Yes, it's a long story, but the Thompsons and I have really gotten close. That's part of what I wanted to talk to Cedric about. I was going to contact him later today, before I knew he was here. I really did come here to see Callie and I didn't mean to make anyone uncomfortable."

Caleb quickly looked back to check if anyone was coming and then said, "Listen, we don't have much time. People are gonna start to wonder where we are. I just wanted you to know that Cedric has been really broken up over everything that happened between you two. It's taken him all the time you have been away to only somewhat recover and even though it may look like he has moved on, I know for a fact that he hasn't. I just talked to him this morning on the phone and he was still talking about you, okay? I didn't want you using the fact that he is here with a date as an excuse to run away from him again. They are not serious. I just wanted to make sure you knew that."

Relief washed over me. "Thank you. I appreciate that." I couldn't contain my smile upon hearing that.

He looked back again and spoke softly. "And Allison, listen…I know he hurt you really badly by not telling you the truth right away, but he didn't mean to cause you pain. His feelings for you were as true as I have ever witnessed. But let me tell you, if your plan was to come back here and ream him out face to face about what happened, I would appreciate it if you didn't. Just walk away from him instead and let him try to move on. Believe me, he understands his mistakes."

Walk away? No.

"Caleb, I wasn't planning on doing that. I had a lot of time to think in Illinois about his reasons for doing what he did. Amanda's parents really helped me through it. I know now that he didn't mean to hurt me, and I still care about him a lot. I just wish I could talk to him right now."

Caleb smiled, looking a little surprised at my admission. "You'll get your chance. Come on, let's head back out."

***

Stephanie was still talking Cedric's ear off when Caleb and I returned to the yard.

At the sound of the sliding glass door, Cedric turned around looked at me and then to Caleb inquisitively. I wondered if he knew we were inside talking. Denise didn't seem fazed, and I had a feeling she knew exactly what Caleb had been up to in cornering me.

My heart clenched when I looked over and saw Stephanie running her fingers through Cedric's hair. It was painful to watch, but I couldn't tear my eyes away. Jealousy swept in like a freight train.

I tried to distract myself by walking over to where Callie was sitting and involved her in a game of tic-tac-toe on her iPad. As we took our turns with x's and o's, I snuck glances over at Cedric and Stephanie who were still seated next to each other at the dinner table and noticed how uncomfortable he looked, stiff and fidgety. He wasn't returning any of her touches and his hands were planted firmly on his lap.

Stephanie's back was turned to me when Cedric's and my eyes briefly met, and I could tell by the look he gave me that he wanted to talk to me, but he didn't know how to break away from her. I needed to communicate to him somehow that I wanted to talk to him, too and that I wasn't mad at him for being here with her, that I wasn't mad at him for anything anymore.

Stephanie ran her fingers through his hair again and then reached over and pulled him toward her, suddenly kissing him on the mouth. I turned away immediately at that sight and could feel the bile rising in me. More feelings of intense jealousy burned up inside of me. It was one thing to see him here with another woman. It was another to see her all over him.

I was done with this, especially after what Caleb told me. If I truly felt that he was happy and moving on, I would have up and left. Thank goodness Caleb confronted me, or I may have been gone by now. But I was determined to stay and determined to send him a signal that I still wanted him…that I needed him, and most of all, that I had forgiven him for not telling me the truth. I couldn't sit here while someone else took something so important from me…while I watched. A primal urge to claim what was mine erupted in me, and I knew I needed to fight for him.

Just as Stephanie put her arm around him, Bettina started clearing the table. Stephanie got up and took some plates through the sliding glass door into the kitchen.

Then, Cedric immediately got up from his seat, started taking in some of the side dishes and was gone into the house.

Callie and I had stopped playing tic-tac-toe and now, she was just looking at You Tube while I sat beside her, playing with her long braid and pretending to focus my attention on anything other than the competition I had mentally started.

Stephanie came back out and returned to her seat, checking her phone, but Cedric remained in the house.

This was my chance.

I got out my phone, scrolled down to find his name and frantically typed.

> I forgive you, Cedric.
> I miss you so much.
> I am sorry for leaving.
> I need to talk to you.

About a minute went by, and there was no response. I hoped he had the same cell phone number and that he even had his cell phone on him.

After another minute, my phone vibrated on my lap.

> Cedric: God, Allison. I'm going fucking crazy. I need to touch you.
> Cedric: This is killing me.

Oh. My. God.

> Allison: Where are you?

> Cedric: In Callie's room. Meet me in here when I tell you to.

> Allison: What if Stephanie comes looking for you?

About thirty seconds passed before he responded.

> Cedric: Ok, when you see Caleb walk over to her, come inside the house.

About two more minutes passed before Caleb walked over to Stephanie and started a conversation about a legal issue his construction company was having. I realized quickly this was a setup and that Cedric had texted Caleb to occupy Stephanie.

My heart began to pound out of my chest, and I walked quickly past them through the sliding glass doors, past Bettina washing dishes in the kitchen and down the hall.

It was as if I floated past everything until I got to Callie's room.

The door wasn't even halfway open when Cedric pulled me into his arms, shut the door and held me tighter than anyone ever had in my life.

"Tell me this isn't a dream," he whispered into my ear, seeming to fight back tears.

Our faces slowly met and he kissed me like his life depended on it, backing me against the door. After about a minute, he broke away suddenly and examined my face. "How could you have become even more beautiful?"

I looked down at the floor, suddenly bashful and emotional and started to tear up. "It's so hard to see you with her. We really need to talk."

Cedric grabbed my chin, pulling it up to meet his icy blue eyes that were burning a hole through me. "Look at me, Allison."

I wiped my eyes as he caressed my chin and said to me, "There has never been anyone who has ever come anywhere close to how you make me feel...not before you or after you. I had been trying really hard to forget you lately, but even so, I didn't get very far. You need to know that I haven't...*been*...with Stephanie or anyone for that matter, sexually, since you, okay? I hadn't even *wanted* to. It just hasn't felt right. I have been so fucked up. It's the longest in my life I have ever gone without—"

"Really? No one?" I interrupted.

"No one. I swear to you, Allison."

I shook my head and smiled. "Me neither."

Cedric kissed my forehead. "Thank God," he said, letting out a deep breath and laughing a bit.

Immense relief washed over me to hear that Cedric hadn't slept with her...or anyone else.

"Where have you been for the past three months? Did you leave town?" Cedric asked as his fingers kneaded the skin on my waist gently.

"God, Cedric, I have so much to tell you." After a brief pause, I said, "I was in Chicago with Ed and Elaine."

The kneading stopped and he shook his head in disbelief. "What?"

"I'm sorry. I told them not to tell you. It was just supposed to be a quick visit to meet them, but then we bonded and I decided to stay and help out with Ed and we got really close and well, it's like they're second parents or something to me now."

Cedric moved back in shock. "Holy crap, Allison. How could I have not known this?"

"It's my fault for keeping it from you. They wanted me to tell you. I just needed time to deal with this alone. It was all too much too fast after the truth came out. But Elaine and Ed, especially Ed, helped me see things clearer. So much else happened out there. I really want to tell you everything later tonight or whenever you can get away from here, but we can't stay in here like this much longer."

Cedric pulled my mouth into his and sucked on my bottom lip slow and hard then released it slowly. "Fuck...I can't let you go, Allison."

I brought his head back toward me for another kiss and our tongues collided into one another.

I pulled back, panting and said, "We should go back outside before someone comes looking for us."

Cedric shook his head and pulled me back into him, sucking on my neck hungrily, his erection pressing firmly against me as he moaned over my skin. "No."

"No?" I asked looking up at him.

"No...just a few more minutes," he said, his eyes turning darker with the strongest sense of desire I had yet to experience from him.

"I missed you so much, Cedric."

Cedric breathed heavily on my neck, "I need to feel you...now."

Upon hearing him say that, my knees got weak as if my legs were going to collapse and my moist underwear felt like it was going to disintegrate on my body.

I opened my mouth against his as our bodies pressed together and felt his hand move under my dress as he abruptly slipped his fingers inside me. Cedric moaned into my mouth as I moved down over his hand.

With the sound of dishes clanking getting louder in the kitchen, he pulled his fingers out of me. "I am sorry, sweetheart. I've just missed you so much. I got carried away.

He held me close as I put my head on his chest and could feel his rapid heart beating against my ear.

"Cedric, we have to leave this room."

"Okay, but I need to see you tonight. Promise me. I'll text you and come pick you up."

I nodded. "Yes."

He kissed me desperately one last time. "You leave first. I have to go to the bathroom and take care of this," he said pointing down to his bulging crotch.

"Okay." I laughed. He was not kidding. He could not go out like *that*.

I started to walk out when he stopped me and grabbed both of my hands and kissed them over and over softly.

"Bye," I whispered, slipping out the door.

CHAPTER 37

CEDRIC

It took longer than expected to get rid of the hard-on. I was so turned on and that wasn't going to change anytime soon.

Five minutes of focusing intently on images from that Sarah McLaughlin animal abuse public service announcement finally did the trick.

When I emerged from the bathroom, Allison was talking to my mother in the kitchen, filling her in on where she had been all of these weeks.

My mother didn't look at me or let on as to whether she knew we were hiding in Callie's room together. I passed them in the kitchen, went through the sliding door to the yard and joined Caleb and Stephanie who were, thankfully, still talking.

When I sat down, Caleb got up and thanked Stephanie for her advice, sneaking me a smirk, as I knew he would.

"Where were you all that time?" Stephanie asked.

"I was in the bathroom, sorry," I said.

"Huh. That was an awfully long time to be in the bathroom."

I lied. "Yeah…sorry, having issues."

Technically, my hard-on was an issue that needed to be dealt with.

Stephanie's eyes lingered on me, and I got the impression she knew I wasn't exactly telling the truth, but she proceeded to change the subject.

"What are we doing tonight?" she asked.

I felt like an asshole and really hated lying. I silently vowed to never lie to another woman again once I could get out of this situation today. But now that Allison was back in my life, I needed to break it to Stephanie that we couldn't date anymore, but this was not the right place or time. I just prayed she didn't try to touch me or kiss me in front of Allison again.

"I don't think I'm going to be able to do anything tonight," I said.

Stephanie raised her eyebrow. "Oh?"

"Yeah, I have a client pitch I am way behind on and forgot about an early morning meeting, so I'm going to need to call it a night after we leave here."

"I could just hang out at your apartment, make a late dinner and stuff while you work," she said.

She was not going to make this easy.

Before I could come up with another excuse, Allison reentered the yard and I could see Stephanie's eyes fixate on her. Allison didn't make eye contact with me and went straight over to sit with Callie.

I swallowed nervously, somehow sensing that Stephanie knew something.

When Stephanie got up to refill her wine, I looked over at Allison. To my horror, I spotted a gargantuan hickey on her beautiful neck.

Fuck.

I tried to signal for her to move her hair over it, but she wasn't paying attention. Callie then moved behind Allison and said, "I want piggy back."

"Callie, you're too big for that," I heard Allison say.

Callie could care less and began climbing on Allison's back.

"Ugh…you're gonna crush me, girl," Allison laughed and lifted up off the chair with Callie now climbing on her back.

Stephanie reappeared and sat down next to me with her legs crossed, sipping her wine, but not saying anything. We sat silently watching the show that Allison and Callie were putting on.

Callie was laughing hysterically, enjoying the ride Allison was giving her around the yard, when all of a sudden she started sniffing Allison's neck.

"Smell…smell…smell like Cedric. Allison smell like Cedric!" I heard

Callie shout as she laughed and sniffed Allison's neck.

This stunned me for two reasons. One: Callie had never used words that well, describing how something smelled. Two: I was fucked.

Stephanie turned to me slowly and glared at me with daggers in her eyes. "You know, I must be the dumbest fucking woman on the face of the Earth. When she walked in the door, I overlooked the fact that your jaw dropped at the sight of her. I overlooked the fact that her name was the same as the one you shouted out in your dreams last night. I overlooked the fact that you were making googly eyes at her throughout lunch and I even overlooked the fact that she disappeared with you and magically emerged from your mother's house with a hickey in the shape of the state of Florida. But that...that...what your sister just said over there...just about seals the deal, doesn't it?"

I was speechless. There was no way to deny it, so I decided to concede to the truth. "Stephanie, I am sorry."

Before I could blink, Stephanie threw her full glass of white wine on my shirt. "Fuck you," she said before grabbing her purse and storming off through the gate.

That was the end of Stephanie.

All eyes were on me as I sat in shock, my shirt soaked. Thankfully, my mother was still in the kitchen with Denise and hadn't witnessed it.

Allison kneeled down slowly so that Callie could climb off her back.

Caleb had his head in his hands while he tried to contain and hide his laughter; he was doing a horrible job at that, by the way.

Allison walked over to me. "I'm sorry. That was really bad."

I squeezed my white Ralph Lauren polo shirt to rid it of the excess wine. "I'm not sorry at all. You shouldn't be either. C'mere." I pulled Allison onto my lap, not caring who was watching and planted a kiss on her lips.

"What are you crazy? We shouldn't do this here in front of everybody," she said.

"Every single person in this house already knows how crazy I am about you."

Her face turned a beautiful shade of pink as she blushed, before taking a piece of my wet shirt jokingly into her mouth. "Mmmm…I love Chardonnay." She laughed. "Seriously, you should go inside and change your shirt."

Caleb wiped his eyes from tears of laughter and walked over to where we were sitting. "Bro, I think I have a spare shirt in my truck."

"Gimme the keys, shithead," I said as I got up and reached for Allison's hand.

We walked through the gate to the driveway at front of the house, where I opened Caleb's backseat to find a navy button down shirt.

I put my hand on Allison's cheek. "I was gonna offer to drive you home, but I just realized we took Stephanie's car here, so I am carless."

"Join the club. Looks like someone's going to have to slum it and take the train like the rest of us." She winked.

"Let me go inside and clean up and then we can leave."

We walked back through the gate and Allison sat down to wait for me while I went into the house and changed. I looked back at her and couldn't believe that this was real, that she was really here. I couldn't wait to get her home and be alone with her.

My mother was just finishing up the dishes in the kitchen while Denise wiped them.

When I tried to sneak past them, my sister-in-law interjected, grabbing me by the shirt. "Uh-uh, no you don't. What's going on out there? You smell like the dumpster behind the pub," she said.

"What do you mean?" I tried to play dumb, but my guilty smirk probably gave me away.

Denise laughed and glanced over at my mother who was also smirking. "Liar. Caleb's been texting me a play by play."

That shithead.

"Stephanie left," I said.

"And?" she laughed.

"And she threw her wine at me."

Denise's jaw dropped. "And that was because…"

I threw my head back and ran my hands through my hair. I just wanted to go to the bathroom, change and get out of here with Allison.

"Because she figured out that Allison and I snuck away after lunch and were making out in Callie's room."

"What?!" Denise yelled as she smacked the counter.

"I knew it," Mom said smiling.

"You knew what?" I asked.

"I knew that the second she walked in that door, that you'd end up together. I could see it in both of your eyes," she smiled. "And I also knew the entire time you two were holed up in Callie's room." She laughed. "I was playing lookout. You just didn't know it." My mother winked.

I knew how she felt about Allison, but found that a little disturbing.

"Thanks, Mom...I think."

"Plus, she has a hickey on her neck that looks like the state of Florida," Ma laughed and Denise and I joined in.

"You didn't take off your shirt, did you?" Denise asked. "If she sees it, she's gonna think you're a psycho, you know that, right?"

"I *was* a psycho...for a while, after she left. And no, she hasn't seen it yet," I said.

When I emerged from the bathroom in Caleb's shirt, Allison was in the kitchen with my mother and Denise. The three of them smiled at me in unison and I knew they had been talking about me. The look on Allison's red face was so sweet and affectionate and I was bursting with love for her, a love I hadn't even ever professed to her directly. I needed to tell her I loved her as soon as the time felt right.

"Ready to go?" I asked.

Allison hugged my mother and Denise and went to say goodbye to Callie and Caleb who were still outside as the sun was setting.

As we walked hand and hand to the train station, Allison told me all about her trip to Illinois. I didn't think my feelings for her could get any stronger, but when she told me how she decided to stay there to help Ed during his cancer treatments, my heart just about blew up. I wanted to tell her then and there how much I loved her, but decided to wait.

The story of how she ran into her brother at Amanda's grave was also unbelievable. If her car hadn't stalled, she would have never met him. It makes you wonder about how divine intervention plays into our lives.

Once on the train, I led Allison to the very back of the car so we would have the most privacy. As we swayed with the movement of the train, we held each other and kissed the entire ride to her stop. The train car was almost empty, but if there were people watching us, we probably didn't notice. Thirty minutes felt like three.

After the train ride, while walking to Allison's house, the skies opened up and rain came pouring down on us. Even though the torrential rain had us soaked from head to toe, we couldn't have cared less and stopped to kiss under the deluge. It was one of the happiest moments of my life.

We laughed in the rain as we ran all the way to her doorstep. I couldn't contain my excitement over being alone with her. Allison told me her roommate Sonia was down the Cape for the night with friends, so when we arrived at her house, I dragged her up those stairs so fast, she almost fell.

We were drenched and I hadn't had sex in months, but it felt like ten years. She was the only woman I wanted from the moment I first laid eyes on her and for a long time, I thought I would only ever be able to experience her again in my dreams and memories. This moment, of being happy here with her like this again, in the same place we first made love, was a dream come true.

CHAPTER 38

ALLISON

Cedric wouldn't let me come up for air and I loved every second of it. From the moment my apartment door burst open, he pressed his rain-drenched body against mine, then moved to the couch on top of me, kissing me passionately. I wanted him inside of me so badly and felt like I was going to burst.

He broke from kissing me only long enough to lift off my wet shirt and loosen my bra, throwing it on the floor, as I pulled off my soaked skirt. When he lowered himself back down, I snuck my hands under his shirt to feel the warmth of his bare skin and his tight abs. I started to nudge his shirt to pull it off and he pushed back, breathing heavily.

"Take it off," I said.

"Wait," Cedric said as he pulled back and kneeled above me, looking down into my eyes. His hair was wet back from the rain and his face was turning red. "I have to explain something first."

I crossed my arms over my bare breasts, suddenly cold. "What do you mean?"

He shook his head. "It's nothing bad. I mean…I hope you don't see it that way."

"Ok, now you're scaring me."

He bent down to kiss my forehead. "No, no, no, no…don't be scared. It's not like that."

"What, then?"

Cedric took a deep breath. "When you told me not to contact you after you read the letter and then you disappeared, I was really screwed up. I was sure I had lost the one thing that mattered to me most. And to be honest, until you told me you forgave me and missed me earlier today, I was sure that I had lost you forever."

I blinked rapidly and sat up. "Okay—"

He continued. "One night, I had gotten a little drunk and was staring at myself in the mirror at the tattoo I got in memory of Amanda and came up with the bright idea that I wanted another one. So, I walked down to Kenmore Square."

"You got a tattoo. Where is it?"

"That's the thing…why I had to tell you before you took off my shirt."

"Ok, let me see it."

"Promise you won't think I'm crazy."

I crossed my heart. "I promise."

Cedric ran his hands through his hair and sighed. "Because…I *was*…a little crazy." He laughed. "But I'm not anymore."

"Can I see it please?"

"Okay…here goes nothing."

He lifted his shirt slowly showcasing his beautiful abs and then as he pulled it over his head, I saw it.

Oh. My. God.

It was of my initials…in same font as the *A.R.T.* on his torso except this tat was higher on his chest over his heart: *A.O.A.* That wasn't all though. Underneath the larger letters of my initials, was a scrolling sentence written in small calligraphy that ran across his chest to his underarm. I struggled to see what it read: *When I saw you, I fell in love and you smiled because you knew.*

I recognized it immediately. "It's Shakespeare," I whispered.

"Yeah…an ode to our middle names."

Words could not describe the amount of love I felt for this man as I rubbed my hand over the words slowly following the path of the sentence.

"It's beautiful." I gasped.

"You really like it? It doesn't freak you out?"

"God, no. I love having a part of me on you permanently. I earned it, dammit," I said as we both laughed. "And you're right. Our connection has always been so strong, from that first moment. I guess deep down inside even though you never said the words, I always did know. That's why I came back."

He kissed me tenderly and said, "I got this tattoo because no matter what happened, I never wanted to forget how you made me feel. I'm not the type of guy who can give my heart to someone twice. You are the only woman who has ever claimed it. It's yours forever, take it or leave it. I love you so much, Allison, more than my life, more than anything."

My heart just about burst into flames hearing him say the words I had longed to hear for so many months. "I love you too, Cedric." I pulled him down onto me. "So much," I said as I held his head to my naked chest.

When he lifted his head to look at me, his eyes were watery. "Sweetheart, thank you for coming back to me," he said.

I wiped the tears from his eyes and from my own and held his face in my hands and said, "You thought you took something from me by waiting to tell me the truth. But you actually gave me the greatest gift: the opportunity to experience what true love was. Your finding me not only gave me you, but Callie, the Thompsons and now, my brother. It's all because of you, Cedric. Because of you, I am not alone anymore."

As soon as the words came out of my mouth, they seemed to ignite something inside him. Cedric kissed me so hard I thought my mouth might fall off and I could feel his pounding heart on my chest.

His hands trembled with need as he pulled my underwear down. His jeans weren't even all the way off when he suddenly plunged into me, moaning into my mouth on impact. I gasped upon the initial burn and almost immediate intense pleasure that followed as he kissed me hungrily while pushing into me repeatedly, deep and hard.

"I fucking love you so much, he whispered over my mouth as he moved inside me. "You have no clue..."

"Oh, God. Deeper, Cedric. I want you deeper." My fingernails dug into his back as I pushed him into me.

"I can't get enough of you…can't get deep enough. I love you…I love you…I love you," he said hoarsely over my mouth.

We were still connected when Cedric flipped us over swiftly, continuing to pound into me while squeezing my breasts hard. He looked intensely into my eyes while I grinded my hips on top of him for several minutes as his eyes seared into mine, never looking away.

Tears streamed down my cheeks as the intensity of what I was experiencing with him overwhelmed me.

His hands moved down to my hips, guiding the motions to push himself deeper into me.

After a few minutes, his eyes moved from mine and seemed to roll back in ecstasy, almost like he was possessed. "I'm gonna lose it. You feel too fucking good. I can't hold out anymore. I want to come inside you," he said.

Hearing him say that made me crazy and brought my orgasm to surface fast. I started to scream as the intense pleasure overcame me. Cedric's loud moan followed, and I felt his hot release as he pulsated inside me.

He turned us over in one movement, so that he was on top of me kissing my face softly, professing his love again with each kiss.

We had sex several times throughout the night after moving from the couch to the bed, then in the shower and even against the kitchen counter when we were supposedly going to have a midnight snack. Cedric was insatiable, and I was a more than willing participant.

CHAPTER 39

CEDRIC

Waking up in Allison's bed was surreal and I had slept like a baby for the first time in months. Despite the fact that we had sex at least six times last night, I couldn't wait to wake her up again. She looked so peaceful, though, so I decided to just stare at her.

It was no wonder she was out like a light. We had spent the entire evening alternating between having sex and drowsy pillow talk.

Allison had told me more about her time in Chicago with Ed and Elaine. The role Amanda's parents played in convincing Allison to give me another chance really touched me. I also opened up to her about the years I spent in Chicago after Amanda's death, something I hadn't really talked about with her before. She was less than impressed to hear how I started my career as the lover of my much older boss. But I vowed to tell her everything about me...no more secrets.

The moment last night when she told me that she wasn't alone anymore because of me, had given me the first sense of real peace and closure since Amanda died. I would never fully forgive myself for the past, but somehow having a positive impact on Allison's life made me feel like I had reversed some of the damage.

It was 11:00 am now and I was itching to wake her up. When she moved and turned herself around, I moved in behind and spooned with her. I was hard as a rock when she leaned into me and said, "Mmmm."

Kissing the back of her neck softly, I said "You know you're going to have to kick me out of here, right? Because I'm never leaving on my own."

"Well, then I guess you're staying a while, because I want to make up for lost time."

"We lost so much time, Allison. Never again, okay?"

She turned herself to me and kissed my nose softly. "Never again."

If being apart from her had felt like my heart was ripped out, at this moment it was safely returned to its rightful spot.

Allison had the day off since she wouldn't be returning to the diner job until tomorrow, and she was still waiting to hear back about being reassigned to her cases at Bright Horizons. So, I called into the agency sick. There was no way I was going to leave her to go to work today when I had just gotten her back.

After we made love two more times in bed, Allison said, "I need to take a shower."

"Can I come with you?" I asked.

She smirked. "Haven't you done enough of that?"

She started to get up when I pulled her toward me and started tickling her. "Let me rephrase that. Can I *shower* with you?"

Allison broke free from my grip and walked to the bathroom, showing off her beautiful naked ass. "Follow me."

Apparently, we were completely incapable of keeping our hands off each of each other. I washed every inch of her body with my mouth and she returned the favor with a happy ending.

It was almost noon and the sun was blazing through the bedroom window.

Allison was in the bathroom blow-drying her hair, and I got dressed into my jeans and back into Caleb's shirt from yesterday.

I was looking up places to get brunch nearby on my phone, when Allison's phone chimed indicating that she had received a text, so I instinctively grabbed it.

My heart dropped as I checked the message.

I can't wait to spend time with you. When are you coming back?

Who was Jake and what the fuck was this? A tremendous cloud of jealousy washed over me instantly and before I could overreact, Allison emerged from the bathroom.

"Who the fuck is Jake?" I asked with the phone shaking in my hands.

She looked panicked. "What's going on with Jake?"

That wasn't an answer.

"Jake can't wait to spend time with you." I threw the phone on the bed. "Who is he?" My blood was boiling.

She ran to grab the phone and looked at me in shock. "Cedric…Jake…is my brother!"

My insides settled and I fell back onto the bed in utter embarrassment. I felt like an ass. "Oh, shit." I smacked myself on the head. "Sweetheart, for some reason, I didn't remember what you said his name was…or that you even said his name at all. I am sorry for overreacting. I thought it was some dude you met while we were apart or something…who was trying to get in your pants. God, I feel so stupid."

She laughed shaking her head. "You know, you had that coming right…with all the girls I've had to witness you with?"

"Come here." I pulled her onto my lap and held her.

I loved her so much it hurt. And just that taste of jealousy was enough to make me almost go off the deep end. I guess I still had a little psycho left in me after all.

CHAPTER 40

ALLISON

Three Months Later

Cosmic bliss is coming your way, and soon Gemini will be the Zodiac's favorite child. You look and feel better than ever, as the stars are aligned nicely. Soon it will be raining lollipops, and that's a good thing, especially for your sweet tooth.

The volume of the music seemed to fade with the feel of the brisk wind that blew in the door when he walked in and sat in booth number three. It wasn't just the fact that most gorgeous man I had ever laid eyes on came in and ordered a salt bagel with butter and a side of coffee. But this stunning man seemed to be staring at me. I could feel his eyes on me when he thought I might not be looking. From the moment I first noticed him, it was like everything turned from black and white in here to color.

So, this was turning out to be a far from typical Monday because this man, the man I loved was here, and I needed to break the news to him.

"Hi honey…you made it! I see Delores already took your order," I said as I walked over to his table.

Cedric smiled. "You know what this reminds me of?"

I grinned. "The first time you came here. You sat right here at this table and followed me around with your beautiful eyes. It was love at first sight for me."

"It was more than that," he said, grabbing my hand. "You owned me from that moment. I fucking ran because I was so scared of how you made me feel. I'm still scared of it."

I bent down to kiss him. "Eat your bagel. I'll be right back."

As I tended to the other customers, Cedric alternated between reading the paper and following my every move.

His stunning beauty never got old. Every time I met his stare, he would flash his beautiful smile at me, and I would melt wondering how I got so lucky.

He would have to get back to work soon, so I asked Max if I could take my break early. I brought Cedric a piece of coconut pie from the kitchen and dressed it with a huge dollop of whipped cream and a maraschino cherry.

"Ah, I get the whipped cream and cherry this time. I'm officially off your shit list...nice!" he joked.

"Yes, honey, you are," I said, planting my lips on his, wanting the world to know he was mine.

Cedric dug into the pie and fed me every other bite as I sat next to him in the booth. He stuck his finger into the whipped cream and dabbed it on my nose, licking it off, and we both laughed.

The past few months with Cedric have been the best of my life. We were inseparable and had talked about maybe moving in together.

I was also back working with Callie two days a week and had given my two weeks notice at the diner to accept full-time hours at Bright Horizons as part of a program where they would also pay part of my tuition to return to Simmons College so long as I agreed to work for them for a minimum of three years post-graduation. I was supposed to be going back in January to start a masters degree program in Applied Behavioral Analysis, a specialized therapy for kids with autism.

During Thanksgiving, Cedric accompanied me back to Illinois where we spent the holiday with Ed and Elaine and took a day trip to the city to finally meet my birth mother. Vanessa was only forty-five and looked more like my sister than my mother. Things were cordial, but I couldn't say I felt the same immediate bond with her as I did with Ed. Vanessa was a good person, but it would take more than a short trip to get to know her and trust her.

Jake, on the other hand, was a different story. My brother and I had developed a real relationship over the past months through emails, texts and Skype. Even though Jake had a rough exterior with piercings and tattooed-covered arms, he was actually quite bright and a straight A student. He would be applying for colleges soon and wanted to major in engineering. We were planning to fly him out here for Christmas and he was thinking of looking at colleges in Boston, like Northeastern. The thought of possibly having my brother here warmed my heart.

So, everything seemed to be going my way lately, until earlier this morning. That's what I needed to talk to Cedric about. Maybe I would wait until tonight when we got home. I didn't want to ruin his pie.

"Sweetie, I have to get back to the office," he said.

"Okay." I sulked.

Cedric kissed my forehead. "Can you get me the bill?"

I shook my head. "It's on the house."

"No, I insist. Get me the bill. I'm going to hit the bathroom. Just leave it on the table."

"Okay."

I walked over to the cash register and wrote up the slip, charging him for the bagel and coffee but not the pie.

When I got back to booth number three, Cedric was still in the bathroom.

On the table was a crisp lone fifty-dollar bill. I laughed as I realized the joke Cedric was playing on me, giving me the same tip he did on that first day.

As I took the money, I noticed the words *"I Love You... Turn Over"* were written on the front. My heart flipped and tears started to form when I saw the words *"Will You Marry Me?"* written on the back.

I covered my mouth with my hands and turned around toward the bathroom. Cedric was walking toward me slowly and landed right in front of me on his knees. His eyes were filled with more love than I could ever hope for and one tear streamed down his cheek.

As I looked around, I noticed that Max, Delores and Mr. Short all had smiles on their faces, and I was pretty sure they were in on this the whole time.

Cedric grabbed my hand and kissed it. "Allison Ophelia Abraham, you are the single most precious thing to me in this entire world. If someone had told me last year, when I first laid eyes on you here at this diner, that you would end up loving me half as much as I loved you from that first moment, I would have thought they were crazy. Something deep inside me then told me that you were my future even if there were going to be many obstacles to get there. When I look at you today, I see everything I have ever wanted. I see my unborn children. I see the person I am going to grow old with. I'll love you til the day I die. Will you marry me?"

I stood in shock with my hand over my mouth as Cedric opened a blue Tiffany box, showcasing a beautiful princess cut diamond.

"Princess cut, two carats. I hear this is what women like," he said.

"Oh, Cedric…it's…it's beautiful," I sobbed. "I love you…so much."

"So, sweetheart…will you be my wife? What do you say?"

Cedric stood up and held me as I started balling.

I needed to tell him. Now.

"Cedric, can we go outside for a minute?"

Cedric's eyes lost their luster as his concern clearly grew. "Sure…sure, sweetheart."

CHAPTER 41

CEDRIC

My heart sank when she didn't immediately say yes to my proposal. She seemed really emotional and the walk from the inside of the diner through the door onto the sidewalk seemed to take forever.

I put the ring back in my pocket as we stood on the sidewalk. The breeze was blowing Allison's hair all over the place and the sun shined into her green eyes, making them almost gold.

My heart pounded out of my chest and the coconut cream pie I had just eaten was starting to come up on me. I couldn't bear it if she was going to tell me she wouldn't marry me. The thought of that was unfathomable.

"Cedric…"

I put my hands on her shoulders and squeezed them. "What's going on?"

She looked so scared as she stared into my eyes and said, "You need to know something before you decide that you want to marry me."

"Allison…nothing could possibly make me not want to marry you. Nothing. Do you understand?" I said as I pulled her toward me.

She started breathing heavily and was trembling my arms.

"I…I need some water," she said.

"Okay…okay, hold on."

All eyes were on me as I reentered the diner. This was definitely awkward, but I could've cared less what they thought. I needed Allison to tell me what was going on.

"Delores, Allison's not feeling well. Can I please have a glass of water?"

She poured it quickly and the door chimed as I made my way back out to her as she waited on the sidewalk with her arms crossed over her chest to mask the chill.

I handed her the water. "Here you go."

"Thanks." She took the glass from me, gulping half of it down and licked her lips nervously.

"Allison, please...tell me what's going on. Are you having doubts?"

"No, Cedric. Of course not...I love you. I'm not having doubts about you. I'm..."

"What? Allison, what is it?" I was seriously about to lose my lunch.

Allison let out a deep breath. "I'm pregnant."

I stood there for a moment replaying what she just said, making sure I heard it right.

Pregnant.

She said pregnant, right?

She was having my baby?

Was this really happening?

I placed my hand over her stomach gently. "You're...pregnant?"

My lips trembled as I pulled her into me, kissing her hard and then releasing her.

"Wait...are you...sure?" I asked.

"Yes...I took a test a few days ago and this morning before work, remember I told you I had a doctor's appointment? Well, it was an ob-gyn. I wanted to be absolutely sure before I told you. He did an ultrasound. I was going to tell you tonight...but then—"

"Oh, my love, come here!" Tears poured from my eyes as I hugged her tightly. "How could you think this would change my wanting to marry you? I want to marry you even more now. I love you so much. This is my dream come true. Don't you know that?" I placed my hand on her stomach. "It's... a little sooner than I expected...but we have nine months to prepare, right?"

"Actually, we have six months to prepare. I'm three months along. I think it happened the night we got back together...one of the several times...that we, you know..."

I took a deep breath from the shock of the news and exhaled with the realization that I wasn't about to lose her.

I was going to be a father.

I grabbed the glass of water from her and gulped down the rest of it before speaking. "Sweetheart...this is wonderful news. Don't you know we can handle anything together? There is nothing I can't handle as long as you're by my side.

"I'm so glad you feel that way, Cedric. Because they'll be here in late May. They'll be Geminis.

The water glass slipped out of my hand and shattered on the sidewalk. *"They?"*

EPILOGUE

Gemini, you are feeling perky and positively elated. Celebration is in the air. You have overcome dramatic obstacles and you may actually be feeling on top of the world. Congrats on coming through the storm.

"Okay, this might be a little hot," Vanessa said as she held the blowdryer to my breasts.

Trying not to laugh at the absurdity of the situation, I clenched my vagina praying not to piss my pants because there was no way I could get these spanx off under my gown.

"This cannot be happening right now. Please tell me it's drying?"

"Patience. We're getting there, baby," she said.

"I can't believe this."

Elaine walked into room holding one of the twins who was sleeping in the infant seat. She looked beautiful wearing a long, sleeveless brown two-piece dress adorned with a corsage. "What on Earth?" she asked.

"Hey, Elaine, come join the fun!" I said sarcastically.

"What happened, Allison?"

"My tits leaked through the satin. I forgot to slip the breast pads into my bra."

Elaine covered her mouth, trying to stifle a laugh. "Oh, honey..."

"Could you imagine Cedric's face if the first thing he saw as I came down the aisle were two giant, wet milk spots?"

Vanessa cracked up and the dryer accidentally blew some of my hair.

"Hey!" I said.

"Sorry, sweetie, sorry," she apologized, stifling her laughter.

Vanessa's long, dark hair was done up in a French twist. I had asked my birth mother to be one of my bridesmaids along with Sonia, Denise and Callie. After all, she wasn't all that much older than me and looked gorgeous in the strapless emerald green satin dress.

"What the—" Jake said, looking at the ridiculous scene in this hotel room as he walked in dressed in a black tux, holding the other baby.

"Don't ask, little brother. Don't ask."

Jake lifted her toward me and said, "Um…Holly just tried to suck my nipple. I think it's time for her meal. What can I feed her?"

"There are some bottles of pumped milk over in the cooler over there." I gestured to a blue cooler in the corner of the room. "I'll pump after the ceremony, so you'll have extra for the reception."

Just then, Ed walked into the room and I smiled. "Hi, Dad."

Ed's eyes began to well up as he caught sight of me in my dress. "Oh, Allison…"

I had pictured this moment for some time…just not with the hot blowdryer on the tits thing.

Vanessa stopped the dryer as I stood up to hug Ed, fanning the tears away from my eyes.

After the birth of my girls, Ed and I had a tender moment at the hospital where he thanked me for making him a grandfather, and he asked me if I would call him Dad. I had wanted to for so long, but hadn't done so until I could be sure it was what he wanted. I knew I could never replace the little girl he lost, but I knew he truly loved me at that moment.

***

Holly Amanda and Hannah Allison came into the world three months ago at the end of May, born naturally at seven and six pounds respectively. It was best day of my life. Cedric was by my side the entire time and when the babies came out, the look of wonder and love on his face, and the tears in his eyes would be an image I'd keep with me and replay until the end of my days. He told me he had never loved me more than the moment I made him a father.

It had been hard balancing summer grad school classes and breastfeeding twins, but with the help of my family, by some miracle, I was able to juggle it all.

My family. It felt so good to say that.

It wasn't a conventional one, but I went from having almost no one just a couple of years ago, to having a true blended family now.

Vanessa had moved to the Boston area to be closer to Jake who just started his freshman year at Northeastern as an electrical engineering major. My relationship with her is still a work in progress, but we have gotten much closer and she and Bettina help watch the twins two days a week when I have classes. On the other days, she works as a waitress at the Stardust. She and Jake moved into my old apartment in Malden when Sonia moved out to live with her now fiancé, Tom.

Jake is everything I could ever want in a brother. He helps out with the twins too and had turned into quite the tattooed "manny." Holly, in particular, had taken a special liking to her Uncle Jake.

Ed continued to be in remission and he and Elaine purchased a summer home in Dennisport on Cape Cod to be able to spend more quality time with us. Ed was able to work remotely from there for his consulting job. Cedric, the twins and I spent most weekends this summer down there. Ed and Cedric like to fetch quahogs and we often steamed the clams for dinner, which we'd eat on the candlelit screened-in porch while listening to Jimmy Buffet on low volume, as the babies slept upstairs.

Denise gave birth to a baby boy named after Cedric's father, Paul. They call him Pauly and his middle name is Cedric. I was excited about my daughters having a cousin so close in age and am sure they'll be wreaking lots of havoc together, like Caleb and Cedric did when they were younger.

Even though I had to stop working with Callie, she's still my favorite girl and refers to the twins, her nieces, as "Teletubbies." (She was watching that show on her iPad, as a matter of fact, as she got her hair done for the ceremony.) She's still as in love as ever with Anderson Cooper.

Cedric and I moved from his condo to a single-family house in the Boston suburb of Brookline. He was promoted to senior agent at J.D. Westock and tries his best to make it home by 6:00 each night, so that I can study in between breastfeeding the girls. I could often be found sandwiched between two heads on a Boppy pillow.

We had decided on a late August wedding and wanted to wait until after the twins were born, so that I could at least try to squeeze into a presentable dress. I had lost about half the baby weight and very voluptuously managed to squirm my way into my dream Pnina Tornai dress that I picked out with Elaine and Bettina during a trip to Kleinfeld in Brooklyn before the babies were born.

Wanting to keep it simple, we opted for an outdoor ceremony with only our family and closest friends. After scouting lots of scenic areas, Cedric and I found the perfect spot by the water in Newport, Rhode Island.

***

The milk spots dissipated just in the nick of time. As the soft sounds of the harp played in the summer breeze, Ed reached out his arm.

Before taking it, I looked up to the sunny cloudless sky and blew a kiss to my mother and sister in heaven. I hoped they were watching over us.

Ed's eyes were watery, and he kissed me lightly on the cheek. "Honey, thank you for letting me be the one to walk you down the aisle. I am so honored. Are you ready?"

"Ready as I'll ever be."

"I love you," he said.

"I love you, too," I said shaking.

"You'll be fine."

"Dad?"

"Yes, Allison?"

"Do you feel like she's here?"

Ed looked up to the sky and then back at me.

"She is here," he said pointing to his heart and then to mine. "She's right here, always."

I smiled, though a part of me still wondered if Amanda would really be okay with my marrying Cedric. It was the one thing I would never be sure of.

"Okay, let's go," I said, clutching my bouquet of pink roses.

The wedding march started and I entwined my arm with Ed's.

As I slowly marched down the aisle, floating past the faces of all the people I loved standing in the sunlight, gratitude overcame me.

Thank you God for the life you've given me.

And then I looked straight ahead, and he took my breath away. Just like that very first day, the most beautiful man in the world.

Blue Eyes.

Cedric was crying tears of joy as I moved closer and closer to him. What did I ever do to deserve to have someone look at me like that, with the intense love I saw so clearly in his eyes?

I kissed Ed on the cheek, and he shook Cedric's hand.

"I love you," I whispered to Cedric as he looked at me in awe.

"I love you so much. You look so beautiful." He was beaming from ear to ear.

The priest began the ceremony amidst the beautiful background noise of our baby girls crying for food. My breasts immediately tingled, and I could feel the milk rushing through them at the sound of the twins crying in unison.

Just a few more minutes, baby girls.

Father Mike started the vows.

"Cedric, will you have this woman as your lawful wedded partner, to live together in the estate of matrimony..."

Cedric lovingly said "I do" and after a minute passed and in the middle of my turn, just as Father Mike asked, *"Will you love him, honor him, comfort him, and keep him in sickness and in health..."* a beautiful butterfly landed on the pink rose boutonniere Cedric wore.

It stayed still, facing me as if it were part of the ceremony.

Cedric looked down and smiled. I wondered if he was thinking the same thing I was. I couldn't be sure.

After I said "I do," amazingly the butterfly moved from Cedric's rose to the skirt of my dress.

It stayed there fluttering its wings and I glanced down at it from time to time as Father Mike spoke.

"Cedric and Allison have consented together in wedlock, and have witnessed the same before God, this company of friends and family, and have given and pledged their promises to each other, and have declared the same by giving and receiving a ring, and by joining hands."

As soon as Cedric and I exchanged rings, the butterfly flapped its wings and landed on top of our joined hands.

Cedric's hands started to tremble a bit, and I realized he knew what I was thinking.

Was it Amanda?

"In the name of the Lord and by the authority vested in me by the state of Rhode Island, I pronounce this couple to be united in marriage. Cedric, you may kiss the bride."

The sound of ocean waves crashing filled the air and we kept still as the butterfly remained on our joined hands as we kissed for the first time as husband and wife.

Just as our faces parted to the cheers of our family and friends, the butterfly flapped its wings, disappearing into the sky above.

FOR MORE TITLES,
VISIT PENELOPE WARD'S WEBSITE:

www.penelopewardauthor.com

Other Standalones by Penelope Ward:

JAKE UNDONE (Jake and Nina's story)
JAKE UNDERSTOOD (Jake #2)

MY SKYLAR (Mitch and Skylar's story)
USA TODAY Bestseller

STEPBROTHER DEAREST
New York Times, USA Today and Wall Street Journal Bestseller

Available Fall 2015:
SINS OF SEVIN

ACKNOWLEDGEMENTS

First and foremost, thank you to my loving parents for continuing to be my biggest fans.

To my husband: Thank you for your love, patience and humor and for finally seeing this as more than a hobby! You take on a lot of extra responsibilities so I can continue to write.

To Allison, who believed in me from the beginning: You manifested all of this!

To my besties, Angela, Tarah and Sonia: love you all so much!

To Vi: I am so happy to have found the other half of my brain! Thank you for your invaluable friendship, support and chats.

To Julie: You are the best writer I know and an even better friend.

To my editor, Kim: Thank you for your undivided attention to all of my books, chapter by chapter.

To my facebook fan group, Penelope's Peeps and to Queen Amy for running the ship: I adore you all!

To Aussie Lisa: We'll always have George. You live way too far from me.

To Erika G.: It's an E thing.

To Luna: Thank you for your passion, the beautiful teasers that help motivate me and for loving Jake!

To Mia A.: How did I ever write before I had you to sprint and procrastinate with?

To Hetty, Amy C., Kimie S., Linda C.: Thank you for your support and pimping.

To all the book bloggers/promoters who help and support me: You are THE reason for my success. I'm afraid to list everyone here because I will undoubtedly forget someone unintentionally. You know who you are and do not hesitate to contact me if I can return the favor.

To Donna of Soluri Public Relations who organizes my book blitzes, handles my p.r. and is an overall awesome person: Thank you!

To Letitia of RBA Designs: Thank you for another stellar book cover.

To my readers: Nothing makes me happier than knowing I've provided you with an escape from the daily stresses of life. That same escape was why I started writing. There is no greater joy in this business than to hear from you directly and to know that something I wrote touched you in some way.

Last but not least, to my daughter and son: Mommy loves you. You are my motivation and inspiration!

ABOUT THE AUTHOR

Penelope Ward is a New York Times, USA Today and Wall Street Journal Bestselling author.

She grew up in Boston with five older brothers and spent most of her twenties as a television news anchor, before switching to a more family-friendly career.

Penelope lives for reading books in the new adult/contemporary romance genre, coffee and hanging out with her friends and family on weekends.

She is the proud mother of a beautiful 10-year-old girl with autism (the inspiration for the character Callie in Gemini) and an 8-year-old boy, both of whom are the lights of her life.

Penelope, her husband and kids reside in Rhode Island.

She is the author of *Stepbrother Dearest,* which spent four consecutive weeks on the New York Times Bestseller List. Other works include, *My Skylar, Jake Undone, Jake Understood, Gemini* and the upcoming *Sins of Sevin* due out in the fall of 2015.

Contact Penelope at: penelopewardauthor@gmail.com on Twitter @PenelopeAuthor or on Facebook on the Penelope Ward Author page. **Guarantee you never miss book news by subscribing to Penelope's updates at the bottom of the page here: www.penelopewardauthor.com**

Made in United States
Orlando, FL
02 July 2022

19368618R00189